WHO KILLED
AUNT MAGGIE?

WHO KILLED AUNT MAGGIE?

MEDORA FIELD

COACHWHIP PUBLICATIONS

Greenville, Ohio

Who Killed Aunt Maggie?, by Medora Field Perkerson
© 2014 Coachwhip Publications
Introduction © 2014 Curtis Evans
First published 1939
No claims made on public domain material.

ISBN 1-61646-274-4
ISBN-13 978-1-61646-274-1

Cover: Oak Alley Plantation © Torsten Karock; Darts © Seamartini

CoachwhipBooks.com

CONTENTS

Blue Murder in Georgia:
The Mystery Fiction of Medora Field
Curtis Evans

MEDORA FIELD (1892-1960), or Medora Field Perkerson, to use her married name, was a prominent Atlanta journalist and the author of a once much-lauded book of Old South domestic architectural history, *White Columns in Georgia* (1952), who near the end of the Golden Age of detective fiction (roughly 1920 to the mid-1940s) wrote two tremendously successful mystery novels, *Who Killed Aunt Maggie?* (1939) and *Blood on Her Shoe* (1942). Both books were bestsellers in hardcover, both sold widely when reprinted in paperback, and both were made into films; yet until now with their republication by Coachwhip, they had remained out-of-print for nearly seventy years. Today Medora Field is best-known for having been a close friend of Margaret Mitchell (1900-1949), author of the mega-bestseller *Gone with the Wind* (1936), yet Field's own two novels merit some renewed attention, as superior examples of women's mystery suspense fiction of the 1930s and 1940s, the leading proponent of which was one of the most popular American mystery writers of all time, Mary Roberts Rinehart (1876-1958). In his 1941 book *Murder for Pleasure*, mystery genre historian Howard Haycraft justly cited Medora Field, along with Mignon Eberhart, Leslie Ford, Dorothy Cameron Disney, Mabel Seeley, Charlotte Murray Russell, Clarissa Fairchild Cushman, Margaret Armstrong, and Anita Blackmon, as one of the most able students in Rinehart's school of mystery fiction. Let us now take a closer look at Medora Field and her two mystery novels.

7

Medora Field was a daughter of the New South, having been born in 1892 to Robert Field (1868-1935) and Mary Frances Abrams (1870-1957) a few miles from the northwestern Georgia town of Rome. The great New South spokesman Henry Grady (1850-1889), managing editor of the *Atlanta Constitution*, had passed away three years before Medora Field's birth, but his impassioned advocacy of the cause of industrialization had not fallen on deaf ears in Rome, where earlier in his career he had edited the *Rome Courier* and where the Rome Land Company had been chartered in 1887, spurring a rush of commercial and industrial development that was in full stride when Medora Field was born. Between 1880 and 1890, Rome's population grew by nearly 80%. Medora's father evidently was an apostle of Henry Grady's creed, for Robert Field in 1901 was instrumental in forming the Robert Field Company, an iron and coke commission business with offices in Columbus, Ohio, and St. Louis, Missouri, that acted as a sales agent for, among other concerns, Sloss-Sheffield Steel & Iron Company of Birmingham, Alabama.[1]

Although he embraced the New South, Robert Field was a child of the Old South. He left this earth north of the Mason-Dixon Line, passing away at an Indianapolis, Indiana, hospital; yet he entered it, three years after the end of the Civil War, on a plantation outside Natchez, Mississippi, a town built on cotton that boasted, visiting tourists are told, the most millionaires per capita in the United States prior to the outbreak of hostilities between North and South. Robert Field's grandfather, also named Robert, in 1822 migrated to Natchez from Princeton, New Jersey. He came of a family of prominence, including among its luminaries his paternal grandparents, Richard Stockton (1730-1781), a Declaration of Independence signer, and Annis Boudinot Stockton (1736-1801),

---

[1] *Rome News-Tribune*, 17 June 1973, 8-B; Michelle Brattain, *The Politics of Whiteness: Race, Culture and Workers in the Modern South* (2001; rpnt, Athens, GA: University of Georgia Press, 2004), 30-33; *The Iron Age* 67 (17 January 1901): 31; *Atlanta Journal*, 27 November 1935; *Find a Grave*, http://www.findagrave.com/cgi-bin/fg.cgi?page=gr&GRid=53441362, accessed 21 October 2014.

a Revolutionary-era poet and intellectual, and a cousin, Robert Field Stockton (1795-1866), a United States naval commodore who helped seize California for the United States during the Mexican-American War. In Natchez, Field married Charlotte Brooks, the daughter and heiress of the owner of Anchorage Plantation, and he became a close friend of Dr. William Dunbar, Jr., a son of William Dunbar (1749-1810), the founder of The Forest plantation and a Thomas Jefferson correspondent and American Philosophical Society member. The younger Dunbar married Field's sister Mary, and Fields and Dunbars remained closely connected in the Natchez area for generations.[2]

With such a family background, it is not surprising that Medora Field wrote nostalgically of the Old South, both in her two mystery novels and in her nonfiction antiquarian study, *White Columns in Georgia*. Yet in her own life she epitomized much that was new. From an early age, Field aggressively pursued a career. She first found salaried employment at the age of fifteen when she became a stenographer to C. E. McLin, founder and president of a large Rome cotton manufactory, Anchor Duck Mills. Her first newspaper job, writing a shopping news column for the *Rome Tribune-Herald*, soon followed. Her great breakthrough came in 1919 when the *Woman's Home Companion* published a story, "The Christmas Spirit Speaks," that Field had based on her experiences masquerading as a homeless woman in Rome. Angus Perkerson (1888-1967), the editor of *The Atlanta Journal Magazine* (later *The Atlanta Journal and Constitution Magazine*), came across Field's article the next year and decided to offer her a job as his assistant. Field accepted the job offer, just as, two years later, she accepted Perkerson's proposal of marriage.[3]

Medora Field at this time has been described as "a dark-haired, square-faced, capable-looking woman with . . . an authoritarian

---

[2] *Atlanta Journal*, 27 November 1935; Ed Field, "Is your neighbor your relative?," *Natchez Democrat*, 6 January 2010.

[3] Harvey Dan Abrams, "Medora Field Perkerson" (undated pamphlet, reprinted from the *Atlanta Historical Bulletin*), 5-8; *The Editor* 52 (25 March 1920): 184.

manner, which some might have called bossiness, a tremendous talent for organization, a social conscience, and a quick grasp of issues. Seasoned reporters would shrink a bit when facing Medora across the desk. . . ." The same year Medora Field married Angus Perkerson, she encouraged him to hire a young lady named Margaret Mitchell as a *Journal* feature writer. During the four years that Margaret Mitchell worked at the magazine, she and Medora Field became fast friends. It was Field who, nine years after Mitchell left the staff, prompted the younger woman to submit her draft manuscript of *Gone with the Wind* to Harold S. Latham, vice-president of The Macmillan Company, who was in the South seeking novels by local authors. Macmillan would, in turn, publish Medora Field's own novel, *Who Killed Aunt Maggie?*, in 1939, followed by *Blood on Her Shoe* in 1942. Though of course neither book came close to the astonishing, once-in-a-lifetime success of *Gone with the Wind*, they both sold extremely well. In Atlanta *Who Killed Aunt Maggie?* was on the bestseller lists for months in 1939 and the next year Republic Pictures bought the rights to the book, which the studio planned to adapt under the title *The Belle Of Atlanta* (happily it was decided to retain the book's title for the film).[4]

Margaret Mitchell, though preoccupied with the filming of her own novel (and all the importunate letters she was getting from aspirants to cinematic success), kept abreast of all that was going on with her good friend's mystery. On May 19, 1939, she wrote George Platt Brett, president of Macmillan, in reference to the premiere that was to be held in Atlanta for *Gone with the Wind*, that she had gone to see Medora, who was president of the Atlanta Press Club, about having a tea in honor of the film. "Fortunately, I arrived some hours before she received the news that The Macmillan Company would bring out her mystery novel, 'Who Killed Aunt Maggie?' on September 15," she humorously noted. "There would have been no premiere discussion had I made my visit later!" On August 8, 1939, Mitchell wrote Brett, "[Medora's] book is coming

---

[4] Anne Edwards, *Road to Tara: The Life of Margaret Mitchell* (1983; rpnt, Lanham, MD: Taylor Trade, 2014), 94; Abrams, "Medora," 10-11, 17.

out on the fifteenth and every friend she has is giving her a party, so it was hard to catch her. . . . everyone who has read [Aunt Maggie], which includes me, thinks it's grand, and we all feel it will have a good sale." The next year, on September 1, 1940, Mitchell informed Katherine Brown, a scout for Gone with the Wind producer David O. Selznick, that Medora had "sold her 'Who Killed Aunt Maggie?' to Republic and she is going West, soon. . . . I thought you might be in California and run into her and think you were having nightmares about being back at the Press Club Tea at the Premiere."[5]

In a 1939 Atlanta Journal article Medora Field notes that she had wanted to write a novel for some time (perhaps, one is tempted to speculate, since Margaret Mitchell's success with Gone with the Wind), but that the "difficulty was that I couldn't think of anything to write about. I had no great message for mankind. . . ." Fortunately Field "happened to think of all the mystery novels that came to me as editor of The Journal's Sunday Magazine book page. . . . Why, anybody can write a mystery! Or so I decided—until I got underway, trying to write one."[6]

Fortunately, when Field's confidence flagged, Margaret Mitchell was there to encourage her, speaking "warm and stimulating words about her friend's writing ability" and reminding her "that self-discipline and hard work are at the very core of any good writing job." With Mitchell's moral support, Field persevered and finished Who Killed Aunt Maggie? (it was not dedicated to Mitchell, however, but to Field's mother, an avid mystery reader). Aunt Maggie was received with acclaim, first from her publisher and then from newspaper reviewers around the country. "Reads as though written by Mary Roberts Rinehart in collaboration with Edgar Allan Poe," enthusiastically (if exaggeratedly) declared a Texas reviewer in the Galveston News.[7]

---

[5] John Wiley, Jr., ed., The Scarlett Letters: The Making of the Film Gone with the Wind (Lanham, MD: Taylor Trade, 2014), 231, 251-52, 352.

[6] Abrams, "Medora," 12. It is possible that Medora Field may have written the short story "Ether," published in Black Mask in May 1921 and credited to Angus Perkerson.

[7] Ibid., 14, 20.

When Republic Pictures was making its film version of *Aunt Maggie*, Field was emphatic about the importance of the titular murder victim. "Aunt Maggie is a familiar type in the South," she informed the film's associate producer. "Almost every family has one. She gets in your hair—true, but she also has her good points. She hasn't changed an awful lot from the Aunt Pittypat of *Gone with the Wind*. . . . everybody grieved that they couldn't have more of Aunt Pittypat in the film."[8] Sadly, not only did the script (by Stuart Palmer, the distinguished American detective novelist who created the spinster schoolteacher sleuth Hildegarde Withers, immortalized on film by Edna May Oliver) heavily alter Aunt Maggie's character, it changed nearly everything in the book, including the identity of the murderer, who is not even one of the book's characters. It is hard to imagine that Field was not at heart disappointed with a film adaptation that flattened her engaging novel into a by-the-numbers old dark house family elimination thriller. Willie Best, on hand as a comic relief butler, is given nothing to do but act terrified; however, Milton Parsons has a great role as the creepy tombstone salesman Mr. Lloyd, though his is yet another character in the film found nowhere in the novel.

In addition to being filmed, *Aunt Maggie* went through nine printings in hardback, was serialized by the Associated Press in newspapers throughout the United States, published in England and Italy, and brought out in paperback by Popular Library in the mid-1940s, eventually selling in that format alone over 125,000 copies.[9] Impressively, in a year, 1939, that saw the publication of Raymond Chandler's *The Big Sleep* and Rex Stout's *Some Buried Caesar*, not to mention novels by the British Crime Queens Ngaio Marsh and Agatha Christie, mystery debutante Medora Field had scored one of the year's greatest publishing successes in crime fiction.

Naturally such success called for a follow-up novel. Soon Harold Latham was importuning Field, "you must get down to the next

---

[8] Ibid., 17.
[9] Ibid. 19.

book." The now bestselling mystery author started work on *Blood on Her Shoe* at the beginning of 1941, but the new novel did not see publication until May 19, 1942. However, it too was a great success, hitting bestseller lists, going through five printings in hardback and actually outselling *Aunt Maggie*. "If you wish to keep your friends let us suggest that it will become necessary to purchase more than one copy of 'Blood on Her Shoe,'" advised a Maine newspaper reviewer. "For despite every protest it's going to be borrowed, passed around, thumbmarked and dogeared ere it finally comes to rest on your bookshelves." Fifteen years later Field wrote a friend and fan, champion golfer Estelle Page (1907-1983), of the scarcity of *Blood on Her Shoe*, indicating that the reviewer's contention was far from fanciful:

> I am so pleased that you liked Who Killed Aunt Maggie [Field had autographed a hardcover copy of the book for Page the previous year], and I do wish I could tell you how to get Blood on Her Shoe. After five printings by Macmillan, a printing of 175,000 pocket book size was made by Popular Library. Where they all went, I wish I knew, because I'd like a few extra copies myself. Every now and then one turns up at the second hand book stores here and I have bought several for relatives, but I haven't seen one in a long time now. . . . I have just talked to Eleanor Keeler [the wife of golf writer O. B. Keeler] and she sends you her love. She promises to send you the name of a bookstore in New York which might be a possibility—or to lend you her copy of Blood on Her Shoe.[10]

In 1944 *Blood on Her Shoe* also was adapted for film by Republic Pictures, happily much more faithfully than *Who Killed Aunt*

[10] Ibid., 19-20; *Lewiston Daily Sun*, 1 July 1942, 4; Medora F. Perkerson to Estelle Page, 2 February 1957, letter in my personal possession.

MRS. ANGUS PERKERSON
1355 PEACHTREE STREET, N. E.
APARTMENT B-8
ATLANTA 9, GEORGIA

Feb. 2 1957

Dear Mrs. Page;

      I can't believe that it was
away last April that I had that nice note from
you.   I meant to answer immediately and you
will just have to forgive me. My mother was
with me at the time, and for a long time afterward,
and was very ill. She is now in a nursing home
and getting along fine but requires constant care.

      I am so pleased that you liked
Who Killed Aunt Maggie, and I do wish I could
tell you how to get Blood On Her Shoe. After
five printings by Macmillan, a printing of 175,000
pocket book size was made by Popular Library.
Where they all went, I wish I knew, because I'd
like a few extra copies myself. Every now and
then one turns up at the second hand book stores
here and I have bought several for relatives, but
I haven't seen one in a long time now. If I
should run across one, I'll be happy to send it
to you.

      I have just talked to Eleanor
Keeler and she sends you her love. She promises
to send you the name of a bookstore in New York
which might be a possibility --or to lend you
her copy of Blood on Her Shoe.

Over   Best wishes, Medora F Perkerson

Correspondence from Medora Field Perkerson
to Estelle Page. (Curtis Evans collection)

Maggie?, as *The Girl Who Dared*. The film benefits from a good tight script by John K. Butler (1908-1964), a prolific writer for pulp crime fiction magazines and B-film westerns and thrillers, such as *The Phantom Speaks* (1945) and *The Vampire's Ghost* (1945). Lorna Gray and Peter Cookson make a handsome couple and quite engaging leads, sultry Veda Ann Borg successfully depicts the twins Cynthia and Sylvia, and Willie Best returns as yet another perpetually petrified butler.

In the meantime Medora Field had begun plotting a third mystery novel, but she set this work aside in favor of the book for which she is best-known today, *White Columns in Georgia*, her history of antebellum homes that survived General Sherman's punitive wartime march though her home state. *White Columns in Georgia* was published in 1952 to much acclaim. Although she lived for another eight years, Field never published another mystery. Yet, as Howard Haycraft indicated at the beginning of Field's brief career in crime fiction, the Georgian made her mark as a notable exponent of the Mary Roberts Rinehart school of mystery, which places a high premium on suspense and atmosphere. Not surprisingly, Field was a great fan of Rinehart's books. She wrote Rinehart an admiring letter in 1940, informing the eminent author that she believed she had read everything Rinehart had ever written. Field's mystery novels also are significant as early examples of female-authored southern regional crime fiction, like the pair published by Arkansan Anita Blackmon (1892-1943) and three of the four mysteries authored by Alabaman Sara Elizabeth Mason (1911-1993).[11]

The Forties Georgia radio broadcaster Para Lee Brock hit upon an essential quality of Medora Field's mystery fiction when she

---

[11] Abrams, "Medora," 20. Anita Blackmon's pair of mystery novels, *Murder à la Richelieu* (1937) *and There Is No Return* (1938) were reprinted in 2014 by Coachwhip and Sara Elizabeth Mason's four titles, *Murder Rents a Room* (1943), *The House That Hate Built* (1944), *The Crimson Feather* (1945) and *The Whip* (1948), are imminently forthcoming from the same press. Together with Medora Field's two mysteries these works constitute a significant body of female-authored southern regional crime fiction from the Thirties and Forties.

discussed the author's *Blood on Her Shoe* on her program "Adventures in Literature." "*Blood on Her Shoe* has a tone of gentility," Brock perceptively observed. In the novel readers find "Chippendale furniture, Georgian silver, Wedgwood china, a bit of classical music, authentic threads of history. . . ." This "tone of gentility" in a murder novel is what many crime fiction fans today designate "cozy," or "cosy," mystery. Over the years many commentators on crime fiction (typically male) have disparaged cozy mystery. Julian Symons, for example, wrote snidely of the mystery novels of Mary Roberts Rinehart, "These are the first crime stories which have the air of being written specifically for maiden aunts." In fact, we know from contemporary reviews that the genteel mystery suspense fiction of Rinehart and her female followers actually was popular with men as well as women, and people of all ages. In this respect, I must take note not only of Field's fan letter from Estelle Page, a middle-aged golf champion, but of a fan letter Field once received from a Cadet Monsalvatge, from the context of the letter evidently a strapping young man. Cadet Monsalvatge had taken time during the Second World War to tell Field how much he had enjoyed *Who Killed Aunt Maggie?*[12] Judging from the sales of the Popular Library reprints of Medora Field's mysteries, these books had scores of thousands of readers. If Field's reading audience did against the evidence consist solely of maiden aunts, these devoted ladies must have been legion.

The comforts of the Rinehart school of cozily creepy mystery are clear enough to this middle-aged male reader, at least. Old money, a mansion, a murder (or more), a maiden and the man she loves (or thinks she loves): it all adds up to a pleasurably suspenseful story. We know that all will eventually work out for the distressed heroine, but it is a fine thing indeed to get one's withers wrung for a spell. Medora Field skillfully employs this time-tested formula in both her mystery novels, particularly *Blood on Her Shoe*.

---

[12] Abrams, "Medora,", 21; Curtis Evans, *Clues and Corpses: The Detective Fiction and Mystery Criticism of Todd Downing* (Greenville, OH: Coachwhip 2013), 193n11; Medora Field Perkerson to Cadet Montsalvatge, 15 November 1944, letter in my personal possession.

Dear Cadet Monsalvatge,

How very nice of you to write me. Of course, I am flattered that you read Who Killed Aunt Maggie? and very pleased to have you say you liked it..

And, of course, I remember you. Didn't I say you reminded

Correspondence from Medora Field Perkerson to Cadet Monsalvatge. (Curtis Evans collection)

Both *Who Killed Aunt Maggie?* and *Blood on Her Shoe* are gen-teel American variants on the highly stylized English country house party mysteries that are emblematic to so many today of between-the-wars detective fiction, when it was in its Golden Age. In *Who Killed Aunt Maggie?* the country house that becomes the locus of murder is fictional Wisteria Hall, located some five miles from Roswell, Georgia, in 1939 a town of some 1600 people with some notably fine antebellum mansions, located twenty miles to the northeast of Atlanta. Today Roswell is part of the sprawling metropolitan Atlanta area and has a population of nearly 100,000 individuals, making it the seventh largest city in Georgia; and readers may be surprised to find, when murder strikes at Wisteria Hall on a dark and stormy night, just how isolated the people gathered there feel.[13]

Having inherited Wisteria Hall from her grandmother, Sally Stuart decides with her husband, Bill, to open the mansion with a house party of a few select friends to celebrate the engagement of beautiful Claire Harper and handsome Bob Dunbar. Also invited are Bob's sister, Alice, and Bill's old Princeton roommate (and best man at Bill's and Sally's wedding), Kirk Pierce, an amiable Yankee who rather admires Claire himself. Sally's Aunt Maggie, a widow who busies herself with abstruse genealogical researches, has a standing invitation to Wisteria Hall, of which she takes advantage in this instance, while Eve Benedict, memorably termed "a twice-divorced man-hunter" by the *New York Times*' Isaac Anderson in his favorable review of the novel, essentially invites herself. "Eve is a sort of forty-second cousin of mine, but I suppose the South is the only section of the country where such relationships can still be used as an excuse to crash a party you haven't been invited to, or indeed are counted at all," explains Sally, the narrator of the story, who does not want the viperish Eve slithering into her house party but decides to try to bear her distant cousin as best she can.

---

[13] Jere Wood, "Roswell creating a great community," 11 July 2014, http://www.bizjournals.com/atlanta/print-edition/2014/07/11/roswell-creating-a-great-community.html?page=all, accessed 21 October 2014.

Front cover of *Who Killed Aunt Maggie?*, paperback edition.

MEET THE AUTHOR

Medora Field

A CHRISTMAS story of Medora Field's which appeared in a woman's magazine induced Angus Perkerson, Sunday Magazine Editor of *The Atlanta Journal*, to hire her as his assistant. Two years later, the newspaper friend who first suggested Miss Field for the job served as one of the ushers when she walked to the altar with her boss.

After the publication of *Gone with the Wind* her friends kept reminding her that Margaret Mitchell once worked at a desk alongside her own. Why didn't she write a book, they asked?

Miss Field, then editing the book page, decided to take the plunge with a mystery. The result was *Who Killed Aunt Maggie?* The original edition went into nine printings and won her a trip to Hollywood as technical adviser for the film version of the book.

Back cover biography of the author

For her part, the sometimes tart-tongued Aunt Maggie makes her feelings clear to all and sundry: "It was bad manners, to say the least, for you to come here uninvited, Evelyn. Bad manners and decidedly bad taste, but I have always contended that it is too late to try to be well born at the age of thirty."[14]

At Wisteria Hall Eve seems to make it her mission to torpedo Claire's and Bob's engagement. Indeed, the reader might be forgiven for expecting that Eve will be the person Sally discovers, at the end of chapter three, choked to death in the ground floor back passageway of the antebellum mansion, but the victim turns out to be Aunt Maggie, who thus exits all too soon from the tale. As Medora Field indicated, Aunt Maggie is the novel's most memorable character, one who would have been familiar to many southerners of her day. Her speech has the authentic tang of an ancestry-obsessed southern matron of seven decades ago, as when she again puts the sinful Eve in her proper place: "Don't give yourself airs, Evelyn Pruitt. You are not a descendant. Your great-great-grandfather was only a second cousin of the Graham who built this house. You are descended from the black sheep of the family."[15]

Fortunately there is still much to hold the reader's interest after Aunt Maggie meets her doom, as the story turns for a time into a classic "old dark house" tale. Wisteria Hall is cut off from civilization, as a thunderstorm hits, the phone line is cut, and the automobile tires are slashed. The house party hosts, guests, and servants spend a frightful night indeed—especially Sally, who, in classic mystery suspense fiction tradition, inopportunely decides to look for clues by candlelight in the early morning hours. Readers will find such additional enticing elements as a rifled dead body, scraps of green paper with mysterious messages writ upon them, a peregrinating cat named Plutarch, a missing eiderdown "puff" and an old rumor of a treasure-laden secret room long-concealed somewhere within the august recesses of Wisteria Hall. Make certain to scrutinize the thoughtfully-provided house floor plan!

14 *New York Times Book Review*, 20 August 1939; Medora Field, *Who Killed Aunt Maggie?*, (New York: Macmillan, 1939), 9, 21.
15 Field, *Maggie*, 30.

When legal authority finally arrives the next day—in the form of the blustering and blundering Lieutenant Gregory and the county coroner, the blind and cryptic Mr. Dodson—Sally and Bill find that they themselves are suspected of Aunt Maggie's murder. A second slaying, committed with a dart right under the eye of law enforcement, does not absolve them of possible guilt in the eyes of Lieutenant Gregory; but providentially Sally stumbles into the solution to both murders, and all ends happily for the innocent, if not for the guilty.

To be sure, *Who Killed Aunt Maggie?* does have some deficiencies as a mystery novel, not unexpected in a debut fictional outing. Though atmospheric, the book at some 82,000 words is rather static, never straying from the confines of Wisteria Hall. As mentioned above, the colorful presence of the murdered Aunt Maggie is much missed. Sally Stuart is likeable enough, but the love interest, crucial in a mystery novel of this sort, rests with the rather bland secondary character of Claire, the object of the attentions and affections of both Bob and Kirke (as well as the animosity of Eve). Additionally, it seems at first that Coroner Dodson will function as the novel's crime solver, until Sally discovers the solution entirely *per accidens*, which is not altogether satisfactory. On the other hand, as Isaac Anderson noted, while the story's ending "may seem a bit artificial," in fact "attentive reading shows that it is foreshadowed more than once in the course of the narrative"—the essence of elegant plot construction in a mystery.[16] The reader has the chance to deduce the solution for herself and beat both Sally and Coroner Dodson to the punch.

Medora Field suffered no sophomore slump with *Blood on Her Shoe*, which is, if anything, superior to *Who Killed Aunt Maggie?* The setting of the novel is another house party at an exquisite antebellum mansion, this one Heron Point, at the other end of Georgia, on St. Simons Island. Heron Point is owned by a brother and sister, Beau (a diminutive of Mirabeau Napoleon) and Chattie (short for Chatfield) Richmond, cousins to the novel's twenty-three-

---

[16] *New York Times Book Review*, 20 August 1939.

year-old narrator and amateur sleuth, Ann Carroll. Besides Ann, the guests at the house party are Ann's older brother, Josh, a lawyer; Ann's attractive heiress friend Pat Fairchild, a Yankee; bond dealer Homer Norton, whom everyone expects Ann to marry (though Ann herself is not so very enthusiastic about this prospect); the twins Cynthia Harrison and Sylvia Scott (known, regrettably, as Sin and Silly); and Sylvia's wealthy estranged husband, David Scott ("I had an idea they were at outs, but here he comes barging in without a word of warning," says Cousin Chattie of Sylvia's spouse, adding philosophically: "He did say he planned to go to a hotel, but of course we can always use another man"). Then there is Rufus Blair, a visitor from the North whom Ann had never met before but nevertheless finds intensely interesting, and an array of black house servants: butler Woodrow, cook Pearl ("part Indian, with bronze skin, high cheekbones, and a lot of natural dignity"), maid Viola, and gardener Zack.[17]

For a lark the house party heads over to St. Simons Island's historic Christ Church cemetery to conduct a midnight ghost hunt, at the climax of which it is a member of the party who gives up the ghost, when this person is stabbed in the back with the antique Spanish dagger that had been conspicuously handled a few hours earlier by the hosts and guests at Heron Point. Two more murders follow this first killing, before Ann, more perspicacious than Sally in *Who Killed Aunt Maggie?*, solves the case (or part of the case, to be precise; there is an additional twist unforeseen by our heroine).

Blood on Her Shoe is a fine Rinehart school mystery suspense novel from the Forties. Ann makes a stronger lead character than Sally in *Aunt Maggie*, serving as more of a genuine sleuth as well as the novel's primary love interest (there is a subsidiary love interest as well with Ann's friend Pat). She also shows some commendable gumption in refusing to allow herself to be married off to a man she finds something less than enthralling and instead securing employment with an Atlanta interior decorating firm. As Ann bluntly puts it, "what with the depression and Father having

[17] Medora Field, *Blood on Her Shoe* (New York: Macmillan, 1942), 17, 101.

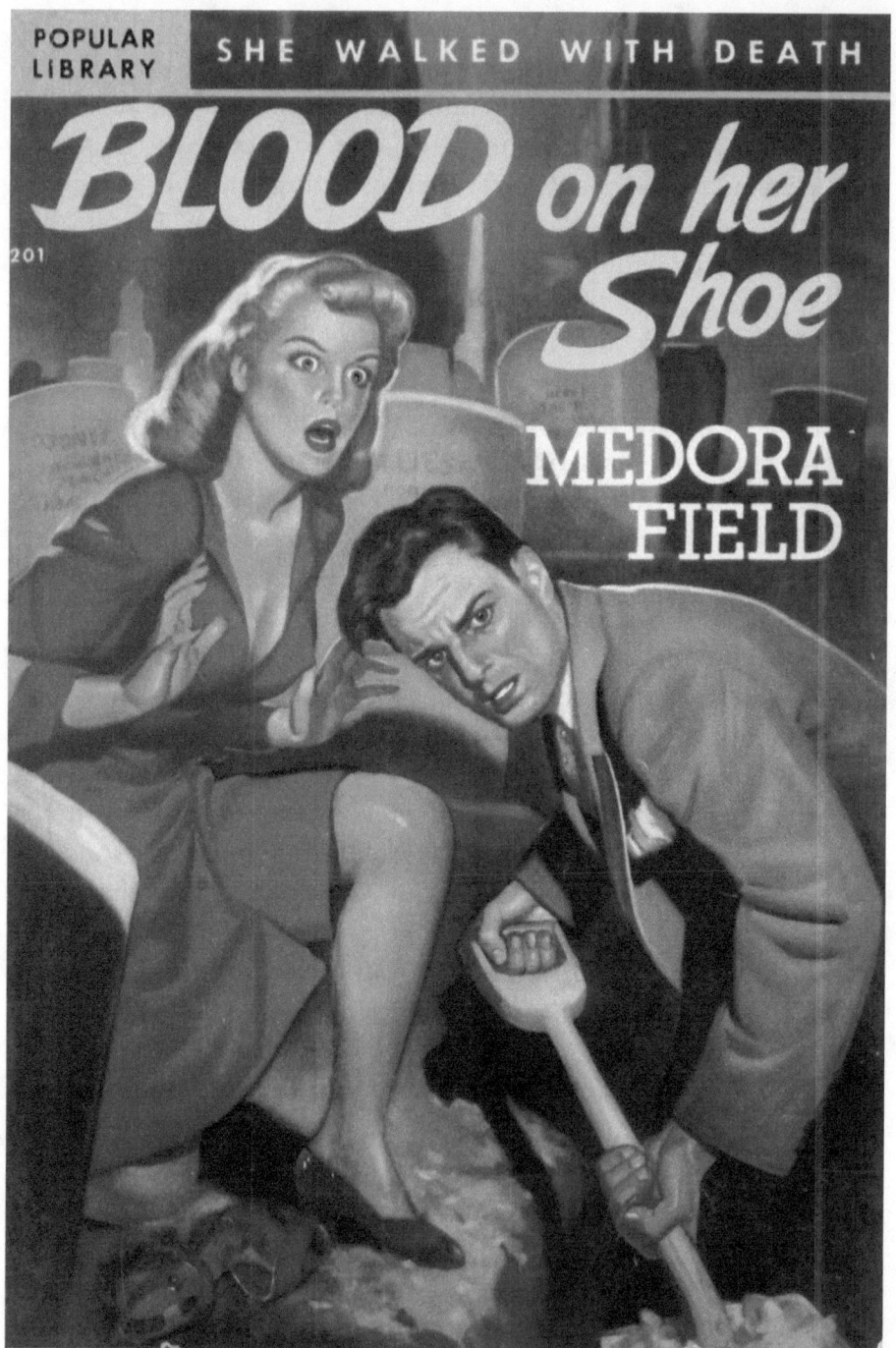

Front cover of *Blood on Her Shoe*, paperback edition.

left our money in a trust fund, I had to do something, or take Mother's advice and marry Homer Norton."[18] Not for nothing was the film version of the novel titled "The Girl Who Dared." There are some changes of scene as well, giving the novel a less static feel than *Aunt Maggie*. Additionally, although some of the clues on which Ann relies to reach her solution are not fairly presented to the reader, there is even greater ingenuity in the plot, which cleverly invokes the novel's title in a metaphorical sense (you will see what I mean when you read it for yourself).

Modern critics of Medora Field's mysteries are likely to point out that in the novels, as in *White Columns in Georgia*, the author writes romantically of what she sees as the glory and grandeur of the Old South. This no doubt is true. A keystone sentence in Field's nostalgic edifice is found in *Blood on Her Shoe*, when Ann and her friends visit Christ Church cemetery, leading Ann to eulogize over graves covered by weathered slabs "that mark not only the end of an earthly sojourn, but the end of an era—that long dead golden age known as the old South." It should go without saying today that not only for many southern whites but clearly for enslaved black Americans the antebellum era was no golden age. Even Medora Field seems to recognize this fact in *Blood on Her Shoe*, when she has Ann, dismissing belief in ghosts, declare: "Anyway, that ghost business was just one of the legends handed down by ante-bellum Negroes. Some of them even believed that certain members of their race rose up in the cotton fields and flew back to Africa. *It was just wishful thinking, of course* [emphasis added]."[19]

Medora Field's portrayal of pre-World War Two black house servants, like that of Leslie Ford in her better-remembered mysteries set in Maryland, will be seen as problematical by many today, it must be allowed. Her black servants "flash" smiles and "roll" eyes, are superstitious (in *Blood on Her Shoe* one chapter details a black character's naïve belief in "mojo"), and are often frightened

[18] Ibid, *Blood*, 4.
[19] Ibid., 33, 102.

by the strange events occurring around them; yet they are by no means unintelligent or lacking in character and resolve. Occasionally through her narrators Field displays flashes of insight, as when both Sally and Ann note the black characters' distrust of the police ("The law never done colored folks no good yet," observes the cook Pearl in *Blood on Her Shoe*) and when Ann notes to herself that younger black house maids like Viola now "sound exactly like the lady of the house when they answer the phone."[20]

Readers who can make allowance for the different social attitudes of a southern white woman writing moonlight and magnolia-scented mystery fiction about her section of the United States three-quarters of a century ago should be able to find great pleasure in reading the crime tales that Medora Field devised. Can you spot *who killed Aunt Maggie* at Wisteria Hall or which woman had *blood on her shoe* at Heron Point? Read on and see!

---

[20] Ibid., 101, 194. I should add that in her new book on the public memory of Sherman's March through Georgia, Anne Sarah Rubin credits Medora Field in *White Columns in Georgia* with "clear eyed understanding," seeing through sanctified southern myths of the march. See Rubin, *Through the Heart of Dixie: Sherman's March and American Memory* (Chapel Hill: University of North Carolina Press, 2014), 166.

WHO KILLED
AUNT MAGGIE?

To that mystery fan
who is my mother,
Mary Frances Field

I

THE QUIET WAS A LITTLE DISCONCERTING as I drove around to the garage back of Wisteria Hall. Of course, its secluded atmosphere and its inaccessibility are among the chief charms of the old place, but I had expected some signs of activity. Where was everybody? Where, indeed, was the station wagon in which the two servants and Aunt Maggie had driven out yesterday to open the house for week-end guests?

I had sounded the horn just as I made the turn in the long driveway where one gets that first glimpse of big white columns through the trees. Now I pressed down on it again, longer and with more force. It seemed almost sacrilegious to rend the peaceful stillness in such fashion. But nothing happened.

The great white bulk of Wisteria Hall stood calm and inscrutable in the December sunshine and, as far as outward appearances indicated, might not have been disturbed since my grandmother's death ten months before, when I first came into possession of the place.

No grinning black face appeared at kitchen window or door. No sign of Andrew, making a great show of bustling down the steps and calling back to his fat wife as he came, "Law, Bessie, here's Miss Sally. Come on, let's help her get her things in the house."

A little impatient at this lack of response, for surely someone must be about, I decided to leave my bags and packages in the car to be brought in later. Perhaps Bessie and Andrew had gone over to Roswell for additional items which might have been overlooked when they brought out supplies the day before.

That would account for the absence of the station wagon. Aunt Maggie was probably dozing in the library or taking a nap in her room.

I glanced at my wrist watch. It was ten minutes after three. I decided I would take the flowers into the house with me, as there would just be time to arrange them, check over the bedrooms and dress before my husband and our guests began to arrive. As I reached for the large florist's box, I heard a sound near the side of the house, as though someone had stumbled on the gravel walk. I might not have noticed it at all, except for the fact that I had been so acutely aware of the surrounding silence.

Thinking that perhaps it was Aunt Maggie, I turned and walked over to where I could see beyond the boxwood hedge and into the front driveway.

Beyond the house and hurrying as fast as he could go toward the gate was a man. Although he was now nearly the length of a city block away, I was almost certain that he was Kirk Pierce, who was to be one of our guests that evening.

But why should Kirk be here at this hour and why should he be running away? Surely he must have seen me.

"Kirk," I called. "Yoo—hoo—oo!"

Did I imagine it, or did he really hesitate for a moment before breaking into a run?

Dropping my box, I also began to run; but he had disappeared around the turn and was out of the gate before I had covered half the distance. When I myself reached the turn, I heard the sound of a motor starting up. This was even more strange. I had seen no car outside the gate as I drove in, though one might easily have been concealed behind the shrubbery.

By the time I reached the gate, there was no car anywhere in sight, but on the fresh country air there was the unmistakable odor of gasoline. And on the fresh red earth, where a section of our private roadway was being worked over, there were tracks showing that a car had turned in from the side.

This private road extends beyond our gate for nearly a mile before it runs into an unpaved country road leading to the concrete highway which is still a mile or so distant. It seemed unlikely that the intruder had made a mistake as to destination, because our private roadway is plainly marked as such and also by the name, Wisteria Hall, on the mailbox.

Our property covers more than five hundred acres and the nearest farmhouse is three miles distant. With Roswell five miles away and Atlanta only twenty, within easy driving distance of my husband's office, Wisteria Hall had seemed ideal when we decided to make certain improvements with the idea of using it as a summer home. But now as the silence once more enshrouded my city soul there seemed something sinister about the place.

Retracing my steps down the long driveway, I noticed that even the sun was hidden by clouds and that there was a hint of rain in the air. Rain would be bad with that piece of road under construction, for cars would surely get stuck in the mud.

The idea of a country house party in mid-winter did not now seem such a grand inspiration after all.

It is my husband's favorite joke that I can be talked into anything, and he once declared that I would gladly agree to attend my own hanging if it were to be held out of town. Looking back to my telephone conversation of the day before with Claire Harper, it seemed to me that there was more than a grain of truth in his joking.

I had mentioned to Claire quite casually that the new basement game room and other remodeling had just been completed and that I thought it might be fun to spend Christmas at Wisteria Hall. Claire, not usually given to sudden enthusiasms, had bowled me over. "Oh, that's just perfect!" she cried. "Listen, darling, I've been trying for several days to get a chance to run over and tell you the big news. But I can't wait. I've finally got Bob to agree to marry me. Yes, that's what I said. We are going to be married. Sally, don't wait until Christmas. Let's go out this weekend. You can give us an engagement party. Just us, you know. You and Bill and Bob and I, and, of course, we'll have to have Alice, since she is Bob's sister. And let's see—somebody for Alice. What about Kirk Pierce?"

Remembering how long Claire had been after Bob, it did not seem just the moment to say that it might all be too much trouble, what with the next day being Saturday. Claire has lots of money and charm and Bob has lots of charm but no money, so it had not been easy, I knew, although Bob had been in love with her for years.

Bob had studied architecture, but had never gone very far with it and had finally stopped trying. His friends helped him to get other jobs, but I have often thought friends can be a handicap, too, when someone is as agreeable as Bob Dunbar.

Friends made it so easy for him to drop things and go off on a hunting trip to South Georgia or to the field trials or on a cruise or somewhere. Hostesses automatically put his name at the head of their lists for cocktail parties, dinners and dances. They asked his advice about redecorating their houses or trading in their cars or their husbands.

What I mean is that when someone has so much charm too many things come easy to him, so that he loses the ability to put forth effort along more serious lines. But, after all, it had not been necessary, for now Bob was marrying Claire.

He could devote himself to architecture without having to bother about the financial returns. Claire said their wedding trip would take them around the world, in order that Bob might study various types of architecture before settling down.

Reclaiming my box of flowers from the ground, I went back to the car, removed my keys and my bag and struggled up the back steps. I found the kitchen door locked, but fortunately I had a key. Once inside, everything seemed to be in order. The place was comfortably warm, indicating that Andrew had the furnace going. The electric refrigerator was functioning. Meats and vegetables and other foodstuffs were in place. Andrew had even been able to find some mint at the market. As a hostess, I began to feel slightly better.

Passing through the big dining room with its twin Sheraton sideboards, I went on to the mellow-toned library. But Aunt Maggie was not dozing by the fire. The fire itself had burned to ashes. Crossing the wide hall, with the lovely old Adam fanlight above the front door, I glanced into the long drawing room, which had been a double parlor before we removed the partition, but this had an even more deserted look.

At the foot of the stairs I called out to Aunt Maggie several times. Only the empty echo of my own voice came back to me.

Leaving my bag on the landing, I hurried up the stairway, wondering if indeed Aunt Maggie had taken one of the third-story bedrooms as she had insisted and if for this reason she did not hear me.

Aunt Maggie is really a dear, but I had not been too pleased when she decided to join the impromptu house party. Hearing our plans when she dropped in to see my two-year-old daughter, Aunt Maggie had insisted that this was just the time for her to check over family records at Wisteria Hall. Although she is what some people would call rich, Aunt Maggie adds considerably to her income by working up family histories for ambitious ladies who wish to become members of the D. A. R., the U. D. C. and similar organizations.

"It amuses me," she often said, "now, that I am a widow." (She had been a widow ever since I can remember.) "I find out such strange things about the best people. Sometimes I think they are more pleased to pay me for what I leave out than for what I put in."

Anyway, Wisteria Hall had been built around 1836 by my great-great-grandfather, and its library contains many rare old documents which Aunt Maggie had itched to get her plump hands on long before my grandmother's death. But Grandmother had refused to be bothered. Each time Aunt Maggie suggested looking them over, she had put her off, saying there was nothing of any value on the place and that it was all foolishness, anyway. I could picture Aunt Maggie in the midst of a perfect orgy since her arrival yesterday.

But where was she now? Certainly she was in none of the six second-floor bedrooms, nor was she in the sitting room. Climbing the rather steep back stairs, the only ones ascending to the third floor, I still received no answer to my call. But papers and books scattered about in the study showed that she had been there.

No doubt she had gone to Roswell with Bessie and Andrew. After all, it was rather spooky to be at Wisteria Hall alone, even in the daytime, as I myself had just discovered. As I turned to leave the study, one of the papers on the desk caught my eye.

It was propped against the inkwell and, yielding to impulse, I picked it up, though I was usually bored with items which so often excited Aunt Maggie. The writing was in a fine, flowing script, probably that of my great-great-grandfather, but the text seemed palpably absurd when associated with the portrait of that austere old gentleman.

It was a sort of jingle about steps and hands and feet and what not, and though I did not examine it very carefully, it seemed to make no sense whatever.

I placed the paper back as I found it, mystified as to why Aunt Maggie should have singled it out, unless perhaps as a curiosity to show that our ancestor had been a riddle addict.

Descending to the stair landing, I brought my bag up to the big bedroom on the second floor which I was to share with Bill. Here again I was arrested by an unexpected bit of paper, this time lying on the old mahogany bureau.

Thinking it only a scrap of paper left there inadvertently by Bessie or Andrew as they put the house in order, I came near tossing it into the wastebasket without looking at it, for it was a bit of green wrapping paper of the sort used by one of Atlanta's largest department stores. Any housewife in the city would recognize it anywhere. But no housewife ever regarded a stranger message on more familiar paper, for upon it was printed in pencil:

"Leave this place at once. Your life is in danger."

Back in town I would have been sure it was a joke, but here alone, my morale already shaken, I stood turning the paper over in my fingers uncertainly until the slamming of a door belowstairs startled me out of my trance. At the sound, relief swept over me like a wave. Here at last were the servants. Or anyway, here was someone. Here was help. Thrusting the paper carelessly into the top bureau drawer, I fairly flew down the stairs, calling out to Bessie, Andrew, Aunt Maggie as I went.

But I received no answer and downstairs I still found no one. Nor did I find any door shut which I remembered as being open when I went upstairs. But outside, the wind had begun to blow and the rain that I had dreaded was already falling.

Seeking haven in the telephone closet under the stairway, I closed the door behind me and tried to reach my husband's office. There was no answer; but when I called the number of our home in Atlanta, the voice of my little girl's nurse was so reassuring that I began to get hold of myself again. Yes'm, little Sally was having her nap. Grandma Stuart was having a nap, too. Mr. Bill had stopped by the house just a little while ago, but said he had some errands to do and Miss Eve to pick up before he went to the country. Yes, ma'am, he said he had to pick up Miss Eve. No'm, there hadn't been no calls from Miss Maggie or Bessie or Andrew.

Miss Eve. Well, that was news. Eve had not been asked to the house party. She had not even been in town when it was planned yesterday. I laughed a little hysterically when I realized that the problem presented by an extra guest had for the moment shoved into the background the thought of that mysterious message in my bedroom.

But it was not just an extra guest, not just an extra woman, so much as the fact that it was Eve Benedict. Everybody knew Eve had been far too fond of Bob Dunbar when she divorced Frank Benedict last year. Eve was never a good loser. And Eve at an engagement party for Claire and Bob meant trouble in anybody's language.

Sometimes it was a little difficult to remember Eve as the thin, rather awkward girl who had been a couple of grades ahead of me in grammar school. She had been known as Evelyn then. Evelyn Pruitt. The thinness had changed to a seductive slimness as she grew up and she had married well both times. As Frank Benedict's wife, we had naturally seen something of her. But Aunt Maggie had never approved of Eve's background, or of what she called her "antecedents."

Aunt Maggie also disapproved quite frankly of her appearance, for Eve's figure now verged on voluptuousness and in the rather bizarre clothes she wore, with her black hair slicked back and her black eyes all made up, she was quite sophisticated looking. Yes, with the engaged pair and Aunt Maggie, Eve would certainly be an addition to the party.

Eve is a sort of forty-second cousin of mine, but I suppose the South is the only section of the country where such relationships can still be used as an excuse to crash a party you haven't been invited to, or indeed are counted at all. I resolved that I would tell Bill a thing or two for not insisting that she telephone me beforehand.

But anyway, I might as well arrange the flowers. First of all, the long-stemmed gladioli for tall vases on the tables in the hall. Then there were the red roses and white stock to be mixed for the dining-room table, and the yellow roses for the library and the drawing room. Busy in the dining room, I stopped dead still for a moment to listen, quite certain I had heard footsteps in the kitchen.

But when I went to investigate, I could find no one. Afterward, as I passed from room to room, I caught myself looking behind me, and in each room I left all the lights turned on. Outside, it was getting dark and the rain, whipped by the wind, beat against the windows and tore at the blinds. As I crouched on the hearth in the library, trying to rebuild the fire, the conviction grew upon me that someone, not friendly, was concealed in the house.

It was all right to tell myself that I was a fool, that it was only the wind and the rain. But, try as I might, I could not bring myself to leave that room and go back upstairs and dress. Finally, darting quickly from one to the other, I did close both doors. But as I sank down in the wing chair by the fire, which somehow failed to warm me, it seemed to me that the light, shining on the silver door-knobs, lent them a gleam somehow sinister. I turned my chair so I could not see either one. So I could not see it turn when something nameless grasped one of those doorknobs from the other side.

Out of doors the wind blew harder and the rain was swept in sheets against the old house. Sitting there, gripped by a paralysis of fear, I wondered if anybody ever would come.

II

THE HANDS OF THE OLD CLOCK on the mantel pointed to ten minutes of five when I heard the sound of an automobile horn in the driveway. At first I was almost afraid to believe my ears, I had strained them so against the moans of the wind, the lash of the rain, listening to hear that familiar sound. But now it was repeated, this time with two short blasts and one long. Our private signal. Bill was here. Everything would be all right.

That tall, red-haired, rather matter-of-fact young man who is my husband was probably a little startled at the ardor of my greeting, if husbands are ever surprised at anything. Eve had preceded him in with a great flourish of silver fox. "Knew you wouldn't want to have a house-warming without me," she announced a little defensively, "so when I heard about it, when I got in from New York this morning, I just called Bill and told him I was coming along."

"You were never more welcome," I said sincerely, for at that moment any familiar face looked heaven-sent. "But it is really not a house-warming," I explained. "That is not to be until Christmas Eve. This is just a little party for Claire and Bob. I suppose Bill has told you the news."

"So the international beauty finally won out," she commented flippantly. This has been Eve's choice designation for Claire ever since one of our Atlanta newspapers had grown fulsome on the subject of Claire's appearance when she was presented at court in London. And it is true that Claire is quite exceptionally lovely, with

37

her Titian hair, her priceless skin and her eyes which are gray, blue or green by turns, depending upon her mood or her costume.

"Well," Eve continued, "love certainly does work wonders, especially love and money. The thought of Bob with a sudden yen for the country in midwinter was just a little too much. I decided I had to come and see for myself. I suppose it all comes from my having left town at the wrong time."

"But where is Andrew?" asked Bill, as he struggled in with the bags.

"That's a funny thing," I said, but before I could explain why it was funny, another car swept up the drive, a car which turned out to be the missing station wagon, and Aunt Maggie was deposited at the front door. Bill's raised eyebrows, as he went forward to meet her, reminded me that this was his first intimation that she was to be among those present.

"How are you, Willie?" Aunt Maggie made things even better by greeting Bill with the nickname he detests.

"Such a day, such a day," she sighed, sinking with self-conscious exhaustion onto one of the library sofas. "And such a wild-goose chase." Pretty, in a rather plump, white-haired, Dresden-china sort of way, Aunt Maggie still gave herself all the airs of her girlhood grace and beauty. Now she pouted for a moment before answering my questions as to where she had been and why.

"You should know," she answered accusingly. "Didn't you telephone Andrew to take Bessie and go and meet the eleven-o'clock bus at Roswell to get a package which was to be sent out from town for you? And didn't you tell him to wait for the next bus if the package failed to come on the first one?"

Aunt Maggie swept along without waiting to listen to my emphatic denial. "Of course, you couldn't know that the second bus would be an hour late and that we would have a flat tire on the way back and that it would rain. And the dampness so bad for my sinuses."

When Aunt Maggie finally ran down, I said again, "But I telephoned no such message."

"Andrew probably just got fed up with the country," Eve suggested with her usual happy gift for facetiousness at the wrong time.

"Still, that's not like Andrew," said my husband. "Better look into it, Sally."

"I should say I will," I declared, starting toward the kitchen without more ado. "Tell Andrew to bring me a little sherry," Aunt Maggie called after me, plaintively. But before I reached the dining-room door, another car-load of guests could be heard arriving and my visit to the kitchen was accordingly deferred.

"Hail, hail, the gang's all here," sang Bill off key, as he ushered them in. And indeed we were all here. Alice, looking more negative and colorless than ever beside a fairly radiant Claire, was followed by Bob Dunbar and Kirk Pierce.

For a moment I thought Alice was carrying a big white muff, then I saw that it was an enormous Angora cat she held in her arms. "I do hope you don't mind my bringing Plutarch," she apologized as she dumped him down preparatory to shedding her wraps. "Since we were to be out here two nights, I told Mamie not to come back until Monday morning and there would have been nobody to feed and water Plutarch."

"Of course, I don't mind," I said, just as I had to Eve and before that to Aunt Maggie, but secretly hoping the rule of three would work a charm and that Plutarch was our last uninvited guest for the weekend.

"You should be wearing hoop skirts, Sally," said Bob, as his eyes looked deep into mine, then swept the wide hall with its graceful stairway and returned to smile at me lightly. "You are just the type, with those big brown eyes and brown curls."

Maybe it is the way he looks at you, as though you were the only person in the room, his eyes startlingly blue against a permanent sun tan. Or maybe it is the way he says things, his voice just above a troubling whisper in your ear. Anyway, Bob's compliments always make a woman feel that she is indeed a very special job. And, of course, Bob is really quite good looking himself in an outdoor, Gary Cooperish sort of way.

By this time we were all in the library, and in the hubbub of general greetings I surprised one of those intimate glances that two people sometimes exchange involuntarily in a crowd. Claire, a little flushed with embarrassment at the hurt look she saw in Kirk's eyes, turned her own eyes away. Kirk, recovering himself, looked away quickly, too. His glance, roving around the room, came to rest above the mantel on that portrait of Great-uncle Fred, complete with saber—a gentleman so fierce of visage that you almost expected him to charge right out of the canvas. "Good heavens, who's that?" Kirk gasped, shrinking back in mock alarm, the general laughter covering any awkwardness which might have arisen.

"That is one of my ancestors," I said. "He was a captain in the Confederate Cavalry."

"Gosh," marveled Kirk, who hails from Pennsylvania, "looking at him, I can't understand how the South lost the war."

Even Aunt Maggie laughed. And, looking at Kirk, I couldn't understand how I had ever thought I saw him running a foot race down the drive that afternoon. There is something so dynamic and forthright about him, something so reassuring about the humorous glint in his dark eyes, that you cannot imagine his being, well, circuitous about anything. Except for the fact that he was born on what Aunt Maggie would consider the wrong side of the Mason and Dixon line, Kirk is the type she would describe as a "black Southerner." Not that he is swarthy, but because of his black hair and his black-browed, keen black eyes. Kirk's quick way of talking rather sets him apart in the South and his eyes have something of that same quick quality, as though they see a lot in a little time and sometimes glance away because they have seen too much. No, it couldn't have been Kirk. And, anyway, hadn't he been my husband's roommate at Princeton, and best man at our wedding, and hadn't we all welcomed him with open arms when he came South a year ago as district manager for a large eastern corporation? Hadn't all our most eligible debutantes and divorcees tried to marry him? All but Claire, that is, who doesn't quite come within either category, of course.

"I knew Bob couldn't be happy without my congratulations," Eve was saying, "so I rushed right out to deliver them in person." Then in an aside to me, as I started once again toward the kitchen, "Of course, I realize it does give you an extra woman, now that everybody is here; but after all, I definitely never am the extra woman."

"I suppose that puts Alice neatly in her place," I couldn't help saying, careful that my voice should not carry beyond Eve's own ear.

"Well, of course, Kirk is rather nice," Eve agreed. "Some other time, perhaps. But for this weekend I should wait until all the returns are in before you are so sure about Claire and Bob."

"Oh, dear life!" Aunt Maggie cried out, shrinking back against the cushions of the sofa. "That horrible creature!" I thought perhaps she had read Eve's lips until I turned and saw the big white cat stalking in as if he owned the place.

"It's only Plutarch," Alice explained. "Come here, kitty darling."

Plutarch paid no attention whatsoever but proceeded to the hearth, where with great deliberation he selected a comfortable spot and curled up before the fire, unconsciously adding that cozy touch that a cat always does give to a room.

"Plutarch?" Aunt Maggie sniffed. "I never heard of such a thing."

"On account of his nine lives," Bob explained with a grin.

"But Plutarch didn't have nine lives," Aunt Maggie objected.

"I'll bet he wished he did have though," said Bob, "instead of just writing lives. That's why it seemed such a good name for the cat."

"I was going to call him Tinker Bell," said Alice, "but now he won't answer to anything but Plutarch. Isn't that just like Bob? And he's really my cat."

"You don't need to tell us that," said Eve, sweetly.

"Well, he'll have to be put somewhere else," Aunt Maggie announced with finality. "You know, Sally, I'm allergic to animal hairs."

"He can have the office," I said, placatingly, referring to the back room from which the masculine head of the house had conducted plantation affairs in days gone by, when the property included a much larger acreage. My grandmother had used it as a sort of morning room, but it was called the office. "I'm going back to the kitchen now," I added, "and I'll send Andrew in for him."

"Don't forget my sherry," Aunt Maggie implored, as though with her last ounce of energy, and this time I actually did get under way.

"Miss Sally," Andrew began the moment the kitchen door swung to behind me, "no package never did come."

"What is all this about a package and meeting the bus?" I snapped crossly. "Has everybody gone crazy?"

"But Miss Sally," Andrew remonstrated with an injured air, "they said it was you yourself said for us to go. For me to go and take Bessie and not come back until I got the package, 'cause it was something you needed for tonight. I couldn't think what it could be. Looks like to me we done brought everything in the world. And they said to get more eggs and to bring a hundred pounds of ice. I got the ice and the eggs all right. Howsomever, I didn't see where we'd need no ice with the electric refrigerator, or no eggs neither, unless you was going to have Bessie make a' angel food cake, and we done got all that fruit cake. Miss Maggie says she ain't going to stay here by herself, so she come with us."

"Andrew," I asked firmly, "who said for you to go?"

"Mr. Charles, at the Biltmore, where you have your hair fixed, said for us to go. He said you was sitting under that there dryer thing, having your nails manicured and you had forgot and there was not much time and for us to hurry."

"I did go to Charles's this morning," I admitted, "but I did not ask him or anyone else to telephone a message. What time did the call come?"

"About ten-thirty, wasn't it, Bessie?" Andrew questioned.

"Yes'm," affirmed Bessie, "'cause we had to hurry to get there in time to meet the eleven o'clock bus."

"And then there weren't nothing on it," said Andrew, with elaborate disgust, "or else that there driver lost it."

"But he couldn't lose it, if Miss Sally never sent nothing," Bessie reminded him.

"I wouldn't put it past him," said Andrew darkly.

Realizing we were getting nowhere fast in this direction, I suggested that a little speed with the mint juleps might not be amiss. I was reminded, as I expected to be, that no such thing is possible if there is to be a proper frost on the glass. Finally they were ready, with Bessie and me lending a hand. Andrew, regarding them with pride, observed, "This here ought to take the damp and the cramp out of all of 'em"—meaning the guests, of course.

When Bill and I were at last in our own room, dressing for dinner, I showed him the note I had found on the bureau. "Somebody must be pulling your leg," he said.

"All right," I agreed, "but who? Nobody but Aunt Maggie and the servants had any right in this house before I came out this afternoon. Which would you pick as the guilty one?"

"What about all those window washers and cleaners?"

"They all finished a week ago. You know we were out here Sunday and made a thorough tour of inspection."

"But it doesn't make sense," he argued.

"None of it does," I agreed, and told Bill about the man in the driveway and the door which I had heard slam downstairs and the footsteps I had thought I heard in the kitchen.

"Poor little kid," said Bill, inclosing me in a nice, comfortable hug, "what a time you have had. But it must have been mostly nerves. Your trespasser, no doubt, just made a mistake about the road, or drove in out of curiosity and decided it was easier to beat a retreat than to explain. And it couldn't have been anything but the wind that slammed the door. A draft somewhere. You know the wind did rise this afternoon. Just listen to it now."

I had to admit that there is nothing like an old house for spookiness, with wind and rain as sound effects. I shivered again, thinking of my long vigil in the library. Thai reminded me of the strange absence of the servants and Aunt Maggie.

Bill was ready to agree by then that there was something decidedly fishy about the entire setup. "Unless possibly some bright soul is trying to stage a practical joke, and even then it doesn't hang together."

"You don't think we had better go back to town?" I asked, feeling a bit foolish, for Bill's presence made everything seem so much more rational.

"In this rain?" hooted Bill. "With the work on that strip of road at its present stage, we'll be lucky if we are able to pull out tomorrow. Besides"—and Bill's voice took on a more serious tone—"if there is anything funny going on, we might as well see it through.

"And speaking of riddles," continued Bill, "did you have to ask Aunt Maggie? I thought this was to be a party. A nice, quiet party, far from the madding crowd and all that, but still a party. Or was it your idea that her monologues on family trees would prove a diversion?"

"Bill Stuart," I said, "don't be simple. You should know she asked herself. She just wanted to look at family papers and use the study on the third floor. Meals on a tray. No trouble. ('You and the guests have a good time, Sally. I'll be busy.') You know."

"Meals on a tray, my eye!" scoffed Bill. "You know how she loves an audience. She'll be in everybody's hair the whole time, and nobody able to walk out because of the downpour."

"But," I argued, "you know, in spite of all that, she is a sweet old soul and I couldn't run the risk of hurting her feelings."

"Humph," grinned Bill, giving me a pinch on my bare shoulder. "What about this favorite-niece business? Nothing there, I suppose? No thought of a nice little legacy. Just your kind heart. I suppose that kind heart is why I married you."

"Well, after all," I chided in the same vein "you could have been said to marry me because of my expectations as an heiress. Anyway, speaking of invited guests, what about dragging Eve out here? Why under the shining sun didn't you make her telephone me first? I would have found some way to head her off."

"Did tell her to. She called back and said she couldn't get you, but she knew it would be all right."

"Well, anyway, have we a gun?"

"Certainly not," Bill reassured me. "And a good thing, too. I don't want you getting scared and killing off our guests, much as I should like to get rid of some of them. I'll go on down and see if Andrew can scare up another round of drinks before dinner."

"Wait a minute," I demanded, applying lipstick hurriedly, "I don't intend to let you out of my sight until we are safely back in Atlanta."

As we crossed the upstairs hall toward the head of the stairs, I heard voices issuing from Eve's room, and when we were even with the door, I noticed that it was slightly ajar. Recognizing the other voice as that of Aunt Maggie, I paused for a moment, intending to announce myself and drop in. But I changed my mind when I heard Aunt Maggie say, "It was bad manners, to say the least, for you to come here uninvited, Evelyn. Bad manners and decidedly bad taste, but I have always contended that it is too late to try to be well born at the age of thirty."

As I hesitated, torn between curiosity and what Aunt Maggie would call good manners, I could not hear what Eve replied, but Aunt Maggie, her voice rising still higher than her usual wont, admonished, "If you don't leave Bob alone, I'll go to Frank. If he knew the truth, you wouldn't be collecting such handsome alimony."

Then I heard Eve say, a deadly venom in her voice, "You do and I'll kill you."

"Hey, what's going on?" stage-whispered Bill, who had been busy lighting a cigarette at the head of the stairs. "No fair for the hostess to eavesdrop. She might hear things about the service."

III

Our other guests were already in the library and Andrew was passing fresh mint juleps when we got down. A few moments later Aunt Maggie made one of her entrances, stately in black lace. Just behind her was Eve, wearing a dinner dress of heavy red satin that did almost too much for her figure. I knew she had worn it with Claire's red-gold hair in mind. But Claire, in green velvet, must have smiled to herself if she shared my thought.

I was not surprised a little later when I found Bob in the dining room, pouring himself a stiff, straight drink from one of the old Waterford decanters.

"I'm so happy about you and Claire," I told him.

"Thanks, Sally," he said, tossing off his drink and pouring himself another without even a pause between. "You know how I've always felt about Claire's money. Nearly always in debt, too. But I'm getting that cleared up . . . little revenue from . . . an old investment. Oh, well, I don't need to be talking like this to you—"

"Of course not," I agreed, and suddenly I knew that it was Claire who had managed this new solvency to pave the way for their engagement. Ever so cleverly, ever so indirectly, no doubt, so Bob would never in the world suspect, knowing Clair, I was sure I recognized her fine Italian hand back of it all. I wondered why she had not thought of it before.

"I'm sorry Eve had to invite herself out here," I apologized.

"Hadn't seen her since she got back to town," he said, wavering a little as he stood. "However, I shouldn't have got myself into such a mess. Seems to be one of the best things I do."

"It's because you are too kind to children and dumb animals," I told him. But I knew well enough how difficult it was for him to avoid complications. Ordinarily he was so full of nonchalance and sparkle, of such gay exuberance, that your own mood lifted merely in anticipation of his approach. He was, in short, what Aunt Maggie called "good company."

She often said such people should be endowed by their less-attractive friends or by the government or somebody, because they did so much to leaven the lump of humanity in general. No doubt, she would have approved of Claire's inspiration.

With a whimsical smile at the drink he still held in his hand, Bob said, "Well, I'm going to turn over a new leaf. Going to settle down. Going to be serious."

"Heaven forbid," I told him. "There are enough dull people in the world as it is."

"Let's have a drink on it," he suggested.

I smiled and shook my head, uncomfortable in the contradictory role of hostess and interested friend who feels that she should raise a restraining hand. We all knew Bob drank a little too much at times, but usually he carried his liquor as he did his troubles, with such casual grace that they both rather added to his attractiveness.

"Well, don't let it bother you about Eve," he said, as he downed his drink. "If any of us could look ahead and see what is likely to happen—"

Instead of finishing his observation, he refilled his glass once more and lifted it to me in a little gesture which might have been a toast or a farewell to bachelor freedom or almost anything gay and gallant, but which I suppose only meant that he was getting a bit too tight to round out his sentences. Anyway, it was plain enough that dinner must be served at once. It would never do to have Bob pass out at his own engagement party. Eve would enjoy that far too much.

But I had hardly begun ladling tomato bisque from the lovely old Spode tureen before Eve was off again, trouble bent. As any normal hostess, I had sat down at the table feeling a natural pride in the beauty of its appointments. The shining surface of old mahogany, high-lighted by the flame of waxen white tapers in Sheffield candelabra—the dramatic combination of blood-red and snow-white flowers—heirloom china and silver. The dependable excellence of the food about to be set before us. Champagne for celebration.

I resented that all this should be needlessly spoiled, not to mention the discomfort to my guests.

In the most dulcet of tones, as though intent upon dispensing sweetness and light for all, Eve had asked, "Been out to the Cavalier Club lately, Bob? Your luck must be picking up if you are able to undertake matrimony."

Bob flushed as he answered briefly, "No, haven't been out lately."

Although Claire went on talking in a low tone to Kirk as though she had not heard, Alice turned a look of open hatred upon Eve, and you had the feeling that everyone at the table was really listening for what Eve would say next. We all knew she and Bob had spent too much time together at the Cavalier Club shortly after Eve's divorce and that while she had won steadily Bob had lost even more steadily—sums which grew more and more spectacular, all things considered.

We did not have long to wait. "How's Big Shot?" Eve asked. "Still being a big shot?"

"Who's Big Shot?" Aunt Maggie wanted to know, and we all laughed because the words sounded so funny when she said them, quite aside from providing a welcome relief from strain.

"Big Shot Anderson," Eve explained. "He runs the Cavalier Club, high-class gambling joint. Oh, yes, strictly illegal. But that's nothing for Big Shot. He used to be a bootleg king. They say he is at the bottom or the top of the numbers racket now. The bug, you know. Or would you? That's Big Shot. Nice person. Nobody you would know."

"But I did know some Andersons," said Aunt Maggie, and we all smiled again. "They came to Georgia from North Carolina and were really quite nice, though rather plain. This, er, Big Shot may be one of them."

"Well, I wouldn't say 'plain' exactly describes Big Shot Anderson," Eve remarked, a little dryly. "He's a big shot because he does things in a big way. Isn't that right, Bob?"

"Oh, by the way," my husband broke in, bent on taking the conversation away from Eve, to everybody's manifest relief, "that reminds me. I heard something today that rather indicates Atlanta is getting a pretty active underworld. Hugh Brannen was kidnapped yesterday."

"What?" we all exclaimed together, or "Kidnapped?" Hugh Brannen is one of our richest citizens and a philanthropist. We could not remember anybody ever having been kidnapped in Atlanta before. Certainly nobody we knew.

"I heard it from Paul Mitchell, of *The Journal*," said Bill. "The papers had just got the story. It seems Mr. Brannen was driving to the office in his Ford as usual when the kidnapers stopped him and took over. Mrs. Brannen kept it quiet until she could send the ransom money, so there wouldn't be any complications about his being released this morning. She requested that nothing be printed Saturday, but it will all be in the papers tomorrow. I didn't find out—"

"That just goes to show," Aunt Maggie interrupted, "what a man's wife can do to him. Hugh Brannen doesn't care a thing about showing off. Won't have a chauffeur for himself and drives an inexpensive car. But she would have him buy that yacht. Got him in all the newspapers down in Miami. I've known Hugh Brannen ever since he was a baby. He was the pokiest little boy I ever saw but, of course, you never can tell by that. His mother was one of the South Carolina DuBoses. Her family was very displeased when she married Walter Brannen. The Brannens were nice people but—"

"Plain," interposed Eve.

"Plain," Aunt Maggie continued, as though Eve did not exist. "And Walter really did make money. Now when Hugh married— Let me see, his wife was Effie Goodrum, of course, but—oh yes, her mother was one of the Virginia Pierces. No money, but very fine family. By the, way, Kirk, did you have any Virginia connections?"

"I don't think so," Kirk smiled, "but thanks just the same."

"Speaking of money," said Eve, "there are all kinds of ways of getting it."

"If you are referring to Bob and Claire," said Aunt Maggie, with great dignity, "I think it is an eminently suitable match. Two charming young people uniting two very old and distinguished families. Their children will have two Signers, since there is one on each side—"

"Oh, Aunt Maggie," Claire broke in, smilingly, "do spare my maidenly modesty."

All of us who had grown up together had in childhood adopted immediate relatives as community property, most often regarded as our common cross. Now we all laughed, but it was plain to see that Kirk Pierce appreciated the humor of the situation more than the rest of us did. It was equally plain to see that Bob had not enjoyed that thrust about money.

"By the way," Kirk asked, obviously trying, as Bill had, to create a diversion, "did anybody hear how Wallace Arnold is getting along? I meant to go by the hospital today, but didn't have time."

"I telephoned," said Alice, "but his condition is still serious."

"Is that Jim Arnold's son?" Aunt Maggie wanted to know. And, "What is the matter with him?"

"I'm not a bit surprised," she went on to tell us when informed that he had been injured in an automobile accident. "His father used to drive the finest team of horses in town and was always having runaways. He broke his leg in two places one time, I remember, and another time he was hung up on a barbed-wire fence with the seat of his pants torn out. Wallace comes by his wildness naturally."

Her opinion was still unchanged when Bill explained that Wallace had not been driving the car at the time of the accident. "Birds of a feather," she remarked, succinctly.

When I'm alone with Aunt Maggie I can take all this sort of thing more or less for granted. It is only when I am conscious of its effects on other people that it annoys me acutely. But we got on toward dessert somehow, some of Bessie's surpassing Tipsy Squire, and were just rising from the table when Aunt Maggie turned to me and said, "Oh, Sally, I almost forgot to tell you. I believe I have found the clue to the secret room."

"What's this about a secret room?" Bill asked as we settled ourselves in the library for coffee, and everybody clamored to hear more about it.

I told them all I knew, which wasn't much. "There is supposed to be one somewhere in the house, but its whereabouts was lost after my great-great-grandfather's death. At least my grandfather and grandmother always said they never had been able to find it. There was a whole generation between, of course. I remember we used to speculate about it when I visited here as a child. I hadn't thought of it for years."

"But why did he want a secret room?" Claire asked. "Was it a Bluebeard room?"

"Nice thought for a bride to be having," chided Kirk, with a grin.

"Search me," I answered. "I think it was because he owned some valuable jade or didn't believe in banks or something. Wasn't that it, Aunt Maggie?"

"It was not at all unusual for houses to have secret rooms back at the time this one was built," she pointed out. "The story, as I always heard it, was that he had to keep large sums of money on the place. And, of course, there was his jade. You know the family moved to Roswell along with the Kings and Bullochs and Dunwodys and others from Darien, Georgia, who established a colony here on account of the climate. Most of the others built in what became the town of Roswell, but your great-great-grandfather acquired this land farther out. The families were all intimate, however. I remember hearing my own grandmother tell about being a guest at Mittie Bulloch's wedding at Bulloch Hall when she married Theodore Roosevelt. Grandmother said they brought ice for the wedding all the way from Savannah. Atlanta wasn't much of a place in those days.

"It was Theodore Roosevelt, Jr., the son of Mittie, who later became President of the United States," Aunt Maggie continued. "Another son was the father of Mrs. Franklin Roosevelt. I remember Mrs. W. E. Baker, one of Mittie Bulloch's bridesmaids, was still living at Barrington Hall when Theodore Roosevelt visited Atlanta as President. He sent word to her that he would be glad to receive her in his private railway car, but she sent word back to the effect that gentlemen called on ladies, rather than the other way around. He may have been President of the United States to everyone else, but he was just Mittie Bulloch's son to Mrs. Baker."

"Wonderful," applauded Kirk, who always egged Aunt Maggie on. "And what did the President do?"

Aunt Maggie smiled at him archly. "He rode the twenty miles from Atlanta to Roswell and called on his mother's old friend, of course," she said.

"Didn't O. Henry write a story about something of the sort?" Kirk asked, while Eve made a moue, indicating her boredom.

"I suspect you are thinking about his story of a Southern literary magazine published sometime after the War between the States," said Aunt Maggie, preening herself on having found such an appreciative listener. "I don't remember exactly, but I believe the editors hesitated about using a very excellent contribution because it was the work of an unknown, named Theodore Roosevelt. Finally, they got around the difficulty with an introduction, explaining that it was written by a member of the well-known Bulloch family, of Georgia—"

"That's all very pretty," Eve interrupted, "but what became of the jade? Is it still in the secret room? I claim my share as a descendant if it is found."

Warned by Aunt Maggie's flush, I hastily began to explain that, as I remembered the story, the jade had been sold after the Civil War when the family hadn't much else to carry on with. But while Aunt Maggie's tone was low-pitched, I could still hear her admonishing Eve, "Don't give yourself airs, Evelyn Pruitt. You are not a descendant. Your great-great-grandfather was only a second cousin of the Graham who built this house. You are descended from the black sheep of the family."

"Was the jade very valuable?" Claire asked politely.

"I don't know," Aunt Maggie admitted regretfully. "He had been a great traveler. I remember hearing that he thought more of his jade than he did of this whole plantation and maybe his family. He kept a journal in which he set down most of his expenditures, but never what he spent for jade. He was also a great reader. He assembled most of the books in this library. It was in one of them that I—"

Just then Andrew came in to collect the coffee things. "Excuse me, Miss Maggie, ma'am," he said, "but here's one of your papers you dropped. Leastwise, I think it is. It looks like one of them old papers you are always working with."

Taking the proffered sheet, Aunt Maggie unwound the chain which held her glasses at the shoulder, adjusted them on her nose and glanced at it hurriedly. "Oh, thank you, Andrew. Yes, indeed," she said. And then, as though suddenly reminded that duty calls, she rose to her feet. "If you will excuse me. I have some work to do."

No duchess could have smiled with more conscious graciousness as the men arose. And so, bidding us an inclusive good night, Aunt Maggie swept from the room.

Eve immediately launched into a dissertation on jade. In spite of her usual gay, sophisticated chatter there have been times when I suspected she should have been a school-teacher. Now she was showing us all how much she had learned about jade while traveling in China. So many grades of jade—pork jade, this and that, before you finally came to the precious jewel jade. . . .

I was not surprised when the group began to melt away. "Some powder," as a polite excuse. "A spot of brandy." Soon only Eve and I were left.

"Let's round up the others and go down and try the new game room," I said, when the subject of jade and I were both exhausted.

"I'd like a little powder," said Eve.

"I'll just speak to Bessie a moment," I answered.

Bessie's ideas and mine agree perfectly about breakfast. I would be as fat as she is if I didn't work so hard on my tennis stroke and swimming. Now we could not decide between chicken hash or country sausage with waffles, so we compromised on both.

"And you know, Miss Sally," Bessie reminded me, "Mr. Bill ain't had nothing, lessen they's eggs."

"All right, scrambled eggs and some of that Virginia ham. And, oh, yes, Bessie, you brought along some of those fig preserves, didn't you?"

"Yes'm, and a jar of that wild-strawberry jam, too."

"Fine, let's have some of both."

This conference could not have consumed more than a few minutes. Leaving the big, spicy-smelling kitchen, which originally had been the dining room, I passed on into the breakfast room. The original kitchen had been a detached building, as was the case with so many ante-bellum houses. Cutting off, at the back, a part of the long central hall to use as a breakfast room had been one of the changes made since the place came into our possession. I was thinking of all this, as I gave the room a final appraising glance before stepping out into the little back passageway beyond, with its steps leading down to the basement and the new game room. From this passageway, back steps also ascend upward. Two other doors open into it, one leading to the office, another to the back porch.

In the passage I stumbled over something that blocked my way. There on the floor at my feet lay Aunt Maggie.

IV

Of course, when I first found Aunt Maggie, I thought she had fainted.

Evidently she had gone upstairs after leaving the library, for she was wearing a Shetland wool sweater over her lace dinner dress. The only explanation I could think of was that she had changed her mind about working and had come down the back stairway because it was a short cut to the game room and that the steep stairs had been too much for her. Or that perhaps she had caught her heel on the step and tripped herself. Like many rather stout women, Aunt Maggie had always been a little vain about her feet and would never give up high heels. Even in that moment of shock, the thought of the high heels led me to wonder about the sweater. Aunt Maggie, a stickler in matters of dress as in manners, would never have worn a sweater over a dinner dress except perhaps in the privacy of the third-floor study for a session with family papers. I was sure she had come downstairs on an errand and not to rejoin the guests.

All these thoughts flashed through my mind as I hurried back through the breakfast room, calling to Bessie, "Bring some water, quick. Aunt Maggie has fainted."

Back again in the passage and endeavoring to find a pulse in Aunt Maggie's wrist, I was startled by the white cat appearing suddenly out of nowhere and fawning against me with a rather disgruntled meow. "Scat," I told him sharply, expecting Aunt Maggie to revive at any moment and faint again at the unwelcome sight.

How had Plutarch got out of the office, anyway? Automatically I glanced toward the door. Yes, it was closed, but, of course, there was another door opening into the breakfast room from the office.

Andrew, who loves to dramatize a crisis, was right on the heels of Bessie's stockinged feet as she padded out with a pitcher of water. While Bessie sprinkled Aunt Maggie's face, I felt for her heartbeat, and Andrew fidgeted, full of suggestions. "If we could just get her on a sofa, Miss Sally. So we could get her feet higher'n her head. It's the blood. We want to get it to her head."

When I could find no heartbeat, I began to feel my first forebodings that perhaps Aunt Maggie had not merely fainted as a result of falling. Even then I thought it was only Andrew's easy excitability when he gasped out, "Law, Miss Sally, she been strangled."

But there were the black marks on her throat.

Sitting back limply on my heels and suddenly feeling very sick, I managed to say, "Get Mr. Bill."

In what seemed no more than a minute the entire house party was crowded there in the little back passageway. Some of them came up the steps from the basement game room. Some came down from the upstairs bedrooms and some from the drawing room. At least they seemed to come from all directions. Feeling faint as I did, it also seemed to me as though someone had come in from the rain outside, but I thought nothing of it at the time. We had not then begun hunting clues for a murderer, and I was too dazed to do more than take in the incredible fact that Aunt Maggie was dead.

I said, as the men went through the same motions I had already tried, "It's no use. We must get her on one of the sofas in the drawing room." There is a sofa in the office and it would have been simpler to take her in there, but I was still thinking of that as Plutarch's hideaway, not realizing that there was now no necessity for his imprisonment.

"Better phone for a doctor," said Bill, still on his knees, doggedly trying to find a pulse in Aunt Maggie's limp wrist. "Kirk, ask the operator at Roswell to get one for us, will you? That will be nearer than Atlanta."

"Dr. Grace was Grandmother's doctor," I said.

"But Miss Maggie done dead, Mr. Bill," Andrew remonstrated. "Ain't nothing no doctor can do. Oh, poor Miss Maggie. Poor Miss Maggie. She was always so proud."

A lump rose in my throat and I turned my eyes away. Andrew had painted an all-too-lifelike portrait of Aunt Maggie. I could not bear to look at her there on the floor.

"Well, we'll need a doctor, anyway," said Kirk. "I'll go and call. Or, Bob, maybe you had better go. I came out here with you. I'm not certain I could tell anybody how to reach the place."

"But anybody in Roswell will know," Bill and I said together. "Just tell them Wisteria Hall." Against my will, my mind went back to the man I had seen leaving the place that afternoon. Could it have been Kirk? Could he be mixed up in all this? Was he now trying to cover up by calling attention to the fact that he was unfamiliar with the neighborhood?

"I'll telephone," offered Bob.

"I don't know what the usual procedure is," said Bill, "but if Aunt Maggie has been choked to death—"

"Choked to death?" shrieked Alice. "Do you mean to say she was murdered?"

I leaned back against the wall as Alice's words brought home the sweeping realization of what had happened. Icy fingers seemed to stop the breath in my throat. Opening my mouth, I tried to speak, tried to say something to Bill about the note and how it had not been a joke after all and that we must go back to town as quickly as possible. But my teeth were chattering so that the words refused to come. Anyway, nobody was paying the slightest attention to me.

They were all staring down at Aunt Maggie, their expressions ranging from blank amazement to horror, and on Alice's face was sheer, naked terror.

Bill got himself to his feet. "I was just going to say," he began again, "that if Aunt Maggie has been— Well, that maybe we should not move her until—until the proper authorities have made an examination." Then his eyes caught mine and he moved quickly to my side, putting an arm around my shoulders. "You shouldn't be standing here, Sally, after such a shock. You are all right, aren't you?" he asked anxiously. And as I nodded dumbly, with the tears burning my eyeballs, he added, "Claire, take her into the library, won't you? All you girls go on in there and let us try to figure out what to do."

I said, swallowing hard, "I don't care what the usual procedure is, I'm not going to leave Aunt Maggie lying here on the floor. I think we should take her into the drawing room."

Just at that moment Bob returned from the telephone. "I can't get the operator to answer," he announced, "The line seems to be dead."

"But it was all right this afternoon," I insisted. "I talked to Atlanta from here."

"Somebody's cut the wires," gasped Alice, and keeled over in a faint. Both Bill and Kirk caught her as she went down and Bill said, somewhat irritably, "I told you girls to go on into the library."

As we were bringing Alice to on the sofa, Eve said, "I can't see why she should be fainting about the telephone."

"It was close in there," I pointed out. "I felt a little faint myself."

"Well, of course, there might have been some excuse for your fainting," Eve agreed, with more tact that one usually expected from her. "After all, it was a nasty shock, finding Aunt Maggie like that."

"Bad enough for Sally," agreed Bill, "but, even so, not quite what a guest would expect as the usual thing, either."

"What nobody seems to realize," said Alice, straightening up and brushing a straggling lock of tan-colored hair away from her pale hazel eyes, "is that a murderer is loose around here. With the telephone out of commission, what are we going to do?"

"It was probably only the wind and the rain that put the telephone out," said Bill placatingly. "You know how these rural lines are. As soon as we move Aunt Maggie, we will see about getting in touch with somebody. You're all right now, aren't you, Alice?" he asked on his way to the door.

But Alice was not all right, for she almost gave way to hysteria when Bob rose from his place at her side. "No, no, don't leave," she begged. "One of the men at least should stay here with us."

"I was only going to see if I could help." Bob patted her hand reassuringly.

"Well," Bill admitted, "I don't think it would be a bad idea for Bob to stay in here. It would make Alice and the rest of you feel better. Kirk and I can take care of—of Aunt Maggie. Then we will see about getting in touch with the doctor or coroner, or somebody."

That picture of Aunt Maggie, crumpled up on the floor, all her proud assurance gone, and with the marks of the killer's lingers on her throat, was a little too much for me at the moment. She had been a part of my background ever since I could remember. I had been named Sarah Margaret for her and had always been her special favorite. Although she had been exacting, she had been indulgent, too, and I was genuinely fond of her. Thinking of all this, I could not help saying, "Who on earth could have wanted to harm poor Aunt Maggie?"

A jumble of questions answered me. How did you happen to find her? Was she already dead? Did you see or hear anything suspicious? How do you think it could have happened? And so on.

Then Eve asked out of a clear sky, "Aren't you her sole heir, Sally? Of course, I know you feel badly about her death, and that this is not just the time for congratulation. But after all, she is dead."

"No," said Claire, "I don't think it is quite the time for such a discussion. It isn't as though Sally was not fond of Aunt Maggie, you know."

To have a third person take sides against her, even in a trivial conversation, was more than Eve could ever bear. Now she turned on Claire spitefully. "It doesn't make much difference what you think," she snapped. "If this is murder, we can expect to have things pretty well aired before it is all over."

Stung as I was by Eve's inconsiderate outburst, I realized vaguely that she was trying to get back at Claire rather than to hurt me but, even so, it was not easy to take. I tried to tell myself that she was desperately unhappy and that this was what made her lash out at people. And that she was unhappy because she either didn't know what she wanted or, perhaps, didn't realize what she wanted until it belonged to someone else.

But, anyway, it would not mend matters for me to lose my head. And there was no gainsaying the fact that she was right about the unhappy consequences which must follow in the wake of murder.

So I said, "Bob, don't you think it would be a good idea to get Alice a sip of brandy? Will anyone else have a drink?"

Bob brought in a decanter and glasses from the dining room and both Alice and Eve took the small drinks offered, after which he downed two quite large ones himself. "And now if you girls will excuse me a moment," he said, "I'll go upstairs and get my pipe."

"Hurry back," Alice told him, obviously braced by the brandy.

"That awful pipe," Eve chided. "Hasn't Claire made you throw it away yet?"

Bob pretended not to hear as he passed through the doorway, and we all settled down in silent gloom before the fire. Claire lit a cigarette and it was then I noticed where Eve had tossed several half-smoked ones to the hearth, their tips smeared with lipstick. There were plenty of ash trays about and, although I knew her carelessness was due to natural nervousness under the circumstances, it did bring back Aunt Maggie's remark about the impossibility of being what she called "well born" at the age of thirty. And that made me think of something else. Of Eve's threat when Aunt Maggie spoke of going to Eve's divorced husband. And of their later passage-at-arms in the library. Yet I believed at the time and I believed now that Eve had not meant her threat literally.

And so we sat and stared into the fire.

"God," Eve ejaculated finally, "what a pleasant little party this turned out to be!"

It was on the tip of my tongue to remind her that she had invited herself, but I decided again that we had enough trouble on hand without letting Eve stir up more. From the way Alice looked at her, I knew she also would like to tell Eve this and plenty besides. But she restrained herself and, shivering slightly, inquired instead, "Why doesn't Bob come back?"

It did seem that Bob had been gone rather longer than his errand required, but just as I was about to say that he no doubt would be along in a moment every light in the house went out, plunging the library into darkness relieved only by the glow of the coals in the fireplace.

Alice screamed, Eve said "Damn," and Claire and I, both reaching out to clasp hands with Alice, found that our own hands had come together instead.

"There are matches on the table," I said, groping for them in the darkness. As I lighted the candles on the mantel and table and secretary to flickering flames, Eve stirred up the coals and put another log on the fire.

"What the devil do you suppose has happened now?" she asked.

"It's the murderer," Alice whimpered. "We'll all have our heads cut off."

"Well, that's no reason why we should lose them beforehand," snapped Eve. "Anyway, it is probably only this damned storm."

"Yes," I hastened to agree. "Of course, it is the storm. I don't suppose Bob will ever be able to find his way down from upstairs. After this I shall certainly provide flashlights for every room."

Eve smiled one of her cryptic smiles and said nothing; but I gathered that what I did about flashlights in the future was of small interest to her, as she obviously did not intend to be among those present.

"You can call it the storm, if you like," Alice quavered, "but after all, Aunt Maggie was murdered. Then there's the telephone. And now the lights."

And there is still more that you don't know about, I thought, as Kirk and Bill came in through the dining-room door, Bill carrying one of the big silver candelabra from the dining room, which he carefully deposited beside the candlesticks on the secretary.

"I've told Andrew to take the station wagon and go to Roswell and report what has happened," he said. "It seemed the most practical thing to do. I knew we would all feel better when somebody from the outside could take the situation in hand."

"Bessie insists that she is going with Andrew," Kirk observed. "And on a night like this. There's marital devotion for you."

"That's not consideration for Andrew," said Bill, dryly. "Bessie's scared to stay alone in the servants' house."

To me there didn't seem anything so strange about Bessie's timidity. I didn't want to be alone anywhere myself right then. That made me think of Bob. "I suspect you had better rescue Bob," I told Bill. "He's probably wandering around upstairs like a lost soul in the outer darkness."

But Bob himself appeared just then, having had matches in his pocket and having located his bedside candle, as he explained. "Didn't I hear you say you had sent Andrew to Roswell?" he asked Bill.

At Bill's assent Bob seemed to hesitate, as though he wished to say something but feared to offend. "You don't seem to approve," Eve remarked. "Any suggestions?"

"No, no," Bob hastened to reply. "Only had anybody thought that we have sent away the two people who were nearest the scene at the time of the—crime?"

"You're barking up the wrong tree there, old man," Bill assured him. "We've had Bessie and Andrew ever since we were married and, while that may not be a life-time, Bessie's mother, who died a year or so ago, was Aunt Ann's cook for thirty years."

"Longer than that," I said. "Your Aunt Ann says she practically raised Bessie."

"There you go. Talking just like Aunt Maggie," Eve cut in. "Family, family, family. After all, it is possible for murderers to have parents just the same as anyone else."

"But it is silly to suspect Andrew or Bessie," Claire chimed in. "After all, if that had been their intention, they had plenty of opportunity last night when they were all out here alone."

"Still," Bob argued, "we might as well face it. Somebody who was in the house at the time has to be guilty. And if not the servants—"

"Then the guests," Eve finished for him.

"Or some outsider," I suggested.

"That's a thought," Bob agreed. "And this outsider may still be inside."

"That's what I've been thinking all the time," wailed Alice.

"We'll search the place," said Bill, determinedly.

"But I don't want to be left alone," Alice wailed again.

At that moment Andrew appeared in the doorway. "Mr. Bill, sir," he announced when all eyes were turned upon him, "I done had a' accident."

"Accident?" we all echoed.

"What do you mean, accident?" Bill demanded.

"Yes, sir, Mr. Bill. First I find a flat tire. I done use the spare this afternoon, so I have to pump it up. Then when I get it changed and Bessie and me are going out the gate, just as we get to where the road been worked on, we skid and run into a tree. I tried and I tried, but I can't get that engine started up again. What I come to ask now is, can I use your car, Mr. Bill, or yet Miss Sally's? I dunno whether I get any farther'n I did the first time, but I try if you say the word. That road's mighty bad. Yes, sir, mighty bad. And it ain't stopped raining one minute since it start up this afternoon."

"Well," said Bill, "we've got to get word to Roswell, somehow. I hate to make you try it on a night like this and over that road, but I suppose you will just have to take my car and see what you can do. It's too bad we have no tire chains."

"Yes, sir, Mr. Bill, thank you, sir," said Andrew and was gone.

"How about that search party?" asked Kirk. "If the girls don't want to be left alone, suppose we divide into two groups, one of us starting in the basement, the other on the top floor and meeting on the second floor."

"Good," said Bill. "Let's all be sure we have plenty of matches, in case our candles go out. By the way, Sally, isn't there a flashlight here somewhere?"

Just like a husband, I thought, expecting you to produce whatever is needed, no matter what the circumstances. Water on the desert. A compass in the wilderness. A flashlight in an unoccupied country house.

"There's one in the compartment of my car," I answered, hoping there was. "And Andrew probably has one in the station wagon."

"I'll tell him to bring one in before he gets away," said Bill, going away toward the kitchen.

"You know, that's a funny thing," he said, when he came back. "My car had a flat, too. Andrew's changing it now. I suppose it must have been all those workmen we had out here. Don't see any point in leaving nails around though."

For our search, which finally got under way, Bill and Eve and Claire decided to start from the basement, while the rest of us climbed to the third floor. I don't think Claire was very keen about going with Eve, but Alice was bent on sticking close to Bob and I somehow couldn't bring myself to face that back passage just then.

In the study I noticed the paper which had been propped against the inkwell was there no longer. But, of course, Aunt Maggie had put it somewhere else. We found her room as neat as could be. Slippers under the bed. Her deep purple dressing gown across the foot. Silver toilet things on the bureau. None of which she would ever use again.

Neither this room nor any of the others showed evidence of having been entered by alien feet.

Back in the hall, the candles cast weird shadows before us and Alice clung more closely to Bob. Instinctively I also moved closer to Kirk, for in the uncertain light it seemed to me that one of the doors of a big armoire moved slightly.

But when we investigated we found it empty.

"Just nerves," laughed Kirk reassuringly.

We had almost finished with the second floor when we met the other crew. Evidently I was not the only one suffering from nerves, for Bill was still kidding Eve because she had brought along one of the darts from the game room.

"For protection," she announced.

"I told her an ice pick would be much more efficient," Bill said.

"But you could do a pretty good job with this, planted right in the vicinity of the heart," Eve argued, flourishing the heavy feather-tipped steel pin to illustrate her point and making Alice wince.

"Shouldn't think it would be long enough," said Bob.

"Oh, yes, the pin is nearly three inches," she pointed out.

Nobody had found anything on the tour. But Andrew had come back into the house. It developed that there were two tires flat on Bill's car. That tires on every car on the place were flat.

Somebody had accomplished this very neatly by removing the valve cores from at least two tires on each car.

V

AFTER A GOOD DEAL of rather pointless discussion as to ways and means, it was finally decided to postpone until morning any further effort to get in touch with the outside world.

And when I say outside world, I am in no way exaggerating the feeling of isolation which completely overwhelmed us, although we were only five miles from Roswell and twenty from Atlanta. No telephone, no electric lights, the automobiles out of commission, the road practically impassable and the rain still pouring. And in the drawing room the sheeted figure of Aunt Maggie, with finger marks on her throat.

So it was not a very gay house-party group gathered around the fire in the library. There have been times when I thought candlelight romantic, but this was not one of them.

Beyond the circle of the firelight the big old room was full of shadows, and beyond these shadows the outer rooms were swallowed in darkness so complete that it was almost palpable. One felt it there waiting, with something ominous in the waiting—fingers, perhaps, which might reach out and draw one into the suffocation of darkness even more final.

In fact, when Andrew opened the dining-room door unexpectedly, Claire, who was sitting with her back toward him, started up with a little involuntary cry of fright. Bob and Kirk both sprang up as though to rush to her defense, furnishing the rest of us a little comic relief from strain and giving all an opportunity to laugh, even though some of us did so a bit shakily.

Andrew, the unwitting cause of it all, was triumphantly holding aloft an oil lamp, and I for one felt like giving him three rousing cheers at the sight. He had remembered the two lamps and can
of kerosene oil which we had moved from the kitchen pantry to
the basement, and he and Bessie had salvaged them and put the
lamps in condition for use.

My grandmother kept them because she never quite trusted
electricity. A search of all the cars had revealed only one flashlight.

"Where you want I should put the other'n, Miss Sally?" Andrew
asked.

"Why not just bring it in here? Even then we won't be any too
bright."

"I thought as how you might want it in the front hall, mebbe,
to light you up the steps."

"All right," I said. As usual, Andrew had worked it all out beforehand. "And please bring in some extra candles, so there will
be enough for all the bedrooms."

"They's already candles in them silver candle dishes on the
bedside tables, Miss Sally."

"Yes, I know, but these are to get us to the bedrooms." Efficient as he is, there are plenty of times when I wish Andrew wasn't
quite so—omniscient.

I felt a little conscience-stricken when Andrew came in again a
few minutes later with fresh coffee and big cups to serve it in this
time. We were all surprised to discover that it was only twelve
o'clock. So much had happened since I looked at my wrist watch at
eight o'clock and decided that dinner must be served at once, lest
Bob drink more than even he could carry gracefully.

Talking it over, we figured that it must have been about ten
o'clock when Aunt Maggie was discovered at the foot of the back
stairs.

"Bessie and Andrew had not finished clearing up when I left
them in the kitchen," I recalled, "and—and found Aunt Maggie."

"I was in the powder room," said Eve.

And at that everyone tried to remember where he or she had been at the particular moment when the alarm first sounded. Nobody, it seemed, had been with anybody else.

Bill had taken Kirk to the game room after dinner, but had left him there for a few minutes to go upstairs for the ping-pong net and rackets, which he had failed to bring down earlier in the evening. Alice was in her bedroom on the second floor. Not even the engaged pair were together.

"I was looking at those miniatures in the drawing room," said Claire. "There is one that looks very much like you, Sally, but I suppose you know that."

Bob said briefly, "I had gone upstairs to my room for a moment."

But none of the three on the second floor had come down the stairs together. Andrew, who had summoned Bill, had followed him down the back stairs. Alice had descended by way of the front stairs. Bob said he had seen her below him in the hall when he reached the landing.

"I heard someone behind me," Alice affirmed. "But I hurried on without looking back."

"It must have happened when I was right there in the powder room," Eve said slowly, as though the idea had just occurred to her. A puzzled look came into her dark eyes, then her expression cleared and she added, "That must be why I thought—"

But as we all turned our attention full upon her, she broke off, leaving the sentence hanging incomplete in mid-air. "Thought what?" Bob asked for all of us.

She laughed a little uncertainly for one usually so belligerently poised. "Nothing," she said. "Just something I hadn't thought of before."

This did not strike me as in any way significant at the time. I was too busy resenting Eve's intrusion at Wisteria Hall, for it had just dawned on me that except for her egotistical dissertation on jade, which had held me in the library, I might have reached the back passageway in time to prevent a murder.

Surely Aunt Maggie could have been dead only a few minutes when I found her.

Aunt Maggie had had her coffee and had left us. The sweater showed that she had returned to her room and had probably meant to spend the evening in the study. Certainly that had been her announced intention.

Something or somebody had brought her downstairs to her death.

These reflections on my part were broken in upon by Bob. "I know this is on everybody's mind," he said, as he refilled and lighted the pipe which apparently had been a bone of contention between himself and Eve, "and, of course, we are all sad because of Aunt Maggie's death. She was really just like a member of my own family. But, after all, there is nothing we can do about it tonight. So let's try to talk about something else. Or better still, why don't we go to bed? Tomorrow is bound to be quite a day for all of us."

Nobody was sleepy, of course. But Bill added his approval to Bob's suggestion. "There will have to be an investigation and probably an inquest," he pointed out. "We will all have to answer questions as witnesses."

"But that's just the thing," said Alice. "There weren't any witnesses. And, anyway, how can anybody try to sleep with a murderer running around loose? We might all be murdered in our beds."

"I figure we are probably safe enough," said Bob. "Why should somebody make sure that we are stuck here, with no means of outside communication, unless he wanted to make his own getaway?"

"That sounds reasonable enough," Kirk agreed. "If anything about the situation can be called reasonable."

"Just the same," said Bill, "I think I'll keep at least one eye open."

"I was just getting ready to suggest that we take turns at sentry duty," said Bob. "And I'll be glad to take the first shift."

"Oh, Bob, must you?" Alice objected.

"And why not, for heaven's sake?" he asked sharply, as though his nerves had finally worn thin from too much sisterly clinging.

Both Bill and Kirk insisted also that they would take the first shift, or remain up the rest of the night if necessary; but Bob, a little grim by now, would have none of it. He would call Kirk at the end of two hours, he promised, and at the end of another two, Kirk would call Bill. There wouldn't be much of the night left after that.

So, taking our candles in hand, we left Bob in the library, with the flashlight and the decanter by his side. And with a thought for old Waterford glass, I hoped that he would not bolster his courage too much.

Alice gave little squeals of fright every time we came to a turn in the stairs or hallway. "Don't lock your door to our bath," she admonished Claire, as we escorted her into her room.

As Bill and I said good night to our guests, we inspected the windows in all rooms and in the hall. The great wisteria vine which gave the house its name sprawled from the front around one whole side of the house, but did not seem to offer close enough connection with any of the windows to be of service in second-story work. Nonetheless, as an extra precaution, we closed and locked the blinds.

It was agreed that we would all lock our doors leading into the hall. Kirk's and Bob's rooms were connected by a bath, as were those occupied by Claire and Alice. Eve's room, which had been my grandmother's and which I had suggested that Aunt Maggie use, had its private bath, as did our own. All the bedrooms had been built with dressing rooms, which in later years had made it simple enough to install modern plumbing.

Eve only laughed a little scornfully when I asked if she would be afraid to sleep in a room alone. "I probably won't sleep, anyway," she answered. "I'll read a murder story. That will keep my mind off the—er—other murder."

In our own room at last, with the door closed, Bill said of Eve, "Even when she doesn't mean to, she rubs me the wrong way."

I told Bill about the conversation I had overheard between Aunt Maggie and Eve shortly before dinner. Neither one of us considered for a moment that Eve could be the guilty one. "But she does get worse all the time," Bill said. "She didn't use to be so bad."

"She was always a little resentful of the rest of us," I remembered. "She seemed to think we lived in some sort of charmed circle.

After she married into the circle, she resented it because we were not more like the movies."

"I don't see any excuse for her," declared Bill, dismissing the subject and starting to blow out the light.

"Wait a minute," I urged, catching his arm. "I've just thought of something. Aunt Maggie's windows. We didn't look to see whether they were open or shut, and the vine goes all the way up to the roof on that side."

"Oh, darling," Bill groaned as he reluctantly heaved himself out of bed and into his bathrobe, "why do you always have to think of things?"

"But I wouldn't sleep a wink unless I knew they were attended to," I told him quite truthfully. "And you wouldn't get to sleep either, with me twisting and turning in the same bed."

Of course, he was no sooner out the door with his flickering candlelight than I had visions of his being cracked on the head by some fiend lurking in the shadows above the back stairway. Or worse still, suppose Bob should mistake Bill for the murderer? I wondered if by any chance Bob had a gun. In fact, I succeeded in making myself pretty miserable until Bill was back again.

"Guess whom I saw going downstairs just now?" he asked as he climbed into bed. And climbed is the word with the beds at Wisteria Hall. Bill's tone was too matter-of-fact for me to think he had seen anything startling. "Eve," he said. "All decked out in fancy pajamas. Going down to have a little session with Bob after Claire is safely tucked in, I suppose. She didn't see me, of course. I was in the back of the hall and she was facing toward the front of the house, going downstairs with her candle."

"So that's the book she was going to read," I remarked, as Bill blew out the light and darkness descended upon us like a velvet pall. I was glad then that my ancestors had slept in big double beds, so I could reach out and touch my husband, feel his protective strength beside me. Blowing out a candle makes the darkness so much more definite and complete than the simple turning of a switch which can as easily be turned on again.

For a long time thoughts raced around in my head like frightened mice, back and forth from one blind alley to another. What
was the meaning of it all? Where would it end? Poor Aunt Maggie.
Finally I felt that I could stand it no longer. The blackness was
closing in on me like a coffin.

"Oh, Bill," I cried out. "I've got to have light in this room. Oh,
Bill, I don't want to die."

"It's all right, darling." Bill pulled himself out of enveloping
drowsiness, groped for matches, lit the candle and took me in his
arms.

He didn't tell me to be sensible or to be reasonable, as some
husbands might have done. And comforted by this unfailing, un-
questioning tenderness, I suddenly felt very sorry for all those
husbands and wives who miss the substance of true marriage while
clinging so tenaciously to the shadow of romance.

I thought of Kirk in love with Claire. Of Claire in love with Bob.
Of Bob, so long in love with Claire, but who tonight had acted so
strangely. On account of Eve, no doubt, who was never really in
love with anyone, but always out for trouble. Of Alice, whom nobody seemed to love but who, I suspected, cherished a secret yen
for Kirk. Well, there I was back at the beginning. What a mess.

Then it occurred to me that instead of wasting sympathy where
it could do no good I might better be sorry for Bill, who swears he
cannot sleep in a lighted room. "I didn't mean to be such a nui-
sance," I told him. "I'm all right now. You can turn out the light."

"Turn out the light, my eye," Bill grunted. "It'll turn itself out
in a moment. That's a candle, my simple sweet."

In spite of his aversion to light, Bill's even breathing soon assured me that he was fast asleep. I myself must have dropped off
shortly afterward, while the candle still flickered in its silver holder.
For we were both aroused from a sound sleep by such blood-curdling screams as I hope never to hear again. One after another they
ripped through the nightmare of returning consciousness, full of
some nameless terror and turning the blood to water in my veins.

The candle had burned itself out and for a moment I don't think
either of us remembered where we were, for Bill kept pulling the

lamp cord at the head of the bed, swearing a little under his breath. Meanwhile the screams continued and it was clear now that they came from the upstairs hall.

Bill finally found the matches and I gave him the candle at the head of my side of the bed.

"Stay here," he ordered, throwing a bathrobe over his shoulders, grabbing up the candle and making for the door.

VI

But, of course, I did not stay there in that dark bedroom alone, with something, I knew not what, going on outside. The screams had stopped now, and when Bill halted suddenly just beyond the door in an effort to get his bearings I was so close on his heels that I bumped into him, almost knocking the candle from his hand.

"For God's sake," he complained in that tone of complete exasperation by which a husband can shift to his wife's shoulders the entire responsibility for whatever has originally upset him.

Other doors were opening. Someone could be heard running up the steps, and in a moment we saw that it was Bob, for he had the flashlight in his hand.

Bob reached the prone figure at the head of the stairs at almost the same time we did.

It was Alice.

She was breathing and there were slippers on her feet and a heavy, quilted robe over her nightgown. Obviously this was no sleepwalking jaunt. It is evidence of my own state of mind when I confess that for a moment, as I looked down upon her, I shrank back a little. Was this our killer? Had Alice suddenly gone mad? At any rate, why was the supposedly timid Alice, afraid of her own shadow, prowling around after everyone else had gone to sleep in a house in which a murder had been committed?

Kirk had brought water and Bill and Bob placed Alice on the hall sofa. I put a pillow under her feet.

"Looks as though she is out for a record," Eve observed caustically. "Two fainting fits in one evening."

74

Nobody paid any attention to her, for Alice had opened her eyes and begun to shudder.

"Did—did you see it?" she gasped.

"See what?" we all asked together.

Alice shut her eyes again and started moaning. "Take me home, Bob," she begged. "We can't stay here in this awful place."

"But, Alice dear," said Bob, patting her hand, "we can't go back tonight. We have to wait until morning. The best thing for you to do is to let us put you back to bed." Not waiting for Alice to say yes or no, he gathered her up in his arms and, with the rest of us trailing behind, carried her to her room and deposited her in the big, canopied bed. We were an odd-looking procession, no doubt, with the women in negligees, Kirk and Bill with bathrobes over pajamas and Bob the only one fully dressed.

Alice had no sooner hit the bed than she buried her face in the pillows and began to cry. "I just can't stand it," she kept saying.

"Here," Bob produced a pocket flask and made her swallow a good dose from it. Sputtering and grimacing and choking, she still managed to keep it down.

"What did you see, Alice?" Eve demanded, and from the insistence of her tone I thought for a moment that perhaps Alice had seen Eve herself, though it is true Eve was not now wearing the fancy pajamas Bill had described. Instead, the flame-colored velvet negligee, wrapped around her with elaborate casualness, revealed rather a lot of astonishingly inadequate white chiffon and lace nightgown.

But, clasping and unclasping her hands, Alice looked from one face to another with a sort of scared-rabbit expression, as though begging us not to think her demented. Shaking her head, she said, "I don't know. Something horrible."

"But what on earth were you prowling around for?" Bob asked the question which was in everybody's mind.

"I thought of something I wanted to ask you, Bob," she said, a little defiantly. "Why shouldn't I go down to the library to speak to my own brother?"

"Well, it was foolish to say the least," Eve reproved, as though she herself had not been prowling also.

Alice gave Eve another of those looks of open hostility which I had seen in the dining room. "I think we should let Alice rest,' said Claire, coming to the rescue. "She's terribly upset and probably doesn't feel like talking. Probably she just had a bad dream that frightened her and that's why she wanted to see Bob."

"I wish it had been a dream," Alice shuddered.

"Would it make you feel better to talk about it?" Claire asked.

"I think I should tell everybody," said Alice, shutting her eyes and shivering again at the thought of whatever it was she had seen. "We must all get away from here. I don't know whether I had been asleep or not," she went on. "But I wanted to see Bob about something. I—I lit my candle and started out. It was very dark in the upstairs hall." Here her voice wavered as the candle must have done. "The lamplight from downstairs made a pale sort of glimmer in the stairwell, but that was all. After I started, I was terribly afraid and almost turned back. But I knew Bob was there in the library and that by the time I reached the head of the stairs I could call down to him without disturbing anyone.

"Then," she continued, "I felt a sort of draft, as though a window or door had been opened somewhere, and"—Alice voice hurried her words, as though she herself was running away from what she had to tell—"my candle went out and something brushed against me in the darkness. I—I touched it with my hand—"

Alice stopped and began to shake so that I was afraid she was headed for hysterics. But Bob made her take another sip from his flask and tried again to persuade her that she should calm herself and go to sleep.

"No, no," she insisted. "I want to finish. Because you will all realize then that we must leave."

"But what happened?" Eve demanded again.

"I must have been almost to the stairway by then," Alice said, "for I saw it going down the steps."

"Saw it?" I breathed.

"Saw what?" asked the literal-minded Eve.

"Oh, Alice, you couldn't have seen anything," remonstrated Bob.

"Yes, I did," she told him. "I—I saw a ghost."

"Oh, no," I heard myself object, as incredulous glances met across the bed.

"Alice, darling, what did you see? Describe it." This came from Claire, in the tone one might use to a child when one hopes to rout an imaginary fear by bringing it out in the open.

"I don't know," Alice admitted. "There wasn't much light. It was just a shape. A big bulk, moving down the stairs. Then is when I screamed and—and the thing ran. I tell you, it ran. And then I suppose I fainted."

"You were just frightened and sick, my dear," Bob tried to reassure her. "Think what you had been through this evening."

"That's it," said Bill. "Sally almost had a spell herself after we got to bed."

I could have killed him cheerfully, but nobody was paying much attention, anyway, for Alice was almost screaming, "No, no, I tell you, I touched it. There was something."

"Could it have been a curtain?" Kirk asked. "You know, a curtain flapping about in the wind?"

We all voted for the long draperies at the window on the stairway landing. In the uncertain light they could have seemed to do almost anything, we told Alice.

"But they couldn't have come all the way to the upstairs hall," she argued, insisting that whatever it was had brushed past her before she had seen it going down the steps.

"Probably just your own robe swishing about," Bob told her. "If you really had seen anything, wouldn't I have met it in the downstairs ball? I was up and out of the library a moment after you started screaming."

"Of course, Alice," Bill reassured her. "Bob would have run smack into it."

"You are sure you didn't see anything?" Alice pleaded, her eyes clinging to her brother's with an almost physical hold.

"Positive."

But Alice still did not appear quite convinced, for she said, with what seemed to me rather pointed logic, "After all, there is always that little margin of time that cannot quite be accounted for. With people moving about at random all over the house this evening, there was still time for Aunt Maggie to be murdered in the back passage."

Claire promised to spend the rest of the night with Alice and the men made another tour of the house, but failed to find anything amiss. When they came back to Alice's room, where Eve and I waited, Kirk looked at his wrist watch and called attention to the fact that it was a quarter after two o'clock and time for his shift as watchman.

"Oh, darling, why do you always have to think of things?" Bill had complained when I asked him to investigate Aunt Maggie's windows. And now that we were back in bed again after Alice's little sight-seeing tour, I had thought of something else.

Indeed, I wondered why I had not thought of it before. Bill, poor darling, had promptly dropped off to sleep for the second, or was it the third, time that evening? Proof of steady nerves and a clear conscience, if the psychologists know their stuff.

My conscience was clear enough, but certainly my brain had been fogged by the rapidity with which events had followed their fantastic course.

Lying there, waiting again for sleep to come to me, the disconnected thoughts which had raced back and forth across my mind earlier in the evening began to straighten themselves out into what might conceivably be called a pattern. Then drowsiness began to creep over me and in that last moment between sleeping and waking, when consciousness hangs poised above the dark abyss of forgetfulness, a thought popped into my head and brought me wide awake again.

Aunt Maggie had announced at dinner that she believed she had found the clue to the long-forgotten secret room. Soon afterward she had been killed. Was it possible there was a connection between these two occurrences?

Could she have been killed while looking for the secret room? Or had there been a struggle with someone who tried to get possession of the clue?

I tried to convince myself that my wits were only woolgathering but, try as I might, I could not help thinking I had hit upon a possible motive. If it was the clue the killer wanted, had he succeeded in wresting it from her? Or had my arrival interfered with his purpose?

Had he fled upstairs, downstairs, out of doors or into the office? I had come through the breakfast-room door, but four exits were still open to him.

And suddenly I knew. Plutarch had told me. Plutarch who had fawned against me when I came back from, my hurried trip to the kitchen for water. When I first came out into the passage the murderer was concealed in the office, and during my brief absence he had escaped. That was how Plutarch happened also to be on the loose.

There is a second door from the office, which opens into the breakfast room, formerly the back hall. This way the murderer could have passed on into the front hall and out the front door or up the stairway. But probably that would have been too risky. To have taken the back stairs, either up to the second floor or down to the basement, or to have gone out the back door would have been much easier and much safer.

If my arrival had prevented the killer from stealing the clue, and the clue was of such importance, there was no time to lose. It must be salvaged for safekeeping.

Why the clue should be of importance to anyone, why Aunt Maggie should be murdered because of it, I, of course, could not figure out. All I really knew was that I could not go to sleep until I had set my mind at rest by making an investigation.

Perhaps already I might be too late. Hours had passed during which everyone had had the run of the house. All unbidden, the thought came that perhaps the nocturnal wanderings of Eve and Alice might have other than obvious explanations. But I put such thoughts forcibly from my mind. It isn't much fun to start suspecting everybody you know of murder.

But I must see about that clue. And as usual my first impulse was to confide in Bill, thus placing the responsibility for action on

his more capable shoulders. Remembering the many times his rest
had already been broken in one night, and that he must get up again
in less than two hours, I managed to restrain myself. Besides, it
was all so wild. How could I expect him to take me seriously? He
would probably tell me to go back to sleep and that everything
would look a lot different in the morning.

And, after all, as Alice had reasoned before me, there would be
someone in the library. I could call to Kirk by the time I reached
the stairway. While I did not believe for one moment that Alice
had seen a ghost, I do not mean to say that I was not frightened at
the thought of venturing out into that dark upstairs hall. But I was
not afraid in the same way that I had been when alone in the house
that afternoon, with the servants and Aunt Maggie mysteriously
missing and with assorted sound effects to provide atmosphere.

It was still raining; but there was a sort of rhythm about it now,
for the wind had subsided temporarily. And although actual violence had taken place since the afternoon, I now knew the house
to be full of people who at one outcry would rush to my assistance.
That Aunt Maggie had been able to make no outcry did not occur
to me until I was actually at the head of the stairway, in the exact
spot where Alice had fainted at what she claimed to be the sight of
a ghost.

But, although my heart swelled even bigger in my throat, it was
easier by then to go on than to turn back. For if my candle went
out, there was the lamp in the hall below. So long as I held onto
the stair rail I would be all right. But it might have been simpler if
I had just turned loose and let myself fall downstairs, for, excited
and hurried as I was, the heavy folds of my long velvet house gown
tripped me at every step and more than once I came near losing
one of my satin mules. I did lose the extra packet of matches I had
brought along.

I groped for it uncertainly, then decided to give it up as a bad
bargain.

As I straightened up and grasped the stair rail again, I stood
petrified in my tracks.

I had heard the front door open and close softly.

VII

MY FIRST IMPULSE, when arrested by that unexpected opening and closing of the front door, was to fly back upstairs. But on halfway ground one course appeared almost as uninviting as the other. Against the forbidding blackness of the upper hall, the lamplight below, sickly though it was, seemed to offer some slight margin of safety. At least one might hope to see what dangers were to be met. And aside from my conviction with regard to the clue, a conviction strong enough to drive me from the comfort and safety of my bed, there was the undeniable pull of feminine curiosity as to what evil business might be afoot downstairs.

So, drawing a long breath, and moving with the utmost caution, I made my way to the lower hall, finally reaching the library door. As I had expected, Kirk was nowhere to be seen. Whether he had gone outside, or had admitted someone to the house, I could not guess. At any rate, the library was empty, with that dreadful emptiness of a room that holds its secrets. It was as though every inanimate object was watching me, jeering a little because it knew more than I did about what was going on in this strange sequence of events and waiting to see what my next reaction would be.

I did not like to turn my back on that room, with the glow of the firelight reflected on the silver candlesticks so that they gleamed like eyes in the gloom. But I had come downstairs on a mission which must be carried out, so I backed away from the door toward the deeper darkness of the drawing room.

Aunt Maggie, I knew, lay on a sofa at the far end, or in what would have been the back parlor before the two rooms were converted into one.

I could walk along the hall to the back-parlor door and have the light of the hall lamp to guide me, but that would also take me in the direction of the breakfast room, through which I had passed from the kitchen when I found Aunt Maggie crumpled on the floor. It would mean, too, that I must pass the coat closet, powder room and telephone closet under the stairs, all of which now loomed ahead as possible harbingers of danger.

Careful to step on the rugs, so my feet would make no sound, I chose the nearer door, with only my candle to light the way down the long room which seemed to stretch before me in ever-lengthening distance. My breath came in such gasps that I was sure the sound would have been audible to Kirk had he been in the library or anywhere on this floor; but I stumbled onward, the candle dripping wax on my pet wine-red house coat.

Eventually I came up short against a black and gold Coromandel screen which had been placed in front of the sofa. When I had edged around it and finally held my candle above Aunt Maggie's sheet-draped form, I knew that I was right in suspecting that the clue of the secret room was in some way connected with her death. And I also knew that I was too late.

For someone had been there before me. Someone who had not troubled to rearrange the sheet after dragging it away from her face and shoulders so that her body was now only half-covered. Both Aunt Maggie's sweater and her bodice had been roughly disarranged. The pockets of the sweater had been turned inside out and left that way.

At this incongruous moment, as I stood looking down at her, I thought of one of the stories Aunt Maggie had been fond of telling. It recounted the misfortunes of a relative who, after the Civil War, got all worn out with supporting "a lot of free Negroes who wouldn't work." So he said to his wife, "We'll go to Texas and leave them here to shift for themselves. Don't say a word to a soul. Let everyone think we are going on a visit." Not a word was said to a soul, but on the day when husband and wife were ready to depart so were all the Negroes. And went right along with them.

I knew that our servants always seem to know everything about us, and that often they reach conclusions about our problems before we ourselves are able to do so. Wasn't this why Andrew was practically the dictator of our household? If the servants in several households had known since Friday of this impromptu house party, how many other people's servants, how many other people might have known, too? It was frightening to consider the potentialities of that grapevine telegraph.

The more I thought of it, the more certain I became that there was something valuable in the secret room and that someone, white or black, knew about it. In the morning I would question Bessie and Andrew. If the person involved was black, they would know nothing and I could question them until I myself was black in the face and they would still know nothing. If he was white, they would likewise know nothing; but if I persisted and promised protection, they might be able to suggest something which would conceivably furnish a clue.

Meanwhile I could at least straighten the sheet over Aunt Maggie. I bent forward, as busy with my thoughts as I was in try-ing to manage the candle, hold back my skirts and arrange the sheet all at the same time. And, of course, I dropped the candle. The light was extinguished, the silver candle dish rolled from the rug onto the hardwood floor under the sofa and in the darkness I could not find it.

Remembering that I had no matches anyway, I gave up the search and, rising to my feet, decided that I would take the nearer door this time and thus sooner reach that beacon of light in the hall.

Even the small ray of light that shone in at the open door at the far end of the room was hidden by the screen and, turning blindly, I walked what seemed the proper distance, hands held out in front of me so I would not crash into the door. I snatched them both back when my right hand encountered something unexpected, something which confused and unnerved me still further until I realized it was a curtain and that I had crossed the floor in the wrong direction.

This meant that I had reached a window instead of the door. I knew that it should be simple enough to turn and retrace my steps, but for the duration of a choking heartbeat I felt as helpless as though lost in the mazes of a nightmare and put my hand over my mouth to keep from crying out. With my other hand gripping the curtain, I leaned against the window, mustering my courage. It was then I saw through a crack between the blinds a red light material-ize in the inky blackness outside. A red light, quite a distance away, that appeared and disappeared between the trees and was gone so quickly I could not be sure I had really seen it at all.

It looked like nothing so much as the tail-light of an automo-bile sweeping around the curve of the road beyond that section now under repair. But why would a car be here at this hour? As I pondered that unanswerable question my heart literally stopped beating, for I heard a stealthy footfall just behind me. Close, so close that I could now feel someone's breath on the back of my neck.

I thought of a good many things in that split second of sus-pended animation while I waited for octopus arms to reach out of the darkness—while I waited for the feel of fingers at my throat. And I needed no one to tell me that I had been the world's biggest fool.

Then Kirk said, as coolly as though discussing the weather. "Don't make a sound. I've got you covered."

"Oh, Kirk," I gasped, "are you crazy?" And practically fell into his arms, for my knees suddenly gave way under me.

"My God, Sally," he exploded, and from the relief in his voice it was obvious that, however else he might be involved in the misfor-tunes that had descended upon our house, at least I had nothing to fear from him so far as my physical safety was concerned.

"How was I to know it was you?" he demanded, still holding on to me with one arm, while he brought the flashlight from a coat pocket with his free hand. "Suppose I had shot you?" he went on, in that rapid-fire way he has of talking. "I couldn't see a thing.

What were you doing in here without a light? I didn't know whether it was Alice's ghost or Alice herself or some lunatic at large from the secret room. Let's get out of here."

Once we were in the hall and it was clear that I could stand unassisted, Kirk's questions began again. "What on earth were you doing in there alone? Why didn't you call me? After all, my dear, this is not exactly a safe house for sleepwalking."

"Aunt Maggie—" I started to explain, then remembered that I must not. "I came down to see if—if she was all right. And somebody had disarranged the sheet."

"What?" asked Kirk, with a puzzled frown. "Disarranged the sheet? Let's have a look." He picked up the lamp from the hall table and we went back into the drawing room and around the screen. "That's darned strange," he agreed. "Why would anybody do that? Or rather, who would do it? Do you suppose Alice's cat— Aren't there stories about—"

"Don't," I shuddered. Still I knew no cat had turned those sweater pockets inside out.

"Oh, Sally, forgive me. How dumb of me. I was only trying to think of some explanation." Kirk carefully straightened the sheet again, then took me by the arm. "Let's go to the fire," he said. "You are shivering."

"My candle," I remembered. "I dropped it and the light went out and it rolled under the sofa."

"So that explains it," said Kirk, as he reclaimed the candle. "Thought I heard some sort of noise from in here."

We were in the library now, seated in front of the fire. I was still shivering from pure nervousness and, while I wanted nothing so much as to be back in my bed, I was so let down that I actually did not feel equal to climbing the stairs at that moment.

"Whew!" whistled Kirk. "What an experience. I don't wonder you feel shot. Don't feel so wonderful myself. Wouldn't a little drink help you?"

"A little sherry," I agreed and, when it was brought, choked a bit, remembering that sherry had been one of Aunt Maggie's last requests. "Why don't you have a drink?" I asked.

Kirk shook his head. "Want to keep my alleged wits about me," he explained.

Strange, the room no longer seemed to mock me. Strange, as the sherry warmed the blood in my veins, my confidence in Kirk should be flowing back, in spite of everything. I wondered if it could be because he is one of those extremely masculine men who seem to influence women without half trying. Perhaps Bluebeard had been like that, I decided. And Dr. Crippen.

I gazed at Kirk covertly. It seemed to me that there was a sort of unnatural gleam in his eyes. I knew it was only the reflection of the firelight which, shining on the candlesticks, had given me that uncomfortable feeling earlier. But in my upset state it made me think of stories of werewolves. Suppose that gleam in Kirk's dark eyes suddenly became more intense? Suppose his lips, instead of smiling, should suddenly draw backward in a snarl?

But this, I knew, was crazy. Determinedly I shook myself out of that mental miasma and made conversation.

"How did you get into that room without my hearing you?" I managed to ask.

"Oh, that was easy enough. I just walked on the rug."

"But—but why didn't you use your flashlight, so you would have recognized me and not scared me to death?"

Kirk laughed, his old, easy laugh, and somehow the sound did a lot to restore the balance of sanity. I was quite sure Bluebeard or Dr. Crippen had never laughed in that wholesome, natural fashion. "How was I to know it was you?" Kirk asked.

"Oh, of course," I admitted, smiling feebly at my own inconsistency.

Kirk put another log on the fire and, taking out his cigarette case, opened and automatically passed it to me. "Keep forgetting you don't smoke," he observed, as he extracted and lighted a cigarette for himself. "Aunt Maggie's idea of a Southern lady, I suppose?"

"If there is such a thing," I agreed. "I liked my grandmother's idea better. She always said if you were born a lady, you didn't have to bother about being one."

Kirk grinned, and smoked a moment in silence. "Going back to the drawing room," he said. "I'm sorry I gave you such a scare. But you see, when I opened the door at the far end of the hall, I couldn't see anything at all at first. The flashlight would have been a dead giveaway, there in the dark. So I kept it in my pocket, as I figured I needed both hands to cope with the situation."

Suddenly, unaccountably, I was struck with the absurdity of the picture and found myself laughing. Kirk looked at me uneasily, as though he suspected hysterics, and certainly they were not far off. But the loosening of tension made me feel better.

"It's too ridiculous," I explained. "First I'm a lunatic at large. Then I'm a situation."

"Every lovely lady is a situation," he said gallantly.

"Why, Kirk," I chided. "This is terrible. You are getting entirely too Southern. I can't believe a thing you say any more."

"That may have been the trouble," he agreed, with unexpected glumness. "Perhaps it was just Southern hospitality on her part, but there was a time when I thought I was making a little headway with Claire. I know this is not the time to talk about it. But, Sally"— he turned to me fiercely—"I can't let her marry Bob."

"Oh, Kirk," I remonstrated, a little shocked at his sudden vehemence, "they've been in love since they were children."

He flipped his half-smoked cigarette into the fire. "Do you think that childhood-sweetheart business has to mean so much?" he demanded. "Couldn't it be just one of those fixed ideas or habits or something, kept alive because of obstacles? In this case the obstacle being Bob's so-called hard luck?"

"That isn't like you, Kirk," I said, but his question and Bob's excessive drinking did make me wonder a little.

"I hope not," he agreed bitterly, "but being myself hasn't got me anywhere in this instance."

As I have said before, there is something so vital about Kirk, something so essentially masculine and compelling, that it rather hurt me to see him sitting there in that dejected fashion, completely minus his usual self-confidence. I forgot all about having compared him in my mind with Dr. Crippen. "You men make me tired," I said.

"Don't you know that, when it comes to love, women are all alike? You look like one of these he-men. Don't you realize that's the way a woman would expect you to act?"

"Sally," Kirk grinned, "you've seen too many movies." But I noticed he straightened his shoulders.

"Maybe," I agreed, "but why do you think people go to movies?"

Because I did not consider it especially flattering to either of them, I refrained from observing that the one flaw in Claire's celebrated good disposition is that her kind heart will never allow her to discourage a suitor until things reach a point where it is far more painful to do so than it would have been in the beginning. Bob was the reason she was still unmarried at twenty-seven. People always said what a grand-looking couple they were. There had been times when I wondered if this influenced Claire unduly. If perhaps she thought Bob completed the picture as no one else could? Now they were engaged at last, and if Kirk thought he could convince Claire she had been fooling herself all these years he had his work cut out for him.

"It is not just that she is beautiful—" As all lovers, Kirk was only too pleased to have an opportunity to rave about the object of his adoration. "It's that she's so beautifully serene."

"Yes, I know," I smiled, while Kirk also smiled self-consciously and lit another cigarette. And it was all true. Claire is beautiful enough and rich enough and sensible enough not to exert herself needlessly. She can go through an entire evening on one word or on three at the most. "Wonderful," she will remark, or, "You are wonderful," to some big, strong, otherwise sensible male and he is reduced to a pulp of admiration, just as in Kirk's case.

But I knew Kirk and I were only wasting our time in idle chatter. Glancing up at the clock, I saw that it was a quarter of four. "Good heavens," I exclaimed, "I must get back upstairs! Bill's bedroom door has been unlocked all this time. Suppose something—"

"I'll light you to your door," said Kirk, rising and reaching for the lamp.

Back in the hall again, we both stopped still in our tracks at the click of an opening door. The sound came from the end of the hall and, as we watched, the breakfast-room door swung slowly inward. Then as slowly, and as quietly, it swung backward and there was the click of its closing. We had seen no one, only the deeper darkness beyond the opened door.

Kirk strode forward, at the same time telling me to go back to the library. "Who's there?" he called.

I did go back to the library, but only to arm myself with the brass poker from the fireside. Then I rushed after Kirk, who was exploring the breakfast room.

As we opened the door into the passageway, we caught a fleeting glimpse of white, and it was all that I could do to suppress a scream. But it was only Plutarch.

How had he got out of that room again? Yes, the door was open. But we found no one inside. Of course, someone could have entered the office by the passageway door and have made his exit through the door opening directly from the office into the breakfast room and thence into the front hall or out the back door. Or, entering from the breakfast room into the office, he could have come out into the passageway and have gone upstairs, downstairs, out the back door or back into the breakfast room from the passage. Heavens, what a place that passageway became, when you considered all its possibilities.

Kirk and I opened doors and listened, but heard not a sound. Once again Plutarch was firmly put back into his lair. We returned to the library by way of the kitchen and dining room, but still saw no evidence to indicate that anyone had been about recently.

"Thank heaven, we both saw it," I said, as I replaced the poker.

Kirk joked about my weapon and at the same time reproved me for running into unknown danger. "Or perhaps," he said, "it was only someone from upstairs who changed his or her mind."

But discussion of this possibility got us nowhere, for why should anybody—any member of the house party, that is—mind running into any other member of the house party?

"I must go," I said, inspired with new urgency at the thought of some strange person wandering around opening doors, for Bill's door was unlocked.

"Wait a minute," Kirk cautioned, his voice dropping almost to a whisper. "Did you hear anything?"

We strained our ears against the beat of the rain, the lash of the wind. "I'll be back in a moment," said Kirk. "I'll take the flashlight instead of the lamp, so my approach won't be so obvious. Don't go moving around now and get me mixed up. Stay right here."

He went out through the dining-room doorway and, scarcely breathing, I sat waiting for his return. I didn't like being there alone. Suppose the murderer came in? Suppose Kirk was really the murderer, after all?

How long I entertained myself with such gruesome imaginings I do not know, but suddenly reality became rampant with the most horrible racket I have ever heard. It came from the hall, just outside the library door; and if all the demons of the netherworld had been unleashed there and begun playing football with the furniture, the noise—to my excited ears—couldn't have been greater, or the effect more demoralizing.

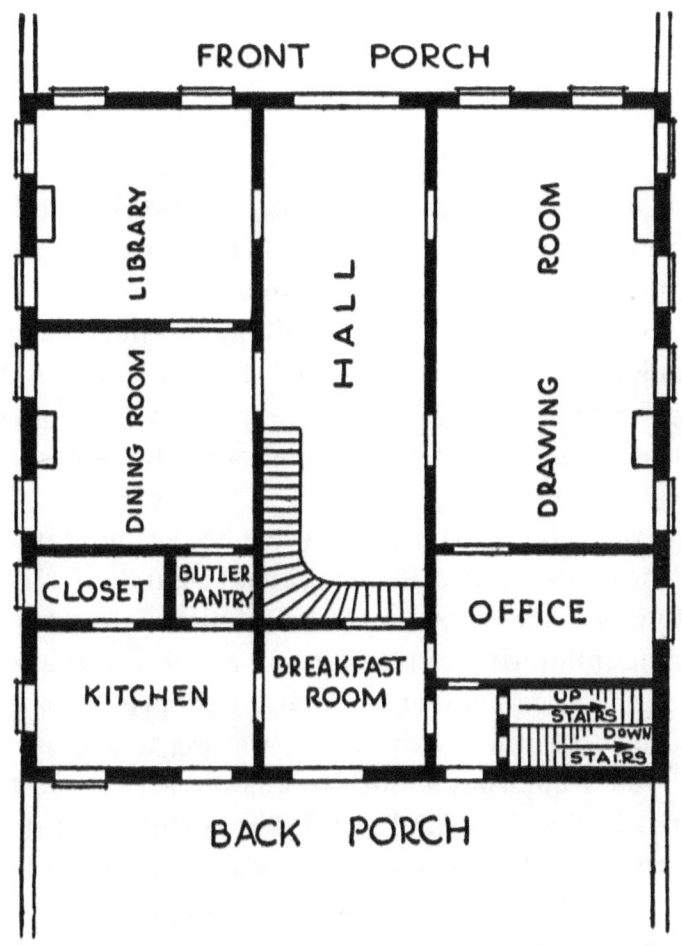

FLOOR PLAN OF WISTERIA HALL, SHOWING PASSAGEWAY

VIII

As I stood, literally frozen in my tracks, I was certain all that horrible commotion in the hall could mean only one thing. The forces of good and evil had come together in mortal combat. There, just outside the door, was the answer to all the inexplicable things that had been happening at Wisteria Hall. Believing Kirk to be in the middle of whatever was going on, and trying to screw up my courage to take a look, I practically fainted when he came charging in from the dining room.

"What the hell?" he sputtered, when he saw me standing there like Lot's wife turned to salt. "Are you all right, Sally?"

There was a final crash in the hall, followed by what sounded like a great splintering of glass. Then, as the reverberation died down, there was a moment of dreadful silence when the whole house seemed as quiet as the grave, waiting to give up its dead. Before I could open my mouth to answer Kirk's question, this silence was broken by sound of a different sort. First there was a human groan, and I grabbed onto Kirk's arm as he strode toward the door. Then the air got thick with profanity, which I recognized with horror as coming from Bill, who was demanding to know who in the blankety-blank-blank had moved the hall lamp.

Kirk and I, already nearly to the door, exchanged guilty glances, for when he had taken the hall lamp to the drawing room Kirk had failed to replace it and had carried it on to the library, where the other lamp already stood on the mantel.

What scene of carnage we had anticipated would be difficult to describe. I am sure I half expected to find Bill in the middle of an army, fending off attacks from all sides; but if there had been an army, he had it fully routed. For there was only Bill himself, grim enough in his struggle to extricate himself from the wreckage of what had been one of a pair of beautiful Chinese Chippendale gilt mirrors. Two chairs and a table, apparently, had been pretty well mixed up in the melee, the tall vase of gladioli had been upset but had not broken and flowers and glass from the mirror were scattered in all directions.

"Watch out, don't get cut," Bill warned, as I rushed forward to fling myself upon him, crying out to know if he was badly hurt.

"Was it you I ran into just now?" Bill demanded of Kirk.

"Ran into?" Kirk echoed blankly.

"Yes, here at the foot of the stairs."

"I was back in the kitchen," Kirk explained. "I had thought I heard a sound from that direction and had gone to investigate. Then I heard all this—"

"Well, let's don't stand here then," Bill cried, galvanized into action in spite of his injuries. "I ran into somebody. Let's go after him."

"All right," Kirk agreed with alacrity. "But which way do you think he went? I saw no one."

"I don't know," Bill admitted dazedly, putting his hand to his head. "I was right at the bottom step. Probably he went through the dining-room door. That's nearest the stairs. I'll go that way and you go through the breakfast room. Sally, stay in the library. If anyone comes in, hit 'em as hard as you can with that poker and yell like hell."

As they gathered up lights for their scouting expeditions, two calls came from the upstairs hallway. "What's going on down there?" in Bob's voice, which sounded quite agitated, while Eve inquired acidly whether anybody ever slept in this house.

Looking upward, I could see the tiny flames of their candles pricking the darkness overhead.

"Bill ran into someone," I explained, shakily.

"What's that?" Bob asked. And, "Why didn't he look where he was going?" from Eve.

Then I could hear Bob trying to persuade Eve to go back to her room and lock the door, while he came down to aid the searching party. "All right," she finally agreed, "but you must come in later and tell me all about it."

I was still in the hall, the lamp which Kirk had handed over to me swaying at an angle of goodness knows how many degrees, when Bob reached the late battlefield. "Gosh," he exclaimed, "what a shambles! How many killed and wounded?" And then without waiting for a reply, "Give me that lamp and let me take a look around."

"You'd better warn Bill and Kirk," I cautioned, "or you may get killed. They told me to stay in the library. Don't let them mistake you for the murderer."

"Murderer," Bob repeated, stopping and staring down at me, as though he had just realized the significance of all that had happened. "Not a pretty word," he agreed. "But we have had a murder, so there's bound to a murderer."

Eventually the three searchers came back to the library fire, greatly disgruntled that they had found no trace of any trespasser.

"Oh, Bill, darling," I cried at the sight of the lump already swelling on his forehead. "How terrible."

"Did you know that you left me in the bedroom without a sign of a candle?" Bill inquired in that long-suffering tone which is so annoying when you already know yourself to be in the wrong.

"Oh," I confessed contritely, "I never thought of that."

"What I can't understand in the first place," Bill went on sternly, "is what you came downstairs for."

"Sally was worried about Mrs. Ambler," Kirk explained. "We went in to see that she was all right and afterward I forgot to replace the lamp. I'm terribly sorry, old man. That looks like a pretty bad bump on your head, too.

"But what happened in the hall?" I had to know. "I never heard such carrying-on in all my life."

"Yes," said Kirk, "are you sure you actually ran into someone and not just a chair?"

"Of course, I'm sure," Bill replied, indignantly.

"Did you see anybody?" asked Bob.

"No," said Bill morosely. "That was the trouble. I couldn't see anything, but I am sure it was a man, for whoever it was gave me a hefty shove to one side. I lost my balance and I think I crashed into a chair. Anyway, all the furniture on the place seemed to gang up on me. I threw out my arms, grabbing with both hands, to try to break my fall and my right hand struck that confounded mirror and brought it down on top of me. Practically brained me and didn't help my hand either," he complained bitterly, taking stock of his injuries.

"Oh, dear, I'm so sorry," I lamented. "And it was my great-great grandmother's mirror, too. But what can we do about your head?"

"Alcohol," Bob suggested. "Applied externally, I mean. All right, internally too, of course. But soak a cloth and hold it over the bump." And, as I looked doubtful, "I've got some in my room," he offered. "I'll go right up and get it."

"I had no notion you would wake up," I told Bill. "Usually you sleep so soundly."

He and Kirk exchanged wry glances. "I wouldn't call this a usual situation," Bill said. "Why on earth should you want to come down to see Aunt Maggie? Of all the foolishness I've ever heard of—"

"I suppose it was foolish," I admitted, glad enough to get off without more detailed explanation at the moment.

"Put me on a pretty spot," said Bill. "Here, I wake up and you are missing. I call but get no answer. So I have to go through all that rigmarole of getting a light. And not a candle anywhere. I look in the bathroom. Nobody home. Then I find the hall door unlocked. Well, I ask, what now? Echo answers why and I decide to take a look. My matches have given out and it is pitch-black in the hall, but I feel my way to the stairs and get down all right. Then just at the foot of the stairs I am run into by a baboon or gorilla or hairy ape and—"

"Here you are, old man," said Bob, back from his quest for first-aid materials. "Do you mean to say this thing you ran into had hair on him?"

"Hair on his chest, anyway," Bill replied, "judging from the force of the shove he gave me. I'd like to get my hands on him"

"Then Alice did see something," I remarked, applying a guest towel, soaked in alcohol, to the bump on Bill's head.

The men looked at one another, but nobody said anything.

"Wow," Bill jumped, "don't let that stuff get in my eye. I've suffered casualties enough for one evening."

"Just a comedy of terrors," I said, thinking of how one mistake inevitably leads to another. "But in both cases the result could have been much worse. Kirk might have shot me if he had had a gun and the mirror might have brained Bill completely."

"But I have got a gun," said Kirk. "Thought it was yours, Bill. Bob turned it over to me when I took his place on night watch."

I looked at Bill, who looked blank, and then we both looked at Bob, who explained a little awkwardly, "Just happened to have it in the car. One of the waiters at the Athletic Club wanted to borrow some money and gave me the gun as security. You know how they are when you start lending them money. Thought I'd have a better chance of being paid back if I took the gun. Found it when I went looking for a flashlight tonight."

"Well, that was luck," said Bill. "But, for God's sake, let's be careful and not shoot one another. Sally, you young idiot, I could spank you for roaming around like that."

"That knot is going to give you a sweet little headache, Bill," Bob told him, tactfully changing the subject. "Hadn't you better go back to bed? I've had my forty winks. I can relieve Kirk."

"Oh, by the way," asked Kirk, "did either of you happen to come downstairs just before Bill had his little run-in with the mirror?"

"What do you mean?" asked Bill and Bob together.

"I mean," said Kirk, "that a few minutes before that time, I started to walk upstairs with Sally and when we got to the hall we both saw the breakfast-room door open and then shut. But we saw nobody. We went and looked all around, but still nobody. Except Plutarch. And he may be a smart cat but I don't believe he is smart enough to turn doorknobs."

"It wasn't Plutarch that I ran into," said Bill. "Probably the same customer opened the door."

"All that noise waked me out of a sound sleep," declared Bob. "I was in bed, so I don't suppose I could have been sleepwalking."

"We heard the click as the knob was turned to open the door," Kirk continued. "That's what made us look."

"Damned funny," Bob observed. Then he turned to Bill with a good-natured grin. "Sure you weren't spying on Kirk and Sally?"

"I only wish I had been," Bill replied with a grimace. "Maybe I'd have missed that damned mirror."

It seemed to me we were working right back to the point where it was all my fault for coming downstairs, so I hastily suggested coffee and sandwiches and we went back to the kitchen en masse to prepare them.

"Odd," said Kirk, "Claire and Alice seem to have slept straight through all the bedlam. Do you suppose they are all right? Hadn't somebody better go and see?"

"I checked up on them when I went after the alcohol," said Bob. "Alice was dead to the world, but Claire came to the door. Said the noise waked her but she thought it was thunder. I guess those two drinks I gave Alice helped to put her to sleep. Anyway, she and Claire are in the same room. I told Claire to keep the door locked and not to open it without the pass word."

Kirk's face had flushed a slow red. I knew he was visualizing that scene between Bob and Claire upstairs, with Claire in negligee as he had seen her after Alice's fainting fit on the stairs. And, knowing Kirk, I was not surprised when he slammed down the bread knife with which he had been cutting slices for sandwiches and announced that it was as dull as the Congressional Record.

"Men never really know how to slice bread," I said, although I had had no previous convictions on the subject. "Let me finish." The knife was actually quite sharp, and I thought that it was not at all the sort of weapon which should be lying around where so many strange things were happening.

Bill insisted that he would take his turn as night watchman, in spite of his injuries. "Don't want to miss that baby if he is anywhere around," he declared.

"Promise you'll be careful and keep the gun handy," I begged as I gathered up a fresh supply of candles and matches. I thought of all the things I wanted to discuss with Bill. The clue to the secret room. The disarranged sheet over Aunt Maggie and the sweater pockets turned inside out. The opening of the front door and Kirk's unexplained absence. The red light beyond the drawing-room window. Of course, Kirk might have been in the house all the time, or there might easily be a perfectly simple reason why he had stepped outside. Perhaps he had gone to investigate suspicious sounds. Perhaps— Well, no doubt, morning would do just as well for my talk with Bill.

In the hall I was properly horrified to think that I had forgotten to mop up the water which had spilled over table and floor when the flowers were overturned. Kirk insisted that he would see to this, and as Bob and I started up the stairs we left him picking up broken glass.

"I think the frame can be repaired," he called after me, with obvious effort to cheer. But, of course, no mirror would be quite the same as the old-fashioned looking glass which had once held my great-great-grandmother's actual reflection.

And I hated to think what Bessie would say when she saw the ruin. "Seven years' bad luck, Miss Sally. Just you mark my words." For seven years I knew she would be anticipating trouble and attributing even the smallest misfortune to that broken mirror. Well, goodness knows, tonight certainly proved that when things start going wrong everything else works at cross purposes.

"Better go and reassure Eve," I told Bob as we took a look around my room and he said good night. "Didn't I hear her say she'd be waiting? Perhaps we should have brought her some coffee and sandwiches."

Bob gave me one of his quizzical glances. "Eve," he said. "Eve in the garden of Eden."

"I'd say she was more like the serpent," I couldn't help saying.

For the third time in one night I went to bed. I left my candle burning, confident that I would remain awake until dawn, but soon found myself quite sleepy and must have dropped off promptly. How much later it was when the nightmare gripped me I do not know.

A cold wind blew across my face. The room was dark and it seemed to me that I heard the door to the hall open and close. At first I only wondered vaguely why Bill should be coming back upstairs. Then I remembered that the door was locked, with the key on the inside.

As I lay there, unable to move or to cry out, the fearful conviction came to me that the secret room opened somehow into this bedroom.

IX

WHEN I AWAKENED at a little after eight o'clock in the morning I discovered that the fastening of one of the window blinds had come loose in the night. This was, no doubt, responsible for the cold draft which had blown across me in my dream, but I still had an uncomfortable feeling that the secret of the hidden room might be somewhere right under my nose.

After all, this was the room in which the warning message had been left.

But a hurried survey revealed no clue. Later, I would make a more thorough examination. Just now I could not hurry fast enough with my bathing and dressing, so anxious was I for the comfort of Bill's nearness, his reassurance that daylight meant a straightening out of at least some of our difficulties.

The rain had stopped in the night, but the sky was leaden, as though a downpour might begin at any moment. On the way downstairs I remembered the matches I had lost the night before somewhere near the landing. They were easy enough to find this morning but, except for the fact that I had automatically looked for them along the way, I should have passed unnoticed a small scrap of rose-colored taffeta which evidently had been snagged off by a nail projecting from one of the rounds supporting the stair rail. Of course, the nail should not have been there in the first place, and it was easy to see that it had been used in a crude attempt to repair a split in one of the delicate rounds.

"Some of Thomas's work," I told myself, with a mental note to have the repair looked after properly. Thomas had been my grandmother's gardener and general handy man for many years, and as she had grown older he had grown a bit slovenly. He and Lindy, his wife, had lived in the servants' quarters back of the house until a month or so ago, when they had moved to a tenant house about a quarter of a mile distant. At Thomas's request we had given him enough land on which to make a crop. It occurred to me now that I might question Thomas along with Bessie and Andrew about the secret room.

Thinking of all this, I picked up the small piece of silk as any housewife would. I noticed that tiny feathers or down clung to the cloth and wondered idly where such a scrap could have come from. Then I remembered that Alice had been wearing a rose quilted robe the night before.

But Alice had said she went only to the head of the stairs.

I stuffed the matches and the bit of silk into a pocket of my red cardigan and hurried on to the dining room. Bill, usually almost too bright and cheerful in the mornings, now looked like death warmed over. The knot on his head had gone down, but the discoloration had spread to the area around his eye.

Nobody else appeared to be up and Bill explained that Andrew had set out on foot for Roswell, "to spread the alarm," and also to try to stir up an electrician and a wrecker for the cars.

"Of course, it's Sunday, and everything will probably be shut up in Roswell," he added. "But, anyway, Andrew can at least find a telephone."

"I'm glad it is Sunday," I said. "Maybe, we can get everything cleared up today and there won't be a lot of wild headlines in the papers."

"Of course, there's the radio," Bill reminded me. "Don't they have news broadcasts on Sunday?"

At the suggestion I could almost hear the suave tones of the announcer:

"Mrs. James Marshall Ambler was found dead last evening at the country home of her niece, Mrs. William Davis Stuart, near

Roswell. Mr. and Mrs. Stuart, socially prominent, were entertain-
ing a group of Atlanta friends at a house party. Great mystery sur-
rounds the death of Mrs. Ambler, one of Atlanta's most beloved
women, whose body was found in the back hall of the house, after
she apparently had been strangled to death . . ."

What little appetite I had disappeared as I followed this gloomy
trail of thought, but at Bill's insistence I forced down toast and
coffee. At the same time I related to him the reason for my trip
downstairs in the small hours of the morning. Neither Kirk nor I
had mentioned to Bill the fact that the sheet over Aunt Maggie had
been disturbed. I had purposely omitted discussing it and Kirk, I
am sure, had refrained out of consideration for me.

This ghoulish detail now impressed Bill where he might otherwise have been inclined to try to explain away my theory that the
secret room was in some way connected with Aunt Maggie's death.
"It's possible you are right," he admitted. "God knows there must
be some reason back of it all. But why on earth didn't you let me
go on this little research expedition?"

"I was trying to let you get some sleep," I said. "Besides, it all
seemed so crazy. I didn't know what you would say. My consideration didn't work out exactly as it should have. But naturally, I
didn't expect you to be running into gorillas or to have mirrors
rise up and sock you on the head."

Bessie padded in, bringing fresh toast. "Funny to me," she
grumbled, "looking glasses jumpin' down off the wall all by theirself
and hittin' folks. Somethin' evil in this here house. Miss Sally, we
goin' back to town today, ain't we?"

Bill and I both said we hoped so and tried to explain that Bill
had knocked against the mirror and that the fastening was no doubt
ready to give way. But Bessie remained firm in her conviction.
"Somethin' evil in this here house," she reiterated, as she went back
to the kitchen.

Bill was as much in the dark as I with regard to the red light
and inclined to think I had imagined it. I was none too sure myself, and yet why would I pick out a red light to imagine? "The trees

are thinner there," I pointed out. "It's that long sweep of lawn with the cherry laurel hedge and the trees and that curve of the road just beyond. It could have been the tail-light of a car."

"But all the cars are in the back yard, just as they were last night," said Bill. "All of 'em with flat tires. And both Andrew and I tried to start the station wagon this morning. Anyway, no car could have negotiated that mud."

"Perhaps it was a car from the outside."

"A car that turned around and went back? I get you," said Bill, "but why?"

"You tell me why," I suggested.

"Look here," said Bill suddenly, "did you have any crazy relatives?"

"All of them are more or less crazy, according to what you've always seemed to think," I answered, with a feeble attempt at lightness.

"No, I mean would any of them be likely to be shut up here in this so-called secret room? You know how people sometimes are about admitting such things. Try to hide the afflicted one away."

"Well, I never heard of anything of the sort," I said. "Of course, Grandmother did die rather suddenly. There wasn't any chance for her to tell anybody anything. That is, of course, if there was anything to tell."

"I only thought of it as a possible explanation," Bill said.

"Speaking of crazy relatives," I said slowly, "that makes me wonder . . . There was some sort of jingle set aside in Aunt Maggie's papers when I came out here yesterday. When I didn't see it last night, I thought she had put it away. Do you suppose—"

"The clue, you mean?" asked Bill, his face brightening. "What did it say?"

"That's the trouble. I can't remember. It was all a mixed-up jumble, something about hands and feet and steps. I thought Aunt Maggie had set it aside as a curiosity. You don't suppose it was a reducing exercise?"

"I don't think they bothered very much about such things back in those days," said Bill. "Sure you can't make head or tail of it?"

I shook my head hopelessly. "Anyway, it may not have been the clue. I'll look in Aunt Maggie's papers. But first I want to speak to Bessie."

"And I want a shave and a bath," said Bill.

In the kitchen I tactfully broached the subject of the secret room. But I got exactly nowhere. Bessie swore she had never heard of any secret room in the house, nor had she heard any sort of remark at any time which might indicate an unseemly interest on the part of anyone else, white or black.

A knock sounded on the kitchen door just as I was leaving, and when Bessie opened it Thomas came shuffling in, hat in hand.

"Mornin', Miss Bessie," I heard him say, and then as he caught sight of me, "Mornin', Miss Sally. I come to see if I could help Andrew and Bessie some, seein' as how Lindy couldn't come. Andrew come over to my house Friday and say you want Lindy to help, but she ain't home. She gone to visit her sick aunt." Like all his people, whatever their usual disregard of the broad "a," Thomas pronounced it a'h'nt. "Yes'm, her a'h'nt is sick."

"I hope she isn't very sick," I said absently. "When did Lindy go?"

Thomas stuttered and seemed unable to remember. "Day before yesterday, I think it was, Miss Sally. Yes'm, she went day before yesterday." While this hesitation struck me as a little odd, I decided that perhaps Lindy had gone after Andrew's visit and that Thomas was embarrassed by the fact.

"Thomas," I said, "have you ever heard of a secret room at Wisteria Hall?"

"Have I ever heard of what, Miss Sally?"

"A secret room," I repeated, knowing very well he had understood me the first time. "Think, Thomas."

"I don't rightly remember, Miss Sally. Seems as how I did hear your gran'ma say somethin' 'bout one."

"What did she say, Thomas?"

"She just say she sho' wish she knowed where it was, if I recollect rightly, Miss Sally."

"Then she didn't know? Did you ever help her to look for it, Thomas?"

Thomas looked really embarrassed this time and stuttered and finally came out with, "Well, no'm; that is, not exactly."

"What do you mean, not exactly?"

"Well, Miss Sally, ma'am, sometimes I sort of looked for it myself, seein' as how anxious yo' gran'ma was to find it."

"Did you have any luck?"

"No'm. I didn't have a bit of luck."

"Thomas," I then asked, "have you seen any questionable characters around the place lately?"

"Any what, Miss Sally?"

"People, men or women or anybody who looked as though they didn't have any business here?"

"Well, Miss Sally, you know they's been some carpenters and folks like that around. I seen them when I come over here to sort of look over the grounds. I knowed it was time to fertilize them lily-of-the-valley beds yo' gran'ma set such store by, what she say was planted a hundred years ago. And, Miss Sally, them carpenters had tromped all over 'em. 'Course them men Mr. Bill hired to fix that bad place in the road been here, but they ain't work on Saturday. And them carpenters been gone a week, ain't they?"

"But have you seen anyone else, Thomas? Anyone who didn't look as though he should be here?"

"No'm, not exactly. I seen a man yesterday, but he went off pretty soon, I reckon. I ain't studyin' much about it, 'cause Andrew done say you all was comin' out and bringin' company."

"What time was this, Thomas?"

"I disremember exactly, Miss Sally, but it was after I eat my dinner. I come to tell Andrew Lindy gone but I look around and don't see no cars and I reckon Andrew gone to the store."

"You didn't see anybody around here later in the afternoon or evening, Thomas?"

But if I had hoped to trip Thomas, I failed miserably. He looked at me with a puzzled frown. "But, Miss Sally, you all was here last night. I wouldn't a' thought nothin' 'bout seein' nobody here then."

"All right, Thomas," I said, giving up, "the reason I am asking you this is because something dreadful has happened, and we have all got to work together to—to get to the bottom of it. Miss Maggie was killed last night."

Bessie, who had kept in the background with utmost difficulty, now came forward to supply the gruesome details and I left them together in the kitchen. As I passed through the butler's pantry to the dining room, the buzzer sounded and I saw that the call had come from Alice's room. This brought my mind back to the scrap of silk on the stairway.

"I'll take Miss Alice's coffee," I told Bessie.

But here again my sleuthing was to meet with no success, for the first thing I saw on entering Alice's room was her quilted robe thrown over the foot of the bed, and even without comparing them, I knew that my sample was of a much deeper shade.

Like Bill, Alice looked rather the worse for wear. More than that, she had a sort of hunted look in her eyes, as though still nervous from her experience of the night before. Her hands shook so that she spilled more of the coffee than she drank, and I decided it was not just the time to tell her that Bill had had a run-in with her ghost.

Sounds of splashing in the bathroom indicated that Claire was up and about, and I remembered that she had spent the latter portion of the night in the room with Alice.

"Sorry I just brought coffee for one," I called. "I'll ring for more right away."

"Never mind," she called back, the lilt in her voice agreeable as always. "I'll dress and go down."

In a few moments more, rosy and fragrant from the bath, Claire herself appeared, trailing her jade-green negligee. Her red-gold hair was fluffed about her head like a halo and her freshness made Alice look even more wan and disheveled. But Claire always looked as though she had just stepped out of cellophane. Sometimes I wondered if her poise and serenity were not somehow implicit in that quality of immaculateness. Now her concern was all for Alice and me. "Brace up, old dear," she told Alice. "We'll be taking you home in a little while now." And, "Sally, it is all so dreadful for you, I know. I almost feel as though I were responsible. The party was my idea, you know."

While I knew Bill would agree with this wholeheartedly, I said she wasn't to feel that way for a moment. "Are you sure you don't want to rest a while and have your breakfast sent up?" I asked.

"Oh, no, I'm coming down. Really, I think it would be much better for Alice if she would get up too."

I left them to settle that question between them and when I was back in the kitchen I dug the bit of silk from my pocket. "Bessie, here's a scrap of cloth I found on the stairs. Have you any idea where it could have come from?"

"How come they any trash on them stairs?" Bessie demanded, instantly on the defensive. "Andrew say he clean 'em up good."

"But look at this," I said. "And these funny little feathery wisps sticking to it."

Bessie wiped her hands on a kitchen towel and took the scrap between her lingers judiciously. "Miss Sally, don't you know what this is?"

Something about Bessie's tone warned me that I was not going to like knowing what it was. "What is it?" I asked reluctantly.

"It's a piece tore out of that new comforter we brought out for Miss Maggie's room. How come somebody tearing up Miss Maggie's comforter?"

How come, indeed?

And yet, of course, an eiderdown puff might have a piece torn out and the explanation still be simple and logical.

"Andrew took it up to Miss Maggie's room still wrapped up and put it on her bed," Bessie recalled.

I remembered seeing it there, on the foot of the big four-poster, when we made our search of the house after Aunt Maggie's death.

I went up to the third floor to take another look. But the down puff was not there now. Nor could I find it in any of the other rooms on that floor. I could not find it anywhere.

X

On the way down from Aunt Maggie's room, I stopped on the second floor for a moment and, in passing, noticed that the doors of the rooms occupied by Bob and Kirk were both open. I decided to look in and see if by any chance one of them might have gone foraging for additional cover in the night.

This did not seem at all probable as I knew there were extra blankets in each room, but it was the only possible explanation I could think of in connection with the missing down puff.

There was no sign of it in either room, but in the bathroom I got quite a start at the sight of a piece of green wrapping paper lying on the floor. But the paper had no torn edges and from the creases I gathered that it was still the original size required for wrapping whatever it had inclosed.

No great amount of detecting was required to decide that it had been dropped there by Bob, for his room was in more or less of a state, while Kirk's reflected the military neatness he had learned in boarding school.

In the downstairs hall again I could hear Bob and Kirk talking in the dining room. As I came nearer the door, Kirk said, "I am afraid this is much more serious than any of us has admitted."

I frankly stopped to listen, for I knew that my entrance would put an end to the conversation and I was curious to know their actual views.

"Why do you say that?" Bob inquired.

"Well, for one thing," Kirk continued, "there were no witnesses to the murder. And for another, not one of us has an alibi. Murder is bad enough in any case, but think what a mare's nest this is going to be when the police start trying to prove each one of us guilty. That is no doubt the line they will take."

"I don't see why they should assume any of us guilty," argued Bob. "The thing that seems most likely to me is that—that it was done by somebody on the outside. Maybe somebody who broke in for the purpose of holding up the place. Aunt Maggie threatened to scream and he choked her to death. Then, overcome with the fact that he has committed murder, he gives up any thought of robbery and makes his escape, first seeing to it that there is no possibility of pursuit."

"That seems logical enough," Kirk admitted. "But the police are going to want to hang it onto somebody. And after all, you'll have to admit your theory is a little far-fetched. Almost nobody knew we were to be here, and even if anybody had, what would a holdup yield, except perhaps some family silver that has been unmolested for a hundred years or so? Of course, the girls have some jewelry, but I still don't believe it would have inspired a planned holdup."

Aunt Maggie's pearls are rather nice, but to save my life I could not remember whether she had worn them at dinner or not. Certainly there had been no trace of them when we found her in the passage, and I had not thought to raise the question. In fact, I was so accustomed to seeing her with them in the evening that they no longer made much impression, for they had been a present from her husband and she wore them constantly. I made a mental note to check on this by calling her house in town when the telephone was in working order.

"It seems to me," Bob was saying, "that one of the first requirements in proving guilt is to establish a motive. I still can't see what motive could be ascribed to any one of us. Love and money are supposed to be two favorite motives in such cases. Can you make either of them fit?"

Going on to the kitchen through the breakfast room, which incidentally we were not using for breakfast, I asked Bessie if she knew where Bill had disappeared to. "He out with Thomas," she told me, "helping him lay planks on the road, so the cars can come through. He ask Thomas is they any cinders or gravel or anything, but they ain't, and then they thought of them planks the carpenters left."

"Well, tell him I'm in the study on the third floor when he comes in, please. And, Bessie, I think for lunch—"

"Miss Sally, is we got to stay here that long? Can't them polices come on out and get everything fixed up so we can go back to town right away? Can't Mr. Bill just fix it up like he done that time when Andrew got arrested in that there crap game?"

"I wouldn't count on it," I answered, "not before lunch, anyway. What I was going to say was that we should plan a sort of buffet lunch, because the police may want to talk to some of us privately and everything will be more or less upset. That baked ham and some sliced chicken and a green salad—"

"Yes'm, and I could make a vegetable aspec."'

"That's the idea. Just fix whatever will be all right cold. Plenty of hot coffee, of course."

"We got to feed them polices, too?" she asked grudgingly.

"Why, yes, if they are here at lunchtime. Wisteria Hall is a long way from anywhere else, you know."

"Too fur to suit me," she muttered. "Don't see why we got to feed the law. Law never done nobody no good as I can see."

I admit that by then I was beginning to feel rather apprehensive about the law myself, for the conversation between Bob and Kirk had given me an idea of what we were in for. It seemed to me that my only hope lay in finding what Bob called a motive. Once we had a motive, maybe, we could find a clue.

So I went back to the third floor again, this time to look through the papers Aunt Maggie had left in the study. I felt reasonably certain she had not considered the secret room of interest except as a family curiosity. This being the case, she probably would not have hidden the clue. If the directions it gave were complicated, she might have had the paper with her when she went downstairs. But if the directions were easy to understand, she had probably left the clue among the other papers or had stuck it somewhere in her room.

But there were no papers in her bureau or desk drawers and nothing of interest in her purse. The collection of papers in the study was formidable. An old family Bible, several volumes of family records, half a dozen packets of letters and a number of loose papers and Aunt Maggie's brief case which inclosed her usual working materials. I sat down in the chair she had occupied and got busy. A lot of reading of old-fashioned, spidery writing was necessary, for I had no idea what the clue she had spoken of might be like.

It was slow work and I had begun to feel pretty hopeless when I heard a step outside. "Here I am, Bill," I called.

But nobody answered and nobody appeared. I waited a minute, for I knew that I had heard someone, then got up and looked out in the hall. But I saw no one. Ordinarily if I had thought I heard a footstep outside a room and found myself mistaken I would have dismissed the matter without further thought. But too much had happened lately for me to maintain any such casual attitude now. I looked first in Aunt Maggie's room, then in all the other rooms on the floor. As usual, I saw no one at all.

But in Aunt Maggie's room it seemed to me that the books and other things on the desk had been moved about. I felt sure of it, for the blotter was askew and surely I would have straightened it automatically when I looked in earlier.

I went back to the study, feeling a little too remote from the rest of the household for absolute comfort, yet anxious to go on with my search. I would make Bill help if he ever got through with his road mending. I worked on and on and to my ears, tuned now to hear the slightest sound, it seemed that the house was very still. I knew that it was only because one whole floor separated me from everyone else; but I found myself listening for noises and, when I finally heard footsteps again, I jumped from my chair and rushed to the door breathlessly.

Kirk, looking very forthright and dependable, was coming down the hall. "Bessie said you were up here," he explained. "I came to ask if I could be of any assistance"

"I was just going through Aunt Maggie's papers to see if they would throw any light on the situation."

"Not a bad idea," he agreed. "May I help? And by the way, Sally, I've been thinking this over, and while there doesn't seem to be any rhyme or reason for it, there's got to be one somewhere. You remember Aunt Maggie told us about finding a clue to the secret room? Do you suppose there could be—any connection?"

I felt my face flush. Here was Kirk suggesting the very thing I had been trying to keep quiet about. I must confess that for a moment I wondered if it were not just the thing the murderer himself might do. But, after all, maybe it was a more obvious conclusion than I had thought.

"I had wondered about it myself," I admitted. "That's why I am looking through these papers."

"Ah, I see. Well, let me help you. Have you any idea what we should be looking for? I mean, did you gather from Aunt Maggie any suggestion as to what sort of clue she had found?"

There was nothing for it but to accept his offer, so I said, "No. No idea at all. Suppose you check through these. I may have missed something."

We worked quietly for a while, then Kirk asked, "You—you don't suppose there's some crazy person hidden in there, do you? Did you ever hear of a relative who was not quite right?"

"Bill asked the same question this morning," I answered. "I never heard anything to make me think so, but it seems that anything is possible."

"I wondered about it when Alice claimed to have seen a ghost," Kirk said. "Of course, we all thought Alice was just imagining things because of overwrought nerves. But Bill ran into somebody in the hall—"

I looked at him guilelessly, but in my heart there was still a question. Could it have been Kirk who collided with Bill? After all, the stairs are nearest the dining-room door and Kirk had come back into the library from the dining room. But he met my glance squarely and it was I who turned away.

"Alice couldn't describe her ghost," I recalled. "She said it was just a—a shape." I shuddered at the thought that perhaps Alice might have been right. That there was some monster concealed in the house awaiting an opportunity to pounce upon innocent victims. Why had Bill used the words gorilla or hairy ape? Had there been something in that brief contact in the hall which had caused him to do so unconsciously? "Its too awful," I said to Kirk.

"I shouldn't have frightened you with such ideas," he said contritely. "If Alice saw anything, it was not a ghost, but something human. By the way," he went on, "was there anyone who might not want you to have this house? Any jealous relative who might have wanted it himself or herself? Anyone who might possibly feel that it was left to you—unfairly, and who would try to scare you away? Has anyone offered to buy it from you?"

"But why? What would that have to do with it?"

"Haven't you heard of cases where people tried to scare off the owners by making things disagreeable for them? Maybe so they could buy the property at a reduced price?"

"But that's too fantastic," I said. "Judge and Mrs. Warren, who live at Roswell, did ask if I would be interested in selling the place. They seemed to approve my decision to keep it and said they had only thought I might be selling it to—Yankees or somebody disagreeable."

"Yankees?" Kirk grinned.

"It's absurd, of course. But the Warrens are very old-fashioned. And these old houses are rather in demand in Georgia because Sherman left so few of them. The judge has been retired for some time and I suppose wanted a house with larger acreage and probably thought he could buy this one very cheaply if we were not interested in keeping it."

"So you don't think the judge is a likely candidate to be putting on a campaign to terrorize the present owners?"

"I certainly don't. And as to relatives, the only one I can think of who might have envied me the house would have been Aunt Maggie and she, of course, was free to come and go as she liked. In

fact, both she and Eve invited themselves this time. However, neither has any direct claim and, as things have turned out, I don't
see how it could be Aunt Maggie."

"Well, that's that," said Kirk, and we both worked silently for
some time. Then Kirk picked up Aunt Maggie's brief case, which I
had already gone through, and started scanning the papers it held.

"Hello, what's this?" he asked suddenly, a note of excitement
in his voice. "Looks like some sort of diagram."

And it was a diagram, with a line beginning at the top left-hand
corner and meandering downward toward the right. Here and there
along the line were names and at certain points there were large
black dots.

I could not help smiling when I saw it and Kirk's eager expression. "That," I told him, "is one of Aunt Maggie's genealogical maps
of Georgia. That black line is Sherman's march through Georgia to
the sea. The black dots indicate towns he burned, or at least towns
in which he burned the courthouses. Aunt Maggie marked them
because it means that all records prior to 1864 have been destroyed
in those towns and it was therefore useless for her to try to trace
family trees through deeds and marriage licenses and other papers
which are usually on record."

"Well, I'll be damned," said Kirk. "You know, Sally, it's a funny
thing. I studied American history, of course, and I know there was
a Civil War. But nobody in the North ever thinks of it one way or
another. What I mean is, up there the Civil War is as remote from
life of today as the Revolution. Why is it so different down here?"

"I suppose the invaded country always remembers longest," I
said. "There are so many things to remind one and so many people
who are determined that nobody shall forget. But all that is changing, even down here. The newspapers call it a 'thin gray line' when
the few surviving veterans of the 'sixties get out to march in the
Memorial Day parade each year. Soon I suppose it will be only a
thin gray line of remembrance—"

"I get you. When you come to think of it, Sherman did leave
rather a lot to remember him by."

"But it was war," I reminded him. "General Sherman was just a
realist, ahead of his time. This was the last of the gallant wars, you

know. When men like Jeb Stuart could wear sashes and plumes and ride rings around a Cavalry that outnumbered his own. Besides, there are lots of stories lying around loose in the state to show that General Sherman had his human side. And think what a grand alibi he has been for a lot of us down here."

Kirk regretfully replaced the diagram. "And I thought I had really discovered something," he lamented. "By the way, Sally, all this genealogy stuff. Could we find a clue there, do you suppose? Aunt Maggie never kept anybody out of the D. A. R or from being presented at court or anything like that by proving the family tree had a few rotten limbs, did she?"

"Oh," I said, "I wouldn't think that was any cause for murder, would you?"

"Well, I wouldn't have until I came South," Kirk admitted with a grin.

"You mustn't judge us all by Aunt Maggie," I told him. "She really had a passion for family research. Tracing a line fascinated her, just as crossword puzzles and chess and golf and other things do some other people. Connecting somebody with a Revolutionary ancestor or with William the Conqueror or somebody, with every link complete, was always a great triumph. I think she enjoyed finding rotten limbs, but she kept them for her private amusement. Tracing the line was the thing."

"You don't think, then, that anybody could have had an appointment with her here, or have followed her out here because of something disgraceful she might have discovered?"

I shook my head. "It would be a perfect solution, but I am afraid it won't do."

Voices came floating in from the hall and a moment later Claire and Alice and Bob crowded in through the doorway. "What's going on?" they wanted to know.

"We are looking for the clue to the secret room," Kirk announced as he rose to his feet. "Would you like to help? We hope it will throw some light on what happened last night."

Well, it was out. Everybody knew now. And, anyway, it probably didn't matter.

XI

"OH," SAID CLAIRE, "I was going to suggest last night before—before anything happened, that we look for the secret room today. It would have been such fun, such a grand way to spend a winter Sunday in the country. We could have offered a reward to the winner."

"Sally," Kirk approved, "that's an idea. We might make more progress if we just tried to find the room itself, without looking for a clue to guide us."

More than once I have marveled at the drama that can be introduced into any atmosphere simply by the entrance of a beautiful woman, and when two men present are both in love with her it is seldom they can agree on even the most insignificant details.

So I was not surprised when Bob said, "Oh, I don't know. Have any of you stopped to consider that there may not be a secret room?"

"What do you mean?" I demanded.

"Well, think of all the changes that have been made in the house since it was built," he said. "Part of the back hall has been converted into a breakfast room. The basement has been changed. You've torn out that partition which separated the double parlors. And, Sally, haven't I heard you say that this entire third floor was originally a ballroom, with a stage at one end for musicians or amateur theatricals as occasion demanded?

"And there's another thing to consider," he went on, as I nodded my head. "I've noticed that the walls of this house are at least three feet thick and that all the chimneys are inclosed. That means, except where there is a recess on each side of the chimney, that there is a good deal of space between walls. How do you know that what was once the secret room may not now be a plain, everyday clothes or storage closet, with no mystery about it at all?"

"Of course, an architect would think of all that," I agreed, more convinced than I had meant to be.

"It seems to me that this floor we are on would be an ideal place for the secret room," Bob continued. "When was it cut up into bedrooms, Sally?"

"My great-great-grandfather built the house," I said. "He was a middle-aged man when he came here from Darien, Georgia. I've always heard that it was my great-grandfather who changed the plan of the third floor. Some relatives from Virginia were coming to visit and more bedrooms were needed. You know how people came and stayed months in those days."

"So that explains it," said Claire. "I had been wondering why most of the furniture on this floor is Empire, while the rest of the house is so definitely eighteenth-century."

"Seems to me it fits perfectly," said Bob. "The chronology, I mean. Aunt Maggie said your grandparents didn't know the location of the secret room. That it was lost between generations."

But if there was not a secret room, the bottom dropped out of all my theories with regard to the murder. I was getting ready to say that perhaps he was right and then quietly follow my own inclination, when Claire spoke up again.

"Oh, let's look, anyway," she urged. "That is, if it is all right with Sally. We might find something. We can sound walls and push panels and examine closets and all that sort of thing."

"All right," Bob agreed, too much his amiable self to argue further. "But, you know, Aunt Maggie didn't say she had found the room. She only said she thought she had found a clue. However, we may as well look. We've got to do something while we wait for the police to come and take us all off in the patrol wagon."

I could see that Alice did not relish Bob's facetious reference to the police. But why couldn't she try to understand that Bob and the rest of us were only trying to do the best we could in a difficult situation? I was beginning to be a little fed up with her, this feeling aggravated by her very appearance of futility. Why will scrawny women economize by knitting themselves suits when knitted suits display all the deficiencies of their figures? And why should Alice insist upon beige, which made her appear more negative than ever?

On the other hand, one always felt that even without beauty or money Claire would still present a smart appearance, for she uses sense about her clothes as she always has about everything else. Except Bob, perhaps. This morning her simple little woolen frock of gray convinced you that only women with reddish-gold hair should ever wear gray at all. And even though she did rather have the look of the cat that has just swallowed the canary, I could forgive her, because she is always so agreeable.

Claire said, "Well, let's be off. How shall we go about it?"

"Let's divide into crews as we did last night," suggested Bob. "Claire and I can start in the basement. We'll give the rest of you the advantage of starting from the floor you are on."

"O. K.," said Kirk smilingly, but I noticed that his hand gripped hard on the chair behind which he was standing.

"But I don't think I want to look," said Alice. "I don't know what we might find in that room if we found it."

"Oh, I wouldn't worry about that," said Bob, giving her a brotherly pinch on the shoulder. I thought Bob seemed a little more himself this morning; yet there was something lacking, for I had to admit that, if I were meeting him for the first time, I might not be so much impressed as women usually were.

"You can help with the records then," I told Alice. "The discouraging thing is that there are tons of them. And they are so hard to read. My relatives seem to have kept everything from the newspaper telling about the assassination of Abraham Lincoln to the tuition receipts for music lessons for three generations of daughters. And just look at the notes on the margins of this Bible. It's almost a diary itself."

"Much simpler to find the proverbial needle in the haystack, or is it the needle in the proverbial haystack?" grinned Bob. "Your work is all cut out for you, isn't it?"

"'Scuse me, Miss Sally," said Bessie, appearing soundlessly in the doorway. "Miss Eve say, can you come by her room? She got somethin' she want to tell you."

"Oh, goodness," I said, "I had forgotten all about her. Isn't Miss Eve up yet, Bessie?"

"Yes'm, she up and had her breakfast. I carried it to her. But she ain't to say dressed. She's layin' on that chafin' lounge."

"Did I hear a'right?" asked Kirk, with a twinkle in his black eyes, as Bessie padded away.

"And wasn't that a perfect description of Eve?" Alice asked. "'She ain't to say dressed.' By the way, Kirk," Alice went on, apparently apropos of nothing at all, "have you ever heard the story of Eve's first husband?"

"Only that his name was Adam and that she persuaded him that an apple a day would keep the doctor away," Kirk answered.

"No, no, I mean Eve Benedict, and her first husband was named Phil Manning."

"Oh, Alice, why bring that up?" Bob objected.

"Kirk might as well be warned," she insisted, "in case he's ever tempted to go on an apple diet." Alice never had learned that belittling another woman doesn't make her any more attractive herself, and in this instance her effort to impress Kirk was embarrassingly obvious.

"Gosh, what happened to him?" Kirk asked, with natural curiosity.

"Nobody really knows," said Alice, pausing for dramatic effect. "There was a story—"

"But nobody knows that it was true," I interrupted.

"Well, I for one believe it," Alice insisted. "You see," she told Kirk, "Eve married Phil Manning because he had position and that was what she wanted. But he didn't have much money. Eve told this part of it herself. She thought it showed she was going to be good for Phil, or that people would think so, or something. Phil had always wanted to go to South America and he had enough money to take them there for a wedding trip. But Eve said they needed the money for other things. They would take a short trip and later when he had accumulated more—"

Alice looked around the circle defiantly. "Well, you all know it is true. She nearly ran him crazy with her demands for money. He couldn't stand it. Less than a year after they were married, he just—disappeared. Eve filed suit for divorce and it wasn't so long afterward that she married Frank Benedict and his money.

"Maybe it was poetic justice," Alice continued, "but it seems Frank Benedict had always wanted to go to South America too. So they went on their honeymoon." She paused again. "Well, the rest of the story comes second—"

"I think this is where we came in, isn't it?" Bob asked Claire. "And so if you will excuse us," making an exaggerated bow, "we'll be off to the South Pole."

"Alice," I said, when they were gone, "don't you think this is a good place to stop?"

"But it is too good a story not to tell," she insisted. "And anyway, I believe it is true." She fixed Kirk with a wide-eyed stare and dropped her voice. "It seems Frank had always wanted one of those human heads—the kind head-hunters collect. You know, how they shrink them down or something to about one fourth their original size and the face is still recognizable?

"Well, as I said, this part of the story came secondhand, and it was first told to somebody in Atlanta by a New York friend. This friend happened to go into a curio shop in Colón or Belize or somewhere. There didn't seem to be anybody about at first. Then she noticed—this New York woman did—a door leading into a back room. Going nearer, she could hear voices. Suddenly a man and a woman came bursting out, the woman screaming and saying she had to get away from there and the man following after and trying to catch up with her before she ran amuck in the street.

"When they were gone and the shopkeeper came out, the New York woman inquired as to the cause of such strange behavior. The shopkeeper was so excited himself that he just threw up his hands and admitted he had illegally offered for sale one of those human heads. He had not wanted to show it, but they had persuaded him.

"Then the shopkeeper told the New York visitor what the woman had said—that it was the head of her first husband."

"But—but," asked Kirk, "how did anybody know it was Eve?"

"The woman saw her later at the hotel and inquired her name at the desk."

"Quite a story," Kirk admitted.

None of which made it any pleasanter to drop in on Eve. And when I saw her, I decided that Bessie's was indeed a perfect description, for she was halfway out of her negligee and a generous amount of bosom was exposed where her white satin slip slid away. She was applying lipstick by the aid of a hand mirror and I thought looked a little haggard in the morning light.

"I always think lipstick is the difference between nakedness and nudity," she observed, watching out of the corner of her eye for my reaction to this witticism.

"I hope you slept well," I said.

"Oh, yes," she replied, airily lighting a cigarette. "I thought I would finish my mystery story before joining the merry throng. How are the two lovebirds? Cooing all over the place?"

And then, as I only waited, "There was something I wanted to talk to you about, but now that you are here I am not so sure what I should do."

"Well, you know best about that," I said, feeling that whatever Eve wanted to talk over with me would be more to her interest than mine, anyway.

She gave me a strange, speculative sort of look. "It's about the murder," she said.

"The murder?"

"Yes. Of course, you know Aunt Maggie was killed by someone in the house."

"I don't know it," I said. "She was killed in the house, of course, but someone from the outside must have done it."

"I think I know better than that," said Eve, calmly blowing smoke through her nose.

"No," I said. It was all that I could manage.

"There is one point I haven't quite figured out," she went on, as I sat and stared at her. "Just a little matter of conflicting evidence, one might say. That's why I think now that I should wait. I may be mistaken. Yes"—flicking ashes into the old Staffordshire pin tray—"I may be altogether mistaken."

I wouldn't have been a woman if I had let it go at that. "But what do you know?" I asked.

"That's the trouble," she said. "The more I think about it, the more I wonder. Don't say anything to anybody until I've had time to straighten things out in my mind."

"But if you really know anything," I said, "it is your duty to tell the police. They'll be here any minute, now."

"Give me time, give me time," she said grandiloquently, and I decided the chances were she didn't know anything but was just giving herself airs.

"Why don't you finish dressing and come down?" I suggested. Then, watching closely for her reaction, "We've all decided that Aunt Maggie's death ties in with the fact that she knew about the secret room, so we are staging a search for it."

I decided I wasn't any good at reading faces. Eve's expression did change, but if it meant any more than interested surprise I was unable to determine. "Why should anybody think that?" she asked.

"For lack of anything else to think, I suppose. The fact that she learned about the secret room is the only unusual thing that happened before her death, so we put two and two together—"

"Without getting very far?"

"Well, we're still hoping. Bob and Claire are working up from the basement and Kirk and Alice are on the third floor. You can take your choice and join either couple, or work independently as I am doing."

"I think I'll begin at the bottom and work my way up," she said, her smile consciously edged with malice.

"Oh, Eve, have a heart," I remonstrated. "Things are bad enough already. Don't do anything you'll regret."

"I never regret the things I do," she told me. "It's only the things I haven't done that I regret."

I thought of a lot of things to say, but once again I kept my mouth shut. There wasn't any use trying to get anywhere with Eve. Eve was—just Eve, and that was all you could do about it. Except,

I did make a mental reservation to the effect that when all this was over I was going to cut completely free from her. Never again would she be able to take advantage of a situation as she had in coming uninvited to Wisteria Hall.

Remembering that earlier resolve to explore my own bedroom as a possible outlet for the secret room, I decided that this was the best of all possible times to do so.

And there on my bureau, where I had found the green note the day before, was another scrap of green paper. I would have thought it was the same scrap, except that the message was different.

This time it said, "Beware of the secret room. Danger."

It was all too absurdly melodramatic, and yet it was happening. One had to take the situation seriously. And that awful feeling of being watched. I raised my eyes fearfully to the mirror, taking in as much as possible of the room, after the manner of the Lady of Shalott.

Over there by the dressing-room door, was the wall moving? No, of course not. It was only my own hand on the mirror frame, pushing it backward. Spinning around on my heel, I went to the door and flung it open, looking up and down the hall. But the hall was empty.

Carefully I searched the room, banging on the walls, measuring space to see that closets and dressing room took up their full quota. The space on each side of the fireplace was blank, except for the windows, and the wallpaper covered it without a break.

I gave up and, taking the two notes and folding them together, put them in my sweater pocket along with the packet of matches and the scrap of silk. As I thought it over, it seemed to me that only two people were above suspicion so far as the notes were concerned. Andrew and Eve. Even Eve could have placed this second note on the bureau in my room. For, after all, there was no reason why she could not have walked the few steps from her room to mine in negligee, timing her visit to coincide with Bessie's trip to the third floor. If she happened to meet anyone, she naturally could explain that she was looking for me.

This was all right, except for one thing. So far as I knew, Eve had been unaware of the hunt for the secret room until our conversation of a few minutes ago.

I stepped out into the hall again and took a look toward Eve's room. The door was opening and Bob was disappearing inside. Turning back toward the stairway, I saw Claire standing in the door of her room. "I had just started out," she explained, "but I waited because I did not want to embarrass Bob. I was to meet him downstairs."

"She probably sent for him as she did for me," I said. "This is evidently her morning to give audiences."

"I wish she was in hell," said Claire between her teeth, startling me half out of my already befuddled wits. I had often wondered at Claire's equable disposition. Somehow it didn't seem to go with the red in her hair. Now I could see the tiger come to life underneath the beauty and charm which, along with her money, had made it unnecessary for Claire ever to fight for anything.

XII

IN THE DOWNSTAIRS HALL we found Bill and an electrician busy at the telephone. Or rather a mild-looking young man in his Sunday best was at work, while Bill looked on.

"Whoever it was did a good job," observed the young man, as Claire and I also stopped to take a look. "Didn't cut it just once, for fear you might be able to fix it, I reckon, but cut it in two places and threw a piece of the wire away. Well, it's all right now, I guess. Wait a minute. That you, Operator? O. K. Ring us back, will you?"

He replaced the receiver and, like magic restored, there was the whir of the telephone bell. "Oh," I said, "how wonderful!"

The young man gave me a grin, thinking no doubt I referred to his prowess with the wires, when in fact, I was concerned only with the blessing of restored communication facilities. It was like getting back one's world.

"By the way, Sally," said Bill, when the electrician had gone and Claire had wandered into the drawing room, "there was nothing wrong with the lights in the house. Somebody simply pulled the master switch. We found it just now when I went with the electrician to investigate."

"Heavens!" I said, thinking of my case of jitters, of Bills collision and various other things which couldn't have happened if we had known the lights were in working order. "What—what about the cars?"

"Andrew came back with the wrecker and they are out there now working on the tires. They got the station wagon out of the mud and back in shape."

"And now that the telephone is in order again," I said, "you'd better phone your mother. She will be frantic if she bears about all this by radio or from somebody who may have happened to pick it up. And I want to hear from little Sally. Thank goodness, Mother and Dad are in Florida. But wait a minute," I added, crowding into the telephone closet with Bill, and closing the door. "Look at this." And I handed him the second note.

"I'll be damned," said Bill. "Another one?"

"Yes, and something else that may not be important, but which certainly seems strange. The eiderdown puff for Aunt Maggie's bed is missing. I found a torn scrap of it on the stairs, but we can't find the eiderdown itself, anywhere."

"Humph," said Bill, and paused for a moment with knit brows. "You know," he said, "I shouldn't be surprised if this is one of those cases where you add two and two. Granted there is a secret room, wouldn't that be the logical place for things to disappear to?"

"But why? You mean somebody in there—got cold?"

"Well, that would be the best reason. Soon as I get through with this telephoning, I'm going to take a look around. But don't you go poking about by yourself, looking for trouble. There's no telling what might have happened to you last night. You stay within reaching distance," he added, putting an arm around my waist and giving me a squeeze.

From the safety of that haven, I asked, "Why don't the police come? You get a wrecker and an electrician, but no police protection."

"The difference, my sweet," Bill explained, "is that the wrecker and the electrician came from Roswell. But Wisteria Hall is not a part of the—er—city of Roswell. It is in Fulton County. The police have to come from Atlanta. And even when they get here, I'm afraid it is not going to be any too pleasant. They will probably assume we were having a drunken party. While we are at this telephone business, I believe I'll call Mr. Marshall. He only handles civil cases, but his advice might be worth having and I don't know anybody else I'd want to call."

Returning to the study, I found Alice and Kirk just finishing up with the last of the papers. "Nothing that seems at all promising," said Kirk, in answer to the question in my eyes. "I'm ready to start looking for the room. Alice, you run on downstairs with Sally. I know you must be tired."

"Oh, no," she remonstrated. "I'm not at all tired. Really this has been fun." Then, "Oh, Sally, I didn't mean it the way it sounded. I only meant—"

"Didn't Mrs. Ambler say something about the books in the library?" Kirk interrupted tactfully.

Alice and I both remembered that she had, but not one of the three of us could remember exactly what it was. "I'll help you look down there," Alice offered.

"Heavens," I groaned, "it would take weeks to go through all those books. There are thousands of them and all printed before the Civil War."

"Wonderful," said Kirk.

"It's true," I said. "All the newer books are in the office or in the upstairs sitting room. My great-great-grandfather collected those in the library—"

"That's it," said Alice. "That's what Aunt Maggie said. Almost those exact words. And she said, 'It was in one of them that I—'"

Alice stopped and we all looked at each other, remembering. For Aunt Maggie had left that sentence unfinished just as she had left her life's work unfinished a short while afterward.

"But even so," Kirk pointed out, "that doesn't mean that the clue is still there. Mrs. Ambler probably removed it."

It seemed all too likely.

Downstairs again, I bumped into Claire and Bob just emerging from the basement. Claire had a smudge of soot on her face, which gave her loveliness a sort of rakish cast. Bob, standing tall and slim beside her, explained that they had even shoveled aside a part of the coal pile in their effort to overlook nothing.

I was touched with all this conscientious industry. "You are both sweet," I said. "I'm sorry you have to be starting your engagement like this."

Claire's eyes sought Bob's as eyes have sought other eyes since time immemorial. But Bob smiled at her only briefly and then said,

"You are the one who should be considered, Sally. All this can't be any fun for you. Have the—er—police put in an appearance yet?"

"No, but the telephone is in working order, in case either of you should wish to talk to anyone in town."

"Good," said Bob. "I would like to make a call."

"And I'd like to shed a little of the coal dust," smiled Claire.

Obviously, she had made no issue of Bob's visit to Eve.

In the library Alice was standing before the bookshelves with an open volume in her hand. At my approach she flushed and replaced it quickly. I noticed that a marker protruded above the pages and resolved to examine the book later. Someone on the place did not want the secret room to be discovered. Could that person be Alice? Could she now be suppressing evidence?

The electric lights, lighting the gloom from outside, shed a sort of diffused half-light over the rows of books. Titles were not always easy to read. And there seemed to be literally thousands of them. I took down one after another, ruffling the pages in the hope that some promising slip of paper might drop out.

"Do you suppose," asked Alice, "that some title or the name of some author might give a clue?"

"That's a thought," I agreed. "It may be that Aunt Maggie only found a key." But how to get anywhere without a key. My eyes ran up and down the shelves. Shakespeare, Balzac, Dante. The Waverley novels. Dickens, Poe. Plutarch's *Lives*. . . . Darn that cat. He probably knew who the murderer was. Whoever opened that door to the office . . .

Gulliver's Travels. Vicar of Wakefield, Arabian Nights. Robert Burns. William Cullen Bryant. Francis Bacon. Tennyson. Longfellow. Goldsmith. *Pilgrim's Progress.* Addison. Chesterfield. *Don Quixote.* Russell's *Modern Europe.* . . . This could go on forever without getting anywhere.

Kirk came in and joined us in the search and, a few moments later, so did Bob and Claire. Bill, I knew, was making his private search for the secret room. "Why all this sudden yen for literature and high thinking?" Bob wanted to know.

"Speaking of high thinking," said Kirk, "look at this."

He had discovered that he could raise the top of a Sheraton reading table which stands in a corner of the room. Inside the table was disclosed a folding ladder. Kirk and Bob together soon had the ladder set up, so that one end rested upon the floor and the other extended upward supported by two stout uprights. Unfolding above this upper half was a rack upon which a book might be placed. Bob was quite fascinated with it and immediately climbed up to take a look around.

"Perhaps," he suggested, "you are supposed to figure it out from the juxtaposition of titles or of authors. Would it mean anything to you that *Robinson Crusoe* has been hobnobbing these many years with Hazlitt's *Life of Napoleon?* And what about Macaulay's *History of England* and de Tocqueville's *Democracy in America?*" Bob paused and smiled down at us in that disarming little-boy way he has at times. "All I can make out," he said, "is that your ancestor certainly could take his punishment, Sally."

"Just listen to this," he went on, "Elliott's *Debates*. Aesop's *Fables. Geography of the Sea.* White's *Historical Collections of Georgia.* Carlyle's *French Revolution. Mormon Government.* D'Aubigné's *History of the Reformation—*"

"Come on down," Alice told him. "You aren't a bit of help."

"Wait a minute," he answered debonairly. "Here is something that makes sense. *Use and Abuse of Liquors* by Dr. Carpenter. Does that suggest anything to anybody?"

"If you mean you want a drink," said Alice tartly, "I think it is still a little early in the morning."

As Bob climbed down, we all looked toward the clock or at wrist watches, as people always seem to do when the time is mentioned. It was a quarter of eleven. The day was certainly moving along, and so far as I could see absolutely nothing had been accomplished.

"All very well," Bob told Alice, "but I need a pickup."

"A little of the hair of the dog that bit you?" Kirk suggested.

"Exactly," Bob replied, opening the door to the dining room. "Join me?"

"A fraction early yet," Kirk answered, but Alice surprised us all by following Bob into the dining room and closing the door behind her.

Claire raised her eyebrows but said nothing.

"I think she's still upset," said Kirk. "Spot of brandy may help her." But we all knew it was not a drink for herself that had carried Alice into the dining room.

"What about this old secretary?" Claire asked. "Might find something there. Weren't they all supposed to have secret drawers and things? Mind if I look?"

"Wish you would," I said as I took down from the shelves the book which Alice had replaced so hastily.

It was a volume of Shakespeare and the marker was placed between the pages of *Venus and Adonis*. The lines my eyes fell upon were:

"Affection is a coal that must be cooled,
  Else suffered, it will set the heart on fire;
  The sea hath bounds, but deep desire hath none."

I understood now why Alice had blushed and also that the evidence suppressed was not what might be called germane to the case.

"Never saw so many old letters," said Claire. "Suppose they are love letters? Anyway, they are all tied with ribbons. And here are some old diaries. It might be fun to read them if anybody ever had time," she added to Kirk, who was standing just behind her chair, looking over her shoulder. Once out of the corner of my eye I saw him reach out as though to touch her, then quickly withdraw his hand.

There was more desultory talk. Bob and Alice came back into the room. I think everybody was beginning to be pretty tired of the whole thing when there was a sharp exclamation from Claire and we all rushed over and crowded about her.

She had found a secret drawer and it was full of tarnished gold coins. Examination showed them to be money coined at Dahlonega, Georgia, when the government maintained a mint at that point back in the days before the rush of the forty-niners made everybody forget gold had ever been discovered in North Georgia.

I remember having been told by my grandmother that it was while making a trip to Dahlonega from Darien that Roswell King,

a banker, impressed with the beauty of the scenery and the eleva-
tion along the Chattahoochee River, decided to establish here the
colony that bears his name. I believe it was first planned as a summer retreat, away from the miasmic swamps of the coastlands, but
by the time of the Civil War a cotton mill and various other indus-
tries had grown up in the vicinity. After the war little industrial
activity was resumed in the ruined plants and for many years
Roswell settled down to something approaching its original serenity. This money, no doubt, had been forgotten, else it surely would
have been spent in those lean years of reconstruction.

We picked up the old coins and let them fall through our fingers. "Question might be," observed Kirk, "whether you will have
to turn this into the government."

But nobody answered, for in the bottom of the drawer we had
discovered a tiny scrap of paper. I think we all wanted to grab for
it. "You look at it, Sally," said Claire.

The writing was so dim that I could barely make it out at first.
There were only two words:

"Jarman. Wills."

It must be a book, we all decided, rushing back to the bookshelves. If I live to be a hundred, some of those titles will still pop
out at me at odd and inappropriate moments. *Encyclopedia Ameri-
cana*. *Lives of the Chief Justices*. *History of American Coloniza-
tion*. Spruzheim's *Phrenology*. Guizot's *Civilization*. . . .

"There isn't any such book," I said dejectedly, after another five
minutes or so of this fruitless search.

"But this sounds hot," said Kirk, standing on the ladder and
reading aloud. "Looks like it might be the right neighborhood.
American Military Law. Bright's *Husband and Wife*. Smith's *Master and Servant*. H'm'm. *Morris on Replevin*. Ah . . ."

"You mean you've found it?" Claire gasped.

"Yes," said Kirk, "but maybe Sally should be the first to look at it."

"I think that's sort of silly," I said as he came down, and they
helped me up the ladder. "Where is it? Oh, yes"—and with shaking
fingers I removed the calf-bound volume from the shelves and
climbed back down again.

The book opened easily in my hands. The pages thus revealed showed plainly the imprint of a marker or paper which was there no longer.

I shook the book in a sort of frenzy, ruffling the pages. Something fell out and a joint sigh of relief went up.

Bob picked up the fallen paper.

It was only a loose page of the book itself.

I sat down on the sofa, with Alice and Claire on either side and examined the page minutely. But we were forced to admit that we could find nothing to suggest the clue Aunt Maggie had mentioned.

Tears were very near the surface as I handed the book to Bob to replace in its niche. My hopes had been so high. "Why don't you all go down to the game room and have a little ping-pong?" I suggested. "It's sweet of you to help, but I don't believe we are going to find anything and it is going to be bad enough for everybody with the police and everything."

Understandingly Claire marshaled them out.

"I'll just fold this ladder back for you," said Bob, lingering behind. As he bent over the table, an exclamation escaped his lips. "What's this?" he asked.

I walked over to the table and looked at the slip of paper he held. Written on it in Aunt Maggie's hand were the words, "Dining-room closet."

"Where did you find it?" I asked, struggling for calmness.

"Here, in the table. You see, the ladder folds over it."

Excitedly I grabbed the bell pull. "Find Mr. Bill and tell him to come to the dining room," I told Andrew when he appeared. "Tell him to hurry."

XIII

Bob and I decided Aunt Maggie had found whatever clue was contained in the book on wills, had made this note and had dropped it as she climbed down the ladder. We were in the dining room itself before I realized there is no closet in the room.

There were the mahogany sideboards, the end tables against the wall, the breakfront china cabinet, the fireplace, the two windows opening out over the side driveway, the three doors opening respectively into library, hall and butler's pantry, but no other door. No sign of any closet anywhere.

Bill joined us in the midst of this fruitless inspection. "What's wrong?" he asked, glancing from one to the other of us.

"We thought we had found something," I said, exhibiting the note and explaining how Bob discovered it. "But it seems to be just another blind alley."

"Wait a minute," said Bob. "Perhaps it is not meant to be visible. Claire and I did look in here for signs of a hidden room, but found nothing of interest. See, there's no break in the wallpaper. Such rooms were usually placed near the fireplace. No, nothing here." His eyes roamed around the room speculatively.

"I've got it!" He snapped his fingers. "It's back of that china cabinet."

"What makes you think so?" asked Bill, his voice taking on some of Bob's excitement.

"Because, don't you see, the door could be concealed behind it. One of those doors cut into the wall and without any frame. You know, like somebody cut through the painting of *The Last Supper?*"

The two men heaved and pushed. I held my breath as priceless china tinkled on the shelves and slid back and forth against the leaded panes of glass doors. Bessie came in to see what was going on. "Sweet Jesus, Miss Sally, they gonna break all yo' gran'ma's china!" she gasped.

At last the tall cabinet stood away from the wall. But if there had ever been a door behind it, no trace remained. The wallpaper covered an unbroken surface. Bill and Bob rubbed their hands across it experimentally in an effort to discover a groove, but without result. Dejectedly they moved the cabinet back into place.

"Maybe she meant the kitchen," I said, without much conviction. "You know, the kitchen used to be the dining room when the old kitchen was a separate building back of the house."

"But Aunt Maggie knew that," Bill argued. "Why would she write dining room if she meant kitchen?"

I couldn't answer that; but we all moved back through the butler's pantry, and it was immediately apparent to anyone with an observing eye that a double wall about five feet wide separated the entire length of the kitchen and dining room and that only a part of this inside space was used as the butler's pantry. In fact, I had always known this, but had not connected the fact with our search for a hidden room.

"But this here space is all took up," Bessie pointed out. "This here's a supply closet," she added, opening a door about midway the length of the room. "And this—"

"Let me see," said Bill, crowding Bessie aside and entering the supply closet. "Yes, but that still doesn't take up all the space. Now what—"

"Bessie, show him," I said.

Bessie stepped to the left-hand side of the supply closet, touched a hidden spring and a wall of shelves pivoted around, leaving space for passage. "It's the silver closet," she explained. "They's a lock to lock it with, too. But nobody never would find it, no way."

Bill and Bob crowded into the small room, which contained nothing but the family silver not already in use, some broken china put aside for mending and several bottles of old wine which had been there goodness knows how long.

"Well here's your secret room," said Bill, disgustedly. "And all this hullabaloo about nothing. What are you going to do now, Sally, with your big idea that the secret room would solve the murder?"

"But I knew about this one all the time," I said. "I can't be sure Aunt Maggie did, though. She and my grandmother didn't get along so well and Aunt Maggie hadn't seen much of the house before grandmother's death."

"Well, your grandparent who built the house seemed to have quite a flair for this sort of thing," said Bill dryly. "He never was mixed up in the smuggling business, was he?"

"That isn't fair," I said. "Back in those days and in a wilderness, every man's house literally was his castle. And he had to have safe places to put things."

"Such rooms were not at all unusual." Bob backed me up. "The tendency is reflected in the furniture of the era. Desks and tables and chests of drawers nearly all had their secret compartments, just as we found this morning."

"What I can't see," said Bessie, "is if they had the kitchen in the back yard, how did they get them waffles and hot breads and things to the dining room without 'em gettin' cold?"

I smiled in spite of myself. "I always understood the cook's young children acted as runners," I told her.

"Yes'm," she nodded, then a look of horror spread over her features. "Sweet Jesus, Miss Sally, do you hear that?

"Of course, I do," I answered crossly. "It's the siren of a police car. And why they should be sounding it as though they were going to a fire, in broad daylight out here in the woods with not a sign of traffic anywhere, I can't imagine."

"They want to be sure the criminal has a chance to get away," said Bob. "You wouldn't want them to run into him unexpectedly, would you?"

Then the law walked in with heavy tread.

"We sure had a heck of a time finding the place," said the older of the two patrolmen, who introduced himself as Hendricks and his partner as Adams. "Nobody in Roswell could tell us where the Stuart place was, but they knew all right when we remembered it was called Wisteria Hall."

"It was my grandmother's house," I apologized. "That's why nobody recognized the name of Stuart. We only came out for the weekend."

"Whe-e-w!" ejaculated Officer Hendricks, "and this is what you get. Orders we picked up on our radio said it was murder."

"Yes," said Bill giving an outline of what had taken place just after dinner the night before and answering a few routine questions put by the two policemen. Then the three of them went in to "view the body," as Officer Hendricks expressed it.

Soon afterward I heard his voice at the telephone. "Better send somebody out to make a complete investigation on this call you told us to look into at Roswell. Yes. Murder and no evidence so far as I can see. No. Nobody here but Mr. and Mrs. Stuart and a house full of company. Mr. and Mrs. Stuart live in town but they were all out here for the weekend.

"Yes, I'd say get in touch with the solicitor's office. Tell 'em to ask for Wisteria Hall at Roswell. Mr. Stuart says there's a nearer way they can come, but they'd better go by Roswell to play safe. It's one of those real old houses, but away off in the woods. About five miles out."

"What are they going to do?" I asked Bill.

"I gather the case is not quite up their alley," he said. "Something that was open and shut and nothing to do but snap on the handcuffs would be all right. But this requires—detecting. They were probably sent out because they happened to be nearer when the call was broadcast. And by the way, when they finish getting the lay of the land, they want to ask everybody some preliminary questions in order to file a report and, I suppose, to have something to turn over to whoever comes out later. Better round up everybody in the library."

"I don't think Eve has dressed yet," I said. "Maybe I had better go and tell her, though, of course, she must have heard that siren."

Eve was still inclined to be airy in manner. "Are they trying to be hard-boiled?" she inquired. "Just wait until I take a hand with them."

"If you really know anything about what happened last night," I said, "for heaven's sake, now is the time to speak up."

But when it came her turn to answer questions as to name, address, occupation and whether or not she could shed any light on the events of the evening before, Eve vouchsafed no more in her replies than the strict letter of the law required. Her main concern seemed to be that the police should be properly impressed with her impersonation of the Lady Vere de Vere. "How terrible," she shuddered, fastidiously, when Officer Hendricks announced that we would all have to be fingerprinted as soon as somebody arrived with the proper equipment.

When the names of the servants were given and the fact came out that Lindy was missing, Thomas was ordered to produce her pronto. "She's probably the one that did it," Patrolman Adams announced to me in a cheerful aside. It didn't seem at all likely to me. Still, there was the fact that Thomas certainly had got himself tangled up when asked about the time Lindy left home.

"I'm going to have to ask you all to stay right here until somebody gets here from town," said Patrolman Hendricks. "Well, maybe not right in this room," as a wave of protest swept over him, "but don't go out of the house. Mr. Stuart, I suppose you are willing to vouch for everybody?"

"Certainly," Bill answered, "but I hope we can get it all over as soon as possible."

Well, that was out of his hands, Officer Hendricks observed, but someone would be along shortly, and meanwhile he would question the servants in the kitchen. I suggested that they use the breakfast room and instructed Andrew to serve the two officers hot coffee and cigarettes.

Eventually the second police car arrived, bringing Lieutenant Jim Gregory; his assistant, Patrolman Roberts; and a fingerprint expert, named Anderson. Lieutenant Gregory immediately went into a huddle with Patrolman Hendricks and Adams and looked very disgusted when he learned they had discovered practically nothing.

They held their conference in the office. Bill and I, waiting in the breakfast room, heard Lieutenant Gregory answer with a skeptical "Yeah?" when Patrolman Adams confided that we "seemed like real nice folks, just as plain as an old shoe." Then the door closed. But we smiled at each other, a little comforted by this homely compliment, even though it seemed to make no impression on Patrolman Adams's superior officer.

Lieutenant Gregory looked more like an athlete than a policeman. He was about thirty-five years old, I should say, quite tall in his well-fitted blue uniform, and had dark hair and piercing dark eyes. I don't know whether his eyes had always had that penetrating quality, or whether it had developed through literally trying to probe down to the truth in other people's eyes. But it seemed a very appropriate feature and one which I was sure could make a guilty person feel quite uncomfortable. In fact, I didn't enjoy it any too much myself, under the circumstances.

"Gentlemen," said Bill, when the office door opened again, "you've come a long way through the cold. I suggest you have some coffee before we try to get down to business."

Lieutenant Gregory looked a little reluctant. But it was cold outside and he had come a long way. Besides, his two companions were plainly more than willing to take this little recess. "Perhaps, it wouldn't be a bad idea," he agreed.

Later he and his retinue and Bill went into the drawing room, where they stayed for quite a while. When they came out, I heard him tell Patrolman Roberts to order an ambulance. Then he went back into the room alone, after which he and the other two officers went out to inspect the back passage. Following a final consultation with Hendricks and Adams, the latter were dismissed and told they could go back on patrol duty. Anderson was instructed to assemble fingerprints, make photographs and gather up any evidence he might discover.

"And now," said Lieutenant Gregory to my husband, with Roberts hovering behind him like an anxious shadow, "I should like to talk to you and Mrs. Stuart. Later we can take the guests and the servants in turn."

We settled ourselves in the office, behind closed doors, a fairly small room furnished somewhat after the manner of the library, except that my grandfather's desk and my grandmother's sewing table give it a more intimate air. And the books are newer.

Roberts found himself a chair near his superior officer and took out notebook and fountain pen. Then Lieutenant Gregory said something which struck me at the time as being quite tactful, but which I later recognized as merely a part of his technique. "In cases like this," he began, "my uniform has the unfortunate effect of making people think of themselves in, well, a convict's uniform. What I mean is that the connection is not pleasant. On the other hand, the most innocent person often looks guilty when being questioned. Because of this, I have learned to discount a lot that looks suspicious. But I would get to the truth a lot quicker and we could clear things up with less trouble for everybody, if people didn't think the law was trying to set a trap to catch them. They get the idea we don't care whom we send to jail, just so we send somebody."

Bill said, "I am even more anxious than you are to clear this up, Lieutenant. Fire away and ask anything you wish. Of course, this has all been pretty much of an ordeal for my wife. She was fond of her aunt, and I hope you won't make it any more difficult for her than is necessary."

"Okay," said Lieutenant Gregory. Then, fixing me with that penetrating gaze, "I believe you found the body, didn't you, Mrs. Stuart?"

I started involuntarily. It was something of a shock, having Aunt Maggie referred to as a body. "Yes," I answered, my voice grown suddenly small.

"From the position of the body, would you say that she died where you found her, or could she have been dragged or carried there from somewhere else?"

"I didn't think of that," I said, "and I don't think anyone else did at the time. At least nobody suggested it. I thought she had fainted or had fallen down the stairs."

"But looking back, what do you think?"

"I—I saw nothing to indicate that she had been dragged or carried. I mean her clothes looked as I imagine they would have if she had fallen or had been allowed to fall."

"What was your opinion, Mr. Stuart?"

"She looked to me as though she had fallen," said Bill, resolutely patient. I knew he thought this was all a waste of time.

"Where were you at the time of her death?"

"On the second floor. I had gone upstairs shortly before to bring down some ping-pong rackets for the game room. In fact, I came up from the basement, passed the place where a few minutes later we found Aunt Maggie, went up the back stairs to the second floor and was there, rummaging around, when Andrew came for me."

Lieutenant Gregory leaned forward toward my husband. "You mean you were on the spot, say five minutes before she was killed, but saw nothing to arouse your suspicions?"

"That is right," said Bill, giving him look for look. "Of course, I can't be positive about the exact number of minutes. But there was certainly nothing to see."

"And when you came out just a few minutes after your husband had gone upstairs," he asked, turning to me, "you saw nothing either, Mrs. Stuart?"

"No."

"And you have no idea of the murderer's identity?" Lieutenant Gregory looked hard at me, then focused his gaze on Bill.

"No," we both said. "Except," Bill said, "some funny things did happen."

"Funny?"

"Yes, odd. Things we couldn't explain." And Bill told him about the telephone call to Andrew.

"What else happened that seemed suspicious?"

"These," I said, extracting the scraps of green paper and the bit of silk from my pocket.

Lieutenant Gregory looked at the notes for a long time. He and Roberts exchanged glances and it seemed to me there was a gleam of excitement in their eyes.

"Odd they should use that paper," Lieutenant Gregory murmured just above his breath.

"That's what I thought, too," I answered.

"How do you mean that's what you thought?" he asked quickly.

"Wrapping paper from a department store," I explained.

"Oh, that?"

"Wasn't that what you meant?" I asked.

Again the two officers exchanged glances. "Suppose we go on to this piece of cloth," Lieutenant Gregory suggested.

I explained that it was undoubtedly torn from the new eider-down comfort brought out for Aunt Maggie's room and that, although it was seen on her bed after the murder, it was mysteriously missing this morning.

He pondered this for a few moments, opened his mouth as if to say something, evidently thought better of it and said nothing. It seemed too bad I could not put him through a third degree.

"Anything else?" he asked.

We told him about the red light, about the door which Kirk and I saw open and close, about Bill's collision in the hall. He listened silently and Roberts kept busy with his pen.

"Can you make any sense out of it?" I asked.

"I'd rather not say just yet," he answered, with something that was as near a smile as I suppose he ever allows himself while on duty. "What's all this about a secret room?"

I told him of Aunt Maggie's conversation the evening before and of how I had come to believe that her murder was in some way connected with the secret room. "The trouble is the only clue we found was a note made by Aunt Maggie, which obviously refers to the silver storage closet in the kitchen."

"That note, where is it?"

Bill produced it from his pocket.

"You are sure this is Mrs. Ambler's handwriting?"

I had been sure enough at the time. I took the note and examined it again. "Yes, it is Aunt Maggie's writing. I'm as certain as one can reasonably be."

Lieutenant Gregory went into the routine questions as to whether Aunt Maggie had any enemies and whether we had cause to suspect the servants or any of our guests. The answer, of course, was no in both cases.

At this point his sandy-haired assistant began to fidget. "What is it, Roberts?" Lieutenant Gregory asked. "Oh, I see. Motives."

Then turning to Bill. "Mrs. Ambler was, I understand, a wealthy woman?"

"She was quite comfortably fixed," Bill admitted.

"You know of no one who might have tried to blackmail her?"

"No."

"Who will profit by her death?"

"Profit?" Bill and I repeated like stupid parrots.

"Who inherits her money?" he elucidated.

"Oh," said Bill. "My wife. Unless Aunt Maggie recently changed her will. Our family lawyer is on the way out. He would know."

While Lieutenant Gregory's expression remained inscrutable, I could feel that Roberts was pleased. I should not have been at all surprised if he had said, "Now we are getting somewhere."

XIV

BUT HOWEVER AGREEABLE Patrolman Roberts's thoughts may have been, they were interrupted by a loud and peremptory knocking at the door. Lieutenant Gregory frowned, but nodded in answer to Roberts's questioning look, and the latter, disapproval eloquent in every movement, arose and stalked over to answer.

Standing outside was our lawyer, Mr. Thomas Marshall, and another man whom I did not recognize. Mr. Marshall's arrival at that precise moment seemed more than mere coincidence to me. I was willing to set it down as a good omen, foreshadowing a speedy disposition of our difficulties.

Bill arose hastily and went to meet the newcomers. "This is Coroner Dodson," Mr. Marshall explained as they shook hands, and I drew my breath quickly, remembering the coroner is blind. I should not have guessed it from his appearance, for he is confident in bearing, vital and alert looking, and though a little heavy is at the same time clean-cut in features and physique.

"I asked Mr. Dodson to come as a special favor to me," explained Mr. Marshall, whose bald head makes his shaggy eyebrows look as though they needed a good manicure. But under those ferocious brows are the large, kind brown eyes of a faithful Gordon setter, which were now turned anxiously in my direction. "I was never so glad to see you," I told him sincerely.

"Mr. Dodson's duties as coroner do not require him to make an investigation in person," Mr. Marshall continued. "All he has to do is preside at the inquest, as no doubt will be necessary in this

143

case. But we have known each other for a number of years. In fact, we play chess together and I have a great respect for his ability and his powers of deduction. So, after your telephone call, I got in touch with him and although, as I said, he is not required to make these visits he is making an exception in this case."

"Very glad to do so," said Mr. Dodson, in his deep resonant voice, as Bill and I expressed our appreciation. "Ah," he added, "I see you have Lieutenant Gregory on the job."

The officer, who had done no more than voice a low remark to his assistant, now came forward, grinning, to shake hands with the blind coroner who had recognized his voice.

"And isn't that Roberts with you?" Mr. Dodson asked, and Roberts, too, arose to pay his respects. "Just a little impetuous sometimes," smiled the coroner, as he shook hands with Roberts, "but with Gregory you make a good team, so I suppose it is all right."

"Have to work hard to put anything over on the coroner," said Lieutenant Gregory, with a noteworthy attempt at lightness.

"You are right, it is hard to put anything over on him," agreed Mr. Marshall, who explained that his purpose in bringing Mr. Dodson was to have him look the situation over and sit in on the questioning.

"He hears more in the human voice than the rest of us do," Mr. Marshall declared.

"Oh, I don't know," Mr. Dodson deprecated modestly, but with a humorous twist to his sensitive lips. "Maybe I just listen more carefully. It is one of the things you learn to do when you cannot depend entirely upon sight."

I remember hearing my father say that Mr. Marshall, while not the most brilliant member of the legal profession, was always smart enough to dig up the right person to do the right thing in his stead. Obviously that was his purpose in enlisting Mr. Dodson's aid. And it did not surprise me that he should feel such confidence in Fulton County's coroner, for Mr. Dodson is by way of being a celebrity and is often in the newspapers.

He is a practicing attorney in addition to his duties as coroner. He goes to baseball and football games, bowls, uses a typewriter and not only dials his own telephone numbers but, by listening when someone else dials, is able to call out the number indicated. Because of his feats as a memory wizard, his skill as a pianist and charm as a public speaker, he is constantly in demand as an honor guest at businessmen's luncheons and dinners. But chess and fishing and symphony orchestras are known to be his great hobbies.

I wondered if by merely listening in on testimony he was able to detect guilt where someone else might fail to do so. Evidently Mr. Marshall believed something of the sort.

"Mr. Marshall," said Lieutenant Gregory, when everyone was seated, "Mr. Stuart says you can tell us about Mrs. Ambler's will."

"What would you like to know?" asked Mr. Marshall, with customary legal caution.

"Who is the chief beneficiary of that will?"

"Ah," said Mr. Marshall, stroking his chin. "Mrs. Ambler was generous, most generous to a number of charities. She also left a fund to both our state and city libraries to be used in the—er—furtherance of departments of genealogy. There are small legacies to both librarians, who have been of great help to her in matters of genealogical research. Mrs. Ambler's faithful servants were also remembered generously. After the distribution of these direct bequests, the residue of her estate accrues to her great-niece and namesake, Mrs. Stuart."

"This—er—residue, what would it amount to?"

"I could not say exactly. You will understand there will be considerable red tape to go through in settling up the estate. There will also be the customary inheritance taxes."

"But roughly speaking, would you say there would still be a considerable sum?"

"That depends upon what you mean by a considerable sum."

"Say, several hundred thousand dollars?"

Mr. Marshall looked very judicious as he pondered his reply. "It is difficult to be definite about real estate," he said, "without a professional appraisal, especially business property. But in securities alone I should say we might safely count on something approximating a hundred thousand dollars."

"Thank you," said Lieutenant Gregory dryly, apparently glad enough to abandon the subject after having finally wrung something concrete from Mr. Marshall's polite evasions. Roberts, who had followed the course of the conversation eagerly, favored his superior officer with one of those I-told-you-so looks, then asked if we should continue with the testimony.

"Shouldn't we explain the situation first to Mr. Marshall and Mr. Dodson?" Bill asked. "I gave Mr. Marshall only the briefest outline over the telephone."

But Mr. Dodson insisted that we proceed, saying he did not wish to delay things and that they could catch up on the details later. "Just where were you when we interrupted?"

Lieutenant Gregory looked at Roberts, who read aloud from his notebook: "Who profits by Mrs. Ambler's death?"

The coroner smiled. "So it was not really an interruption?"

Mr. Marshall coughed apologetically. "I should like to advise Mr. and Mrs. Stuart," he said, "that they are not compelled to answer questions which, er—"

"May be used against them," Lieutenant Gregory finished for him. "Right. I was only going to ask"—he turned to Bill—"whether you or Mrs. Stuart have enemies of your own?"

"Enemies?" Bill echoed. "Why—why, I don't know. It never occurred to me to think so. If I do have, I don't know it."

"And you, Mrs. Stuart?"

I shook my head. "If I have any, I don't know it."

"You can't think of anyone who might try to get back at you for something? Revenge, you know. Somebody who would try to get you on a spot. Some person who would know you were going to inherit your aunt's fortune and could make it look like you killed her?"

I had an all-gone feeling in the pit of my stomach. "Oh, no!" I cried, more in protest than denial.

"Lieutenant," said my husband, and his voice had grown suddenly harsh, "don't you think this is going a little farther than is necessary?"

"Now, now," the lieutenant soothed, casting an anxious look in Mr. Dodson's direction, "I only asked if you thought there was a possibility somebody might try to make things look bad for either of you."

"But you don't think it looks as though I could have killed her, do you?" I asked, still pretty well overcome with horror at the thought. It had never occurred to me that anyone might think that.

"Just on the face of it, no," agreed the officer. "It would take a pretty strong woman to strangle another to death, even though the victim was a much older woman."

"Mrs. Stuart is city tennis champion," said Roberts.

Outraged, both Bill and I turned on him at once. I, wounded to the quick that anyone should seem so anxious to make me out a criminal, my red-headed husband ready to fight. "Either you apologize for that, or get out of this house," Bill ordered.

"Apologize," Lieutenant Gregory growled to his subordinate, "and then keep out of this."

"Sorry," Roberts mumbled; red to the roots of his sandy hair. "I just—"

"That'll do." Lieutenant Gregory cut him short. "Now, let's all try to keep our shirts on," he said. "I tried to explain at the start that some of the questions I have to ask may sound—er—as though I was trying to set a trap, but this is not the case. I have drawn no conclusions about anybody and am only interested in clearing things up. But in order to do this, I am going to need everybody's help. You see," he went on, "we've got to get something, somehow, to work on. Frankly, from the situation as a whole, the inaccessibility of the place, it looks like an inside job. Yes, I know Mrs. Stuart thinks she saw the tail-light of a car last night. But that was long after the murder was committed, and you say you had searched the place several times. Mr. Stuart ran into somebody in the hall, but in the dark it could have been anybody. What about your guests, Mr. Stuart?"

"Do you mean, do I think I ran into one of them? Because, of course, I wouldn't know positively. But I don't think it was one of our guests."

"Have you cause to suspect any of them?"

"No," said Bill.

Lieutenant Gregory turned to me. "And you, Mrs. Stuart?"

I have never had what is known as a poker face and I felt myself flush. But I said, "No, I have no real cause to suspect anyone."

A lot of things went through my mind as Lieutenant Gregory held my gaze with those probing black eyes. Eve's conversation with Aunt Maggie. The man on the walk whom I had mistaken for Kirk. The nocturnal perambulations of Eve and Alice. Bob's excessive drinking. The opening of the front door and Kirk's unexplained absence.

"Isn't there something you are not quite sure about, Mrs. Stuart?" Lieutenant Gregory asked politely. "We'll get to the bottom of this a lot quicker if everyone will put his cards on the table."

"Bill," I said, "you know everything about this that I do. Do you think we have left out anything which Lieutenant Gregory should be told?"

Bill looked thoughtful for a moment. "What about your visitor on the driveway?"

"Oh, yes," I said, "when I was taking things out of the car in the back yard, I heard someone on the walk at the side of the house. I went over to see who it might be and a man was running away. At first I thought—" I stopped, realizing I had gone further than I meant to.

"Yes?" asked Lieutenant Gregory.

I looked at Bill, who nodded. "I thought it was someone I knew, but when I called him he only ran faster, so, of course, I knew I had been mistaken."

"Are you so sure now?"

"Yes. Oh, yes," I said.

"Just the same, I should like to have you name that person," he insisted. "The person you thought you recognized."

Mutely my eyes sought Bill's again. "It couldn't have been," he said.

"Lieutenant Gregory," I asked, "may I wait until you have finished questioning the others? Then if you still feel that it is necessary, I will give you the name. I am so firmly convinced that I am mistaken that I should not like to feel I had created any false impression in your mind."

"So?" said Lieutenant Gregory, and his eyes took on an extra gleam.

"So what?" asked Bill, a bit belligerently.

"So it was one of your guests?"

I fell back weakly in my chair. "I only said I thought I recognized the person," I pointed out. "I could not possibly swear to his identity."

"I'm not asking you to swear to anything," the officer reminded me. Then, changing his tactics, he asked Bill whether there had been much drinking the night before.

"No one got drunk, if that's what you want to know," Bill told him shortly. I was glad Bill had not seen Bob take all those extra drinks.

"This party," said Lieutenant Gregory, "I judge it had not been planned very long in advance?"

I wanted to ask, "And how did you get that idea?" But after all, it would have been easy enough to find out from the servants, or probably the question had already been asked Bill by the first two patrolmen. So I only said, "No."

"How did you happen to come out on such short notice?"

"Oh," I said, knowing how futile I sounded, "we very often do things like that. I mean, pick up and go out of town for a weekend just because somebody thinks it would be pleasant. One of my guests, Claire Harper, suggested that it would be fun to come out here. I had expected to open the house next week, anyway."

"I see," said Lieutenant Gregory. "Then it was just an impulse?"

"I suppose you could call it that."

"I see."

But I did not and said so. "I don't see what difference any of that can make," I told him. "Anyway, nobody knew Aunt Maggie was coming. That is, none of the other guests knew. I was really the only person who knew in advance, except her servants, for she— came at her own suggestion."

"You mean you didn't really care to have her come?"

I felt myself flushing again.

"It hadn't occurred to me to ask her. She was free to come if she wanted to."

"Thank you," said Lieutenant Gregory noncommittally, adding that I might take a recess if I cared to.

I went out of the room in more of a fog than ever.

XV

As I ENTERED THE DINING ROOM, Andrew stopped his table setting to tell me that Lindy was in the kitchen and very anxious to see me, "privately."

"Send her in," I said, and as Andrew opened the door of the butler's pantry the sound of high-pitched voices came from the kitchen, in marked contrast to the usual chatter and laughter which, to the housewife, is such a pleasant overtone of domestic harmony. But with the police in the office and Anderson wandering around, poking into every nook and corner, why should I expect harmony anywhere in the house?

Then the door of the butler's pantry opened again and Lindy, a rather slight, dark woman of about thirty, flounced in, her black eyes snapping fire. "You go on back," she commanded Thomas, who was right on her heels.

"But they ain't no sense in yo' botherin' Miss Sally," he argued, stubbornly following her into the room.

"Now, what's all this about?" I asked firmly, resolved that I would make short work of any marital mix-up I might be called upon to mediate.

"Miss Sally—" they both began.

"Suppose we let Lindy have her say first," I suggested.

"Ain't no use in botherin' Miss Sally," Thomas repeated doggedly.

"Botherin', humph," snorted Lindy. "Miss Sally, Thomas done got me here on account of them police. He says they thinks it's

151

funny 'cause I run off last night. But I ain't gonna stay home and get in no trouble. Now he say I can't tell 'em why I leave home, but I ain't goin' to no jail on account of that no-'count Eph of his."

"I thought Thomas said you left Friday," I said, somewhat irrelevantly.

"That's just another one of his tales, Miss Sally. I never left till yesterday evenin'. That no-'count Eph come around and I ain't goin' stay home and get in no trouble."

"But who on earth is Eph?"

"Eph's my son Ephraim," said Thomas. "And Eph ain't no bad boy. Miss Sally, don't you remember Eph? He's been gone away from home a long time."

"Oh, yes," I recalled, "but I haven't seen him since he was a little boy and I had forgotten his name."

"He's his son by one of them first wives of his," said Lindy vindictively. "Eph done run away from the chain gang and come home. I ain't gonna get in no trouble by bein' here when they come after him."

"Is this true, Thomas?" I asked.

"No'm. Eph done serve his time in the chain gang last year. Eph's a free man."

"He don't never come home lessen he in trouble," Lindy argued. "Or else maybe he want somethin'. Come and talk Thomas out what little money he got, then play it on the bug and ain't nothin' left."

"He ain't so," Thomas contradicted. "He come 'cause he sick."

"Well, what business he got comin' over here to the big house when I tell him you ain't here?" Lindy demanded.

"He just come lookin' for me," Thomas insisted.

"You mean Ephraim was over here yesterday afternoon?" I asked, trying to keep my voice normal.

"Yes'm, Miss Sally. I tell him Thomas out lookin' after his set hooks on the river, but I see him comin' on over here, anyway. He say he don't feel good and want Thomas should phome for the doctor man."

"Fine way to treat a sick boy," Thomas accused. "When I come home, you ain't there, and Eph layin' on the floor like he dead. I get him in bed and give him a little corn I got at the house and he lay there and talk out'n he head. About six o'clock I come over here, Miss Sally, and get Andrew to call Dr. Grace what always wait on yo' gran'ma."

"About what time was Ephraim over here?" I asked.

"He come home about three, Miss Sally," said Lindy. "He come over here just a little while after."

"But why should he come here, if he knew you were somewhere else?" I asked Thomas.

"Miss Sally, Eph want somebody phome for the doctor man, that what I think. But I guess he don't find nobody."

"You are sure of the time?" I asked Lindy.

"Yes'm, 'cause I take that short cut through the woods to go to my a'h'nt's house and it was after four when I get there."

Ephraim's visit, no doubt, solved the mysterious footsteps in the kitchen and the door that slammed when I was upstairs. I did not want to jump to conclusions, but it did occur to me that while Lieutenant Gregory was conducting his investigation in the office I was probably solving the murder, much less formally, in the dining room.

"Thomas, why didn't you tell me about this when I talked to you this morning?" I asked.

"Miss Sally, ma'am, I ain't know till Lindy tell me this morning that Eph been over here. Anyways, he never come back here last night, Miss Sally. I was with him the whole time. But, Miss Sally, that man I tell you about seein' here yesterday, I forgot to tell you he had a long knife in his hand and he was lookin' all around the house like he want to cut somebody's throat."

It seemed to me that I could follow Thomas' train of thought perfectly, but I asked him to describe the blood-thirsty-looking visitor.

"He was a big tall man with a black mustache, Miss Sally." Well, the black mustache clinched the matter. Thomas was merely concocting a smoke screen. "Why didn't you tell me this to begin with?" I asked.

"It 'scaped my mind, Miss Sally. But Ephraim, he ain't had nothin' to do with makin' no trouble over here, Miss Sally. Eph ain't no bad boy."

"Did the doctor ever come?" Strange that Dr. Grace should pass so near the house and not drop in, and on such a night, too.

"Yes'm, he come. That young doctor man what help Dr. Grace. He been here before when my misery was bad," Thomas explained. "He say Eph done got in—in—"

"In what?"

"Well, Miss Sally, seems like he got cut in a fight. And the place it ain't got well yet. The doctor man say it in—"

"Infected? Well, how is he today?"

"The doctor man say to keep him in bed. He still just layin' there with a high fever and don't know nobody."

"What time did the doctor come last night?"

"I don't rightly remember, Miss Sally. It was kind of late. All the time I worry about Eph and think maybe no doctor not get here at all on account all that rain. But finally, here he come."

"Did you tell the police about Ephraim, Thomas?"

"No'm. They never ask me nothin' about Eph. They just want to know where Lindy is or anybody else that suppose to be 'round here. Well, Eph ain't suppose to be 'round here. Leastwise, he don't what you'd say live here, Miss Sally."

"All right, but from now on I think it would be best if we all tell the police everything we know. And, Thomas, don't try telling them more than you know. Don't go making up stories about men with black mustaches and long knives, because they will be sure to catch up with you and then they won't believe anything you say."

"I sho' am goin' to tell 'em the truth," said Lindy, giving Thomas a scornful look.

I knew exactly what I was going to do when the door swung shut behind them. I would telephone Dr. Grace, learn the name of his assistant and check on the time he visited Ephraim last night. That would either give Ephraim an alibi or place him at the head of the list of suspects.

But with my hand on the doorknob, I was halted by Bessie, who evidently had been waiting for Thomas and Lindy to finish their interview.

She came over close, looked around in all directions and whispered, "I done found a clue, Miss Sally."

"What do you mean, clue?" I asked, Thomas and Ephraim still on my mind.

"It's somethin' I found," she went on cautiously. "You know this mornin' when I was makin' up the beds and cleanin' up the bathrooms, with Thomas to help me 'cause Andrew went to town and then was busy when he come back—"

"Yes, yes, Bessie, what is it?"

"Well, we finish all the rooms, 'cept Miss Eve's and she still in there, but she say I can come in and straighten up. And, Miss Sally, I found somethin' ain't got no business in there, else I'm crazy."

"But what is it?"

"Didn't that man what come to fix the phone say it done been cut in two places and a piece of wire throwed away?"

"Yes, he did say something like that."

Bessie opened her mouth, seemed to be struck speechless by some thought that hit her all of a heap and, turning, made a waddling dash for the door. Completely mystified, I started to follow, but at that moment the library door opened and Alice wandered in. "I'm looking for Plutarch," she explained. "He was up in my room just after breakfast and now I can't find him."

"He'll show up," I consoled her. "You can't lose a cat, you know. Here comes Bessie. Maybe she knows something about him."

"I give him his breakfast in the office," Bessie told us as calmly as though she had not apparently had a fit two minutes before. "He et a good breakfast and drunk his water, too. I shut him up in there when I come out and I ain't seen him since."

"Well, of course, the police are using that room now," I reminded Alice. "He's probably upstairs."

"I've been up there. Poor thing, he's probably scared to death. I'll go and see if somebody left the basement door open." And she wandered out again.

"What in the world happened to you just now?" I asked Bessie sternly.

She looked puzzled for a moment, then her face cleared. "Oh, Miss Sally," she grinned, "I just remembered my Sally Lunn muffins in the oven. But they all right. Just a little brown. I don't know what come over me, puttin' them muffins in the stove 'fore you all was at the table."

"But what was this about a clue?"

Bessie looked around the room again, then her voice dropped to a whisper. "Miss Sally, you reckon Miss Eve kill Miss Maggie?"

"What on earth makes you ask that?"

Bessie reached into her apron pocket and pulled out a piece of telephone wire about half a yard long.

"Where did you get it?"

"In Miss Eve's room, all hid away."

"What do you mean, hid away?"

"Well, you might just as well say hid away, Miss Sally. When I empty the wastebasket, I notice they was a pair of stockin's in there. Miss Eve had thowed 'em away 'cause they was a run in 'em and then I see this package. Looks like she would have give me them stockin's without throwin' 'em away, don't you think so, Miss Sally?" Bessie interrupted herself to ask indignantly. The fact that she weighs about a hundred pounds more than Eve and that her feet must be several sizes larger had nothing to do with her feeling in the matter.

"Perhaps she didn't think they were worth offering to you," I placated. "What about this package? Was it in the wastebasket, too?"

"Yes'm. It and some cotton and them tissues you take cream off with. And then I see this package wasn't just some paper wadded up like I first think. So I unwrap it and find that piece of wire. Well, bless sweet Jesus, I say, what for Miss Eve got this old piece of wire? Then I remember about the telephone."

"Where were you when you unwrapped this package, Bessie?"

"In the back hall, where I take the wastebasket to empty it in the big one to bring downstairs so Andrew can take it to the furnace."

"Then nobody saw you unwrap it?"

"No, ma'am."

"You are sure you didn't find it in the big wastebasket, after you emptied the small one? You are sure it came from Miss Eve's room?"

"Yes'm. Miss Sally, I see it when I pick up them stockin's. I ain't goin' to run no risk gettin' them tore no worse by emptyin' 'em in the big wastebasket."

"All right. Don't say anything about this until I've had time to talk to Mr. Bill."

The telephone rang and I said that I would answer it. At Wisteria Hall my grandmother had only the one phone and that in the hall closet. It was the old-fashioned box-on-the-wall variety and the piece of wire obviously had been cut from the extension cord reaching up from the floor to the box.

As I took down the receiver, I hung the loose piece of wire over the telephone.

Someone who introduced himself as Jamieson said he thought I might be interested to know that on Saturday at around eleven o'clock a man in a convertible coupé had inquired at his garage in Roswell the direction to take in order to get to Wisteria Hall.

Mr. Jamieson said he thought nothing of it at the time; but since getting word that morning through Andrew of what had happened the night before, he had recalled the incident. Evidently Andrew had talked a good deal, or maybe the news had just got around, for Mr. Jamieson knew of the fake telephone call and the fact that the rest of us did not arrive until late afternoon. He described the man as being dark-haired and dark-eyed and said that he believed he would recognize him. Unfortunately he did not take the license number. Mr. Jamieson seemed all too willing to continue the conversation, hoping, no doubt, to learn further details of the morning's events, but I thanked him and hung up.

The description fitted Kirk, even to the convertible coupé. Though, of course, there are plenty of dark-haired and dark-eyed men and convertible coupés.

I called Dr. Grace and, after offering his services in any way that they might be needed, he gave me the telephone number of his young assistant, Dr. Martin Bates. But this gentleman was not at home and his wife had no idea when he would return. He was on an obstetrical case out in the country, she said, and there was no near-by telephone, but she promised to have him call as soon as she heard from him.

Next I called my own home in town. I wanted to ask Bill's mother, who had come over to spend the weekend with little Sally and the nurse, whether she had talked to anyone who might have called me on the telephone Saturday morning. But Julia, the nurse, had taken all calls, she told me, and Julia was accordingly put on the wire.

"Yes'm," Julia remembered. "They was a man called. He wanted to know where you was and I told him you was goin' to the Biltmore to get your hair fixed and he said he would call you there. No'm, I didn't recognize his voice. Andrew most generally answers the telephone and he might know."

But since Andrew had not been at home to take the call, this naturally did not get us very far. "Were there any other calls?"

"A lady wanted to know where you was, too, and I told her, but she didn't give no name."

"Do you think you would recognize the voices if you heard them again?"

"I couldn't say for sure, Miss Sally. I might remember the lady. She talk in a sort o' dress-up way."

Eve, of course. Talking to a servant after what she imagined to be the manner of a great lady. But who could the other call have come from?

Bill's mother had already notified the servants at Aunt Maggie's house of what had happened the night before. I waited on the line while Minnie, her maid, went to make sure about the pearls.

"Yes'm, they in her little safe in the wall," she reported. "Miss Maggie always said it was bad luck when she forgot 'em. Oh, Miss Sally, seems like I can't stand it with Miss Maggie gone."

Then Andrew was at my shoulder, saying, "Miss Sally, the dead wagon, I mean the ambolance, done come for Miss Maggie."

I forgot all about the piece of wire and left it hanging on the telephone.

XVI

WHATEVER ELSE HAD HAPPENED or might happen, the lunch gong sounded the same. I sat down at the table, wondering whether I had been taken in too easily by Thomas and his story of Ephraim's illness. How did I know Ephraim was as sick as Thomas made out? Even now he might be making good his escape.

If I had only been able to reach Dr. Bates by telephone. If I had only had an opportunity to speak to Bill, who now sat the length of the table away from me, separated by the flickering flames of the candles which had been lit because of the all-pervading gloom of the weather. Their light did brighten things somewhat, but it seemed to me that it also emphasized the sense of strain apparent on faces around the table by casting into high relief some features and lengthening the shadows on others. There were candles burning on the sideboards too, with their silver dishes of food, but Andrew would not be there to pass these dishes. Lieutenant Gregory had asked if he and his assistant might be served separately in the breakfast room. "This will give us time to check up on where we stand," he had said, "and I can question the servants. I'd like to start with the butler. After lunch I'll interview the guests individually."

I thought it a little unfortunate that he should choose this particular time to put Andrew through the third degree. Andrew was not only needed elsewhere, but goodness knew what might happen to my cherished old Spode if Lieutenant Gregory tried to be too casual in his questioning.

As Thomas blundered around the table, I strained my ears for the sound of the telephone bell, knowing all the time it was far too soon to be expecting a call from Dr. Bates. Then I remembered the telephone wire. What on earth had I done with it? Oh, yes, the telephone closet. "Lindy," I said, as she passed hot Sally Lunn muffins which were only a shade too brown on top, "ask Bessie to step in here when she can."

Bessie came, and as I whispered instructions about the telephone wire her skittish glances at Eve made it all too plain that here was her choice as number one candidate for the electric chair. I wondered if she could be right. If Eve, now being so consciously charming to Mr. Dodson, really possessed guilty knowledge, as she had hinted. And if that knowledge involved someone else now seated at this table.

With these thoughts in mind, I was more than a little startled when Mr. Dodson, seated on my left, asked in a low tone if all our guests were assembled in the dining room. "Yes," I told him, "that, as you know, is Eve Benedict on your left. On her other side is Bob Dunbar and just below Bob is Claire Harper, seated on the right of my husband, who is at the end, On Bill's left is Kirk Pierce and between Kirk and Mr. Marshall is Alice Dunbar, Bob's sister."

"Thank you," he murmured, "that will help to give me a little preliminary line-up on the situation."

"Line-up, indeed," caroled Eve, who apparently had overheard Mr. Dodson's remark. "He is the most amazing man, Sally. Do you know, he just now told me the color of my hair and eyes?"

Mr. Dodson chuckled. "That is fairly simple," he declared. "I don't always hit, of course. But radio tests, for instance, have shown that the voice has a great deal to do with personality and coloring. In one of these tests listeners were asked to describe speakers they had never seen, and a majority of the descriptions were fairly accurate. As I recall, listeners have also identified photographs by voices, with a fair average on the credit side."

By way of making conversation when Eve turned again to Bob, I asked Mr. Dodson, "In a case such as this, would ordinary table talk be—what shall I say—revealing?"

I had not really sought information and the gravity of his reply rather gave me pause. "Yes," he said, "sometimes."

"But how?" I asked, my entire attention now engaged, and I lowered my voice quite unnecessarily, for Eve was being vivacious for the benefit of the table at large. "Is it a note in the voice? Fright, desperation, defiance—what is it?"

"Ah, but that I cannot tell you. It may be something that is said. Some statement, you know. It may be a laugh. It may be no more than a nuance—an overtone, perhaps. There may be nothing at all. One can only listen and hope. One can only encourage conversation—"

So I sat and tried to listen with ears attuned differently from my usual bent. Tried to listen as I imagined Mr. Dodson was listening. Tried to see myself and my guests as he was seeing us, without the aid of eyesight and from sound alone.

Eve, it appeared, was being charming to everyone. I thought it a pity Mr. Dodson could not see her in her slinky black crepe and pearls, since she was so obviously putting herself out for his benefit. She herself had chosen to sit next to him, but perhaps that was only because Bob was on her other side.

Quite unnecessarily, she was arranging Mr. Dodson's food for him, making sandwiches and serving his plate, for when it pleased her to take thought of others she must have her way. Under cover of conversation ostensibly general, she was using Claire and Bob as targets, leaving them now and then to return to Mr. Dodson, as though his welfare and interest were her chief concern. He was plainly flattered, as any man is when a woman exerts herself to be attractive to him, but it was also plain from the half-smile that hovered around his mouth, that he was in no way taken in.

Eve's double offensive was interrupted by Thomas and the platter of vegetable aspic, which he unfortunately presented from her right. "Other side," she told him condescendingly, so flustering poor Thomas that when she attempted to serve herself, he jogged the dish against her elbow and the entire serving was deposited on her napkin instead of the plate.

Instantly Eve flared, opening her mouth to make some caustic remark, then, remembering the role she had set herself to play, subsided with a smile of conscious good-sportsmanship which included the entire table. "Just take this napkin and bring me another," she told Thomas, with elaborate politeness.

What surprised me even more than Eve's unusual amiability was Alice's being arch for the benefit of Mr. Marshall. She had assumed that bright, artificial animation with which unmarried men seemed always to inspire her, and I could not figure out the reason until I remembered belatedly that Mr. Marshall was a recent widower.

Claire, as usual, was lending a shell-pink ear and two expressive eyes by turns to the gentlemen on her left and on her right, now and then raising her eyes to meet Kirk's black-browed, brooding gaze across the table. Because of her gray dress, Claire's eyes were gray, but something in their depths suggested also the gray of stormy skies. I wondered how much longer she would be able to stand Eve's impossible goading.

But already Mr. Dodson had taught me something. I now recognized Claire as a listening person, even as he was himself. Claire heard more and, accordingly, men considered her "understanding." It occurred to me that perhaps for no more than that some people are considered psychic.

All the men looked a little grim, but it seemed to me there was reason enough for this, aside from the murder. Bill, with his black eye resulting from that hit-and-run encounter in the dark hall. The two triangles raying out from the engagement of Claire and Bob. Although I was certain Bob did not consider Kirk an actual rival, I knew he was none too easy in his mind about Eve. How much claim Eve had, I could not guess, nor how much it meant to Bob.

Everyone seemed to be making a desperate effort to talk without mentioning the things uppermost in everybody's mind. Someone had struck on food as a safe subject. Kirk, bent on helping along the makeshift conversation, was saying that the best place to lose all your illusions about Southern cooking is in the South—

"I mean," he added hastily, "in restaurants and places which advertise old time Southern cooking. Fried chicken, for instance. Either half raw inside or tough and tasteless, with a coat of cement on the outside. More crimes"—he hesitated, as though he would like to bite back that word crime, then continued doggedly—"are committed in the name of fried chicken than any other one dish."

"But," Mr. Marshall pointed out with a pontifical gesture, "that is only because the real article is so superb. Imitation, you know, is the sincerest flattery."

"I'm so sorry there's only cold baked chicken today," I said. "With the police here, I had an idea we might be eating, one at a time, in snatches."

"But, ah, this hot shrimp pie," Mr. Marshall rushed gallantly to the rescue. "And I've eaten so much of the baked ham I feel I must send you one from my farm in Virginia. Nothing like country ham, is there?" Then he turned to Kirk, judiciously, obviously determined that no outlander should fail to be informed as to the true state of affairs. "Your point is well taken, young man. The traditional Southern cooking and hospitality flowered in an age of leisure. A golden age, some of us think. Today it survives only in a few fortunate homes, such as"—he paused to make a little bow to me.

"Page Bessie," said Eve sardonically.

Ignoring the implication of her remark, Mr. Marshall continued, "Of course, there are many reasons for this. Economics, machines, commercialism, dieting, wives who are more interested in other things than the art of cooking. Too few people realize that eating is one of life's fine arts as well as one of its greatest pleasures. Most regrettable, this latter. I am minded of an apt passage in a book by one of my favorite authors, Thomas Love Peacock. A reverend gentleman, describing what he evidently considers the ideal woman, says, 'She has the greatest of all female virtues, for she superintends the household and looks after her husband's dinner.'"

"After all," asked Alice coyly, "what could be more important?"

Mr. Marshall beamed on her approvingly, while I tried not to meet the look of amused disdain in Eve's eyes. I knew it couldn't be very long before she would break out one way or another. And knowing, too, that Mr. Marshall could go on in this vein forever, giving both chapter and verse, I tried to divert the conversation into other channels. "I didn't know," I said, "that Thomas Love Peacock was one of your favorites."

Mr. Dodson turned his face toward me and smiled as Mr. Marshall replied, "He writes so appetizingly of food, my dear Sally. Quail and lobster and ham and the good Lord knows what else for breakfast. Yes, I greatly fear that where I once read for style and—er—other literary considerations, I now read either for the food or the murders." Realizing how his witticism must sound under the circumstances, he grew quite red and apologized hastily, "I'm very sorry, Sally. I'm like the boy on the bicycle, who tried so hard to miss the tree that he ran smack into it."

His distress was so genuine and the picture of Mr. Marshall on a bicycle trying to miss a tree was so provocative that we all laughed. "I suppose no one ever thought of dieting in those days," Eve observed, with unexpected tact.

"Oh, no, they simply ate what they wanted and resigned themselves to gout," Mr. Marshall agreed.

"We've got the evidence in the library," said Bill, "a gouty stool designed by Mr. Sheraton himself so it can be raised to different elevations to support the ailing foot or leg. No home complete without one."

"Hold on to it, old boy," advised Kirk, with a grin in my direction. "You'll need it, unless you divorce Sally."

"Not if he keeps up his golf," said Mr. Marshall, who is as serious about his game as he is about his food. I prayed he would not get started on that subject.

"The only thing I can't enjoy about books written such a long time ago," said Eve, reverting to Mr. Peacock, "is the smell."

"The smell," Mr. Marshall repeated, greatly mystified.

"Oh, don't you know?" Eve explained with characteristic airiness, "the lack of bathing facilities."

Mr. Marshall looked a little embarrassed, but Mr. Dodson smiled and said he had always thought that was how perfume happened to be invented.

Bessie came in with the coffee and whispered in my ear that she couldn't find the piece of telephone wire. "I look on the floor and outside and all about, but it ain't nowhere."

"We'll look again when lunch is over," I told her, "and wait a moment—Thomas has forgotten the cheese." Involuntarily I glanced at Mr. Dodson, wondering if with his preternaturally trained hearing he had picked up the conversation about the telephone wire. But if so, his expression gave no indication, for he seemed to be listening to Mr. Marshall, who was off again.

Down the table, Bob was fidgeting with his food and eating practically nothing. I knew from that half-humorous, half-reckless look on Bob's face that Mr. Marshall's ponderous discourse was due to wreck itself shortly against a facetiousness which he might not understand, and I girded myself mentally to jump into the breach. Bob had been drinking too much for a hostess to feel safe about him.

"Speaking of commercial products," Mr. Marshall droned on, "many of these are quite excellent. But there are certain dishes of the homemade variety which cannot be equaled. Take soup, always the test of good cooking. Where was there ever a canned soup to compare with that made at home with a good base of meat stock and so thick with vegetables that it is a meal in itself? Indeed, it requires almost a day to simmer down to the proper consistency—"

"But," Bob broke in, "why all this heavy accent on food when it is drink which brings us our most transcendental moments? What is a man without a drink?" He looked up and down the table challengingly. "A mouse," he announced, in answer to his own question, and, rising, stepped over to the sideboard and brought to the table the tray holding the decanter of brandy and glasses.

"Join me?" he asked of the table at large.

"Why not?" Eve replied. "I don't suppose you've any corner on these transcendental moments."

The ringing of the telephone bell came faintly through the closed hall door and I felt myself relaxing with relief. Dr. Bates at last. But when Lindy came back after answering the call, she said it was Mr. Dunbar who was wanted.

Those of us who did not take brandy lingered over a second cup of coffee, perhaps unconsciously trying to postpone as long as possible the time when we must face Lieutenant Gregory and reality.

Bob came back from the telephone with a harassed look on his face and said that he really should go in to town to attend to a matter which had come up. "Could you arrange it for me?" he asked Mr. Marshall as casually as though he had not a few moments before stepped on that gentleman's toes. Mr. Marshall assured him rather stiffly that only Lieutenant Gregory could grant such permission.

"Why should you have to be going back to town?" Claire asked in a low voice, which nonetheless revealed an unexpectedly sharp note. "Didn't you come out to stay until Monday morning?"

But even more surprising than Claire's outburst was Alice's look of undisguised impatience turned on Bob. Evidently she was counting on the Harper money even more than it had occurred to anyone to think.

What crosscurrent of feminine influence could be calling Bob to town? I wondered. There were so many ladies who counted on Bob for so many things. How would he be able to arrange all that to fit in with matrimony? Quite plainly Claire was not going to like it, even though he might be just flitting from flower to flower. I did not hear what he said to Claire in answer to her question, for Eve, rising to her feet and holding her brandy glass high, proposed a toast.

"To the bride," she said, with a little supercilious bow to Claire. Then downing the contents of her glass, she asked, "Whatever made you think, Claire, that Bob would want to be taken seriously as a marrying man?"

We looked at her in shocked silence, and Alice said, "If you mean to be humorous, Eve, I don't think that is very funny."

"You wouldn't," said Eve, sweeping out of the room and looking back over her shoulder to say, "But take it any way you like."

I did not want to look at Claire, yet instinctively I had, and I saw cold fury gather in her eyes as she turned to watch Eve from the room. Then she looked around the table and smiled. Except for that glance, I should not have known how much the smile cost her, but inwardly I applauded her self-control.

I had been right about Eve. She had not been able to keep it up. She really hated us all. This and her natural lack of self-restraint had been too much for her.

"Suppose we go to the library," I suggested, and under cover of the general movement I asked Mr. Dodson almost under my breath, "What do you think of her—of Eve?"

"I can see she would be a popular choice," he said noncommittally.

"But could you—did you get any idea at all? It seems as hopeless as ever to me."

"Perhaps a glimmer," he cautiously admitted.

"Tell me," I begged.

"No, no," he said, "you must not press me like this. Too much is involved. We must not run the risk of a mistake, or of letting your sympathy block the path of justice. Besides, I have an idea that I wish to test. If that works—"

"Yes?"

"I think the facts will then be apparent to all."

XVII

As the dining room cleared, Mr. Marshall, who had lingered for a word with Bill, came forward to guide Mr. Dodson to the library.

"Wait a moment," I whispered to my husband, "there's something I want to tell you."

"Wish somebody would tell Bob something," he complained, digging for his cigarette case. "Seems to me he ought to have sense enough to know this is not the time to try to drink up all the liquor in sight."

"It's all Eve's fault," I excused.

"But why should he let himself in for such things?" Bill grumbled. "Why can't he use a little sense?"

"Everybody is not as direct as you are, darling," I reminded him, as he glared at his empty cigarette case as though it, too, had failed in deportment suited to the occasion. "There are plenty of cigarettes in the library," I added, knowing that it would be like trying to hold a restive horse until he had had his smoke.

"Well, just a moment. I'll be right back—"

But he was not to be right back, for as I followed him to the library door we both saw Roberts, who was waiting to tell Bill that Lieutenant Gregory wished to see him in the office.

"Again?" asked Bill, in some surprise. "Thought I told him all I knew."

"It's about something that has come up since then," Roberts explained smoothly.

"All right," Bill agreed, "but I hate to keep everybody else waiting. You are sure we can't go to town and finish all this tomorrow?
None of us is going to run away, you know."

"Perhaps it won't take so long," said Roberts, and something
in his voice caused me to look at him quickly, but his expression
was unrevealing.

"You mean you've got something?" asked Mr. Dodson, who had
also caught that note of what might have been restrained excitement.

"Suppose we go along to the other room," Roberts suggested,
leading the way, and Mr. Marshall, taking Mr. Dodson by the arm,
prepared to follow.

"Can't I come, too?" I asked.

"Let's wait and see," said Mr. Marshall, giving me a little pat
on the shoulder. "Anyway, don't worry. Everything is going to be
all right soon."

Which, of course, is just what one would expect from a family
friend and legal adviser. But it made all the more astounding what
he came back to tell me a little later.

Just how much later it was I do not know, for the day, which at
times seemed to fly, at others seemed to drag on leaden feet. Eve
evidently had gone directly upstairs from the dining room. Claire
had excused herself soon after we went into the library and, I think,
had also started upstairs, but Bob, rising quickly to his feet, had
followed her from the room and must have persuaded her to go
into the drawing room. Anyway, from where I sat with Kirk and
Alice, I could hear the faint tinkle of the piano.

When Mr. Marshall appeared at the door there was nothing in
his manner to indicate that his request to speak to me privately
was of any great importance. And as we walked down the hall toward the breakfast room, I was struck with the irony of Claire's
musical selection, for the air was one familiar from my childhood.
Perhaps she had only opened at random that bound collection of
old sheet music, but she was playing "Sweet Memories Waltz,"
which, according to the inscription penned thereon, had been presented to one of my feminine ancestors in 1857. Had Claire selected

it in order to punish Bob? I wondered. Was she listening to his pleading as she played, her gray eyes now and then looking upward into his, or was she ignoring him by a pretended absorption in the yellowed sheet of music before her?

So busy was my mind with such thoughts that I did not turn my attention to Mr. Marshall until we had reached the breakfast room and he had closed the door behind us. Then I looked up and saw that his face, with the kind setter eyes, was contorted as though he were suffering great physical pains.

"What is it?" I cried. "Do they think I did it?"

"No, my dear," he answered. "They think Bill did it."

I stared at him incredulously. "But that's absurd," I said. "Bill is the last person on earth who might have done such a thing."

"I'm afraid they have a pretty good case against him," Mr. Marshall admitted unwillingly.

"Oh, no!" I cried, his own obvious alarm communicating itself to me. "They couldn't have. It—it's impossible."

"Sit down, my dear," said Mr. Marshall gently, "and let me get you a glass of water."

"No, no, I'm all right. I must go to Bill."

"But I'm not sure you can see him yet," Mr. Marshall protested uncomfortably. "They hadn't finished when I came out. I—I wanted to prepare you."

"But they are crazy," I told him. "Bill didn't do it. He couldn't have. Oh, Mr. Marshall, you know Bill well enough to know it is impossible."

"Yes, yes, my dear, of course. Now try to calm yourself. We'll take care of Bill. We'll get Wade Allen to defend him."

"But I am calm," I insisted. "You—you know it can't be as bad as all that." Even I knew Wade Allen is considered the best criminal lawyer in the South.

"No use taking any chances," Mr. Marshall told me soothingly. "I am afraid you are going to have to make up your mind that all this is going to be pretty—disagreeable, and try to keep a stiff upper lip."

"All right," I said, "but right now I'm going to see Bill."

"I don't know that you should try to just yet," he objected, like an anxious mother hen, but I was already knocking on the door. Roberts, opening it a mere crack, admitted grudgingly that Mr. Marshall could come back in, but otherwise he assured us that they positively could not be disturbed.

I said, "Will you please tell Lieutenant Gregory that I wish to speak to him?"

About to object further, Roberts was interrupted by Lieutenant Gregory himself, who came to the door and, motioning Roberts out of the way, stepped into the breakfast room, pulling the door shut as he did so.

"I want to see my husband," I told him.

"Mrs. Stuart," he said not unkindly, "it would be much better if you would wait until we have finished our questioning. I did not know Mr. Marshall had gone out to see you or I should have objected."

I am afraid I rather lost my head at that, for I said, "This is my house and my husband. Lieutenant Gregory, may I pass?"

He opened the door and stood aside. "You are only making this harder for yourself," he said.

My eyes flew to Bill, sitting in a chair by my grandfather's desk, his red hair tousled and his blue eyes full of a sort of belligerent bewilderment. It was astonishing how much more blue his left eye looked than the right, with its dark circle caused by the bruise. I knew the expression on his face so well. It is always there when Bill comes up against stupidity. He finds it so difficult to believe that people are not all as honest and decent and straightforward and intelligent as he is himself.

He came to his feet when he saw me and we met halfway across the room. "Oh, Bill," I said, as we gripped each other's hands tightly, "this is so silly."

"Very silly," he agreed through set teeth, "but I can't seem to convince Lieutenant Gregory of the fact."

I looked around that small, intimate, friendly room which has stood for a hundred years of family security and gracious living. I looked at Lieutenant Gregory, waiting to resume his seat at my grandfather's desk. And for a dreadful moment the room ceased to be a part of Wisteria Hall and became the close, cramped quarters of a storm-rocked boat, with great, angry waves, dashing hungrily against its sides.

"Here, here," said Bill quickly, "sit down." And as I collapsed in a chair, "Are you all right now?"

"Oh, yes," I assured him, trying to smile, then, turning to Mr. Dodson, I asked in a voice that I somehow could not raise above a whisper, "You don't believe any of this foolishness, do you?"

"What do you mean, foolishness?" Lieutenant Gregory interrupted grimly.

"Don't upset yourself too much, Mrs. Stuart," said Mr. Dodson, and his calm, kind voice steadied me immediately. "You never can tell from the way a case starts out just how it will end."

"But what's it all about?" I demanded. "Why does anybody think Bill did this terrible thing?"

"Andrew," said Bill testily. "Something Andrew thinks he overheard, just before you went out to the back passage and found Aunt Maggie."

"Andrew?" I repeated stupidly.

"I questioned your butler as he served our lunch," Lieutenant Gregory explained. "At first he denied knowing anything at all remotely connected with the murder. I accused him of trying to shield the family and saw that I was on the right trail. He finally broke down and confessed that last night while in the breakfast room he heard voices in the passage outside and what sounded like an argument. He recognized Mrs. Ambler's voice, but while he knew her to be talking to a man, he was unable at first to identify the man's voice. Or rather, he says he did not pay much attention until he heard Mrs. Ambler raise her own voice and call Mr. Stuart by name."

"What?" I asked weakly. "I cannot believe it. Andrew is mistaken."

"I am afraid not," said the officer dryly. Then, turning to Roberts, "What was it Andrew says he overheard Mrs. Ambler say to Mr. Stuart?"

Roberts flipped the pages of his notebook, cleared his throat, moistened his lips and read: "'Don't you dare lay hands on me, Willie.'"

"But it is impossible!" I cried.

"And yet someone did lay hands on Mrs. Ambler," I was reminded inexorably. "It was the natural thing for her to say under the circumstances. And there was no one else known to be on the premises whom she would have addressed by that name."

"I don't care," I argued. "It's all wrong. Bill wouldn't do such a thing. Mr. Dodson, you said you had a glimmer. Surely you know better than this—"

"We must not interfere with Lieutenant Gregory's investigation," he told me. "There are still others to be questioned, you know. When he has finished, we will see what we can do."

"But Andrew could so easily be mistaken," I insisted. "After all, he admits that he was not paying much attention. There are other words, other names, that sound like Willie. It was just an association of ideas in his mind. Aunt Maggie was one of the few people who call Bill by that name. Andrew, of course, knows this as well as anyone, and if she said anything sounding at all like Willie he would naturally jump to the conclusion that that was what she meant."

"You are just wasting your breath, my dear," said Bill. "I've been over it all with Lieutenant Gregory. I've tried to convince him that I had no reason to kill Aunt Maggie and no desire to, or to kill anyone."

"I'm afraid you are going to have to try to prove that to a jury, Mr. Stuart," said Lieutenant Gregory. "And in view of these new developments, Mrs. Stuart, wouldn't you like to amend your own story? Are you sure that you gave a correct statement of the facts when you said that you saw no one else in the passage when you stepped out there shortly after the murder?"

"Sally, you don't have to answer that question," cautioned Mr. Marshall.

"But, of course, I will answer it," I said. "I did not see anyone."

"All this is very unnecessary," Mr. Marshall told Lieutenant Gregory. "Assuming that Mr. Stuart is guilty, which I do not, I suppose you are aware that, according to law, a wife is not compelled to testify against her husband."

"But I'm telling the truth," I repeated. "Mr. Dodson, you believe me, don't you?"

"Yes, Mrs. Stuart," he said simply, "I do believe you."

"Thank you," I choked, suddenly very near to tears. Bill squeezed my hand hard and for a moment no one spoke. The silence was so heavy you could feel it. Or rather you could feel all sorts of vibrations in it—vibrations that met and clashed there in that quiet room as definitely as words that are said or swords that are crossed.

I looked around the circle of intent faces. Roberts, fidgeting with his notebook and so obviously resentful of what he considered special privilege. Lieutenant Gregory, stern and hard-bitten, unremitting in his vigilance lest he be taken in by a too-plausible story. Mr. Marshall, his features etched in lines of deep distress, his eyes full of incredulity that two people he had known since their childhood could have become involved in such an unthinkable predicament. Bill, still puzzled and impatient, but wearing a fighting look as well. Only Coroner Dodson's countenance, with the unseeing eyes, was serene.

He said now, and his voice was like oil poured on troubled waters, "Lieutenant, may I beg an indulgence? I was not present when the butler was interviewed. Would it delay matters too much to have him brought in and let us go over his testimony?"

We waited in hushed expectancy for Lieutenant Gregory's reply. After all, it would not have been unreasonable for him to refuse. But he said finally, looking at his wrist watch, "I have no objection to your questioning the witness, provided you will be brief."

There were tears on Andrew's black cheeks when he was brought in, and at sight of them I almost broke down myself. "Oh, Miss Sally, Mr. Bill," he cried, "fo' God, they could've drug me over red-hot coals of fire and I wouldn't 've told, but they just scared it out of me."

"Never mind, Andrew," I said. And from Bill, "We know you only told what you believed to be the truth, but how the hell could you have thought it?"

"Yes, sir. Yes, sir, Mr. Bill. That's right. But I sho' didn't want to."

"Suppose," said Coroner Dodson, in his pleasant, deep voice, "you tell us exactly what did happen, Andrew."

"Check this testimony," said Lieutenant Gregory to Roberts.

Andrew looked appealingly first at me, then at Bill. "Well, sir," he began, "I was in the breakfast room after dinner last night. I done went in there to put up some linen we brung out from town what belong in that room. We been so busy I forgot all about it. Then I see it in the kitchen after dinner and I say to Bessie, 'Law, Bessie, if Miss Sally see this, she'll git after me, sho'.'"

"All right, Andrew," Lieutenant Gregory prompted. "You can skip that. Just tell us what you heard."

"Yes, sir. Yes, sir, but I just want to show how come I was in that room. I wasn't tryin' to hear no white folks' business. At first I didn't pay no attention to talkin' outside the door. Natchully they is passin' and repassin'. Then I notice Miss Maggie's voice and it seem to me she sound worried about somethin'. She talk louder, but I still don't hear what she say. I hear a man, too"—Andrew looked over at Bill, as though he realized fully the import of what he was saying and did not wish to go on.

"All right, Andrew," Lieutenant Gregory prodded.

"Well, I can't understand what the man say. Seem to me they arguin' about somethin'. I never can tell who the man's voice is. Then I hear Miss Maggie say, 'Don't you dare lay hands on me, Willie.'"

Bill, whose eyes had been fixed on Andrew ever since his recital began, now asked, "How can you be so sure she said 'Willie,' Andrew?"

"'Cause, Mr. Bill, she say it louder'n she done say anything else. Like she plum scared."

"Did you hear anything else, Andrew?" Mr. Dodson asked.

"No, sir. I sell out and get away from there. I know when white folks light, it ain't no place for me."

"What did you do afterward, Andrew? Did you tell anybody about this?"

"No, sir. When I go back to the kitchen, Miss Sally in there talkin' to Bessie 'bout what we goin' to have for breakfast next mornin'. Bimeby, Miss Sally go on out through the breakfast room and find Miss Maggie dead on the floor. She call Bessie to come there quick 'cause Miss Maggie fainted. We brung along a pitcher of water, but we ain't able to revive her. She done dead. Then I know I must not say nothin' to Bessie never. 'Cause women can't keep no secrets."

"You mean," asked Mr. Dodson, "that you didn't intend to tell anyone about all this?"

"No, sir. When folks gets mad, they liable kill somebody 'thout meanin' to. Mr. Bill wouldn't harm nobody in his right mind. And Miss Maggie could be right worrisome sometimes."

"How do you mean, worrisome?" asked Lieutenant Gregory quickly.

Andrew scratched his head. "Just worrisome," he repeated, "like old folks is sometimes. Miss Maggie, she talk about family trees all the time and she want everybody to look after her."

"Not quite grounds for murder, you will agree, Lieutenant," said Bill.

"Any more questions, Coroner?" the officer asked. "All right, you can go, Andrew. But stay within call."

"Oh, Mr. Bill," Andrew begged from the doorway, "please don't think hard of me. They could have drug me over red-hot coals—"

"That's all right, Andrew," Bill interrupted. "I know."

XVIII

"I CAN EASILY SEE ANDREW'S POINT," said Mr. Dodson when the door had closed. "Andrew can understand violence when it is not the premeditated variety. After all, the white race has had thousands of years of the discipline of civilization and law and order. A hundred years ago Andrew's ancestors were savages or slaves. That's why the South has such a high homicide rating. It doesn't indicate that we are any more vicious than other sections, but only that many of our citizens are still more or less children so far as morals are concerned. Their acts are largely governed by their emotions—"

Lieutenant Gregory cleared his throat. Evidently he had heard all this before. "I'm afraid we had better be getting on," he said.

"So we should," Mr. Dodson agreed, "but it is a subject that interests me deeply. Pardon my digression, Lieutenant."

"I should like to ask Mr. Stuart," Lieutenant Gregory resumed, "what paper was burned in the right-hand fireplace in the room where Mrs. Ambler was taken after her death?"

"Paper?" Bill and I echoed together.

"Yes. One of my men found the ashes and a scrap of the unburned paper there this morning."

"I have no idea," said Bill, "unless—"

"Unless what?"

"Sally, do you think it could have been the clue to the secret room?" Bill asked.

"May I see the scrap that was left?" I requested Lieutenant Gregory.

177

"Here it is," he said, pointing to the desk. And there it was, a very small scrap of yellowed paper, along with a scrap of rose-colored silk and two small pieces of green paper. A queer collection. Like pieces of patchwork. But how on earth were we ever going to get them fitted together to find an answer?

I picked up the bit of paper, with its scorched edges. "And not a sign of a word on it," I grieved. "Just this little fringe of letters that are the ends of lines, I suppose. Not enough to do any good."

"Do you mean," Lieutenant Gregory asked, "that you think someone may have burned the clue to the secret room you have been trying to locate?"

"I'm afraid so," I said.

"One thing I forgot to tell you," Bill said to Mr. Marshall, "is that Sally came downstairs last night after everyone had gone to bed. She got the idea that the clue to the secret room was in some way connected with the murder. That being true, she should also have got the idea that clue hunting was not the safest indoor sport at that time of night."

"But I didn't find anything," I admitted disconsolately. "Except that someone had been there before me and had searched Aunt Maggie, not even bothering to replace the sheet over her." Andrew's words came back to me, 'She was always so proud.' I could not help thinking Aunt Maggie would have minded death itself less than all the indignities which had been heaped upon her.

"Whoever that was, probably burned the clue." Bill's voice jerked me back into the immediate present.

"Are you sure you did not burn the clue, Mr. Stuart?" Lieutenant Gregory asked, fixing his piercing black eyes on Bill with an intensity calculated to make him squirm but which did not.

"Quite sure," Bill answered, the pupils of his own blue eyes like points of steel.

"And you, Mrs. Stuart, you did not burn it either?"

"But—but why? Haven't I just been telling you that I wanted more than anything to find it and then try to find the room? Why would I burn it?"

"Perhaps because you did not want someone else to find the secret room."

"But that's absurd," I objected. "Why should I mind anyone else finding the room when I myself do not know where it is or what it contains?"

Lieutenant Gregory's eyes were boring holes in my skull. "Are you sure you do not know what it contains?" he asked, his words measured so that each was a separate, ominous threat.

I felt control slipping, as the sands of the shore are swept from under one's feet by the tide. Covering my face with my hands, I fought the desire to scream a denial.

"Officer?" Bill demanded peremptorily, and there was a note in his voice that I cannot easily describe, something fierce and primitive, which might first have been heard at the entrance of a cave.

Some inner reserve of strength must have been tapped by that involuntary exclamation from my husband. It might be Bill and I against the world. But it would always be Bill and I together. Removing my hands, I raised my head and faced Lieutenant Gregory squarely. "I know no more about that than you do," I told him.

Irritably he turned toward Bill. "Come across," he ordered. "Where is that room?"

"If I knew," said Bill, and although his words may have sounded flippant, his tone did not, "nothing would give me more pleasure than to lead you to it."

"But," said Lieutenant Gregory, abruptly changing his tack, "you did kill Mrs. Ambler."

"You don't have to answer that, Bill," Mr. Marshall interposed.

"But you haven't got a leg to stand on," Lieutenant Gregory drove on. "You admit that you passed the place of the murder only a few minutes before it must have occurred. By your own admission there was a witness to this fact, left behind in the game room. And Mrs. Ambler was heard to call your name."

Bill looked at him for a long moment with eyes that never wavered, then shrugged his shoulders, helplessly. "What's the good of all this?" he asked. "You believe I'm guilty. I know I'm not. We could go on like this forever. All right, have it your way. Only let's get it over."

"So you admit it?"

"I admit nothing of the sort. I simply want to get through with all this argument."

"Very well, then. Why not give us the whole story? Everything is there—motive, opportunity, witnesses. You'll save yourself trouble and make it easier for your guests if you lay all your cards on the table and, as you say, get it over with. Think what a strain this must be for Mrs. Stuart."

Bill regarded him grimly; "Very considerate of you," he said. "What do you mean by motive?"

"Quite simple. Your wife inherits Mrs. Ambler's money."

"But that's absurd!" I cried.

"Absurd, eh?" Lieutenant Gregory mocked. "Well, murder is not absurd, and whether or not you are interested in clearing up the death of your aunt the law will see things through."

Bill strained forward, half rising from his chair, but I pulled him back. "No, no," I whispered, and providentially at that moment a knock sounded on the door.

"Telephone call for you, Mrs. Stuart," said Roberts, after having opened the door and poked his head out cautiously.

"Dr. Bates," I breathed thankfully. "I—I think this may change things."

"You mean you know something you haven't told?" Bill asked incredulously.

"No, not exactly. I tried to tell you just after lunch, but didn't get to. Then all this other sort of—knocked me silly. Lieutenant Gregory, would you mind going with me to the telephone?"

I tried to explain briefly about Ephraim. "I know he was here yesterday afternoon. But Dr. Bates came to see him last night—"

"You mean you think the time may be important?"

"Yes, something like that."

Dr. Bates told me that he left Thomas's house at exactly fifteen minutes after nine Saturday evening. "I looked at my watch," he said, "because I was expecting a call at any time from an obstetrical case, and I remember remarking that it was later than I had thought. Ephraim's temperature registered one hundred and three and he was delirious. I gave him a hypodermic injection to quiet him. In my opinion it would have been impossible for him to leave his bed and go to Wisteria Hall at the time you mention."

"It's so important to be sure about it," I insisted. "You think he couldn't possibly?"

"I couldn't swear it, of course, if that is what you mean. But in my opinion it is just about the last thing that was likely to happen."

I replaced the receiver forlornly. "I—I had wanted you to talk to him," I said, "if it seemed that Ephraim might—have been the one."

"We'll look into it, anyway," he said. "Why didn't you tell me this before?"

"But I hadn't a chance. Besides, you would have learned of Ephraim's presence when you questioned Lindy. That's why she left home."

"Guess we'd better look into that before we go on with the guests. Ah, here's Anderson. Found anything else?"

"This," said Anderson, holding out the piece of telephone wire.

"Oh, so it was you who removed it from the telephone? I mean from where I had hung it over the telephone box."

Anderson and Lieutenant Gregory both regarded me with puzzled expressions. "What do you mean?" Lieutenant Gregory asked.

"I mean that Bessie found that piece of wire that had been cut, and gave it to me," I explained. "I had to answer the telephone just afterward and left it hanging in the closet. Later, at lunch, I sent Bessie to look for it and she couldn't find it. I suppose you had already picked it up," I suggested to Mr. Anderson.

"No. I found it in a pocket of one of the overcoats in that closet," he told us, pointing to the little room.

"Suppose we finish this discussion in the other room," said Lieutenant Gregory. "Come along, Anderson."

But, of course, I first had to explain to Bill about Ephraim and what I had hoped to learn from Dr. Bates.

"Roberts, suppose you telephone in and see what they've got on him," said Lieutenant Gregory, after inquiring Ephraim's full name. "If he's got much of a record, have an ambulance come out and take him to Grady Hospital, where we can keep him under observation. And now about this telephone wire, Mrs. Stuart—"

"Bessie found it in one of the wastebaskets upstairs."

"You mean in one of the guestrooms?"

I looked at Bill and then at Mr. Marshall. "Oh, this is dreadful," I said.

"Might as well not try to shield anybody," said Mr. Dodson.

"But—" I hesitated.

"Was it in your husband's room?" asked Lieutenant Gregory.

"Would there be fingerprints on it?" I asked.

"Wouldn't show up."

"Then I suppose it doesn't matter. Bessie says she found it in the wastebasket in Mrs. Benedict's room."

"But, of course," said Mr. Marshall, "whoever cut the wire in the first place naturally wore gloves."

Bill looked at Mr. Marshall and grinned suddenly. "Getting to be a pretty good criminal lawyer yourself," he suggested.

Lieutenant Gregory chose to ignore the interruption. "Anderson, which coat did you find the wire in?" he asked.

"I'll show you," Anderson replied, disappearing through the door and returning a few moments later with a dark blue llamacloth topcoat. Bill and I looked at it and then at each other.

"I take it you recognize the coat," Lieutenant Gregory observed.

"Certainly," said Bill. "After all, there were only two coats besides my own and both worn by men I see frequently."

"Then it is not your coat?"

"It is Kirk Pierce's coat," Bill told him. "Naturally I am aware that you could easily establish this fact without my telling you."

"Anderson," Lieutenant Gregory instructed, "please ask Mr. Pierce to step here."

Kirk came in, looking puzzled, but interested too. I suppose it had been pretty boring, Just sitting around waiting or trying to make conversation with Alice. He glanced about the room in that quick way of his. "Sally," he said, nodding in my direction, then sat down in the chair Anderson pushed forward for him. His eye caught sight of the coat thrown over a chair slightly in the background. "Looks like my coat," he observed casually, "but I guess not. Hung mine in the closet."

"It is your coat," Lieutenant Gregory told him. "We brought it in here because of something in one of the pockets. Would you have an idea what that would be, Mr. Pierce?"

"Could be most anything, I should think," grinned Kirk. "Gloves. Cigarettes. Papers. Handkerchief. Rolls of camera film. Might even find a cigar."

"No," said Lieutenant Gregory. "Guess again."

Kirk turned to me, "Not the clue, Sally?"

"Oh, no," I answered. "I only wish it were."

"Mr. Pierce," said Lieutenant Gregory, "have you seen this piece of wire before?"

Kirk looked at the wire blankly. "Looks like a piece of telephone wire to me," he said. "No, if I have seen it before, I am not aware of the fact."

"You did not put it in the pocket of your coat?"

"I'm afraid I am past the age for collecting pieces of wire, Lieutenant," he replied, smiling.

"This is a serious situation, Mr. Pierce," he was rebuked. "The sooner you and the others here realize that fact, the better. We are trying to clear up a murder."

Kirk instantly wiped the smile from his face. "I assure you that you have my entire cooperation," he said.

"Perhaps then you will tell me what you know about the events of last night."

Kirk raised his black eyebrows. "I know nothing," he said, "except that I thought I heard some sort of commotion and came up from the game room to that little room at the head of the stairs."

"And what did you find when you came upstairs?"

"Practically everybody else crowded together and Mrs. Ambler on the floor."

"Aside from the fact that Mrs. Ambler was dead, did you notice anything else that struck you as unusual?"

Kirk hesitated for a moment, as though trying to recall the scene in all its details. "No," he answered. "I don't think so."

"Before or since that time, have you seen anything which might shed some light on the situation?"

"Nothing that would shed any light—no."

"Be more definite, please. You saw something which—"

"I saw a door open and close with apparently no one behind it," said Kirk. "At least I found no one. Mrs. Stuart was with me at the time."

"Yes," I nodded. "I've already told them."

"Have you any suspicions with regard to the identity of the murderer, Mr. Pierce?" Lieutenant Gregory questioned.

"I have not," said Kirk positively.

"You have no cause to think that Mr. Stuart might have murdered Mrs. Ambler during the time he was absent from the game room?"

"What?" Kirk cried, half springing from his chair. "Certainly not."

"Thanks, old man," said Bill. "The Lieutenant seems to think differently."

"But it's impossible," Kirk insisted, even as I had done. "He couldn't have."

"Why do you say that he couldn't have?" asked Lieutenant Gregory.

"He is not the sort of person to do such a thing."

"I've found that almost anybody is capable of murder under the proper set of circumstances," Lieutenant Gregory remarked dryly.

Roberts was back from the telephone. "Anderson has kept your notes for you," Lieutenant Gregory told him. "What did you find out?"

"Ephraim Johnson has a record, all right. Fights. Robbery. Stolen automobile. Served two hitches on the gang. But nothing very recent. Told 'em to send out and take him to Grady."

"Okay," said Lieutenant Gregory. "And now about this piece of telephone wire. It might not be amiss if we had Mrs. Benedict come in and tell us how it found its way into her wastebasket."

I reached for the bell pull, then decided that I did not wish to call Andrew just then. He would still be protesting about red-hot coals. "She went upstairs just after lunch, I believe," I told Lieutenant Gregory. "I'll go for her myself."

Roberts, being near the door, rose to open it for me. But I did not pass through the door. Not just then. For at that moment there came from somewhere overhead the sound of a perfectly ghastly scream.

As we all stood uncertainly, there was another scream, broken off suddenly.

Then silence

XIX

"STAND BACK, EVERYBODY," ordered Lieutenant Gregory, drawing his revolver from its holster and dashing through the door as I shrank back into the room and attached myself to Bill's arm. Roberts and Anderson were right behind their superior officer as he charged out and up the stairs.

And, of course, none of the rest of us stood back, though Bill did make an effort to park me in the library. By the time I reached the top of the stairs at the tail end of the procession, the police were coming out of mine and Bill's room and crossing over to the other front bedroom, which was occupied by Eve.

This time they did not come out, and when I crowded in behind everyone else I understood why, for what I saw was a tableau of horror.

Eve, who evidently had decided to take an after-lunch siesta, lay motionless on the chaise lounge, her face twisted in the awful agony of death. There was a dark red stain on the front of her white chiffon nightgown, a stain that spread and clashed oddly with the flame color of her negligee.

Standing over Eve as she lay there were Claire and Alice. Bill says that when he first reached the door, ahead of the police because he had not stopped to look into our room, Claire was holding Alice with both arms and had one hand over her mouth to stop her screaming.

This, no doubt, is why that second scream had broken off in the middle.

"Hold on, there," warned Lieutenant Gregory as Bob and Kirk surged toward the two girls now cowering backward from the chaise longue. Someone turned on additional light and we saw what he meant. On the floor, where it might have dropped from Eve's hand, lay the feathered dart which she had brought up from the game room, "for protection."

Its steel pin was red with her own blood and even the pale yellow of the feather tips was beginning to be stained crimson.

"For God's sake, Bill," gasped Mr. Marshall, who had lumbered up the stairs just ahead of me, "what sort of place is this? What has happened to everybody since you came out here?"

I could well understand his horrified bewilderment, for my own knees knocked together and I put out a hand to the nearest shoulder in order to steady myself. The shoulder happened to belong to Roberts, and I was so embarrassed when I discovered this fact that I found myself quite able to stand without support, even to murmur an apology.

But he gave me a wintry half-smile that was almost human and said, "Pretty raw. Better go back downstairs, Mrs. Stuart."

The grisly sight which met our eyes seemed to me all the more awful somehow because of the setting. That stately old room in which my grandmother had died, less than a year ago, had certainly known its joys and sorrows and all the things that go to make up normal living. But through the years no alien forces had been able to threaten the foundations of its dignity, never had there been wanton invasion of its privacy. And now, violence and murder.

Nobody replied to Mr. Marshall's question, for Anderson had stepped forward and was trying to find a pulse in Eve's wrist. Had he placed a hand above her heart he must have drawn it back, dripping with blood. After a moment he pulled back one of her eyelids and had a look at the pupil of the eye. "Dead," he said matter-of-factly.

I don't think I have ever seen anyone more angry than Lieutenant Gregory appeared when Anderson made his announcement. "All right," he barked, wheeling and facing us, his piercing dark eyes resting first on one and then another, "which one of you did it?"

It was plain to see that he didn't care very much for any of us just then.

That old expression that you could hear a pin drop falls far short of describing the complete silence that followed his question. You could literally hear the sands of time dropping in a mythical hourglass. And nobody said anything at all.

Lieutenant Gregory turned to Roberts. "You and Anderson search the house and grounds. Check on the servants. Make sure there's no one here who is unaccounted for. Telephone in and find out why nobody's come out from the solicitor's office. And tell 'em to send an ambulance."

I will never know whether Bob meant to go to the assistance of Claire or of Alice; but when Lieutenant Anderson said "Dead," it was Alice who practically fell into Bob's arms. Perhaps we had all been too stunned to think until that moment. Bill and Kirk, one on each side of her, led Claire from the room.

In the movies I have always had to turn my head away from those medieval scenes showing victims on the rack and I had to turn it away now. For I could not bear the look on Bob's poor tortured face. That look made me all the more certain Alice had killed Eve. And if she had killed Eve, she must be in some way responsible for Aunt Maggie's death. That was the only possible explanation of her strange behavior from the time of the discovery of Aunt Maggie's body. I had always thought Alice a bit silly, but I had never known her to be such a bag of nerves. The only ray of light I could see was that this must surely show Bill as innocent.

Remembering Eve's broad hint with regard to the identity of the murderer, I wondered if she had done more than hint to the person suspected. It seemed likely and that her own death had been the result.

No doubt she had gone upstairs because she realized she would be unwelcome among the other guests after her behavior in the dining room. Completely disregarding the fact that she might be called at any moment for questioning by the police, I could imagine her calmly deciding upon a nap. She was always like a cat for comfort. And, of course, she would not have minded making the police or anyone else wait while she dressed. Indeed, she would have told them that if they were in a hurry they could come to her room.

Something else Eve had disregarded was the fact that we had a murderer in our midst.

And now, as we all stood huddled together indecisively in the half-dark of the upstairs hall, I heard Alice saying to Bob, "She had the dart in her hand when I came in the room. She had it in her hand."

Nobody asked who had the dart in whose hand, because a deep, pleasant voice just behind us said, "So we've had a second casualty, with the police and the coroner in the house?" We had all forgotten Mr. Dodson, but he had found his way upstairs and evidently had arrived in time to hear most of what had been said.

Lieutenant Gregory was trying hard not to say anything he might regret. "It's an inside job, all right," he admitted sourly. "Either one of the people standing right here is guilty, or someone who is concealed in the house. I'm going to find that person even if we have six more murders while we are about it."

"That would make it just about unanimous, Lieutenant," said Bob, but the was none of his customary jauntiness to match the words.

"What do you meant" Lieutenant Gregory barked. "This is no time for humor." Then, incongruously enough, he started counting us after the fashion of a conductor on a sight-seeing bus. "That's everyone, isn't it?" he asked Bill. "You told me there were eight of you."

"There were eight of us, including Aunt Maggie," Bill affirmed. "There are six of us left."

"And which is this latest victim?

It seemed an odd question for Lieutenant Gregory to be asking, but of course, he had not yet got around to interviewing the guests, though he did have the list of names and other information and Anderson had taken fingerprints of all of us.

"Mrs. Benedict," Bill told him. "Eve Benedict."

"Ah," breathed Mr. Dodson, "but she rather invited it, didn't she?" At his low-voiced remark you could feel the tension tighten until it seemed that soon we would be hearing it crackle and seeing sparks as from electricity.

"What's that?" Lieutenant Gregory snapped.

"That's right," drawled Mr. Dodson, "you insisted on lunching alone and—making hay. You didn't hear the lady's parting shot when she left the dining room."

"Are you saying that she made some threat which would have inspired her murder?"

"Well, hardly that," Mr. Dodson replied. "But I rather gathered there was more than met the eye in a good many things she said. She didn't seem to be overly fond of anyone present."

"All right," agreed Lieutenant Gregory resignedly. "We'll go into that a little later. Just now I want everybody to go downstairs and wait for me in that room we've been using for conferences. Mr. Stuart, will you send Anderson up? I want him to check for fingerprints."

"Fingerprints?" Claire repeated strangely.

Lieutenant Gregory glanced at her quickly. In fact, we all did, and I will admit that her words gave me a queer feeling of suffocation. Why did Claire, who talked so little, have to go saying things at a time like this?

"What do you mean?" Lieutenant Gregory asked harshly.

I don't suppose in all her life Claire had seen a man glaring down at her like that and she dropped her eyes, so that the long lashes lay quivering on her cheeks, and shrank back against Bill. "Nothing," she whispered. "Why—why should I mean anything?"

"Can't you see she's upset, officer?" Kirk demanded, as though the fault lay entirely with Lieutenant Gregory. And Bill added his oar by inquiring truculently why we were all standing there, anyway.

As we trooped down the stairs, I thought Mr. Marshall looked decidedly the worse for wear. Certainly this was a far cry from his usual quiet Sunday with a round of golf and a midday dinner followed by an afternoon nap. Though goodness knows he had had a generous enough equivalent of that midday dinner. But he said one thing that cheered me a little and verified my own conclusions about the situation. "Well, anyway," he panted, "Bill couldn't have committed this one. He hasn't been out of my sight since we left the dining room."

"And," I chimed in, "don't you think this goes to show that he could not have had anything to do with the other one either?"

We had reached the bottom of the steps and, as the others went on into the library, Mr. Marshall beckoned Bill and me into the privacy of the drawing room. "I would feel much better if Bill had a good, watertight alibi," he confessed. "But Allen will fix that up. Sally, are you sure the doctor is right about that colored boy? I'm going to suggest to Gregory that we call him in for more complete questioning."

"Call in Dr. Bates?" I repeated. "Well, that's all right, of course. But it would look more plausible, I mean that Ephraim could be guilty, if the doctor had seen him after ten o'clock instead of after nine o'clock. Dr. Bates assured me that he left Thomas's house at a quarter after nine. If Aunt Maggie was killed around ten, that would eliminate Ephraim, for he had a temperature of one hundred and three, was delirious and the doctor had given him a hypodermic."

"You think if the doctor had found him in that state after ten instead of after nine, that Ephraim would be a more likely suspect?"

"Dr. Bates didn't seem to think it possible he could have got out of bed at the time he left him."

"Still, people do wander around when they are out of their heads," Mr. Marshall insisted. "Maybe"—his face brightened—"the doctor could be mistaken about the time. Maybe his watch was slow. Such things do happen. Oh, well, Wade Allen will go into all that. We'll be in capable hands."

"Isn't it just about as good as a confession of guilt when you hire Mr. Allen?" Bill asked, and for the first time I began to realize what all this was going to mean to my husband unless he could promptly be cleared of suspicion. Fine and decent as he is, the respect of his fellow man is something Bill has always taken for granted and is just as necessary to him as the air he breathes. If this case came to trial, no matter if he were exonerated, there would always be people who would believe him guilty. Questions would follow us all our lives. There would be whispers behind our backs. And the money. We would never be able to use it as Aunt Maggie intended as long as there was anyone in the world who might insinuate that it was blood money.

"Listen, my boy," Mr. Marshall was saying, "circumstantial evidence has convicted more innocent people than all the guilty ones Wade Allen has been able to save. We are not going to take any chances."

"Thanks," said Bill, giving Mr. Marshall one of his straight-from-the-shoulder looks and bringing a lump into my throat. "Suppose I'd better be trying to find Anderson."

"Yes, yes, by all means. Sally, shall we join the others in the library? We can all go to that back room later. It is a little brighter in here with the fire—" Poor Mr. Marshall, who so loved his comfort, was trying to make the best of things.

We found Alice weeping on Bob's shoulder as they sat together on the sofa. Bob was saying helplessly, "There, there," and, "Try not to think about it."

"Is there anything I can do?" I asked. "Alice, would you like a little ammonia or some sherry or something?"

"No, no," she sobbed. "I only want to get away from this horrible place."

"What about you, Claire?" I asked. "Are you all right?"

Claire, sunk in the big wing chair on the right of the fireplace, looked up absently and made a valiant effort to smile. "I'm all right," she said. "What about you, Sally?"

"Oh, I'm all right," I answered, with a conviction that I was far from feeling, and sat down in the chair Kirk placed for me between himself and Mr. Dodson. As Kirk's eyes strayed quickly from one to another of the group, I had an uncomfortable feeling that he was trying to read our various expressions for some secret purpose of his own and succeeding far better than we ourselves would have thought possible.

It also struck me as a little strange that we were not discussing the murder. Then I realized that perhaps this was because we all felt that Alice was guilty. But what had Alice meant when she said to Bob, "She had the dart in her hand when I came in the room"?

Did she mean that Claire or Eve had it?

It was a question I would have to wait for Lieutenant Gregory to ask.

Bill came in, pulled up the gouty stool and sat down between Kirk and me. "They are certainly turning everything upside down," he said. "Searching the servants' quarters, even looking in the automobile trunks. Must think the murderer is a contortionist. I got to the kitchen just in time to see Roberts having a fit because Bessie couldn't produce the fugitive when she opened the silver storage closet for him. From the look in her eye I think she was pretty well tempted to lock him in there. He kept on asking if there were any old wells about. Probably be going down the coal chute next."

"Oh," said Alice, suddenly straightening up and looking around at us with a sort of drowned expression. "Do you suppose that's where Plutarch is? I could hear him when I was in the basement, but I couldn't find him. At least I thought I heard him. Perhaps he was out of doors."

The crying hadn't helped Alice's looks and her lipstick was all smeared, giving her mouth a grotesque twist to one side. "Here," I said, digging into my pocket for a handkerchief, "let me fix your lipstick—"

"I'll get a towel," Bob offered, rising to his feet.

"You'll find plenty in the powder room," I told him.

For we could see—we could all see—that it was not lipstick, but dried blood, on Alice's cheek. Claire glanced away quickly, and a moment later I saw her take a surreptitious look at the palms of her hands, then close her fingers into tight fists in her lap.

As my eyes met those of Mr. Marshall, I knew that he also had seen that strange gesture of Claire's.

Who else might have been looking, I did not know. Bob was back now, bathing Alice's face with a wet towel.

"I'll bring you some powder," I told Alice. "Claire, wouldn't you like some powder, too?"

"Yes," she answered, not looking at me, and we went out of the room together.

"I'll wait until you've finished," I told her at the door of the powder room. "Then I'll repair my own damages. It's such a cubbyhole."

I knew now what Alice meant when she said, "She had the dart in her hand."

XX

I WENT BACK TO THE LIBRARY and gathered up the towel Alice had used and when Claire emerged from the powder room I took that towel, too, and delivered them both to Bessie with instructions to hide them in the silver closet. Since that room had already been searched, it seemed a safe place, and I had read too much about blood stains on towels to leave them lying around where the police might find them.

Bessie took the towels without a word and padded off. Why I should be trying to suppress possible evidence I did not know and Bessie did not ask, but we understood each other. And, of course, if it came to a question of establishing Bill's innocence, I could always produce them.

When I returned to the library again, feeling almost as guilty as though I had just disposed of the corpus delicti, it gave me quite a start to find Lieutenant Gregory waiting. Mr. Marshall, it seems, had persuaded him to conduct his inquiry in the more cheerful surroundings of the library, and Roberts had already seated himself at the reading table and was fidgeting with notebook and pen.

Alice, still concerned about Plutarch, was insisting that the coal chute be more thoroughly investigated and everything had to be delayed until Andrew could be summoned and told to make a search.

"All I got to say is he sho' won't be no white cat if that's where he's at," Andrew mumbled as he went his reluctant way.

Lieutenant Gregory, who had been bearing things as patiently as possible, took his seat at the reading table. "Can anyone tell me whose property this is?" he asked, holding up a man's handkerchief for inspection. "It has a 'P' in one corner," he announced as we all straightened up and stared at the square of white linen.

"It looks like one of mine," said Kirk, as he rose and went over to the table in order to examine it more closely.

"Recognize it, eh?" the officer said.

"Of course, I can't be absolutely certain," Kirk said. "But I don't know anybody else here who would be using that initial. I have a batch of handkerchiefs just alike."

"We found it on the floor of Mrs. Benedict's room," Lieutenant Gregory announced, portentously.

Kirk's face turned a fiery red and he looked pretty flustered for a moment.

"Will you," Lieutenant Gregory asked, "kindly explain its presence in the room with the murdered woman?"

"I—suppose," Kirk stumbled over his words, "I dropped it there, though I—don't remember having a handkerchief in my hand at the time."

"At what time was this?" Lieutenant Gregory probed inexorably.

"Some time after lunch," Kirk confessed slowly. "I don't remember exactly."

"Try to remember as nearly as you can."

"Well," Kirk replied, "I smoked a cigarette here in the library after lunch. Mrs. Stuart and Miss Dunbar were here at the time. I believe Bob and—Miss Harper were in the room across the hall. Anyway, someone was playing the piano. Then sometime later Mr. Marshall came and asked to speak to Mrs. Stuart and she left the room with him. Shortly after this, Miss Dunbar said she was going upstairs and also left. I walked out on the porch and smoked another cigarette. Then I—went upstairs. On the way to my room I stopped to speak to Mrs. Benedict. I knocked on her door and she told me to come in."

"Was Mrs. Benedict—er, dressed at the time?"

"Is it necessary to go into this?"

"I should prefer that you answer my question."

"Mrs. Benedict said she had meant to take a nap. But she found herself—wakeful. I think she had been reading. Anyway she was lying on the chaise longue and had a book in her hand."

"Is it customary for men guests at house parties to visit the rooms of ladies who are"—the officer paused uncertainly, and I thought of Bessie's expression, "not to say dressed"; then he added—"not formally attired?"

Kirk's jaw tightened, but he strove for calmness. Not once had he glanced in Claire's direction since the catechism began and I was glad he missed the look of rather sick disgust on her face.

"It was not a rendezvous, if that is what you mean," he told Lieutenant Gregory. "I simply wanted to speak to Mrs. Benedict, and when she called out to me to come in I opened the door and stepped inside."

"You closed the door?"

"Certainly. I did not wish to be—overheard."

"I gather you wished to discuss something urgent with Mrs. Benedict?"

"What I wanted to discuss with Mrs. Benedict was—personal," Kirk said.

"You would save yourself and all of us a lot of time if you would be frank," he was warned. "Everything that happened immediately preceding Mrs. Benedict's death is important and this is no time for polite evasions."

"I did not kill Mrs. Benedict," said Kirk, biting out his words, "and this being the case, I fail to see where my conversation with her could have any bearing on the matter."

Lieutenant Gregory shifted himself in his chair. "You are sure she said nothing whatever which might shed some light on the cause of her death?" he asked. "Did she seem nervous or in any way afraid?"

"No," said Kirk positively.

Lieutenant Gregory focused his gaze first upon Alice, who squirmed like a scared rabbit, and then on Claire, who might easily have passed for Lucia di Lammermoor in one of her sleep-walking scenes. "Will you kindly tell me how you happened to be in the room with Mrs. Benedict?" he asked Claire.

There was a long pause and still Claire said nothing.

Alice whispered, "I found her in there."

"Found who in there?" Lieutenant Gregory asked.

"Claire—Miss Harper."

"Yes?" he questioned. "Is this true, Miss Harper?"

Claire came out of her trance. "Yes, oh, yes. But—"

"She had the dart in her hand," Alice interrupted.

"Who had the dart in whose hand?" The fatal question had been asked at last.

"Claire had it," Alice went on nervously.

I couldn't bear to look at Bob or Kirk.

Bill squeezed my hand. "Now, now," he whispered.

"What was she doing?" Lieutenant Gregory asked, trying to make his voice sound casual.

"She was just standing there—looking down at Eve—Mrs. Benedict. And she was saying something. I stood there at the door, too shocked to move or to say anything at first."

"What did she say?"

"I said"—Claire took up the narrative, and if there was a tremor in her clear, lovely voice, I could not tell—"'It is just too bad, Eve. But you'll never get in my way again.'"

We sat in a sort of frozen silence. Then Alice said, "Yes, that's what she said. Can you blame me for screaming when I saw Eve all covered with blood—and Claire started toward me with that horrible dart in her hand?"

"I had no intention of hurting you, Alice," said Claire, her voice edged with contempt. "I just wanted to stop your hysterics, if possible."

"But the dart," interposed Lieutenant Gregory. "It was lying on the floor when we came upstairs."

"It fell," Alice explained. "I tried to take it away from her and it fell."

"Miss Harper," said Lieutenant Gregory, leaning toward Claire in that way I had learned to dread, "suppose you tell us exactly what happened from the time you first went to Mrs. Benedict's room."

"You don't have to go through this, Claire," Kirk interrupted savagely. "Just refuse to answer."

Claire gave him a curious look, then her gaze shifted to Lieutenant Gregory and under his probing stare her face went white and her hands flew to her throat. "Oh," she gasped, "you think I killed her. But I didn't."

I drew a long, choking sigh of relief. In fact, there was an audible lessening of tension in the room. It was like a scene in the theater, actually, where everyone has been sitting on the edge of his seat and then suddenly the play is over and the lights go on and you realize it was all just make-believe.

Only, in this instance it was not a play. I may have imagined it, but it seemed to me that even Lieutenant Gregory seemed a little relieved at Claire's horrified denial. Certainly his voice had lost a shade of its gruffness when he said, "But the dart? How did you happen to have it in your hand?"

"Don't—don't ask me that," Claire shuddered.

"But Miss Harper, you must remember, we are trying to clear up a murder."

"I know—I know. But it is so horrible."

"Can't we postpone this?" Bob demanded angrily. "Miss Harper has just told you she didn't kill Mrs. Benedict. Isn't that enough?"

Claire smiled at him wanly. "It's all right," she said. "I'll try not to be so silly." Claire's hands pushed back her Titian hair; she shut her eyes, and long dark lashes swept her cheeks. Then looking up at Lieutenant Gregory in unconscious appeal, she said simply, "When I thought Eve failed to hear my knock, I pushed open her door and went in." Again Claire's hands flew to her throat. "She wasn't quite dead—"

"Did she say anything?" Lieutenant Gregory demanded, straining forward. And I think we all held our breath, waiting for Claire's answer.

Slowly she shook her head. "Not—not anything I could understand. But her eyes—they seemed to be begging me to do something.

I saw the dart—and the blood. I knew she wanted me to—remove the dart. At first I thought I could not bear to touch it, but I knew I must—"

"She didn't say anything?" Lieutenant Gregory asked again.

"No, she didn't say anything. I asked her who did it. I said, 'Who, Eve, who?' But she could not speak; and as I stood there with the dart in my hand, there was a strange, gurgling sound in her throat and her head slipped to one side and I knew she must be dead.

"It was horrible." Claire shuddered. "I knew I should be sorry for anyone who was so hated that she had been murdered. But I couldn't be. Not just then, anyway. And I thought that at least she would never bother me again. That—that was when I said—what I did. Then I heard a sound which I thought came from the bathroom, and I was terribly frightened, for I was sure it must be the murderer. I didn't know what to do. Then I realized Alice was in the room and I knew I must have been mistaken about hearing anyone in the bathroom."

"Please tell us how you were standing when Miss Dunbar came in the room. Could you see both the bath and the hall doors?"

"I couldn't see either. But"—as though she suddenly realized where his question might lead—"I am sure Alice came in from the hall. That door was—was much nearer. Besides, it was open when I turned around and saw Alice, and I had pushed it shut before I saw Eve on the chaise longue."

"What was the purpose of your call on Mrs. Benedict?"

"I just wanted to speak to her."

"You were just dropping in for a little—social chat?"

"Yes—no—that is, not exactly."

I dug my nails into Bill's hand until he winced and gave me an indignant frown. But why couldn't Claire have stopped when she said "Yes"?

"What do you mean, not exactly?" Lieutenant Gregory bore down.

This time it was Kirk who broke the lance for Claire, and I thought Lieutenant Gregory was going to try to break him in two with his bare hands right there. But he restrained himself and in answer to Kirk's hot-headed interference as to why the question should be asked, Lieutenant Gregory patiently reminded him that we had had two murders in less than twenty-four hours. "The situation warrants a little discomfort for the guests, if necessary in clearing things up," he added sarcastically. Turning again to Claire, he asked, "Miss Harper, do you mind telling us the nature of your call on Mrs. Benedict?"

"Yes, I do mind very much," Claire admitted, "but I suppose I must. Mr. Dunbar and I"—and she paused to seek courage in a glance toward Bob—"had just announced our engagement to be married. Mrs. Benedict had been—interested in Mr. Dunbar for some time—"

"Mrs. Benedict is unmarried then?"

"She is divorced," Claire explained. "She disapproved of our engagement and—was most insulting at lunch today."

"Yes?"

"I went to see her to tell her . . ." Claire's voice trailed off into silence.

"To tell her what?" Lieutenant Gregory barked, and I was not so certain now that he believed in Claire's innocence. Beauty in distress might sway him as any mortal man, but murder was murder. And, as he had so aptly expressed it, we had had two murders in less than twenty-four hours.

Claire gazed around the room helplessly and her face, which had been so white, was now dyed crimson. "I wanted to tell Eve"—her voice sank to a throaty whisper—"to keep hands off."

"And what did she say?"

"Don't answer that, Claire," Kirk cried out quickly.

Claire gave him a little smile of gratitude, while Lieutenant Gregory turned on him furiously. "Mr. Pierce, I must ask you to keep out of this or I shall have to place you under arrest."

"But, Officer," Mr. Marshall interposed reasonably, "Miss Harper has her legal rights. Without advice of counsel, she is not compelled to answer questions which afterward might be used against her."

"It's all right," said Claire weakly. "I've already told you what happened. I knocked on the door, then called out to ask if I might come in. When I got no answer I opened the door, thinking Eve was in the bathroom. And there she was." Claire shut her eyes again and the long dark lashes lay quivering on her cheeks. "What I meant to do when I removed the dart and saw that she was dead was to go downstairs and tell somebody—"

"But you did not?"

"No, I've told you. Alice came in and—got excited."

"When you asked Mrs. Benedict who had stabbed her, why did you think she had been murdered? Why didn't you think of suicide?"

Claire's eyes widened and she shook her head. "It just wouldn't occur to anyone who knew her," she said.

"Explain that remark, please."

"But—but—"

"Lieutenant," asked Bill, and Lieutenant Gregory turned toward him impatiently, "may I speak for Miss Harper? What she means is that Mrs. Benedict was not very popular. She had an unfortunate gift of sarcasm and an equally unfortunate desire to put people in their places. I think she rather enjoyed stirring up trouble at times."

"She had a knack for making enemies?" the officer suggested.

"Something like that," Bill agreed.

"But she wasn't like that all the time," I somehow felt called upon to say, I suppose in justice to the dead. "Sometimes she could be quite generous and agreeable. I know she often acted without much self-control, but I think the cause was deeper than just a desire to be disagreeable. I think"—I floundered—"that perhaps she had an inferiority complex. She seemed to want things just because someone else wanted them—just to show that she could have them, I suppose."

I happened to glance at Mr. Dodson, who had spoken no word since the questioning began. He was nodding his head. "I rather think Mrs. Stuart is right," he said.

"But," Bill went on, "naturally when she went around stepping on people's toes, they were not going to sit down and try to figure all this out and feel sorry for her."

"And this time," Lieutenant Gregory concluded, "she stepped too hard on somebody's toes?"

"Oh, I don't know about that," I babbled. "Perhaps it was just an accumulation of things. Perhaps it was suicide. Or maybe she knew too much. She told me this morning that she thought she knew who killed Aunt Maggie."

Trying to cover up on any inadvertent suggestion that it was Claire's toes Eve had stepped on, I blundered along, realizing too late by the electrified atmosphere of the room that I had—as Bessie would say—"opened my mouth and put my foot in it."

XXI

STRANGE TO SAY, Lieutenant Gregory did not immediately follow up the opening I had given when I mentioned my conversation with Eve. Instead of ordering that I inform him forthwith whether or not she definitely had committed herself and the name of the person involved, he gave me a long, speculative look and said, "We will go into that a little later." It seemed to me that everybody in the room appeared a bit deflated by this anti-climax and that Lieutenant Gregory derived some hidden satisfaction from the fact.

"Just now," he continued, "I should like for Miss Dunbar to tell me how she happened to go to Mrs. Benedict's room. And before we start I want to say that unless we can conduct this inquiry calmly and without a lot of interruption it will be my duty to have the lot of you sent to the tower and held on suspicion."

"The tower?" Kirk echoed uncertainly.

"The county jail, the big rock," Bill explained.

"Right!" said Lieutenant Gregory.

We all sat there dumbly. This, we had begun to realize, was no ticket for traffic violation which we could hand over to Uncle Henry or to some other member of the family who had "influence." This was something we had to take—or go to the tower.

"Now, Miss Dunbar," said Lieutenant Gregory, "will you answer my question?"

"What—what was it?" Alice gulped.

"Why did you go to Mrs. Benedict's room?"

"Oh! Well, I went there for the same reason Claire did. I—that is—well, you see Claire and my brother are to be married. Eve Benedict came out here uninvited for the express purpose of breaking their engagement. She was a terrible person. She had no scruples and she appealed to the very worst in a man. She had been after my brother since before she divorced her second husband—"

"What happened to her first husband?" Lieutenant Gregory asked. "Did she divorce him?"

"Not—until afterward. I mean not until after he disappeared."

"What do you mean, disappeared?"

"He just disappeared and nobody knows what happened to him, except—"

"Stick to the facts, Miss Dunbar."

"Well, I was just thinking," said Alice, and a look of quickly veiled craftiness came into her eyes, "that he must have hated her terribly. Do you think he might have come back and killed her?"

The question seemed to be addressed to no one in particular, but I prayed Lieutenant Gregory would hold Alice to his original line of inquiry. With all that had happened at Wisteria Hall I did not feel that I could listen to two recitals of that ugly story in one day.

"Do you have any reason to think he might have come back, Miss Dunbar?" Evidently my prayer was not to be answered.

"I do not believe this can possibly have any connection with Mrs. Benedict's death," my husband objected.

Lieutenant Gregory, immediately suspicious, turned on Bill angrily. "We were to conduct this inquiry without interference," he reminded.

"Sorry," Bill acknowledged. "My mistake."

"Now, Miss Dunbar—"

"Well, you see," Alice began, and the spiteful gleam in her eyes showed plainly how much she enjoyed this opportunity to give what she considered the low-down on Eve, "it all began with her first honeymoon—Eve's, I mean."

When the story was finished, Lieutenant Gregory looked just a little sheepish as he inquired the whereabouts of Eve's second husband. No doubt, he guessed by then that Alice had simply been trying to divert suspicion from herself.

"I suppose Frank Benedict is in town," Alice told him casually.

"Make a note to get in touch with Frank Benedict as soon as we are through with this inquiry," Roberts was told.

"But—" I began, then stopped, remembering Lieutenant Gregory's edict.

"Yes?" he asked.

"I was only going to say that I don't see how he could have anything to do with Eve's death."

"Was she collecting alimony?"

"Oh, yes," Alice breathed. "Loads of it."

"Pretty good motive, anyway," said the officer. "Miss Dunbar, when you went to Mrs. Benedict's room, I gather that you meant to tell her to keep off the grass?"

"Yes. I wanted to tell her to leave my brother alone. She—"

"Don't, Alice," Bob pleaded.

"But it is true." Alice's voice rose shrill and high. "She would have got you back. Oh, she was vile, vile. Why did Bill bring her out here uninvited except that she is the sort of woman that men—"

"Alice," I cried, indignantly, as Bill opened his mouth to speak, then shut it resolutely, "you know that isn't true!"

"Of course," said Bob placatingly. "Alice is just upset and doesn't know what she's saying."

Lieutenant Gregory held up his hand for silence. "Let's leave personalities out of this," he told Alice. "Did you have any success with Mrs. Benedict?" I realized that his voice was far too casual, but Alice rushed recklessly on.

"I went to her room twice before I really went in," she said. "The first time, as I came out of my room, I saw Bob leaving—" Alice put her hand over her mouth, stopping the words too late.

"Why, Alice," said Bob quickly, "why didn't you say this before? Perhaps you've given me an alibi."

"Yes, of course," Alice agreed eagerly. "I was going to say so, but all this has been so upsetting." Then she explained to Lieutenant

Gregory, "I didn't want Bob to know I had seen him, so I stepped back inside my own door."

"What did you do next, Miss Dunbar?"

"I waited a while. Then I went to Eve's room. But I did not go in, because I heard voices."

"Please go on with your story."

"I did not really see Eve alive after lunch," she admitted reluctantly.

"But the voices. Did you recognize them?"

"I recognized Eve's, of course. She was talking to a man, but his voice was low. I thought at first that I recognized the man's voice and then I was not sure. Naturally," she added self-consciously, "I did not stay to listen."

"And then what, Miss Dunbar?"

"But that's all. I thought that for some reason Bob had gone back again to Eve's room. But, as I said, I was not sure. Now I know it must have been Kirk's voice I heard."

Nobody looked at anyone else as Alice made this pronouncement. Lieutenant Gregory grunted. "Seems to have been a sort of convention in that room," he observed. "Wonder how you kept from falling over each other. We will have to get straight on the time element. As it is now, any one of four people in this group could have killed Mrs. Benedict. Mr. Dunbar, will you tell us as nearly as possible the time of your visit to her room?"

Bob reddened. "If I cannot, does it mean I will be under suspicion of having committed the murder?"

"You are already under suspicion. Everyone in the house who cannot account for his or her whereabouts at the time of the murder is naturally under suspicion. But I would suggest that you answer my questions."

"I am trying to think. If Sally had only installed a watchman's clock for all of us to punch at given intervals, it would be so much simpler—"

Lieutenant Gregory jerked his head impatiently. "Answer the question," he ordered tersely.

"Let me see . . ." Bob still hesitated a long time, and Claire gazed at some point just above his head. Evidently she could not bear to think that he had gone directly from that little session at the piano to a tryst with Eve. "But"—Bob's expression brightened—"Alice has just told you she saw me come out and that later on she heard Eve engaged in conversation with someone else."

"Very easy for a sister to get mixed up, under all the circumstances," said Lieutenant Gregory. "Mr. Dunbar, I suppose your conversation with Mrs. Benedict was also—"

"Personal," Bob finished for him.

"And you, Miss Dunbar, with all your various trips to Mrs. Benedict's room, are you sure you heard nothing that aroused your suspicions in any way? You saw no one in the hall at any time whose behavior might have struck you as strange?"

Alice looked from one door to the other, as though seeking some avenue of escape, then back at the stern-faced officer, and her eyes dropped beneath his scrutiny. "I have told you everything I know," she said, a little sulkily.

Lieutenant Gregory turned again to Claire. "Miss Harper, are you quite sure you saw no one in the bathroom when you thought you—heard a sound from that direction?"

Claire seemed completely nonplused by this new attack. "Oh, no," she insisted. "Why do you ask?"

"Because," Lieutenant Gregory told her, "someone did go in that bathroom. Whether that person was there or not when you were in the bedroom remains to be proved. But at some time after Mrs. Benedict was killed, somebody went into her bathroom and washed his or her hands and left a slight trace of blood on the towel. The towel was still damp when I examined the room just after the discovery of the murder."

Apparently all my efforts at disposing of towels had been in vain.

"But," Mr. Marshall pointed out, "if there had been someone in the bathroom when Miss Harper went in the room, wouldn't he have had to remain there? You would have found him. There would have been no chance for him to escape, would there?"

"There is a door leading from the bath directly into the hall," Lieutenant Gregory explained patiently. "Or rather the bath opens into a kind of dressing room or closet or something which opens into the hall. Mrs. Benedict seems to have occupied the only room with a bath from which you can go directly to the hall." He gave me one of his searching looks, as though trying to decide whether I might have had some ulterior motive in assigning Eve that particular room.

"There was nothing strange about that," I felt called upon to explain. "It is the room formerly occupied by my grandparents. I hadn't meant to use it, unless perhaps for Aunt Maggie—until Eve came unexpectedly. My grandfather had the door cut because he liked to get up early, and in this way he could dress in the bathroom and leave without disturbing my grandmother by passing back through the room."

"I see," Lieutenant Gregory nodded. "And you, Mrs. Stuart, did you also go calling on Mrs. Benedict after lunch?"

"I'm sorry," I told him, "but I suppose I have what you call an alibi. Anyway, I have not been alone for one moment since lunch. I was with Alice and Kirk in the library—in this room, that is—until Mr. Marshall came to tell me about—about Bill."

Mr. Marshall cleared his throat. "Lieutenant," he asked, "doesn't this second murder make it plain enough to you that Mr. Stuart is not guilty of the charge you have made against him?"

"What charge?" Bob asked quickly, and I realized with a little shock that all our guests were not yet aware of the fact Bill was Lieutenant Gregory's number-one suspect for the first murder.

"Just a little charge of homicide," my red-headed husband explained bitterly. "He thinks I killed Aunt Maggie."

Lieutenant Gregory waited for the exclamations and ejaculations to subside. "I cannot see how the situation has changed with Mrs. Benedict's death," he said, "except that it is plain I am going to have to take you all one by one to thresh this thing out. Nobody's told all he knows yet." He paused, looked over at Mr. Dodson and asked, "Any suggestions, Coroner?"

"Not at the moment," Mr. Dodson answered. "I was going to ask you to let me try a little plan of my own, but perhaps it would be best to go on with your individual questioning."

"What was your plan?" Lieutenant Gregory asked, a bit testily.

"We can still try it if nothing definite has developed when you have finished," Mr. Dodson explained. "I should like to hold what might be considered a sort of inquest rehearsal. My idea would be to assemble all the surviving members of the house party and the servants in this room, question each briefly and let him or her testify with regard to the two murders."

"An inquest rehearsal," Lieutenant Gregory repeated doubtfully, while looks of consternation spread around the room, "with everybody under oath, just as they would be at the inquest? What's the use, if you are going to have to hold an inquest, anyway?"

"I believe this will obviate the necessity of a formal inquest," said Mr. Dodson quietly.

"You mean you believe the murderer will confess?"

"I should like to discuss that with you privately," Mr. Dodson replied.

XXII

THE STORM BROKE THEN, with everybody demanding to know if we hadn't been through enough without having to submit to an unnecessary third degree. Bob was especially resentful. "My sister cannot stand much more of this," he told Lieutenant Gregory. And knowing Alice, I thought it quite likely that she might at any moment fling a fit and fall in it, as Bessie would say. Certainly I had had all of Alice's dramatics that I cared for.

I think Lieutenant Gregory was of half a mind to refuse Mr. Dodson's request until he saw how distasteful the idea was to everyone else. Bob had just asked whether such a proceeding was legal and Kirk had said he was less concerned over that point than whether it was really necessary. "Of course, we all want the situation cleared up, but it does seem to me we have had rather a lot of cross-examination already," Kirk added.

"How do you think such situations are cleared up?" Lieutenant Gregory asked grimly.

"I think," said Mr. Marshall placatingly, "that it would be best to follow Mr. Dodson's plan. After all, don't lose sight of the fact that he came out here as a favor to me. What he is doing is because of friendship, rather than—er—animosity or the desire to make anyone uncomfortable. When his little—séance is over, I believe we can all hope to go back to town, can we not, Officer?"

"Back to town, yes," agreed Lieutenant Gregory and I don't think any of us missed his meaning, for it was plain to see that he did not expect us all to go back to our accustomed habitats.

"All right," he said, glancing around the group, "we can take a little recess now. But everybody must stay within call—that is, in the house. And by the way, Mrs. Stuart," he added, as the general exodus began, "may I speak to you a moment?"

Bill remained with me, of course, and when the room was clear Lieutenant Gregory said, "In your testimony a little while ago, you said Mrs. Benedict intimated that she knew who committed the first murder?"

"She did," I admitted, "but—"

"I did not press the point," he interrupted, "to ask whether she actually gave you any idea of her suspicions or possible knowledge. I—er—had a reason for this. But first, please repeat to Roberts as much of your conversation with Mrs. Benedict as you remember."

"But that's all," I said. "She simply hinted at things, and when I tried to get her to be definite she began to hedge and said she might be mistaken."

"Just what did she say exactly?"

"I believe she said something to the effect that she wanted to get things straight in her own mind, or that she wanted to check up on something. I cannot remember exactly, because at the time I got the impression she was only giving herself airs. She always liked to appear important."

"Too bad you didn't make her go into detail," said Lieutenant Gregory.

"But I did try," I told him again, "and when she shut up I told her it was her duty to tell the police what she knew."

"Why didn't you tell me this when I first came? I could have had her down for questioning immediately."

"I—naturally thought you would wish to conduct your investigation in your own way. That you would question her yourself and—"

"Now, now," said Bill, reading my mind as he so often does. "Don't you go getting any idea you are responsible for Eve's death. Whoever killed her had good and sufficient reason."

"But there is just a possibility," Lieutenant Gregory went on, "that she was killed because she knew too much. The chances are more than good, however, that her murder had nothing to do with Mrs. Ambler's death."

"But it seems perfectly logical that the same person committed both crimes," Mr. Marshall argued. "After all, there cannot be a house full of murderers running around loose." Involuntarily he looked back over his shoulder as though he expected an assassin to appear from behind the ambush of the wing chair.

"I don't see it that way," said the officer stubbornly. "True, when a man or a woman has killed one time, it is much easier to kill again. And, after all, you can die only once, no matter how many crimes you commit. But usually a murderer follows pretty much the same technique in his activities. And usually all his murders can be traced to the same motive. That's why I think these were committed by different people and probably amateurs at that. If you will analyze the two cases, you will see that there is no apparent connection. Mrs. Ambler was strangled to death. I believe monetary gain to be the motive. But Mrs. Benedict was stabbed, and the only motive we have been able to uncover so far is personal dislike."

"But if she were killed to cover up on the first murder, you would need no other motive," Mr. Marshall told him.

"I admit that. But there is another reason why I do not believe the two crimes were committed by the same person. Mrs. Ambler's death was the result of cold calculation. But Mrs. Benedict was killed while the police were in the house. No one, except in the heat of passion, would take such a chance."

"I believe," said Mr. Dodson, "that he was taking what he believed to be the lesser of two chances."

"He?" asked Bill quickly.

"Just a convenient pronoun," Mr. Dodson smiled.

"Thought perhaps you had reached some definite conclusion," Bill explained, his feathers visibly drooping.

"He probably has," said Mr. Marshall. "That's why I feel we should give him all the cooperation we can."

"Of course, I can guarantee nothing," Mr. Dodson deprecated.

"If you have definite suspicions, you should say so," Lieutenant Gregory told him crossly.

"Don't ask me to commit myself yet. It will be better for all concerned if I keep my own counsel. And even if my suspicions are confirmed, we may still have the job of proving our cases, which is not always easy to do."

"Lieutenant," Bill asked, "why do you think these murders are the work of amateurs?"

Lieutenant Gregory gave Bill one of his deep, probing looks. "Well," he said finally, "take those two notes left around for you to find, Mrs. Stuart. No professional crook would be guilty of such old-fashioned methods."

"If he has committed two murders and eluded detection, he can't be such an amateur now," Mr. Marshall observed.

"There's more than one person mixed up in this," Lieutenant Gregory insisted. "Wouldn't surprise me to find the whole house party involved. Lots of things they are all going to have trouble explaining when the case comes up for trial."

"Oh," I asked, suddenly remembering, "were there fingerprints in Eve's bathroom?"

"Who's conducting this inquiry, anyway?" Lieutenant Gregory asked, with a dry grin. "I've been answering too many questions and getting nowhere. What I want to ask you to do, Mrs. Stuart, is to let me know if anyone shows undue concern about what Mrs. Benedict may have said to you this morning."

"You mean—if anybody tries to find out whether she really told me anything definite?"

"Exactly. If anybody wants to know whether she named names or anything of the sort, tell them anything you like but report to me immediately. And by the way," he added, "I wouldn't wander off alone. May not be too safe for you if anybody suspects you know something."

"But, Officer," Bill protested, "do you realize what you are letting my wife in for?"

"Never mind," I said, "don't you see this means Lieutenant Gregory admits the possibility that someone else may have killed Aunt Maggie?"

"Well, now, I wouldn't go as far as that," the officer remarked cautiously. "But I will admit that this second killing does complicate things considerably."

"Just keep a bodyguard handy, my dear," Mr. Marshall advised. "You and Bill can sort of stick together, you know."

"Except that would probably prevent any questions being asked," I pointed out.

The arrival of an ambulance and a police doctor made it necessary for Lieutenant Gregory to declare another short recess. Mr. Marshall, Mr. Dodson, Bill and I joined the others in the drawing room, which in spite of battle, murder and sudden death still smelled faintly of dried rose leaves in Sevres potpourri jars, just as it had ever since I could remember.

The lights in the crystal chandeliers had been turned on and Andrew had made fires in both fireplaces. In my grandmother's time one room had been a yellow parlor and one a green, the old mahogany furniture upholstered in yellow and green silk damask, respectively. "It makes such a nice contrast with the double doors open on days when I receive," she said. After her death, when we tore out the partition and did the walls in chalk-white, we hung warm rose draperies at the high windows and mixed the yellow and green furniture to make a balanced effect in the long room with its gray Aubusson rugs. Here was background for formal gaiety, for ladies who flirted behind fans and stole glances at themselves in the tall pier-glass mirrors, for gallants who pledged undying devotion and perhaps also cocked an eye at their own reflections.

What a strange contrast was offered by that serious-faced little group huddled at the fireplace nearest the front of the house and farthest from the black and gold Coromandel screen which still concealed the sofa on which Aunt Maggie had been placed after her death. I knew that my own face was just as serious. That all our minds were filled with dark thoughts and dread suspicions.

My throat was as dry as though I had a fever and all of us looked as if we needed a pickup of some kind. "Let's have tea," I suggested to Bill, who rang for Andrew, instructing him also to bring whisky and soda.

Everybody brightened perceptibly at the appearance of refreshments, even Mr. Dodson. "The English certainly had the right idea," said Kirk as he decided on tea. Bob mixed himself a whisky and soda with the remark that he had "been taking too many straight drinks lately."

Claire refused the thin bread and butter sandwiches, but Alice took a second, apparently without realizing that she had not touched her first one. "By the way, Sally," she said, with assumed nonchalance, "you never did tell us what Eve told you."

I almost strangled over my tea when Claire seconded the motion. "That's right, Sally," she said, "you didn't tell us."

This was certainly going straight to the point. Of course, it might be no more than feminine curiosity, but I decided to make things a little difficult. I could feel myself the center of all eyes as I hesitated. Even Mr. Dodson's face was turned toward me and I had a sudden, foolish notion that his ears were actually bent back.

"What Eve told me when?" I asked perversely.

"Oh, what she said about Aunt Maggie," Alice prompted. "You know, you said she hinted that she knew something."

Did I imagine it, or was there an unusual tenseness in that general attitude of listening. "Oh, that?" I said casually. "You know Eve. How she liked to appear important. I—just didn't pay any attention to her."

"If she really knew anything I rather imagine she would have gone to the police as soon as they arrived," Mr. Dodson cut in, before anyone else could speak, and I knew he did so deliberately. "Mrs. Stuart, may I beg another cup of tea?" he asked.

Andrew brought in more hot water, and as I busied myself making fresh tea and filling cups the subject was effectively sidetracked. "Take some sandwiches and drinks to the library," I told Andrew, who looked as though he would like to add a sizable quantity of arsenic as well, but he refrained from comment in the presence of Mr. Dodson. Both Andrew and Bessie apparently regarded Mr. Dodson as a sort of cross between a witch and a policeman and no doubt stood in fear of being "cunjured" any moment.

I will have to admit that my own idea was not so very different in some respects. Curious to know more of Mr. Dodson's unusual methods of "detecting," I said, under cover of Mr. Marshall's drone, "I still don't see how you can tell so much, just from listening. . . ."

"It is not as complicated as it sounds," he answered, matching his tone to mine. "When you lose one of your senses, the others are sharpened. Not just your hearing, but all of them. And not all at once, of course. You learn to think more and to reason. In this modern age of automatic conveniences, most people seldom find it necessary to think at all. Everything has been thought out for them and they lead purely automatic lives, punching a button here, another there. They would be horrified, of course, if they realized how completely they depend upon their eyes. I have a friend, a neurologist, who bears me out in. this. He says the average person has scarcely any call to develop his mental resources."

"But," I said, "doesn't a lawyer usually study the face of a witness in drawing conclusions? Mr. Marshall has told me that you lost your sight when you were just a child and that you later memorized law by listening to other students read aloud. I think that is wonderful. But how do you find a substitute for—for seeing the change of expression on faces?"

"Well, as I've told you, the voice is very revealing. But I also make a study of what I call manner. Manner can be misleading, just as facial expression sometimes is. But I find most revealing of all the witness who tries to conceal evidence. Reading over an investigation of some twenty years ago, I was impressed anew with the fact that witnesses seek to answer any question rather than the one asked.

"Through the years," he went on, "I have developed a sort of technique for sticking to the subject. Not being able to see with my eyes, I am perhaps less easily diverted from the point at issue and do not allow a witness to wander."

Andrew was at my elbow again, waiting to tell me I was wanted on the telephone. Bill arose and went with me, and when I found that it was his mother I put him on the wire. The newspapers had called her, and in this way she had learned of Eve's murder. Now she was anxious for us to come back to town as soon as possible, for, like Mr. Marshall and like Bessie before him, she was beginning to feel that there was something wrong about the place itself. I was thankful she had no intimation Bill had been accused of Aunt Maggie's murder.

"I suppose the newspapers will be out here next," I said to Bill.

"Yes," he admitted, "they've already been calling: up, but Mr. Marshall has told Andrew to say we are not answering the telephone. I'm afraid that really does mean they will be here as soon as they can find the place. Just don't say anything, no matter what they ask. Let me talk to them or, better still, we will let Mr. Marshall handle that situation."

Lieutenant Gregory called to Bill from upstairs, and just as Bill went to join him Bob appeared. I had an instant, unpleasant feeling that he had been waiting until the coast was clear. "Thought I'd do a little telephoning myself," he explained. "Sally," he said, hesitating a little, "there's something I'd like to speak to you about. Don't want to upset you, but has it occurred to you that you may be rather on a spot?"

"What do you mean?" I asked.

"I mean if Eve told you anything. Just wanted to warn you. Lots of things been going on, you know." Bob's eyes, usually filled with dancing lights, were now quite serious.

"But she didn't tell me anything," I said. "I never meant to give the impression that she did."

"Well, it might not be a bad idea to give a rebroadcast," he said, patting me on the shoulder. "Can't run the risk of anything happening to you, my dear."

Before anything further could be said, Kirk came through the drawing-room door and Bob, excusing himself, stepped into the telephone closet. Instead of returning to the drawing room as I had intended, I turned into the dining room, for no other reason than to see if Kirk would follow. And I couldn't help wondering if Bob had faked that telephone errand.

The lights had been turned out in the dining room and it was almost dark, with cavernlike recesses of shadow on all sides. As I groped my way nervously across the room toward the light switch, which for some strange reason had been placed at the library door, I was startled out of all proportion when I heard Kirk's voice and realized that he was just behind me.

"Look, Sally," he asked, "may I speak to you a moment?"

I turned; the room was a little lighter now that I was accustomed to the change, and it seemed foolish to insist upon turning the light up before pausing to listen.

"What is it, Kirk?" I asked, striving to make my voice sound natural.

"Nothing much," he answered. "I just wanted to say that if I were you I wouldn't go around talking about that conversation with Eve. Might not be safe to let everybody know if she told you anything."

I said again, "But she didn't. I thought I made that plain."

"No," said Kirk, "no, you didn't. Anyway, just thought I'd mention it."

I looked up into Kirk's eyes and it seemed to me they had that same strange gleam which had made me uneasy in the library the night before. That gleam that could make me think of a werewolf. It was odd, because there were no lights in the room now, except that pale shaft from the hall. Powerless to move, I stuttered, "I—I was—going to turn on the lights."

"Where's the switch?" he asked, and the sound of his voice made everything normal again. With light flooding the room, I knew I had been letting my imagination run wild.

"You were pretty mysterious about your own conversation with Eve," I reminded him.

"Oh," Kirk laughed, a little self-consciously, "you see, I was meddling. It wasn't what that policeman tried to intimate, because I never did like Eve a little bit. I was a fool, I suppose, but my mission seems to have been similar to Claire's and Alice's and maybe Bob's, too." Kirk's face got red and he looked embarrassed. "You see, I had an idea that perhaps if I used a little of that he-man stuff you recommended that I could persuade her to lay off Bob and Claire. Does that sound too foolish, Sally?"

I looked at him with my mouth open. "Kirk," I said, "I think you are a fool, but a fool who has nice instincts."

He took both my hands in his, looked deep into my eyes for a long moment, and I was sure he was on the verge of telling me something. Then the door from the kitchen opened and Andrew came in. Kirk let my hands fall. "Thanks, Sally," he said.

XXIII

ALTHOUGH I SOMETIMES SUSPECT it requires a bit of conniving on Andrew's part not to miss anything that goes on, such was not actually the case when he interrupted my interview with Kirk. He was legitimately on his way to answer the front doorbell. As I followed him, intending to return to the drawing room, I saw that Bill was already at the door and heard what might be described as the overtones of a commotion.

Curiosity drew me farther and there on the porch were, of all people, Judge and Mrs. Warren. The judge was indignantly expressing his opinion to a carload of photographers and reporters who had arrived simultaneously. Apparently, just as a whole battery of cameras was trained on the stretcher which bore Eve to the ambulance, the judge and Mrs. Warren had unwittingly come between and were now a part of the picture.

What a time for callers, and especially such callers. Instantly my mind had flown to Kirk's suggestion of that morning.

Could it be possible that the Warrens were trying to smoke us out in order to buy the place as a bargain?

I put the thought resolutely from my mind and stepped forward to greet them. These were old friends of my grandparents, so solid and respectable that it was impossible to associate them with anything underhand. The judge, looking all the more squat in morning coat and striped trousers, is very much the old-style Southern gentleman, even without a goatee. His white-haired wife, taller by a head, is one of those sweet, soft-looking old ladies who can be as hard as nails when it comes to getting her own way. How I should have loved to duck and run.

The judge was still vituperating. "Impudent young whipper-snappers," he sputtered. "Like to have them come up before me in court. Ah, Sally, my dear, such distressing news. Such distressing news. We came to see if we could be of any service."

"Such a terrible thing to happen in your grandmother's house," said Mrs. Warren, who is quite deaf, yet never raises her voice. "I cannot believe that it is true. Have you really had a murder, my dear?"

"Two," I said, automatically holding up two fingers and motioning her into the drawing room. The judge followed, leaving Bill to deal with the gentlemen of the press, who seemed pleased enough to see the judicial coat-tails turned in their direction.

"Dear me!" Mrs. Warren ejaculated. "What have you done to this room? Or am I seeing double? There certainly are two fire-places in here."

I explained to her as fully as I could that we liked the idea of one long room instead of two square ones and that I thought it gave a beautiful effect of spaciousness.

"Spaciousness," she sniffed. "Looks like the state apartments at Windsor Castle to me."

"Oh, no," Bob objected with one of his whimsical smiles, "not nearly enough gilt for that."

The men, of course, had risen and had to remain standing while each name was repeated twice for Mrs. Warren and she had got everybody's family relationships straight. She insisted upon calling Kirk Mr. Price and asking if he was related to the Prices of North Carolina. "Glad to hear it," she said inexplicably when it was finally dinned into her head that he was neither a Price nor a North Carolinian.

"And how is your dear grandmother?" to Claire. "We went to school together in Switzerland, you know. You are really just like her, except that her hair was dark while yours has that lovely Titian shade."

"Can't see what the young men can be thinking about to let such a beautiful girl stay single," the judge remarked with intended gallantry.

"May I give you some tea?" I asked, as Roberts came in to say that Bill was wanted in the library again. Mr. Marshall hastily arose and made his excuses, and so did Mr. Dodson, both glad to escape the callers even though it meant a session with the police. The judge, learning with something akin to horror that the police were actually encamped in the house, was instantly on his feet, insisting that he would speak a word to whoever was in charge. "I knew your father and your grandfather," he told me benignantly. "I will see that you are not inconvenienced any more than is necessary, my dear."

"That's very sweet of you," I acknowledged, knowing that it was useless to try to stop him. I could imagine him telling Lieutenant Gregory, with great dignity, that the charges against Bill were absurd because he had known Bill's wife's grandfather. Of course, he was right in a way, but it wasn't a way that went very far any longer.

As Mrs. Warren sipped her tea she plied us all with questions, to which most of the answers had to be shouted several times. "I should think you could not bear to think of staying here after all that has happened," she told me, her keen old eyes watching my every expression.

"Oh," I said, "I love the house. I spent practically all my summers here as a child, you know."

"Yes, of course, but how do you feel about it now?"

I looked her squarely in the eyes and said, "Well, I'm still planning to have little Sally make her debut here. This room is perfect for it. The receiving line can stand between these two fireplaces."

"How old is she now?" she asked.

"Only two," I admitted. "I hope all this will be forgotten long before she's old enough for a debut. Anyway, I just plainly do not believe in haunted houses. Some human agency is responsible for what has happened this weekend. Not the house itself."

"Roswell has never had such a scandal," Mrs. Warren observed with relish. I could picture her serving it up to her bridge club, a choice morsel, equal to breast of guinea under glass. "You are sure, my dear, that you have no suspicions?"

"Oh, well," I answered, "I'm getting to the point where I suspect my own shadow. Take care I don't start suspecting innocent callers."

She met my inane smile with a shrewd look from her bright old eyes, stirred her tea and sipped again. Glancing around at the group, she said unexpectedly, "I can see where it does rather place you in a delicate position. No one to suspect but your guests."

Andrew came in softly, made a pretense of raising the lid of the hot-water kettle and whispered, "Miss Sally, ma'am, can you come out in the hall quick?"

I looked at him questioningly, but his eyes were politely noncommittal. "If you will excuse me," I shouted to Mrs. Warren, "some trouble in the kitchen."

"She's gone, Miss Sally," Andrew burst forth in a sibilant whisper the moment we were outside the door.

"Who's gone?"

"Miss Alice. I see her slip out the back door with her coat and hat on. I think she just gone for a walk. But it ain't safe with all what's goin' on, so I keep my eye out and I see her run over to Mr. Bob's car and get in and start it up. Next thing I know, she off like a shot out of a gun."

"Oh, dear," I said, staring at Andrew stupidly. Harassed by Mrs. Warren, I had not even missed Alice.

"If you tell them polices, they sho' will bring her back," he reminded me. Right or wrong, Andrew could not find it in his heart to take sides with the police.

"Andrew," I asked, "do you know anything about this second murder? Miss Alice . . ."

"No'm, Miss Sally. I ain't had no time to be upstairs since lunch. 'Sides, I was feeling too bad 'bout what them polices made me tell—"

"All right. Don't say anything to anybody about Miss Alice until I've had a moment to think."

Should I go to Bob or to the police? As I stood there, it seemed to me there was only one thing I could do. Dismissing Andrew and walking across the hall as calmly as I could, lest eyes be watching, I paused for a moment outside the library door. Should I knock? No, that would mean going through preliminaries which would consume more time. And Alice was racing along that darkening road toward town or toward oblivion. Her driving had always been notoriously bad. She might wreck herself at any moment. That big tree at the turn—

If Alice were guilty—or even if she only knew something—and her car was wrecked by accident or design, where would the rest of us be? All this went through my mind like lightning, actually in the small space of time between grasping the silver handle of the library door and turning it.

"Excuse me," I said, leaning against the door as I closed it behind me, breathless as a runner caught up in midsprint, "but Alice— Miss Dunbar—has gone. I thought you would want to know."

Lieutenant Gregory, already on his feet, went into action like a machine gun, issuing orders in all directions even before I could answer the questions he asked. "How did she get away? Go after her, Anderson. What sort of car is it, Mrs. Stuart? Maroon sedan. What color is that? Brownish-red, Anderson. You wouldn't know the license number, would you, Mrs. Stuart? All right, Anderson, if you don't catch her before she reaches the highway, pick up the number when it is broadcast. Roberts, tell headquarters to get the number and have county and state troopers look out for the car."

"Bob would know the number," suggested Bill. "Or he would have his ownership certificate."

"Never mind," Lieutenant Gregory waved him aside. "I want Anderson to be on the way before we have any relatives messing up things."

Of course, Bob went into a tailspin when he heard the news. "It's all this damned third degree," he stormed. "My sister isn't able to stand it. You've scared her out of her senses and she'll probably wreck the car and be killed. If anything like that happens"— he glared at Lieutenant Gregory for a moment, then finished in a voice grown suddenly calm—"I'll kill you."

In all the excitement, I don't know when it was that I missed Mrs. Warren. She was not in the drawing room where I had left her, nor was she with the judge in the library. Thinking back again to that offer to buy the place and the possibilities suggested by Kirk, it occurred to me in my upset state that her movements might bear watching. Perhaps Mrs. Warren knew about the secret room. Perhaps she was even now establishing contact with the person responsible for all our troubles.

Looking in one after another of the downstairs rooms, I was on the point of starting upstairs when I saw her coming down the back steps from the second floor. She looked a shade embarrassed when she first sighted me, but regained her composure instantly and smilingly explained, "I just wanted to see your dear grandmother's room. I've visited in it so often with her." Then smoothly putting me on the defensive, "But it was in a terrible state of confusion, my dear. I should think you would wish to speak to the servants."

"I should think it would be in a state of confusion," I told her, a little maliciously. "That's where Eve Benedict was killed just a few hours ago."

"Oh," she said. "Well, I wouldn't let the servants be getting slack. You have to keep right behind them, you know."

I stood there, feeling completely baffled. Of course, it was the natural thing for her to come to call when she heard that the grandchild of an old friend was in trouble. It was possible, I knew, that her upstairs tour could have been prompted by nothing more than curiosity to see an old friend's room and incidentally to pry into my housekeeping and whatever changes we had happened to make on the second floor. But my grandmother's room was at the front of the house and she had come down the back stairs.

It was a relief to have the judge appear opportunely and say he thought they should be starting home. And it was then we discovered that Alice had not escaped in Bob's car, but in the one driven by the Warrens, which was an identical model.

This meant more dashing about and more telephoning to headquarters. It meant, too, that Alice had more than a head start on her pursuers. And it meant that we had the Warrens on our hands indefinitely. Bill offered to drive them home or to have Andrew do so, but Lieutenant Gregory would not allow it. "Looks a little funny," he grumbled, "that key being left in the lock."

"But people often do that in the country," Bill reminded him. "Besides, they'll be in everybody's hair, including your own."

"Can't be helped."

Nor did he relent when the judge went to him and threatened to have him discharged. "Sorry, sir. I didn't mean to give you the idea you yourself were not at liberty to go. But I do not wish any-one who was on the place at the time of either of the murders to leave. I am sure your car will be returned shortly and you will then be free to go or remain as you like."

"I've been trying to get the judge to trade in that car," Mrs. Warren mourned. "Now it will probably be wrecked and we will be accused of manslaughter or sued or something."

Mr. Marshall inquired of Lieutenant Gregory if he might use the telephone long enough to tell his butler to keep the dinner warm, but that request also was denied. "Got to hold the line open," he was told.

"Be funny, if it were not so damn serious," Bill whispered in my ear.

Lieutenant Gregory drew us both aside. "What about our little test?" he asked me. "Were you—er, approached by anyone, on the subject of your conversation with Mrs. Benedict?"

"By practically everybody. Alice asked me about it while we were having tea and Claire backed her up. But, of course, women have so much curiosity. I never did say definitely though, thanks to Mr. Dodson breaking into the conversation at the psychological moment."

"Then Miss Dunbar may have gone away with the impression that you had definite information?"

"Perhaps, but her brother knew differently. At different times, both he and Kirk warned me that such knowledge put me on the spot. I told them both that I knew nothing whatever."

"I'm a little sorry about that," he said. "It might not have been a bad idea to let everybody think—"

"And have something happen to Sally," Bill cut in indignantly. "No, thank you. I didn't care for the idea in the beginning."

Lieutenant Gregory again took up his individual questioning in the library and I took up the white woman's burden in the drawing room. Aunt Maggie murdered. Eve murdered. Bill suspected. Alice off on a tangent. And I must still sit and shout small talk to two elderly bores who, so far as I knew, might be the diabolical cause of it all.

No prosecuting attorney could have thought of more questions to ask about the murders than Mrs. Warren fired at me. And with clocklike regularity her mind reverted to the subject of the misappropriated automobile. I could only hope that she did not visualize Alice as I did. At every curve or turn of the road, rushing headlong to disaster. The car a mass of ruins. Alice herself thrown clear, but lying still and white, her lips never to open again.

Vaguely I noted when Claire came back from the library and sank limply into a chair a little removed from our group. Kirk left us then and Bob moved over to sit by Claire. If they spoke at all, it was in whispers but, anyway, they could not have talked above our own hullabaloo. Bob must have been called out eventually, for when I glanced in that direction again I saw that it was Kirk who sat by Claire.

The telephone rang, shrill in the stillness. Each of us, save Mrs. Warren, started up involuntarily, then settled tensely to wait. "What is it?" she asked, conscious of the change in atmosphere.

But we were all too busy listening to answer. Andrew and Roberts met outside the door, both on the way to the telephone and we heard Roberts say that he would take the call. Then he evidently pulled the door of the little closet shut, for we could hear nothing. And when he came out, he strode back to the library without a word.

"Have they found her?" Mrs. Warren demanded.

I looked hopefully at the judge, but obviously he had had enough of Lieutenant Gregory and said we would have to wait and see.

Well, so had I had enough of Lieutenant Gregory. And why should he be concentrating so on Bill? Did he hope to break him down finally, perhaps by confronting him one by one with his supposed accomplices? I could not have told which was more tormenting, Mrs. Warren's conversation or my own thoughts, but the combination was rapidly becoming unbearable.

They brought Alice back finally. In handcuffs.

"What the hell?" roared Bob. "Take those things off my sister."

"All right, all right," Anderson agreed calmly. "But we had to get her back some way. And we had to bring along three cars. Hers and mine and the troopers'. There wasn't nobody to hold her and her fightin' and scratchin' like a wildcat."

"Ask him if our car is all right," Mrs. Warren instructed the judge in a stage whisper.

"Yes'm," said Anderson, turning politely.

"He says it's all right," boomed the judge.

"She went off the road," Anderson explained, "just after she reached the highway, but just down into a little gully and the mud was too slick for her to get out again."

"I'd have been all right," Alice told him spitefully, "if you hadn't come along. These nice highway policemen were getting the car out for me. At least, I thought they were nice then."

She glared at the two inoffensive young men, who blushed dark red under their tan, and one of them rubbed his hand across a long scratch on his cheek.

In spite of her upset state, Alice apologized prettily enough to Judge and Mrs. Warren when she found she had taken their car. Mrs. Warren prescribed milk punch and bed immediately and offered to stay and sit with her; but when Lieutenant Gregory fixed Alice with his eagle eye and said he wanted to wind things up, she was surprisingly docile.

As Judge and Mrs. Warren took a reluctant departure, Bill said, "I'll go and see if Andrew has the cars ready to travel, just in case we ever need them again."

I followed him as far as the dining room, where I told him about Mrs. Warren's surreptitious visit upstairs. "It's silly," I acknowledged, "but do you think they could possibly be trying to scare us into selling at a bargain?"

"Ask me any Tuesday, Wednesday or Thursday and I would say that you are crazy with the heat, full of prunes and drunk on Coca-Cola," said Bill, passing his hand wearily through his red hair, "but on this weekend I am beginning to think anything can happen."

"Anything can happen," I agreed, "but you didn't kill Aunt Maggie and we have got to find some way to prove it."

"That reminds me," said Bill, "I'm beginning to think we got a bum steer this morning. You know that note about the silver closet? I suppose it was Aunt Maggie's handwriting all right, but I believe it was planted—"

"Planted?"

"I mean somebody thought if we were diverted to the silver closet that we would stop looking for any other secret room. How did you happen to find the note?"

"Bob found it, but that doesn't mean anything. It was Kirk who opened the table. And it was Kirk who went through Aunt Maggie's papers this morning—"

As we stared at each other uncomfortably, Claire came in and Bill excused himself and went on to the kitchen. "I suppose this proves Alice did it," she said tonelessly.

"You mean, her running away?"

"Well, yes, that and things in general. She's acted so strangely the whole time. I believe she knew Eve killed Aunt Maggie."

I looked at Claire in astonishment. "Why do you say that?" I asked.

"Well," she went on calmly; "Aunt Maggie told me last night before dinner that she and Eve had quarreled and that Eve had threatened to kill her. Then this afternoon I saw Alice coming out of Eve's room just before I went to call on Eve myself. I didn't want to run into her, so I went back inside and waited a moment."

Lieutenant Gregory had expressed wonder that Eve's visitors did not fall over each other. This obviously explained why. They had all been too cautious.

"You told them this, in the library?"

"Oh no," said Claire. "Of course not."

The door from the library opened and Mr. Marshall came in, looking embarrassed and, it seemed to me, hungry. At any rate, his eyes strayed wistfully toward the covered silver dishes of cold food on the sideboards. Then he took out his handkerchief, wiped his forehead and said:

"Miss Dunbar has confessed."

XXIV

THERE WERE FIFTEEN OF US gathered there in the library following the rather sketchy and perfunctorily eaten supper which Mr. Marshall had insisted upon "for the sake of our health."

Now, as we grouped ourselves for what we referred to with hollow facetiousness as "the séance," someone asked Mr. Dodson if he wished us to sit so that we might clasp hands in a circle. But he said, quite impersonally, that this was not necessary.

The four servants were ranged in a dark row near the book-lined wall next to the dining room. Lindy, although presumably absent at the time of the first murder, was there with Thomas and Andrew and Bessie. Andrew had raised his eyebrows disapprovingly when I suggested that straight chairs be brought in for them from the dining room, but I said, a little impatiently, "Of course, you'll have to sit. This may go on for quite a while."

"For years and years," said Bob, with a ghost of his old lightness. "We'll all probably grow long beards while we sit. I hope you brought your razor, Andrew." And from Andrew's sheepish grin it was all too obvious that he had.

Rather strategically, it seemed to me, Anderson sat near the dining-room door and Roberts near the hall door, which is exactly opposite the fireplace. The sofa, on which I sat with Mr. Marshall on one side and Bill on the other, had been placed so that the group really did form something of a square circle, with the servants in the background. Alice was in a chair on Bill's other side and next to her was Bob, then Claire and then Kirk nearest to Lieutenant

231

Gregory. In this way, Kirk and Bob and also Alice and Claire, of
course, sat with their back to the hall door. On Lieutenant Gregory's
other side sat Mr. Dodson in the wing chair next to the fireplace.

The fire had burned low on the hearth and nobody thought to
replenish it, for, of course, the room was comfortably warm from
the furnace heat, not to mention that extra warmth which is always generated by the proximity of human bodies. Andrew had
placed a tray, bearing a silver pitcher of water and goblets, on the
library table, where the light from one of the reading lamps shone
on them and brought out an additional gleam. The yellow roses,
nodding in their crystal bowl near by, were the only reminder that
we had expected to pass a quite different weekend.

An almost abnormal quietude hung over the room as we waited
for Mr. Dodson to begin his questioning. Shifting himself in the
deep-cushioned chair and turning his head as though to take an
inclusive view of the group, he said, "I should like to ask everyone
to stay put while we are conducting this little investigation. I don't
mean that you must sit like statues, but I don't want anybody
moving from his or her chair or about the room. In other words, I
don't want any unnecessary sounds or movements to distract my
attention or to interfere with my hearing. If you will shut your eyes
for a moment, I think you will come nearer having some concep-
tion of how important sounds become when sight is absent."

Involuntarily we all closed our eyes, and I think we must all
have held our breath too, in a concerted effort to remain perfectly
quiet, for in another moment you could quite plainly hear the sound
of full-time breathing resumed.

"Good," approved Mr. Dodson. "I think we are all now what
the spiritualists would call en rapport."

Claire shivered and looked around the room and both Bob and
Kirk put out a hand to reassure her.

"First," said Mr. Dodson, "I want to say that we will not go into
unnecessary detail. You are not under oath, as this is not an official inquest. Of course, if anyone should wish to give a signed confession, this can be sworn to, as already has been done in the case
of Miss Dunbar. It is my hope and I may say that it is my belief

that this session will make an official inquest unnecessary. Roberts holds the signed confession of Miss Dunbar, but let us disregard that document as though it did not exist. We have had two murders. We have a confession for only one. I do not believe Miss Dunbar could have committed the first one, yet I believe that there is a connection between the two. Lieutenant Gregory does not agree with me as to this. He believes that the murders are the work of different people. If such is the case, then more than one person is behind what has happened here since Mrs. Ambler came down those back stairs last night to meet her death in the narrow passage at the back of the house.

"In other words"—Mr. Dodson paused for a moment before going on—"I repeat that I firmly believe there is a connection between the two murders, and therefore if more than one person is guilty a thorough sifting of the evidence in one case should bring to light evidence against more than one person."

"I think we are wasting our time," Lieutenant Gregory remarked with more than a little show of irritation. "After all, we have a confession in one case and in the other we have evidence sufficient to justify an arrest. What more can you want? Put Miss Dunbar and Mr. Stuart behind the bars and this case will break wide open. My job is done and I have other work to look after. I'm not supposed to spend my life on an open and shut case."

"But you agreed to indulge me," Mr. Dodson reminded, with an ingratiating smile, "and perhaps you will not regret the waste of time."

"All right, but let's get along with it."

"Very well. Technically we do not have an actual witness. We have someone who heard, but who did not see the principals in the first murder. Andrew, will you stand and repeat your story of what you heard last night?"

"Yes, yes, sir," Andrew replied in a scared voice. "Yes, sir—" Grasping the edge of the reading table, Andrew tried to steady himself and his voice at the same time.

"Go on," said Mr. Dodson kindly.

"Mr. Bill—" Andrew looked at Bill beseechingly.

"That's all right, Andrew," said Bill. "Go on."

So Andrew told his story again, haltingly and with many lapses into silence, from which he had to be prodded by Lieutenant Gregory or Mr. Dodson, and I must say that it had the ring of truth, nor did it vary from that earlier version as I remembered it and as Roberts had it written down in his notebook.

When Andrew came to that part where Aunt Maggie was said to have cried out, Mr. Dodson stopped him. "I want you," he said, "to imitate as nearly as possible the tone and expression of Mrs. Ambler's voice." And then as Andrew hesitated, looking vague and even more helpless, Mr. Dodson explained, "Say it as nearly as you can like Mrs. Ambler said it."

Andrew's face cleared. "Yes, sir. 'Well,' she say, 'Don't you dare lay hands on me, Willie.'" And with the Negro's special gift for mimicry, Andrew's voice rose at the end so that what had begun as a command ended as an entreaty. It was, in fact, the whole gamut of emotion, from arrogant self-confidence to desperate panic.

Mr. Dodson nodded his head. "That will do, Andrew," he said, and I wondered if Mr. Dodson's reaction in any way approached my own. For there was something about that last utterance of Aunt Maggie's that seemed wrong to me. It was not in the words. I felt confident that they were her own. Nor was it in the tone, exactly. Whatever it was eluded me, but I felt that if I had the time in some less hectic atmosphere, or maybe possessed a little more brains, I could figure it out. "I'll probably think of it after I've gone to bed tonight," I told myself. There would be plenty of time for thinking if Bill were taken to jail. How would I ever sleep again with such a cloud hanging over our lives?

Mr. Dodson's face wore a sort of hooded look. With sight, I decided, he probably would have made a marvelous poker player. He asked me to repeat my own part of the evening's performance, which I did. I told of finding the house deserted, of seeing the strange man in the driveway, of hearing footsteps in the kitchen and a downstairs door slam while I was upstairs. I told of the telephone message which Andrew said he received. Of the green scrap of paper with its sinister warning. Of the quarrel overheard between

Aunt Maggie and Eve. Of finding Aunt Maggie dead and of discovering later that her body had been disturbed. I told of seeing the red light and of the door which Kirk and I had seen open and close. I told of finding the second message on green paper and of the scrap of paper which Bob found. I told of being asked to settle the argument between Lindy and Thomas about Ephraim and said that while I was reasonably certain it was Ephraim's footsteps I heard in the kitchen, and Ephraim who slammed a door, I had no notion otherwise as to any explanation of anything that had happened.

"When only yourself and Mrs. Benedict were left in this room after dinner, you say that she told you she was going to the powder room, which is in the hall?" Mr. Dodson asked.

"I don't believe she said that exactly. As I remember she said she was going to powder her nose, which might have meant a trip upstairs. It was later, when we were all trying to recall where we must have been at the time that Eve said she had been in the powder room. And that's a strange thing, but she said then that it reminded her of something, or rather that it explained something."

"Can you be a little more definite, please, Mrs. Stuart?"

"I don't know," I hesitated. "I rather got the impression that something that had puzzled her when she was in the powder room was explained by the murder or something in connection with it. We had been trying to figure the exact time it occurred. I remember she did not finish what she was saying and that one of us asked her what she meant."

"And what did she say then?"

"I don't remember exactly. It was an evasive answer. I think she said, 'Oh, just something I hadn't thought of before,' or something like that. I thought she was just trying to be mysterious. And thinking, too, that if she hadn't kept me in the library I might have reached the passage in time to prevent—Aunt Maggie's murder."

"Does anyone else recall exactly what Mrs. Benedict said?" asked Mr. Dodson.

Everybody seemed to be waiting for someone else to speak, then Kirk said, "I believe Sally has quoted her correctly, at least so far as the meaning of Mrs. Benedict's statement is concerned."

"Thank you," said Mr. Dodson, "and now, Mrs. Stuart, do you remember who asked Mrs. Benedict to complete her unfinished statement?"

As I looked around, trying to remember, I wondered if Mr. Dodson felt that the identity of that person might provide a clue to Eve's murder. While I pondered this question, Bob said, "It was I who asked her what she had started to say."

"Ah," said Mr. Dodson, "then everyone present had some intimation that Mrs. Benedict might know something. Your question and her evasion of a direct answer would have made this fact all the more pointed."

"Yes," Bob admitted, "but I did not think of it that way at the time."

"Your question was a perfectly natural one," Mr. Dodson agreed. "I dare say if you had not asked it, someone else would have. In fact, I am surprised that one of the ladies did not beat you to it." Then turning to me again, "Mrs. Stuart, it did not occur to you that Mrs. Benedict might have passed on through the breakfast room and have met Mrs. Ambler in the passage, even when you knew they had quarreled before dinner?"

"I didn't take their quarrel seriously. But yes, it did occur to me later on, though I knew that it didn't make sense."

"Yet the prospect of losing her alimony might provide a very strong motive," said Mr. Dodson, apparently more to himself than to anyone else.

Bill was questioned then and the time element discussed. Andrew had testified that Bill had the ping-pong rackets and net and balls in his hands when he found him upstairs in our room and was just ready to start back downstairs.

Everyone else in turn gave an account of his or her whereabouts, Alice fretfully complaining that she thought she should not be questioned again after having signed a confession. Bessie and Thomas and Lindy were questioned too, but nothing came out which seemed to shed any further light on the situation. "Can't us go, now?" Bessie asked when that was over.

But no, Mr. Dodson wished us all to stay put as he again expressed it. "Miss Dunbar," he asked, "would you mind explaining why you ran away when you knew that you had no possible chance of escape?"

"Because I couldn't stand any more of this horrible inquisition. I wasn't trying to escape. I only wanted to go where I could be quiet. These policemen are fiends. They don't care whether anybody is guilty or not. All they want is a confession." Alice looked from one to another vindictively, her eyes blazing. I had never seen her have so much color or fire.

"Is that why you signed the confession?"

"Yes, I signed it so I could have some peace, but I'm not getting it."

"And not because you were guilty?"

"No"—Alice bit her lip but caught herself up quickly—"I mean, of course, I am guilty, but—"

"Roberts," asked Mr. Dodson, "will you check Miss Dunbar's statement with the confession? And now, Miss Dunbar, please tell us how you killed Mrs. Benedict."

"With the dart, of course," said Alice. "I—I stabbed her."

"Yes, we know, but tell us what you did before that. What passed between you and Mrs. Benedict when you first went to her room, and any other details that led up to the—er, killing."

Alice had that scared-rabbit look again and I thought, she is right, they should not torture her this way. After all, she had made a confession. "Oh," she cried, "it's all there in that paper. I've told it once. I won't go through it again."

"Is this necessary?" Bob demanded hotly. "My sister committed no murder. Any confession obtained from her under stress is without value."

"What did you say when you went into Mrs. Benedict's room, Miss Dunbar?" Mr. Dodson asked quietly.

"I told her she had to stay out of my brother's life," said Alice: Then the words came tumbling out, "I said I knew something that would stop her alimony if I told her husband. She said she would

kill me if I told him. She started toward me, and I grabbed up the
dart and stabbed her with it and she fell back on the chaise longue.
I—I killed her in self-defense."

"Roberts," asked Mr. Dodson, "does that statement check with
Miss Dunbar's previous one?"

"No, sir, the conversation is different and in her previous statement Miss Dunbar makes no mention that Mrs. Benedict made any
move toward an attack. She says that Mrs. Benedict just laughed
at her when she told Mrs. Benedict to stay out of her brother's life.
She says Mrs. Benedict told her she (Miss Dunbar) had no attrac-
tion for men. Besides, Mrs. Benedict was struck while lying down
on the sofa in a more or less relaxed position."

"You are all just trying to tangle me up," Alice spit out the
words, her eyes roving from one to the other.

There was a moment of waiting silence. Then Claire spoke up.
"It's all right," she said. "Don't badger her any more. Alice didn't
do it. She couldn't have, because—because I did it."

Sternly, Lieutenant Gregory's voice rose above the confused
babble which followed this startling announcement. "Why didn't
you admit this when questioned earlier, Miss Harper?" he asked.

Claire looked at him appealingly and, even in the face of all the
circumstances which may prevail against her, it is remarkable how
appealing a beautiful woman can be. I was sorry Mr. Dodson could
not see her. "Because," she said, "I did not know that anyone else would
be accused. But naturally I cannot let—Alice—suffer in my place."

"Don't pay any attention to her, Officer," Kirk ordered. "It's
impossible. She couldn't have done it."

Lieutenant Gregory turned on him with that look of a tiger
ready to spring. "And why not?"

Kirk's mouth dropped open and he stared at Lieutenant Gregory, obviously at a loss. "Why—why, because it is impossible," he
said finally.

"My witness," Mr. Dodson politely called the situation to order,
and Lieutenant Gregory settled back into his chair unwillingly.
"Miss Harper," Mr. Dodson asked, "will you please tell us how you
killed Mrs. Benedict?"

It was Claire's turn to look blank, then she brightened and said, "I prefer not to discuss the details now. I don't have to, do I, Mr. Marshall?"

Mr. Marshall cleared his throat, hesitated and Claire, cheeks flushed, raced on, "Isn't it enough that I—I killed her? I will make a statement later through my—my lawyers. Of course, I killed her in self-defense, but my lawyers can go into all that. Now, can't we go home?"

In a way, it was all just like Claire, to think that even the consequences of murder could be arranged to suit her convenience. In another way, it didn't sound at all as I should have imagined Claire would react to such circumstances. But evidently both Bob and Kirk believed her. There was, however, a subtle difference in their expressions. Bob's, it seemed to me, was all horror, while that of Kirk was a mixture of anguish and compassion.

"You wish to sign a confession?" Lieutenant Gregory asked impersonally.

"No," cried Bob and Kirk in unison.

"No," said Mr. Dodson. "I want you to tell us first how you killed Mrs. Benedict."

"She didn't kill her," Kirk burst out.

"Do you really know something about this case, Mr. Pierce?" Mr. Dodson asked mildly.

Kirk lost his belligerent look. "Yes," he said slowly. "Enough. I killed Eve Benedict."

"Your motive?"

"Oh, just a misguided sense of—of chivalry, I suppose," Kirk answered. "Just a gesture."

"What the hell do you mean, just a gesture?" Lieutenant Gregory demanded angrily.

Kirk gave him look for look and suddenly Kirk's own eyes were full of a reckless, smiling deviltry. "Effect of the old South, you know. This house. White columns. Magnolias. Hospitality. Haven't you felt it too, Officer? Rather dying out down here. Too bad."

"He's drunk, Mr. Dodson," said Bill.

"No, he's not drunk," declared Lieutenant Gregory. "Roberts, put the handcuffs on him."

"No, no!" Claire cried, as Roberts laid down his notebook, stood up and reached into his coat pocket. And "No" someone else said.

"It's all foolishness," Bob added. "I killed Eve Benedict. After all, nobody had a better motive. She had it coming to her and I'm not sorry—"

As we all sat there in a sort of stupefied silence, Lieutenant Gregory said, "Four confessions. This is carrying politeness a little too far."

Bob remarked, as casually as though he were really seated in a movie theater. "Well, this seems to be where I came in. Shall we be going?"

"Yes," Lieutenant Gregory began, "we'll all go to the tower and—"

Then three things happened in such rapid succession as to seem almost simultaneous. Although no one in the room appeared to move, the door to the hall opened, all the lights in the house went out and something whizzed past overhead and came to rest with a sort of thud in the wall above the mantel.

There were screams and muttered curses and general confusion as we all came to our feet and milled about in the dark. I grabbed Bill and held on to him and Lieutenant Gregory yelled out to Roberts to "catch him." But Roberts, at the door, shouted back that no one had gone past.

Then somebody struck a match and somebody else struck one and candles were lighted. Roberts touched with an experimental finger the button of the electric switch at the door and the light came back on in spite of the fact that the hall and library remained dark.

"Look above the mantel," Mr. Dodson commanded.

We all looked. There, stuck in the canvas of Uncle Fred's portrait, right through that fierce old gentleman's beard, was a feather-tipped dart, similar to the one that had killed Eve Benedict.

XXV

"THAT TIES IT," SNARLED LIEUTENANT GREGORY, when he saw the dart buried in Uncle Fred's beard. "First, we have a murder when only the house-party guests are present. We have another when the police are in the house. Now, a third is attempted when the entire group—and the police—are gathered in one room."

"But nobody in this room could have opened the door and turned out the light," Roberts objected. "They might have thrown the dart, but they couldn't have opened the door. I was right here and I'd have seen them."

"And I'd have heard them," said Mr. Dodson conclusively. "There was no unusual movement in the room before the door opened and the light was turned out. I couldn't be sure about just afterward, for everybody began to shift at once and sounds were all mixed up. Somebody in here possibly could have thrown that dart. Or it could have been thrown from the hall."

"Then what are we waiting for?" Lieutenant Gregory demanded, with the anguish of a bull who finds himself tethered in a china shop. "Roberts, Anderson, nothing to do but search the damned place again. I'm going to telephone for more men. I'll get to the bottom of this if I have to call out the national guard."

Anderson and Roberts, with drawn revolvers, were already outside the door and Anderson shouted back from the drawing room that the light there and in the hall had only been switched off and that nothing was wrong with the current. Apparently whoever turned out the library light had first turned out all the others, and reaching in to press that button had been able to step backward into a dark cloak of invisibility.

"Guess we might as well lend a hand, too," Kirk suggested. "How about it, Lieutenant?" he asked, as the disgruntled officer paused in the doorway. "Do we go or stay? I mean, as a confessed murderer, do I have the run of the premises?"

"You're all getting a big kick out of those confessions, I guess," Lieutenant Gregory observed surlily. "No, everybody stays in this room until the place has been thoroughly searched. Mr. Marshall, I hold you responsible for the presence of everyone until I have had time to telephone for reinforcements. Ought to be somebody here from the solicitor general's office any time now, even if he got lost a couple of times on the way."

The deep distress on Mr. Marshall's face was almost more than I could bear. He looked as though his kind setter eyes might overflow at any moment. "But—but—" he sputtered, "that's all foolishness. I'm no detective, but what has just happened makes it plain to me that nobody in the room could be guilty. There's some outside person back of all this. What his purpose is, I can't imagine. But it seems to me that there's no further use in holding everyone here for somebody to take potshots at them with these—er—darts or to strangle them on stairways. I admit I don't feel any too safe myself. Wouldn't it be the sensible plan to let us all go back to town and you take over the place for as long as necessary? We can be reached at our respective homes. I assure you that nobody will make any attempt to escape. I—I feel that I can be just as responsible as though we remain here."

"Sounds like a sensible idea to me," said Bill. "This place has been searched a dozen times already and no results. I'll stay here with you if necessary, but I see no reason for further inconvenience for everyone else."

"But I won't let you stay," I shuddered, "unless I stay too."

Everybody, white-faced and some of us more than a little shaky, looked hopefully at Lieutenant Gregory. The servants, quiet now in their little huddle, added a petition. "Please, Mr. Policeman," implored Thomas, "just let us get out o' here alive."

For a long moment Lieutenant Gregory stood there and it was something to see the look of indecision on that usually determined face. "No," he said finally. "You can't go yet. I was ready to call things off and go to town. But Mr. Dodson insisted on his pretty little tea party. And where does it land us? One of you confesses and then everybody else says, 'Oh, no, she couldn't be guilty. I did it with my little hatchet.' Everybody so polite. Everybody so ready to say it was all his fault. Or maybe everybody decided if they would just confess right quick, we'd have to shut up shop and go home.

"Well," he announced, "we are not going to. Maybe those confessions were just a little leg pulling to break up the show. It may be that somebody on the outside did open the door and turn out the lights. Maybe, he even threw the dart. But somebody in this house party knows who it was. Maybe you all know. All these wholesale confessions look like it. And I'm going to clean things up before anybody leaves this place. I'm tired of all this funny business." And with that Lieutenant Gregory stalked from the room. A few minutes later we could hear him growling into the telephone.

Bob closed the door and turned the key in the lock. "Feel a little safer that way," he said, with an attempted grin. "Andrew, lock that other door, please. At least we can make the police knock when they want to come in."

There was nothing to talk about or there was too much to talk about. For what is there to say to four people who have all confessed themselves guilty of the same murder? Besides, we had all been under severe nervous strain for nearly twenty-four hours. We had struggled to maintain an outward appearance of casualness but that was no longer possible. I was tired even of trying to think. If Alice were guilty of Eve's murder, had she killed Aunt Maggie too? Had Alice really seen something on the stairway before she fainted? And even though Ephraim conceivably might have killed Aunt Maggie or anyone of us have killed Eve, who could have opened the door and turned out the lights while we all sat together in this room? And last, but somehow puzzling too, where was Plutarch? That luxury-loving animal would never have remained out of doors.

So we sank into the lethargy of waiting. Once I roused myself sufficiently to ask Mr. Dodson, "Are we going to find out anything before we are all murdered?"

He smiled. "I don't think that dart was really meant for anybody," he said, "unless perhaps for Gregory or me. I think it did just what it was intended to do, at least to an extent. That is, it has broken up the meeting. But if its purpose was to persuade Gregory to go back to town, it doesn't seem to have succeeded very well."

I don't know how long we sat there before Lieutenant Gregory finally came back and told us we could have the run of the house but not to go outside. I must have slept finally, slumped on the sofa with my head against Bill's shoulder, for I know it took me a moment or two to reorganize things when I heard Lieutenant Gregory's voice. He hadn't appreciated the humor in locking out the police. And they had found no one in their search of the house or grounds.

"No need to wait for anybody from the solicitor general's office," he concluded. "Going to finish this up. Mr. Stuart, want to question you again. We'll take the rest in turn. Stay within call," he ordered tersely.

"What time is it?" Claire asked listlessly, as a disconsolate move was made toward the drawing room. "You mean what year is it?" I heard Bob reply. And, indeed, it was all horribly like something that has been happening over and over for at least a hundred years. I lingered a moment to reassure the servants, who were reluctant to leave. When they were gone, I turned to Mr. Dodson. "May I ask a question?" I begged, in the face of Lieutenant Gregory's frown.

"It seems to me," I told Mr. Dodson, "that there was something wrong about what Andrew said Aunt Maggie said. Did it sound all right to you?"

"Ah," said Mr. Dodson, and I noticed Lieutenant Gregory and Roberts stiffen a little at his tone. "So it didn't sound exactly right to you? What seemed to be wrong?"

"I don't know," I confessed helplessly. "I thought perhaps you could figure it out."

"I think he told us what she said, all right," Mr. Dodson admitted. "But you are right, there was something a little wrong about it." He paused, seemingly to enjoy the effect his words produced, or perhaps to prolong the suspense, and it is true that we were all looking at him with bated breath. There was an expression of mingled bafflement and exasperation on Lieutenant Gregory's face which seemed to say, "He's at it again."

"What was wrong," said Mr. Dodson finally, "was the interpretation given by Andrew and everyone else to what Mrs. Ambler said. To me it was perfectly clear that when Mrs. Ambler called out 'Willie,' she was not speaking to her assailant. She was calling for help against him. Who more likely for her to call than her niece's husband?"

"Oh, yes, yes," I cried, "that's it! I see it now."

"She was calling to your husband in a desperate plea for him to come to her assistance," Mr. Dodson went on, "but unfortunately he was too far away to hear her and before she could call out again for anyone else to hear, the murderer had stopped her voice with his hands at her throat. I don't know whether murder was the original intention but, if not, I think he realized after he had gone so far that he could not turn back. So he strangled Mrs. Ambler and hurried away, perhaps just in time not to be discovered by you, Mrs. Stuart, as you came out through the breakfast room to the passage. He would not have gone into the breakfast room, knowing that the servants might be there. But, as you have shown me, there are four other exits through which he might have stepped into anonymity and comparative safety."

I was a little limp when Mr. Dodson finished speaking. "Oh, thank you, thank you!" I cried fervently, while Bill wrung his hand and Mr. Marshall said, with great satisfaction, "I knew he'd save the day."

Surprisingly, Lieutenant Gregory did not seem as pleased as the rest of us.

"But you do see that it is all right?" I insisted. "That's the way it must have been."

"Sounds very pretty," he admitted. "But you haven't proved anything. No evidence to support all this. Still got to find your murderer. If Mr. Stuart is not guilty, let him produce the killer and I'll be the first to congratulate Mr. Dodson."

Even Mr. Dodson raised his voice in protest, but Lieutenant Gregory was not to be moved. He had had a perfectly good murderer taken away from him, and unless another could be provided it was just no sale. But he finally agreed that he would make no actual arrest that night and with this we were forced to content ourselves.

"I suppose you realize, Mrs. Stuart," he grimly informed me, "that if your husband is freed of suspicion, you become the next most likely suspect unless, of course, someone else has been proved guilty in the meantime."

Bill got pretty red-headed at this, but we were all a little more accustomed to the idea of being regarded as killers and were ready to forego useless argument. And so far as my personal feelings went, there didn't seem to be much difference whether it was Bill or I who was accused. Either way, my life looked equally rosy.

"Did you draw any other conclusions?" I asked Mr. Dodson. "I mean about Eve's murder?"

Before he could answer, Lieutenant Gregory cut in, "If you will excuse us, Mrs. Stuart, I should like to finish my little talk with your husband."

In the hall I stopped by the powder room and gazed at my strained countenance, making what repairs were possible at the moment. Again my mind started its round of vicious circles. If I could only find the secret room. Why couldn't I remember that crazy jingle? Where could Plutarch have got to?

I remembered Alice had thought she heard him when she went to the basement, but Andrew had not been able to find him in the coal chute. How was it Plutarch was always escaping from the office? Because someone had opened the door, of course. The office—I sprang to my feet. Perhaps—perhaps there was an entrance from that room to the secret room.

Andrew had economically turned off the light in the office. As I touched the switch button and the interior of the small room sprang into being before my eyes, I involuntarily stepped backward, stifling a scream.

A strange man was standing in the middle of the floor. Apparently he found the encounter as awkward as I did, for we both stood there silently, staring at each other.

My first wild conclusion was that here at last was the suspicious character we had all been looking for. But even in that moment of initial shock and surprise, I was conscious of a feeling of anticlimax, inspired no doubt by his commonplace appearance. Here was no movie villain. Here was no devil with horns and tail. Here was no gorilla or-hairy ape. Here was only a stockily built young man of perhaps thirty, a little on the hard-boiled side and rather flashily dressed, it is true, but otherwise not at all remarkable-looking.

But appearances are often deceiving, of course, and I told myself that I must be very clever and engage him in unsuspecting conversation until I could pull the bell cord and summon Andrew. I could scream, if necessary, but it would be much better to be calm and take him unaware. So I said, somewhat weakly, "I didn't know there was anyone in here."

He grinned, disclosing an impressive gold tooth. "Place is lousy with police."

"What?" I asked stupidly.

"Plain-clothes man," he explained, flipping his coat lapel.

"Oh," I said, not quite convinced, but remembering that Lieutenant Gregory momentarily expected someone from the solicitor general's office. It could be true.

"Then," I suggested, trying to keep the doubt out of my voice, "you'll want to see Lieutenant Gregory."

"Yes," he agreed, "in a few moments. Just doing a little reconnoitering. Like to go over the ground and form my own conclusions, you know."

"Oh," I said again, inanely.

"'S'right," he reassured me. "Call Gregory if you want to. Just delay things is all." As I hesitated, he went briskly on, "But you can help me if you will. You want to get this cleared up, don't you? Now, I gather the bedrooms in this shack are on the next floor. How about sort of giving me the layout of who has which room?"

"If you'll wait a moment," I offered, "I'll have the butler show you around. Wouldn't that be better?"

He hesitated, then said, "Okay, but I could do better alone."

I rang for Andrew, and as we waited I led the way into the back passage and explained that the bedrooms on the right of the back stairs were occupied by Bob and Kirk and Bill respectively and those on the left by our feminine guests, one of whom had been murdered that afternoon.

"Pretty wholesale slaughter around here, looks like," he observed.

As Andrew did not appear immediately, I said I would step to the kitchen and ask the cook to locate him. "Oh, never mind," my visitor told me airily, "I'll get along all right."

"I'll send Andrew along later," I promised as he vanished up the back stairs.

"Them bells is ringing in all directions," Bessie explained, as I entered the kitchen. "Andrew's done gone to the front door and I was comin' to the office just as soon as I could get my apron changed."

"It's all right," I told her. "Just tell Andrew that a plainclothes policeman is snooping about upstairs and that I would like it if he would sort of keep an eye on him and see that he reports to Lieutenant Gregory. I'll tell Mr. Bill if he ever gets out of the library."

I went back to the office but I still could find no sign of any hidden entrance. I would try the basement stairs and see if I could hear Plutarch as Alice had claimed.

It seemed to me that the single bulb which lit the back passage had never cast so pale a light nor the little room itself seemed so remote from the rest of the house. But I must go on if that hunch about Plutarch was to be investigated. I opened the door cautiously and began the descent to the basement.

And there on the landing, a line from the jingle came back to me.

"Steps up, steps down . . ."

Steps? Steps could be stairs, of course. Perhaps I had thought of it because of the fact that I was standing with stairs above and below. But, of course, that was true of so many places in the house. All the way from the basement landing to the third floor by way of these same back stairs. Aunt Maggie had been killed in the passage with steps leading up and down. . . .

In a fever of excitement I decided that I would go and drag Bill from Lieutenant Gregory's clutches. Somewhere around some of these stairs . . .

Then it was that I seemed to hear, ever so faintly, a series of muffled meows. But try as I might, I could not decide which direction they came from.

"Plutarch," I called. "Plutarch."

Faintly the answer came back, but I was just as much at sea as ever.

Here again is evidence of what might be considered my great-great-grandfather's eccentricity. Straight in front of me, as I stood on the landing, was a door leading down into the game room. To the left is another, leading to the furnace room.

In my ancestor's day a part of the game room had been a wine cellar. The present furnace room had provided space for provisions. It was because he wished them to be entirely separate that he had individual stairways built down from the landing.

I opened one door, then the other, calling out to Plutarch as I did so, but no sign of any white cat. I called again, and again heard Plutarch's plaintive meow. But where could he be? On my right was only a wall which I had always thought stood flush against a wall of earth. But as I looked at it now, I saw that it, too, was fashioned to look like a door, except that there was no door handle. Of course, this might have been simply to provide a uniform effect.

But suddenly I was certain that Plutarch's cries had come from behind this wall. Here, I knew, was the secret room. The answer to everything that had happened.

Caution whispered to go back and wait for Bill. But, I thought, no harm just to see if it is the door. Just to see if it will open.

I banged on the paneling. Was that a hollow sound that came back? In my excitement I could not be sure. I sought in vain for some secret spring to press. I ran my hands up and down the outside of the frame. Perhaps somewhere . . .

Then suddenly an abyss opened under my feet and I was falling . . . falling . . .

XXVI

A STEEP FLIGHT OF STEPS broke my fall somewhat. Except for this and the fact that I had thrown out my arms and happened to grasp the stair rail on one side, there is little doubt that I would have landed on the brick floor with a broken neck.

Even so, I was sure that I was just a nice little bag of broken bones, afraid to move lest I find that I could not. As I lay there in the dark, for the opening through which I had fallen had closed behind me, something soft and alive rubbed against me and I screamed at the top of my voice. Also I involuntarily drew away, and this showed me that at least I could move.

My scream was answered by a loud and petulant meow close at hand, and I realized with hysterical relief that it was Plutarch who had rubbed against me. "How did you get here?" I asked him, as he rubbed against me again. And although Plutarch could not tell me, the answer, of course, was that somebody had opened that concealed trap door on the landing and Plutarch either had followed that someone down the steps or had been brought down. The latter supposition did not sound very plausible, for after all there was no reason to conceal the unlucky animal. Nor was there reason to think that Plutarch had followed anyone in particular, for he is a fairly friendly cat with the usual feline curiosity and would have trailed anybody who did not actually kick him aside. The presence of Plutarch, therefore, was no clue to the discoverer of this underground retreat, which I knew must be the secret room.

251

Alone at last with the object of my frantic search—the secret room—my one desire was to escape: I had no wish to linger in the dark or to be discovered there by the murderer. But having landed with my right foot doubled under me, the ankle was giving me various and assorted fits. Otherwise, I seemed to have no injuries beyond bruises. I tried to rise, but the ankle hurt so badly that I was forced to sink down on the bottom step.

"Just an old-fashioned girl," I told myself in bitter disgust. "A sprained ankle."

But I knew I could not remain on that bottom step indefinitely. Grasping the stair rail, I was able to pull and drag myself upward, while waves of faintness swept over me, caused by the pain in my ankle. Finally reaching the top step, I groped about, trying to locate the spring or handle or some means by which to open the trap door. But so far as I was able to discover, there was nothing. Nor could I push upward the door itself.

I called for help as loudly as I could, but it seemed to me that my voice fell backward as from physical impact against the floor above me. Even though I had left open the door from the passage, I knew the chances of being heard were pretty slim, unless someone happened to be going through that little back hallway. I tried beating my fists against the trap door. It did no good, but I kept on. And I was grateful when Plutarch came and sat on the step beside me.

My hands were bruised from the futile pounding and I was all out of breath from yelling, so we just sat there for a little while. Horrible thoughts came to keep me company along with Plutarch. Suppose not even the murderer returned to this underground lair? Suppose I was left there in the dark to starve to death. Perhaps to suffocate. Panic seized me and I screamed again for help.

But even this near approach to hysteria wore itself out and reason began to reassert itself. I noticed that, although the place had a closed-in atmosphere and was fairly cold, the air did not seem tainted. Naturally my ancestor, God rest his quaint soul, had provided some source of supply when he had the place built. What made his plan so fiendishly clever was the fact that secret rooms always bring to mind the thought of secret panels and hollow walls.

Who would think of looking for a trap door on that unlikely land-ing? Nobody, I told myself bitterly, visualizing my own skeleton entombed centuries hence.

Then I remembered the lost packet of matches I had reclaimed on the stairway that morning. By some lucky chance they were still in my pocket. I clawed at them as a starving man might grab for food or a drowning man for a straw. In this clumsy haste I broke the first one. But I was able to strike the second and from this pin point of light the near darkness receded unwillingly.

The all-important objective, of course, was to locate the spring or catch that controlled the opening of the trap door, but as I burned one match after another in fruitless effort I realized that the supply would soon be consumed and my situation unimproved. Other basement rooms had been wired for electricity long ago, but before this was done the location of the secret room had been lost or forgotten.

Finally I remembered to tell myself that I would be missed by someone abovestairs. Andrew, if no one else, would soon be spread-ing the alarm. The thing to do was to wait quietly until I heard footsteps overhead and then yell for all I was worth.

Why hadn't I thought of it before?

All very well, of course, except that the murderer might arrive ahead of the searching party. But I sat down again and waited for what seemed hours, Plutarch in my lap purring contentedly, then rousing himself to meow questioningly. Even he seemed to realize that there was something wrong about the situation, or perhaps he was only hungry and thirsty. I was pretty thirsty myself, what with all my panic and yelling.

So we waited. But nobody came.

Pandora-like, I began to wonder about the secret room. How big was it? What did it contain? As I pondered these and other questions, the room itself seemed to stretch away from me into infinite space, full of unknown dangers, then to close in on all sides, like the walls in a horror movie.

It was Plutarch who kept me fairly calm. His even breathing. The comfort of his warm body against mine. There were six matches left. My social security against what need I could not guess. I moved my ankle experimentally. Thank heaven, the pain was considerably less. I could even stand if I did not place my full weight on the right foot. Plutarch complained as I set him down, but he kept close to my side and we moved slowly down the steps together. Curiosity had got the better of me as it had of Plutarch.

Why on earth hadn't I thought to arm myself with a flashlight when I started on this mad pilgrimage? Why hadn't I— All idle recrimination, of course. At the bottom of the steps I lighted one of the precious matches and found myself standing in what appeared to be a narrow passage, for brick walls came close on either side. With my free hand stretched out in front I followed the passage for about six feet, when it ended plump against another wall.

Hastily I struck a fresh match and in its light was revealed a door, just an ordinary door, with an ordinary knob that turned in my hand and opened inward.

Pausing, with the door only a few inches ajar, I stood listening. Like Mr. Dodson, I was learning to rely more on my ears. But I still had to listen consciously, just as some of us have to look consciously if we are to see details. What I heard did not help my morale any.

Someone, or something, alive was in that room, for I heard breathing. But such breathing. Loud and labored as though some giant were recovering from a hang-over. Or perhaps it was some great watchdog, sleeping now by fortuitous good luck, but ready to spring to life at a sound. My impulse was to pull shut that door and get away from there.

Then I realized Plutarch had already pushed his way inside.

I waited breathlessly for a moment, but there was no growling, no spitting, no sounds of mortal combat between ancient enemies.

There were only four matches now. I must open the door wider before lighting the next one, lest the slightest movement blow out its feeble flame. This I did and the sound of that heavy breathing almost unnerved me again, but I forced my feet across the threshold.

I found myself in a room about nine feet wide and twelve feet long, and almost the first thing my eyes fell upon was a small table on which was a stub of a candle in a pewter holder. If before this time anyone had told me that I would squeal with delight at the sight of a mere stub of candle, I would have sworn he was crazy. Too late I remembered and stifled the cry in my throat, lest I waken that dreadful sleeper.

Touching the dying match to the wick, I picked up the candle and moved about, cautiously exploring. There was a fireplace, with ashes on the hearth but no fire. Even as my gaze took in this fact, I also noticed that part of the small room was cut off by a big screen and it was from behind this screen that the sounds of heavy breathing emerged.

With my heart doing all sorts of violent gymnastics, I tiptoed around to take a look behind the screen. The first thing to arrest my gaze was my own rose taffeta puff. Only secondarily did I notice that the puff was spread over a prone figure on a low cot.

Moving fearfully nearer, I saw that the eyes of the sleeper were covered with tape, and I guessed that he was probably bound to the cot or that his hands and feet were tied. He was lying on one side in an obviously uncomfortable position and now and then moaned a little in his sleep.

Dragging my eyes away to inspect more thoroughly the screened-off section of the small room, I understood why the screen was there, a strange place for such a piece of furniture. Built into the wall just above the cot was a safe. Obviously this was where my ancestor stored his valuables. I decided that the room was probably under the back yard, rather than the house, and that its ventilation came through the chimney or perhaps by way of some other arrangement as ingenious as the trap-door entrance.

It was dumb of me not to have realized at the very first that the sleeping figure on the cot was the core and center of all that had happened recently at Wisteria Hall. But I suppose it was feminine curiosity that made me try to orientate myself before going into the situation more thoroughly. So far I had not come near enough to determine whether the man on the cot was anyone I might identity.

Now I ventured forward timidly, pausing every moment to listen for footsteps on the stairway. Then, as I stood still at the head of the cot, its occupant stirred and groaned loudly, so that I practically jumped out of my skin and came near dropping the candle.

As the helpless figure struggled and half turned, I cried out in horror. For I recognized the man. Even with his eyes bandaged I knew that he was Hugh Brannen. It was all simple enough.

That story Bill had told last night at dinner about Mr. Brannen having been kidnapped— Obviously his abductors had used our place as a hide-out and, when we arrived unexpectedly, their plans had been upset.

Bill had said Mr. Brannen was to be released Saturday morning, but evidently the schedule could not be carried out. No doubt, that telephone call to Andrew had been an effort to clear the way.

But who—

Ah, of course. One of the workmen who had remodeled a part of the basement as a game room had somehow discovered the hidden room. Yes, that must be the answer. But how would he have known of our sudden plans to open the house? That would be easy, I realized, if he happened upon the station wagon Friday. No doubt, he would have a lookout.

I examined the rose puff more carefully. Yes, there with the down spilling out, was the place where it had been snagged on the stairway. Could this explain Alice's ghost? Had the kidnapper, perhaps afraid to replenish the fire and also afraid that his prisoner might develop pneumonia and die, gone foraging for cover and used the down comfort as a concealing domino in which to escape from Alice?

I shuddered as I pictured him on his search for that extra covering. Stealthily turning doorknobs in the night until at last he found one that yielded to his touch. Suppose our bedroom doors had not been locked? Would he have invaded them and what would have happened, had he been discovered? It was all too horrible to think about.

"Mr. Brannen," I called softly, then more loudly, but he did not stir. I shook his shoulder, but he only moved restlessly and mumbled something that I did not understand. Gradually, the cause of that heavy breathing began to dawn on me.

He had been drugged.

In the act of tearing away the tape from his eyes, I withdrew my hand. Should the kidnapper return, undoubtedly it would be better for him to find his prisoner as he had left him. Conscious, Mr. Brannen might be able to help me plan some method of escape, but so long as he slept that terrible sleep there was no hope of any assistance.

Walking back around the screen, I spied, by the light of the fast-decreasing candle, a piece of green paper on the floor near the table. It had a jagged edge and was no doubt the piece from which the scraps had been torn for the notes planted in our bedroom. It was all beginning to fit together.

The jigsaw puzzle made up of scraps of paper and scraps of silk.

Could the kidnap notes have been written on this same sort of paper? Was that why Lieutenant Gregory had regarded with such interest the notes we received and why he had refused to answer questions about them? If so, it was no wonder he had gone after Bill so relentlessly.

Picking up the paper with the tips of my fingers, I carried it behind the screen and shoved it under the cot. Perhaps there would be fingerprints on it, even though there had been none on the notes themselves.

But what to do? Plutarch seemed to feel the same way, for he looked at me questioningly. Then I noticed that he was sniffing at a milk bottle full of water which stood on the floor with a cup turned over it. So thirsty that I forgot all about fingerprints or germs, I poured myself a drink and then filled the cup for Plutarch, who lapped greedily, stopping now and then to look up at me with that same questioning look in his eyes.

"Yes," I said, "I know it is Mr. Brannen's cup, but maybe we will be out of here before he needs to use it again." Plutarch switched his tail and we moved together into the open part of the room.

The candle was almost burned out now and there were only three matches. Although kindling and wood lay on the hearth, I did not dare make a fire, for fear of its effect on the kidnapper. In the back of my mind was the thought that when he came I might be able to escape by hiding under the stairway and watching to see how he opened the trap door on the way out.

But why on earth hadn't I tried to find the opening while there was enough of the candle to guide me? And, I realized sickeningly, it was possible that in my preoccupation with exploration I had failed to hear footsteps if they passed along the landing above the stairs.

Standing there, completely discouraged, I admitted to Plutarch that I was the world's biggest fool. My ankle, forgotten until that moment, began to broadcast uncomfortable twinges. Panic was crowding close again.

Oh, well, I would go to the stairway and listen, sitting in the dark and hoarding my infinitesimal bit of candle and the three matches. Every now and then I would call for help. If no one came finally, I would still have the matches and scrap of candle to light me back to the room, where I would make a fire. Surely next day someone would see the smoke and try again to find me. Beyond that, my thoughts did not dare to travel.

As I reached the brick passage leading from the room to the stairs, a faint slit of light told me that the trap door was being opened. But silently. Not as a rescuer comes, with shouts and re-assurances.

Shrinking back inside the doorway as the slit widened, I tried to tell myself that it was all right. But I knew that it was not, and as I heard footsteps descending the stairs I hastily blew out the candle and hid myself behind the screen, realizing that I was following blind instinct and that my hiding place offered no real protection.

Then I held my breath and waited, certain that the kidnap-murderer was coming nearer every moment.

XXVII

THE DOOR OPENED, and beyond the screen I saw the bobbing beam of a flashlight. Certain that my time had come, I almost cried out, unable longer to stand the suspense.

There was a scuffing of footsteps and then a voice said, "Smells sort of smoky in here."

It was a voice that sounded somehow familiar, yet I could not quite place it.

"What was that noise?" the same voice asked and I recognized it then.

The alleged plain-clothes man.

To think that I had met the murderer face to face and had let him get away. In fact, had helped him. Now, unless unexpected intervention came, I would meet him face to face again, but—

"Just that damn cat," said another voice, a voice pitched so low that it was almost impossible to hear, what with the pounding of my heart.

So there were two of them. But that was not surprising. One man could hardly handle such a job alone.

"I told you he followed me down here," the second voice resumed, a little louder now. "And why the hell didn't you stay down here, too? Don't you know the house is full of policemen?"

My heart stopped beating and the world rocked under my feet, for this time I recognized that voice. "No, no," I whispered over and over to myself. Something wet dropped on my hand and I realized that I was crying.

But even in my shocked horror and grief, I knew that I must be careful. Perhaps, oh, perhaps, they would go away and later I would be rescued and could tell of finding Mr. Brannen. I could say quite truthfully that I did not see the men who came into the secret room.

"Gettin' scared, are you, Buddy?" sneered the first voice. "What'd you expect me to do, wait down here all night? I know how to keep out of the way of the police. 'Sides, they ain't got a thing on me. Why shouldn't I come out here to call on a friend? How'm I to know he's committed a coupla murders?"

"Damn you, Spike." The second voice was loud and angry beyond all sense of caution now. "Whose fault is it you didn't come back last night like I told you to? We could have got him out of here all right if you had had the car ready."

There was the sound of a chair scraping across the floor and almost simultaneously a quick feline wail and indignant spitting, which made it all too plain that Plutarch had got in somebody's way. A moment later, tail lashing and full of protesting meows, Plutarch rounded the screen and was rubbing against my leg, but I did not dare reach down to comfort him for fear of knocking against the cot or screen and thus revealing my presence.

Spike's raucous laughter finally died down and he resumed the conversation. "How the hell was I to get the car here? I see that wrecked truck thing and that road that looked like it was knee deep in mush and I know I'd never get no car out of it if I come any further. Had a hard time turnin' around and gettin' out as it was."

"Didn't seem to bother you much that I was left with the bag to hold. And the dope just about all gone, too. Had to give him so much he'll probably wander around and get run over if we turn him loose on the highway tonight. That is, if the police ever get out of the house."

"Your little stunt didn't seem to do much good, did it?"

"No, just messed things up worse, I suppose. But it seemed to me if they thought somebody outside the room was mixed up in it all, they would realize there was no sense in holding everybody indefinitely."

"Well, I done my part. How'd you get such a fool idea, anyhow? Didn't think it'd work when you wanted me to do it."

"Oh," wearily, "just a play I saw when I was a kid. *Thirteenth Chair*. Only it was a knife—"

"Now, you're talkin', Buddy. With a knife you've got somethin'. Them damn dart things, they ain't no good. Say, when I was throwin' knives in the circus, like I tell you—"

"Yes, I know. You've told me you were good. But you haven't told me yet how we are going to get Hugh Brannen out of here. Has it dawned on you for a moment that I was to have no connection with this job except to furnish the hide-out? You and your pal were to get him here and get him away. You were to handle the kidnap notes. Everything. Like hell, you did."

"'S what you get for messin' things up with murder. 'S what I get for mixin' with society. Guess your fine friends would eat this up, Mr.—"

"Shut up, damn you. I've told you not to call my name. How do we know he may not hear?"

"All right, Buddy, all right. But what I can't see is what you wanted to do the old gal in for?"

"Hell, I told you she was on the way here. She had found the key—that damn rhyme. I tried to dissuade her. Tried to convince her it was just a crazy riddle. But there was no stopping her. She started to scream. Then—then I did stop her. And when I put my hands on her—there was nothing to do but finish the job. Ugh—"

"Can't take it, can you, Buddy?" taunted Spike. "If you'd a-done like I was in favor of, we'd finished the old man off when we brought him out here. Then when we got the money, we'd've been through. And everything safe. But you wasn't goin' to have nothin' to do with murder. No, sir, old man Brannen was goin' to be took care of. No blood on your hands. Well," he snarled, "just look at 'em now."

"Damn you, Spike. I never meant to kill anybody. If you had done your part—"

"Okay, Buddy, okay. But that don't get us nowhere now. What the boss sent me out here to get is the ransom money. When the police shell out, I'll take the dough in and you can come on later and get your cut when you've turned the old man loose. Or you can just leave him here for all I care."

"No, you don't, Spike Sellers. I take that money in myself or it stays here in this safe. Nobody else knows the combination."

"Reckon the boss wouldn't have no trouble gettin' a good safe cracker out here," Spike remarked confidently. Then his tone changed, as though he might be wheedling a child. "But listen, Buddy, you'll get yours, all right. Maybe you don't know it, but you're on a spot, right now. They ain't been able to pin nothin' on you yet, but you can't tell. Somebody ought to have that there money to take care of it. The boss just—"

"I've got my own reasons for holding onto that money. I don't trust you and I don't trust your boss. Your boss has something that belongs to me. And he's going to hand that over to me before anybody touches that hundred thousand."

"So that's the way it is? Well, get this straight, Buddy. I'm not here to take no funny business. Before I leave, you are going to open that safe and hand over the money. Then you can get on back upstairs with your cronies and the cops. When the coast is clear, I'll do my fade-out. You can come back later tonight and let out the old man if you want to take a chance on it. Just drop him here in the yard if you are scared to take him to the highway. My advice is just to forget him."

"Still leaving me all the dirty work, I see."

"Well, who messed things up? Who was it knew about this fine hide-out? Secret room. House goin' to be empty till summer. Everything just swellelgant. Oh, yeah? Who was it popped the old gal off? Aw, hell, let's get goin'. Come on now and open that safe."

This was the end. The hair literally crawled on my head. Could I possibly slip around one side of the screen as they came from the other direction? But from which direction would they come? Could I crawl under the cot? No, it was too low, and anyway, they would be sure to hear me. What could I do?

Then I breathed again. The argument was still going on. ". . . told you I wouldn't let anybody touch that money until I've got what belongs to me."

"You won't, eh. Oh, yes, you will. March, Buddy— Now, now, don't be a fool. Fold up that gun."

"Who's being a fool? You stay here, Spike Sellers, as I told you to, until the police are out of the house. I'm going back upstairs."

One of those long, quiet moments followed, punctuated by the quick breathing of the two men on the other side of the screen. Then there was a sudden movement, a gasp and the writhing, rasping sounds of a struggle. They were close, so close that I expected the screen to be knocked down any moment. Something dropped to the floor and rolled beyond the edge of the screen, shedding an innocent little pool of light in this inferno of darkness. Did I dare grab for it? Luck was with me, for the wrestlers on the floor were too absorbed in their struggle to be aware of anything else.

Nerving myself to make a dash for the stairway, hoping with the aid of the flashlight to be able to locate the spring which would open the trap door, I was instantly stopped in my tracks by the sound of a deafening explosion, followed by a horrible groan. With the smell of smoke and powder all about me, I waited in a vacuum of suspended animation to see which one of the combatants had been shot.

"All right, Buddy," I heard Spike say hoarsely. "Didn't mean to do it, but you asked for it. Well, you and the old man can stay here and rot together. I'll come back and get the dough when the place is clear." Only a groan answered him.

"Where's that damn flashlight?" Spike grunted. "Guess it broke when it fell. Ah . . ." A long sigh of satisfaction and a scratching sound seemed to indicate that he had found matches in his pocket, then above the screen was the sickly glow of a feeble light.

"Want to make you a present, Buddy," said Spike throatily, "just in case they ever find you. Gonna let it look like suicide. Sweet of me, ain't it? Well, I ain't so keen about runnin' into cops with the wrong gun on me at a place like this. Not under all the circumstances." Heavy breathing and fumbling sounds made it all too easy to imagine what must be taking place on the other side of the screen.

"All set now," Spike said finally, muttering a curse as his light died out. "Last one I had. How'm I gonna find that damn trick door catch in the dark? May have to wait a while, anyway, if the cops are too plentiful."

Spike shuffled through the door, evidently feeling his way. I was shaking from head to foot, but I knew what I must do. I waited until he reached the steps, then I dashed around the screen with my flashlight and, averting my eyes from that figure on the floor, I grabbed up the gun and was behind Spike in a flash.

"Hands up," I ordered. "I've got you covered." Perhaps, I had learned that from the movies, but it must have sounded convincing, for with the flashlight trained on him I could see Spike's hands waver slowly upward, while he swore beneath his breath. Thank heaven, I was able to hold that flash fairly steadily too.

"All right," I said, "go on. Open that door, but keep your hands up."

"Hell," he growled. "how'm I gonna keep 'em up and open the door?"

Perhaps he was not dissembling, but I wasn't trusting. "One little move the wrong way," I warned, "and it will be good night for you."

Watching closely in order that I might note the location of the trap-door spring, as well as any false move on his part, I managed to keep both the flash and the gun trained on him without undue wavering. Ah, so that was why I could not find it. A lever off to the right apparently controlled the action of the door, for with his hands still above his head Spike reached out and grasped it. No doubt, in my wild grabbing as I fell, I had touched that lever and thus closed the door behind me.

The trap door was opening. Now I had my greatest danger to face. Walking up the stairs behind him as I was, it would be easy for him to turn and rush me. Or with equal facility, once he was on the landing above, he could close the door in my face and make a dash for it.

"All right," I ordered, when I was halfway up the steps, "march." Unconsciously I was handing back to him the words he had used only a few minutes before in the secret room.

It seemed to me that he hurried just a little more than was necessary. Perhaps it was only that I myself was pretty near the breaking point. Anyway, I turned loose and fired a shot off to his right.

Let him run now, if he chose. Let him shut the door behind him. That shot would bring others running.

He let out an unearthly yell as the bullet whizzed past, a yell that met and mingled with another that was also like nothing I had ever heard before, a strange, blood-curdling, atavistic cry that could have come only from the wild heart of Africa. As my head emerged above the opening I could hear Andrew, even before I could see him. "Don't shoot no mo', Miss Sally!" he screamed, his voice full of savage exultation. "I got my razor on him."

Doors were opening. Feet were coming from all directions. Roberts was the first to reach the scene, and even in all the excitement I was struck with the look of bewilderment on his face. But he lost no time in putting handcuffs on our whimpering, cringing prisoner.

"I thought—" said Roberts, his tone all perplexity, "anyway, he's gone and Mr. Dodson was so sure—"

"Down there," I said, pointing toward the still open trap door. "Get a doctor—"

They told me afterward that it was Roberts who caught me as I, who had been so calmly confident a short while before, crumpled weakly in a faint.

When I opened my eyes again, I was lying on the library sofa and there was a burning in my throat and a warmth in my stomach as of brandy. Claire was stroking my wrists, while Bessie hovered just within range of my rather blurred vision.

"Bill," I whispered. "Oh, Bill—"

"He tole me to let him know, just as soon as she come 'round," said Bessie, padding out of the room.

"But I want to see him," I argued, trying to sit up, while Claire gently pushed me back. "I'm all right. I can go."

"No, no," said Claire. "You mustn't go out there. It's too awful."

"Did they get a doctor?"

"Yes, you know Mr. Marshall had insisted on having Dr. Bates come out to check up about Thomas's son. So he was already here. We let him look at you first. You had us all scared, with that shooting and everything. But he said you'd be all right when your face was washed. It was so dirty."

I realized Claire was trying to divert me from the main subject, for her eyes dropped beneath my scrutiny and the long dark lashes swept her flushed cheeks. Though she was fairly calm now, I knew she had been crying. "I've seen him," she admitted. "He—talked to me."

"Then he isn't dead?"

"No, but the doctor says there isn't a chance. That's why they are letting him talk now, while they wait for the ambulance."

"Oh. And Mr. Brannen?"

"Still unconscious, but the doctor said he would be all right."

It was perhaps half an hour later that Bill and the others came in. Andrew was serving coffee again, but Lieutenant Gregory stopped only briefly to pay his respects. Odd, but it seemed to me now that his piercing dark eyes were rather attractive. And when Roberts shook hands with me there was real friendliness in his glance.

It was all rather like the end of an ocean voyage when you've had a stormy crossing. People you had never seen before sailing and perhaps would never see again suddenly seemed like old friends.

The ambulance had arrived and taken Bob to Grady Hospital. Alice, following in the car with Mr. Marshall, Mr. Dodson and Plutarch, would go later to the home of an aunt.

The police were delivering Mr. Brannen to his own fireside and the ransom money would be held as evidence. Bob had given them the combination of the safe.

A tear that was even hotter than the coffee dropped into my cup. "Just like Bob," I gulped, "to smuggle that comforter down to Mr. Brannen. I can't think he meant to do anything wrong."

"He just got into such a corner," Bill agreed. "You know he never could say no to anyone. And all that gambling with Eve. One thing brought on another. Big Shot Anderson had a lot of his checks that were no good. Bob held him off with the promise of getting a loan from Mr. Brannen. You know he was such a good friend of Bob's father. But the loan didn't materialize and one day when Bob was pretty drunk he gave Big Shot a note, with Mr. Brannen's name

forged as endorser. Bob said he had been sure he could finally persuade Mr. Brannen to lend him the money to take up the note.

"Big Shot, it seems, doubted the endorsement, and when he
threatened to call Mr. Brannen Bob confessed. Then Big Shot had
him. It must have been about that time that one of Big Shot's men got
into some kind of trouble. Afterward, it seems Bob happened to mention to Big Shot that the secret room would have been a good place to
have had this henchman disappear to until the storm blew over.

"Well, apparently all that got to working in Big Shot's master
mind. You know, the note with Brannen's name on it, the hideaway, Bob as a sort of lookout man. Bob thinks that was how the
idea of the kidnapping was born. He wasn't to do any of the dirty
work, you know. Mr. Brannen wasn't to be harmed. And Bob would
get his note back and a little stake besides. He said he meant to
settle down afterward—"

"I think"—Bill paused—"in all justice, Bob must have been
pretty well shot last night when he—met Aunt Maggie. I didn't think
about his drinking so much until I happened to notice the vanish-
ing liquor supply this morning."

"But," I asked, "how did Bob know about the secret room?"

"He told us while he was giving Gregory his confession. You
know he came out here with me several times while we were planning the game room and other changes. Nobody but an architect
would have guessed it. Bob says he couldn't figure out that extra
chimney attached to the end of the house where there were only
back stairways—except on the third floor, of course. Then he saw
those three doors on the basement landing, or rather two doors
and an imitation door without a knob. He had no trouble locating
the spring. He said I was out in the yard at the time with the con-
tractor and he fully meant to tell me as soon as he came out. Then,
on second thought, he decided it would be fun to wait until we were
all out here sometime and he would produce the secret room as if
from a silk hat. You know Bob—"

"But what about that piece of telephone wire?" Kirk inquired
dryly. "Planted first on Eve and then on me. That doesn't seem
exactly friendly."

"Bob didn't do that," Bill told us. "That was Andrew, both times, trying to cover up for me. I pinned him down just now and he admitted it. Said he didn't know whose coat he parked it in, except that it wasn't mine."

"Tell me just one thing," I asked Kirk. "It was you out here early yesterday afternoon, wasn't it?"

"Yes," he admitted. "Now that it is all over and Alice has gone, I can tell you. The sudden house party plans threw the kidnapping schedule out of joint, as we know. Mr. Brannen was to be released Saturday morning. It was Friday night when Bob learned of the projected party, and the servants were already here. Saturday morning Alice overheard enough of a telephone conversation to gather that he was mixed up in some sort of mess out here. And Alice knew he owed Big Shot twenty thousand dollars. She didn't know about the forged note or the kidnapping. Nothing definite. So she asked me to slide out and try to get a line on things for Bob's protection. I got here before noon, but didn't see anything until you almost saw me, Sally, though twice I thought I heard a car. That's why I lingered on.

"Of course," he added ruefully, "there's little doubt that my presence prevented the kidnappers from releasing Mr. Brannen. After they had contrived to clear the place of Andrew and everybody, here I was—"

"No, no," the quick unexpected exclamation came from Claire. "That was Alice's fault, not yours."

Nobody looked at anybody else and Bill said, "I suspect we'd have to go back even farther than that to find where the fault really began, but—"

"But let's don't," I begged.

"Well, anyway," said Kirk, "I owe you an apology, Sally. Naturally, I couldn't explain this before without giving Alice away. And I was never sure that any of it was connected with Aunt Maggie's murder."

"And I owe you an apology," I said, "for more than half the time I was wondering if you were the—the—" I stopped, remembering Bob and finding myself quite unable to say the word, murderer.

Kirk smiled. "Makes us even," he said.

"I suppose it would all have gone through well enough," Bill observed, "if Aunt Maggie hadn't found the secret room. Or even if she had been willing to postpone her investigation."

"That's true," Kirk agreed. "Bob and Sellers would have got Mr. Brannen out of the house somehow. This is no doubt why Bob was scouting around when he ran into you at the foot of the stairway."

"And those green notes?" I asked.

"Were the same as the kidnap notes," Bill nodded. "That's why Gregory was bearing down on us so."

"But where does Eve fit in?"

"She heard Bob and Aunt Maggie talking and recognized Bob's voice, but turned back to the powder room in order to miss Aunt Maggie. In the powder room she probably did not hear Aunt Maggie's call, but she pieced it all together afterward, Bob said, and threatened to expose him unless he broke his engagement. She didn't want to marry him herself, you know—just—" Bill stopped abruptly.

"It's all right," Claire assured him. "Bob had already told me that our engagement was—a mistake. When he said he wanted to save me any unpleasantness, I thought, of course, he meant Eve." Color suffused her face, but she forced herself on. "I refused to release him and then he said it never would have worked out. That I only wanted to have my way. I suppose—he was right."

At this awkward pause Andrew appeared at the door, all his old aplomb restored. "'Scuse me, Mr. Bill. We'se ready to ride. Me and Bessie done got all the bags packed and in the cars. We put Miss Alice's—and all the other bags in the station wagon. But seein' as how they was two cars, we put yourn and Miss Sally's bags in one and Miss Claire's and Mr. Kirk's in t'other, so they'd be a gen'leman to drive each one."

There it was again. Bessie and Andrew always one jump ahead.

COACHWHIP PUBLICATIONS

COACHWHIPBOOKS.COM

BLOOD ON HER SHOE

MEDORA FIELD

ISBN 978-1-61646-275-8

THE WINE ROOM MURDER

STANLEY VESTAL

ISBN 978-1-61646-247-5

COACHWHIP PUBLICATIONS

COACHWHIPBOOKS.COM

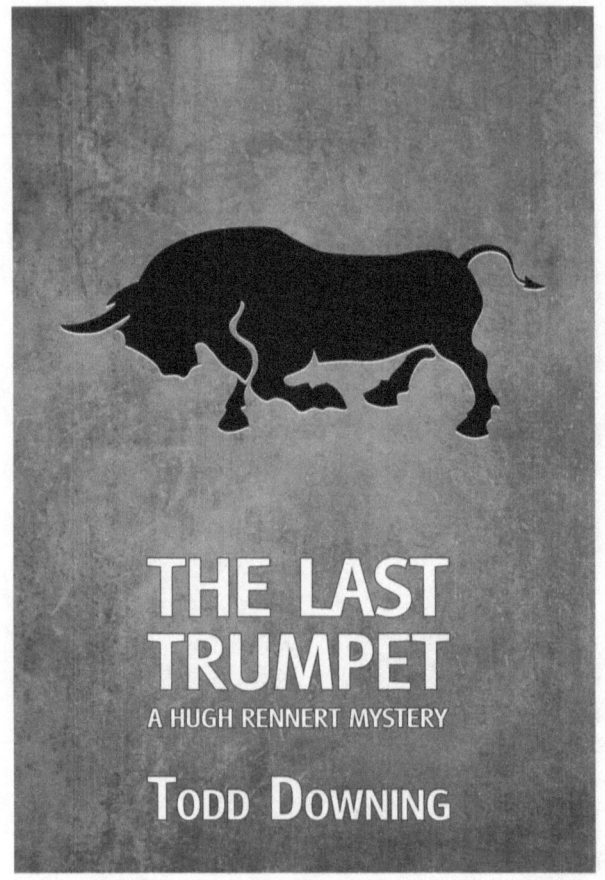

ISBN 978-1-61646-152-2

THE QUINNY HITE
MYSTERIES

CHINESE RED · HERE LIES THE BODY

RICHARD BURKE

ISBN 978-1-61646-247-5

COACHWHIP PUBLICATIONS

COACHWHIPBOOKS.COM

THE MUMMY
CASE MYSTERY

DERMOT
MORRAH

ISBN 978-1-61646-250-5

COACHWHIP PUBLICATIONS

ALSO AVAILABLE

THE
**MUSEUM
MURDER**

JOHN T. McINTYRE

ISBN 978-1-61646-252-9

COACHWHIP PUBLICATIONS

COACHWHIPBOOKS.COM

THE
DEATH
OF A
CELEBRITY

HULBERT
FOOTNER

AN AMOS LEE MAPPIN MYSTERY

ISBN 978-1-61646-263-5